NECROPOLIS

LOGRIS, MERYN AND Nehn, working forward with a handful of Vervun Primary troopers, almost ran into a Zoican fireteam in a drain-away under one of the main derrick rigs. Hearing the commotion over his microbead, Varl charged in with several other Tanith, spiking the first ochre-suited soldier he met with his silver bayonet.

Major Rodyin came in behind, shooting his autopistol frantically. He seemed pale and short of breath. Varl knew Rodyin had never been in combat like this before. In truth, the man had never been in combat at all before that day.

Three desperate, bloody minutes of close fighting cleared the drain-away of Zoicans. Logris and Nehn set up solid fire positions down the gully, overlooking the dock causeway. Rodyin took off his glasses and tried to adjust the earpieces with shaking hands. He looked like he was about to weep.

'You alright, major?' Varl asked.

Rodyin nodded, replacing his spectacles. 'The more I kill, the better I feel.'

Nearby, Corporal Meryn laughed. 'The major sounds like Gaunt himself!'

More Dan Abnett from the Black Library

• GAUNT'S GHOSTS •

Colonel-Commissar Gaunt and his regiment the Tanith First-and-Only struggle for survival on the battlefields of the far future.

FIRST AND ONLY
GHOSTMAKER
NECROPOLIS
HONOUR GUARD
THE GUNS OF TANITH
STRAIGHT SILVER

• THE EISENHORN TRILOGY •

In the nightmare world of the 41st millennium, Inquisitor Eisenhorn hunts down mankind's most dangerous enemies.

XENOS
MALLEUS
HERETICUS

• OTHER NOVELS •

RIDERS OF THE DEAD
HAMMERS OF ULRIC (with Nik Vincent and James Wallis)
GILEAD'S BLOOD (with Nik Vincent)

A WARHAMMER 40,000 NOVEL

Gaunt's Ghosts

NECROPOLIS

Dan Abnett

For Steve White, master-at-arms and knower of stuff

A BLACK LIBRARY PUBLICATION

First published in Great Britain in 2000

This edition published in 2003 by
BL Publishing,
Games Workshop Ltd.,
Willow Road, Nottingham,
NG7 2WS, UK.

10 9 8 7 6 5 4 3 2 1

Cover illustration by Adrian Smith
Map by Ralph Horsley

A CIP record for this book
is available from the British Library

ISBN 1 84416 006 8

Set in ITC Giovanni

Printed and bound in Great Britain by
Cox & Wyman Ltd, Cardiff Rd, Reading, Berkshire RG1 8EX, UK

See the Black Library on the Internet at
www.blacklibrary.com

Find out more about Games Workshop
and the world of Warhammer 40.000 at
www.games-workshop.com

IT IS THE 41st millennium. For more than a hundred centuries the Emperor has sat immobile on the Golden Throne of Earth. He is the master of mankind by the will of the gods, and master of a million worlds by the might of his inexhaustible armies. He is a rotting carcass writhing invisibly with power from the Dark Age of Technology. He is the Carrion Lord of the Imperium for whom a thousand souls are sacrificed every day, so that he may never truly die.

YET EVEN IN his deathless state, the Emperor continues his eternal vigilance. Mighty battlefleets cross the daemon-infested miasma of the warp, the only route between distant stars, their way lit by the Astronomican, the psychic manifestation of the Emperor's will. Vast armies give battle in his name on uncounted worlds. Greatest amongst his soldiers are the Adeptus Astartes, the Space Marines, bio-engineered super-warriors. Their comrades in arms are legion: the Imperial Guard and countless planetary defence forces, the ever-vigilant Inquisition and the tech-priests of the Adeptus Mechanicus to name only a few. But for all their multitudes, they are barely enough to hold off the ever-present threat from aliens, heretics, mutants – and worse.

TO BE A man in such times is to be one amongst untold billions. It is to live in the cruellest and most bloody regime imaginable. These are the tales of those times. Forget the power of technology and science, for so much has been forgotten, never to be re-learned. Forget the promise of progress and understanding, for in the grim dark future there is only war. There is no peace amongst the stars, only an eternity of carnage and slaughter, and the laughter of thirsting gods.

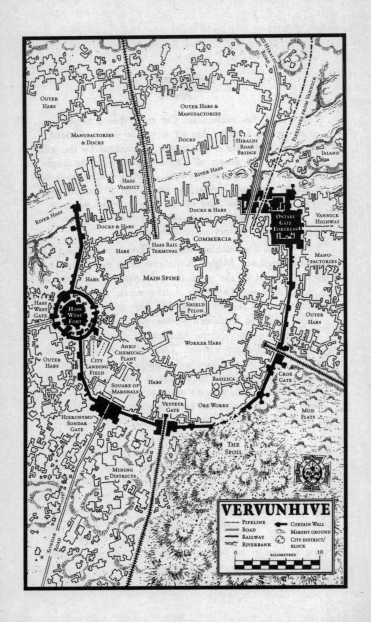

OUTER
HABS

OUTER HABS &
MANUFACTORIES

MANUFACTORIES
& DOCKS

DOCKS

HIRALDI
ROAD
BRIDGE

ISLAND

River Hass

Hass
Viaduct

River Hass

DOCKS & HABS

DOCKS & HABS

ONTABI
GATE
FORTRESS

VANNICK
HIGHWAY

HABS

Hass Rail
Terminal

COMMERCIA

MANU-
FACTORIES

HABS

HABS

MAIN SPINE

SHIELD
PYLON

OUTER
HABS

HASS
WEST
GATE

HASS
WEST
FORT

WORKER HABS

ANKO
CHEMICAL
PLANT

OUTER
HABS

CITY
LANDING
FIELD

SQUARE OF
MARSHALS

HABS

BASILICA

CROE
GATE

MUD
FLATS

HIERONYMO
SONDAR
GATE

VEYVEYR
GATE

ORE WORKS

THE
SPOIL

MINING
DISTRICTS

SONDAR ROAD

VERVUNHIVE

- - - - - Pipeline
▦▦▦▦ Road
▦▦▦▦ Railway
〰〰〰 Riverbank

■━■━ Curtain Wall
Marshy ground
City District/
block

KILOMETRES

0   10

AFTER THE VICTORIES *at Monthax and Lamacia, Warmaster Macaroth drove his forces swiftly along the trailing edge of the Sabbat Worlds cluster and turned inwards to assault the notorious enemy fortress-worlds in the Cabal system. Successful conquest of the Cabal system was a vital objective in the Imperial crusade to liberate the entire Sabbat Worlds group. To achieve this massive undertaking, the warmaster sent the line ships of his Segmentum Pacificus fleet forward in a pincer formation to begin the onslaught, while assembling and reforming his enormous Imperial Guard reserves ready for ground assault.*

'It took close to eight months for the troop components to convene at Solypsis, thousands of mass-conveyance transports carrying many million Imperial Guardsmen. There were many delays, and many minor skirmishes to settle en route. The Pragar regiments were held up for six weeks engaging the remnants of a Chaos legion on Nonimax, and a warp-storm forced the Samothrace and Sarpoy troop ships to remain at Antioch 148 for three whole months. However, it is the events that took place on the industrial hive-world of Verghast that are of particular interest to any student of Imperium military history...'

— from *A History of the Later Imperial Crusades*

ONE
ZOICA RISING

'The distinction between Trade and Warfare is seen only by those who have no experience of either.'
— Heironymo Sondar, House Sondar,
from his inaugural address

THE KLAXONS BEGAN to wail, though it was still an hour or more to shift-rotation.

The people of the hive-city paused as one. Millions of eyes checked timepieces, faltered in their work, looked up at the noise. Conversations trailed off. Feeble jokes were cracked to hide unease. Young children began to cry. House soldiery on the Curtain Wall voxed in confirmation and clarification requests to the Main Spine command station. Line supervisors and labour-stewards in the plants and manufactories chivvied their personnel back into production, but they were uneasy too. It was a test, surely? Or a mistake. A few moments more and the alarms would shut down again.

But the klaxons did not desist.

After a minute or so, raid-sirens in the central district also began keening. The pattern was picked up by manufactory hooters and mill-whistles all through the lower hive, and in the docks and outer habs across the river too. Even the great ceremonial horns on the top of the Ecclesiarchy Basilica started to sound.

Vervunhive was screaming with every one of its voices.

Everywhere, hazard lamps began to spin and flash, and secondary storm shutters cycled down on automatic to block windows. All the public-address plates in the city went black, erasing the glowing lines of weather, temperature, exchange-rate data, the local news and the ongoing output figures. They fuzzed darkly for a few seconds and then the words 'Please stand by' scrolled across all of them in steady repeats.

In the firelit halls of Vervun Smeltery One – part of the primary ore processing district just west of the Spoil – rattling conveyers laden with unprocessed rock shuddered to a halt as automatic safeties locked down. Above the main smelter silo, Plant Supervisor Agun Soric got up from behind a file-covered desk and crossed to the stained-glass window of his bureau. He looked down at the vast, halted plant in disbelief, then pulled on his work-jacket and went out onto the catwalk, staring at the thousands of milling workers below. Vor, his junior, hurried along the walk, his heavily booted feet ringing on the metal grill, the sound lost in the cacophony of hooters and sirens.

'What is this, chief?' he gasped, coming close to Soric and pulling the tubes of his dust-filter from his mouth-clamp.

Soric shook his head. 'It's fifteen thousand cubits of lost production, that's what the gak it is! And counting!'

'What d'you reckon? A malfunction?'

'In every alert system in the hive at once? Use your brain! A malfunction?'

'Then what?'

Soric paused, trying to think. The ideas that were forming in his mind were things he didn't really want to entertain. 'I pray to the Emperor himself that this isn't...'

'What, chief?'

'Zoica... Zoica rising again.'

'What?'

Soric looked round at his junior with contempt. He wiped his fat, balding brow on the back of his gold-braided cuff. 'Don't you read the news-picts?'

Vor shrugged. 'Just the weather and the stadium results.'

'You're an idiot,' Soric told him. And too young to remember, he thought. Gak, he was too young himself, but his father's father had told him about the Trade War. What was it, ninety years back, standard? Surely not again? But the picts had been full of it these last few months: Zoica silent, Zoica ceasing to trade, Zoica raising its bulwarks and setting armaments up along its northern walls.

Those raid-sirens hadn't sounded since the Trade War. Soric knew that as a bare fact.

'Let's hope you're right, Vor,' he said. 'Let's hope it's a gakking malfunction.'

IN THE COMMERCIA, the general mercantile district north of the Main Spine, in the shadow of the Shield Pylon, Guilder Amchanduste Worlin tried to calm the buyers in his barter-house, but the sirens drowned him out. The retinues were leaving, gathering up servant trains and produce bearers, making frantic calls on their vox-links, leaving behind nothing: not a form-contract, not a promissory note, not a business slate and certainly none of their funds.

Worlin put his hands to his head and cursed. His embroidered, sleet-silk gown felt suddenly hot and heavy .

He yelled for his bodyguards and they appeared: Menx and Troor, bull-necked men in ivory-laced body-gloves with the crest of Guild Worlin branded on their cheeks. They had unshrouded their laspistols and the velvet shroud-cloths dangled limply from their cuffs.

'Consult the high guild data-vox and the Administratum links!' Worlin spat. 'Come back and tell me what this is, or don't come back at all!'

They nodded and went off, pushing through the packs of departing traders.

Worlin paced back into his private ante-room behind the auction hall, cursing at the sirens to shut up. The very last thing he needed now was an interruption to trade. He'd spent months and a great deal of Guild Worlin funds securing mercantile bonds with Noble House Yetch and four of the houses ordinary. All of that work would be for nothing if trade – and income – went slack. The whole deal could collapse. His kin would be aghast at such losses. They might even strip him of his badge and remove his trading rights.

Worlin was shaking. He crossed to the decanter on the wrought-brass stack table and was about to pour himself a hefty shot of ten-year-old joiliq to calm his brittle mood. But he paused. He went to his desk, unlocked a drawer with the geno-key that he kept around his wrist on a thin chain and took out the compact needle pistol.

He checked it was primed and armed, then fetched the drink. He sat back on his lifter throne, sipping his liquor and holding his badge of credit – the mark of his rank – gazing at the Worlin crest and its bright ornament. He waited, the weapon in his lap.

The klaxons continued to wail.

AT CARRIAGE STATION C4/a, panic had begun. Workers and low-classers who had ventured into the mercantile slopes for a day's resourcing began to mob every brass-framed transit that trundled in along the cogged, funicular trackway. Carriages were moving out towards the Outer Habs and the Main Spine alike, overloaded, some doors only half closed.

Crowds on the platforms, shivering at each yelp of the alarms, were getting fractious as more and more fully laden transits clattered through without stopping. A slate-seller's stall was overturned in the press.

Livy Kolea, hab-wife, was beginning to panic herself. A body-surge of the crowd had pushed her past the pillars of the station atrium. She'd kept a firm grip on the handles of the child-cart and Yoncy was safe, but she'd lost sight of Dalin.

'My son! Have you seen my son?' she asked, imploring the frenzied crowd that washed around her. 'He's only ten! A good boy! Blond, like his father!'

She grabbed a passing guilder by the sleeve. A rich, lavish sleeve of painted silk.

'My son–' she began.

The guilder's bodyguard, menacing in his rust-coloured mesh, pushed her aside. He jerked the satin shroud off the weapon in his left hand, just briefly, as a warning, escorting his master on. 'Take the hand off, gak-swine,' his vox-enhanced larynx blurted gruffly, without emotion.

'My son–' Livy repeated, trying to push the child-cart out of the flow of bodies.

Yoncy was laughing, oblivious in his woollen wrap. Livy bent down under the segmented hood of the cart to stroke him, whispering soft, motherly words.

But her mind was racing. People slammed into her, teetering the cart and she had to hold on to keep it upright. Why was this happening – to her – now? Why was it happening on the one day a month she carriaged into the lower Commercia to haggle for stuff? Gol had wanted a new pair of canvas mittens. His hands were so sore after a shift at the ore face.

It was such a simple thing. Now this! And she hadn't even got the mittens.

Livy felt tears burst hot onto her cheeks.

'Dalin!' she called.

'I'm here, mam,' said a little voice, half hidden by the klaxons.

Livy embraced her ten-year-old son with fury and conviction, like she would never let go.

'I found him by the west exit,' a new voice added.

Livy looked up, not breaking her hug. The girl was about sixteen, she reckoned, a slut from the outer habs, wearing the brands and piercings of a hab-ganger.

'He's all right though.'

Livy looked the boy over quickly, checking for any signs of hurt. 'Yes, yes he is... He's all right. You're all right, aren't you, Dalin? Mam's here.'

Livy looked up at the outhab girl. 'Thank you. Thank you for...'

The girl pushed a ringed hand through her bleached hair. 'It's fine.'

The girl made Livy uneasy. Those brands, that pierced nose. Gang marks.

'Yes, yes... I'm in your debt. Now I must be going. Hold on to my hand, Dalin.'

The girl stepped in front of the cart as Livy tried to turn it. 'Where are you going?' she asked.

'Don't try to stop me, outhab! I have a blade in my purse!'

The girl backed off, smiling. 'I'm sure you have. I was just asking. The transits are packed and the exit stairs are no place for a woman with a kid and a cart.'

'Oh.'

'Maybe I could help you get the cart clear of this press?'

And take my baby… take Yoncy for those things scum like you do down in the outer habs over the river!

'No! Thank you, but… No!' Livy barked and pushed the gang-girl aside with the cart. She dragged the boy after her, pushing into the thicket of panic.

'Only trying to help,' Tona Criid shrugged.

THE RIVER TIDES were ebbing and thick, ore-rich spumes were coursing down the waters of the Hass. Longshoreman Folik edged his dirty, juddering flatbed ferry, the *Magnificat*, out from the north shore and began the eight-minute crossing to the main wharves. The diesel motor coughed and spluttered. Folik eased the revs and coasted between garbage scows and derelicts, following the dredged channel. Grey estuary birds, with hooked pink beaks, rose from the scows in a raucous swirl. To the *Magnificat*'s port side, the stone stilts of the Hass Viaduct, two hundred metres tall, cast long, cold shadows across the water.

Those damn sirens! What was that about?

Mincer sat at the prow, watching the low-water for new impediments. He gestured and Folik inched the ferry to starboard, swishing in between the trash hulks and the river-sound buoys.

Folik could see the crowds on the jetty. Big crowds. He grinned to himself.

'We'll make a sweet bundle on this, Fol!' Mincer shouted, unlooping the tarred rope from the catheads.

'I think so,' Folik murmured. 'I just hope we have a chance to spend it…'

MERITY CHASS HAD been trying on long-gowns in the dressing suites of the gown-maker when the klaxons first began to sound. She froze, catching sight of her own pale, startled face in the dressing mirror. The klaxons were distant, almost plaintive, from up here in mid-Spine, but local alarms shortly joined in. Her handmaids came rushing in from the cloth-maker's vestibule and helped her lace up her own dress.

'They say Zoica goes to war!' said Maid Francer.

'Like in the old times, like in the Trade War!' Maid Wholt added, pulling on a bodice string.

'I have been educated by the best tutors in the hive. I know about the Trade War. It was the most bloody and production-costly event in hive history! Why do you giggle about it?'

The maids curtseyed and backed away from Merity.

'Soldiers!' Maid Wholt sniggered.

'Handsome and hungry, coming here!' squealed Maid Francer.

'Shut up, both of you!' Merity ordered. She pulled her muslin fichu around her shoulders and fastened the pin. Then she picked up her credit wand from the top of the rosewood credenza. Though the wand was a tool that gave her access to her personal expense account in the House Chass treasury, it was ornamental in design, a delicate lace fan which she flipped open and waved in front of her face as the built-in ioniser hummed.

The maids looked down, stifling enthusiastic giggles.

'Where is the gown maker?'

'Hiding in the next room, under his desk,' Francer said.

'I said you'd require transportation to be summoned, but he refuses to come out,' Wholt added.

'Then this establishment will no longer enjoy the custom of Noble House Chass. We will find our own transport,' Merity said. Head high, she led her giggling maids out of the thickly carpeted gown-hall, through drapes that drew back automatically at their approach and out into the perfumed elegance of the Promenade.

GOL KOLEA PUT down his axe-rake and pulled off his headlamp. His hands were bloody and sore. The air was black with rock-soot, like fog. Gol sucked a mouthful of electrolyte fluid from his drinking pipe and refastened it to his collar.

'What is that noise?' he asked Trug Vereas.

Trug shrugged. 'Sounds like an alarm, up there somewhere.' The work face of Number Seventeen Deep Working was way below the conduits and mine-head wheels of the mighty ore district. Gol and Trug were sixteen hundred metres underground.

Another work gang passed them, also looking up and speaking in low voices.

'Some kind of exercise?'

'Must be,' Trug said. He and Gol stepped aside as a laden string of ore-carts loaded with loose conglomerate rattled by along the greasy mono-track. Somewhere nearby, a rock-drill began to chatter.

'Okay…' Gol raised his tool and paused. 'I worry about Livy.'

'She'll be fine. Trust me. And we've got a quota to fill.'

Gol swung his axe-rake and dug in. He just wished the scrape and crack of his blade would drown out the distant sirens.

CAPTAIN BAN DAUR paused to button his double-breasted uniform coat and pull the leather harness into place. He forced his mind to be calm. As an officer, he would have been informed of any drill and usually he got wind even of surprise practises. But this was real. He could feel it.

He picked up his gloves and his spiked helmet and left his quarters. The corridors of the Hass West wall-fort were bustling with troop details. All wore the blue cloth uniform and spiked helmets of the Vervun Primary, the city's standing army. Five hundred thousand troops all told, plus another 70,000 auxiliaries and armour crews, a mighty force that manned the Curtain Wall and the wall forts of Vervunhive. The regiment had a noble heritage and had proved itself in the Trade War, from which time they had been maintained as a permanent institution. When foundings were ordered for the Imperial Guard, Vervunhive raised them from its forty billion-plus population. The men of Vervun Primary were never touched or transferred. It was a life-duty, a career. But though their predecessors had fought bravely, none of the men currently composing the ranks of Vervun Primary had ever seen combat.

Daur barked out a few commands to calm the commotion in the hallway. He was young, only twenty-three, but tall and cleanly handsome, from a good mid-Spine family and the men liked him. They seemed to relax a little, seeing him so calm. Not that he felt calm.

'Alert duty stations,' Daur told them. 'You there! Where's your weapon?'

The trooper shrugged. 'Came running when I heard the– Forgot it… sir…'

'Go back and get it, you dumb gak! Three days' discipline duty – after this is over.'

The soldier ran off.

'Now!' cried Daur. 'Let's pretend we've actually been trained, shall we? Every man of you knows where he should be and what he should be doing, so go! In the hallowed name of the Emperor and in the service of the beloved hive!'

Daur headed uptower, pulling out his autopistol and checking its clip.

Corporal Bendace met him on the steps. Bendace had a data-slate in one hand and a pathetic moustache on his upper lip.

'Told you to shave that off,' Daur said, taking the slate and looking at it.

'I think it's… dashing,' Bendace said soulfully, stroking it.

Daur ignored him, reading the slate. They hurried up the tower as troopers double-timed down. On a landing, they passed a corporal tossing autoguns from a wall rack to a line of waiting men.

'So?' asked Bendace as they started up the final flight to the fort-top.

'You know those rumours you heard? About Zoica going for another Trade War?'

'That confirms it?'

Daur pushed the slate back into Bendace's hands with a sour look. 'No. It doesn't say anything. It's just a deployment order from House Command in the Spine. All units are to take position, protocol gamma sigma. Wall and fort weapons to be raised.'

'It says that?'

'No, I'm making it up. Yes, it says that. Weapons raised, but not armed, until further House Command notice.'

'This is bad, isn't it?'

Daur shrugged. 'Define "bad"?'

Bendace paused. 'I–'

'Bad is your facial growth. I don't know what this is.'

They stepped out onto the windy battlements. Gun crews were raising the trio of anti-air batteries into position, hydraulic pistons heaving the weapon mounts up from shuttered hardpoints in the tower top. Autoloader carriages were being wheeled out from the lift-heads. Other troops had taken up position in the netted stub-nests. Cries and commands flew back and forth.

Daur crossed to the ramparts and looked around. At his back, the vast, smoke-hazed shape of the Main Spine itself rose into the sombre sky like a granite peak, winking with a million lights. To his right lay the glitter of the River Hass and the grimy shapes of the docks and outer habs on the far bank. Below him, the sweeping curve of the vast adamantine Curtain Wall curved away east to the smoke pall of the ore smelteries and the dark mass of the Spoil hunkered twenty-five kilometres further round the circumference of the city skirts.

To the south, the slum-growths of the outer habs outside the wall, the dark wheel-heads and gantries of the vast mining district, and the marching viaducts of the main southern rail link extended far away. Beyond the extremities of the hive, the grasslands, a sullen, dingy green, reached to the horizon. Visibility was medium. Haze shimmered the distance. Daur cranked a tripod-mounted scope around, staring out. Nothing. A pale, green, unresolvable nothing.

He stood back and looked around the ramparts. One of the anti-air batteries on the wall-top below was only half raised and troopers were cursing and fighting to free the lift hydraulics. Other than that, everything and everyone was in place.

The captain took up the handset of the vox-unit carried by a waiting trooper.

'Daur to all Hass West area positions. Reel it off.'

The junior officers sang over the link with quick discipline. Daur felt genuine pride. Those in his command had executed gamma sigma in a little under twelve minutes. The fort and the western portion of the wall bristled with ready weapons and readier men.

He glanced down. The final, recalcitrant anti-aircraft battery rose into place. The crew gave a brief cheer that the wind stole away, then pushed the autoloader-cart in to mate with it.

Daur selected a new channel.

'Daur, Hass West, to House Command. We are deployed. We await your orders.'

IN THE VAST Square of Marshals, just inside the Curtain Wall, adjacent to the Heironymo Sondar Gate, the air shook with the thunder of three hundred tank engines. Huge Leman Russ war-machines, painted in the blue livery of Vervun Primary, revved at idle in rows across the square. More vehicles clanked and ground their way in at the back of the square, from the marshalling sheds behind the South-Hive barracks.

General Vegolain of the First Primary Armoured, jumped down from his mount, buckling on his leather head-shield, and approached the commissar. Vegolain saluted, snapping his jack-booted heels together.

'Commissar Kowle!'

'General,' Kowle replied. He had just arrived in the square by staff limousine, a sinister black vehicle that was now pulling away behind its motorbike escorts. There were two other commissars with him: Langana and the cadet Fosker.

Kowle was a tall, lean man who looked as if he had been forced to wear the black cap and longcoat of an Imperial commissar. His skin was sallow and taut, and his eyes were a disturbing beige.

Unlike Langana and Fosker, Kowle was an off-worlder. The senior commissar was Imperial Guard, seconded to watch over the Vervunhive standing army as a concession to its continued maintenance. Kowle quietly despised his post. His promising career with the Fadayhin Fifth had foundered some years before and against his will he had been posted to wet-nurse this toy army. Now, at last, he tasted the possibility of acquiring some glory that might rejuvenate his lustreless career.

Langana and Fosker were hive-bred, both from aspiring houses. Their uniform showed their difference from Kowle. In place of his Imperial double-eagle pins, they wore the axe-rake symbol of the VPHC, the Vervun Primary Hive Commissariat, the disciplinary arm of the standing army. The Sondar nobility was keen on discipline. Some even said that the VPHC was almost a secret police force, acting beyond the reach of the Administratum, in the interests of the ruling house.

'We have orders, commissar?'

Kowle scratched his nose absently and nodded. He handed Vegolain a data-slate.

'We are to form up at company strength and head out into the grasslands. I have not been told why.'

'I presume it is Zoica, commissar. They wish to spar with us again and–'

'Are you privy to the inter-hive policies of Zoica?' Kowle snapped.

'No, comm–'

'Do you then believe that rumour and dissent is a tool of control?'

'No, I–'

'Until we are told it is Zoica, it is no one. Is that clear?'

'Commissar. Will… will you be accompanying us?'

Kowle didn't reply. He marched across to Vegolain's Leman Russ and clambered aboard.

Three minutes later, the Sondar Gate opened with a great shriek of hydraulic compressors and the armoured column poured out onto the main south highway in triple file.

'WHO HAS ORDERED this alarm?' The question came from three mouths at once, dull, electronic, emotionless.

Marshal Gnide, strategic commander of Vervun Primary and chief military officer of Vervunhive, paused before replying. It was difficult to know which face to answer.

'Who?' the voices repeated.

Gnide stood in the softly lit, warm audience hall of the Imperial House Sondar, at the very summit of the Main

Spine. He wished he'd taken off his blue, floor-length, braid-trimmed greatcoat before entering. His plumed cap was heavy and itched his brow.

'It is necessary, High One.'

The three servitors, limp and supported only by the wires and leads that descended from the ceiling track-ways, circled him. One was a thin, androgynous boy with dye-stained skin. Another was a voluptuous girl, naked and branded with golden runes. The third was a chubby cherub, a toy harp in its pudgy hands, swan-wings sutured to its back. All of them lolled on their tubes and strings, blank-eyed.

Servos whined and the girl swung closer to Gnide, her limp feet trailing on the tiled floor.

'Are you my loyal marshal?' she asked, in that same flat monotone, that voice that wasn't hers.

Gnide ignored her, looking past the meat puppet – as he called it – to the ornamental iron tank in the far corner of the room. The metal of the tank was dark and tarnished with startlingly green rust. A single round porthole looked out like a cataract-glazed eye.

'You know I am, High One.'

'Then why this disobedience?' the youth asked, atrophied limbs trembling as the strings and leads swung him round.

'This is not disobedience, High One. This is duty. And I will not speak to your puppets. I asked for audience with House Ruler Salvador Sondar himself.'

The cherub swung abruptly round into Gnide's face. Sub-dermal tensors pulled its bloated mouth into a grin that was utterly unmatched by its dead eyes.

'They are me and I am them! You will address me through them!'

Gnide pushed the dangling cherub aside, flinching at the touch of its pallid flesh on his hand. He stalked up the low steps to the iron tank and stared into the lens port.

'Zoica mobilises against us, High One! A new Trade War is upon us! Orbital scans show this to be true!'

'It is not called Zoica,' the girl said from behind him. 'Use its name.'

Gnide sighed. 'Ferrozoica Hive Manufactory,' he said.

'At last, some respect,' rattled the cherub, bobbing around Gnide. 'Our old foes, now our most worthy trading partners. They are our brethren, our fellow trade-hive. We do not raise arms against them.'

'With respect!' snapped Gnide. 'Zoica has always been our foe, our rival. There were times last century they bettered us in output.'

'That was before House Sondar took the High Place here. Vervunhive is the greatest of all, now and ever after.' The youth-puppet began to drool slackly as it spoke.

'All Vervunhive rejoices that House Sondar has led us to domination. But the Legislature of the Noble houses has voted this hour that we should prepare for war. That is why the alarms were sounded.'

'Without me?' the girl hissed, flatly.

'As it is written, according to the customs, we signalled you. You did not reply. Mandate 347gf, as ratified by your illustrious predecessor, Heironymo, gives us authority to act.'

'You would use old laws to unseat me?' asked the cherub, clattering round on its strings to stare into Gnide's face with dead eyes.

'This is not usurpation, High One. Vervunhive is in danger. Look!' Gnide reached forward and pressed a data-slate against the lens of the tank.

'See what the orbitals tell us! Months of silence from Zoica, signs of them preparing for war! Rumours, hearsay – why weren't we told the truth? Why does this spring down on us so late in the day? Didn't you know? You, all-seeing, all-knowing High One? Or did you just decide not to tell us?'

The puppets began to thrash and jiggle, knocking into Gnide. He pushed them off.

'I have been in constant dialogue with my counterpart in Ferrozoica Hive Manufactory. We have come to enjoy the link, the companionship. His Highness Clatch of House Clatch is a dear friend. He would not deceive me. The musterings along the Ferrozoica ramparts were made because of the crusade. Warmaster Slaydo leads his legions into our spatial territories; the foul enemy is resisting. It is a precaution.'

'Slaydo is dead, High One. Five years cold on Balhaut. Macaroth is the leader of the crusade now. The beloved Guard legions are sweeping the Sabbat Worlds clean of Chaos scum. We rejoice daily that our world, beloved Verghast, was not touched.'

'Slaydo is dead?' the three voices asked as one.

'Yes, High One. Now, with respect, I ask that we may test-start the Shield. If Zoica is massing to conquer us, we must be ready.'

'No! You undermine me! The Shield cannot be raised without my permission! Zoica does not threaten! Clatch is our friend! Slaydo is not dead!'

The three voices rose in a shrill chorus, the meat puppets quivering with unknowable rage.

'You would not have treated Heironymo with such disrespect!'

'Your brother, great one as he was, did not hide in an Awareness Tank and talk through dead servitors… High One.'

'I forbid it!'

Gnide pulled a glittering ducal seal from his coat. 'The Legislature expected this. I am empowered by the houses of Vervunhive, in expediency, to revoke your powers as per the Act of Entitlement, 45jk. The Legislature commends your leadership, but humbly entreats you that it is now taking executive action.' Gnide pushed the puppets aside and crossed to a brass console in the far wall. He pressed the centre of the seal and data-limbs extended like callipers from the rosette with a machined click. Gnide set it in the lock and turned it.

The console flashed into life, chattering runes and sigils scrolling down the glass plate.

'No!' screeched the three voices. 'This is insubordination! I am Vervunhive! I am Vervunhive!'

'You are dethroned for the good of the city,' Gnide snapped. He pressed the switches in series, activating the power generators deep beneath the hive. He entered the sequences that would engage the main transmission pylon and bring the Shield online.

The cherub flew at him. He batted it away and it upturned, tangling in its cords. Gnide punched in the last sequence and reached for the activation lever.

He gasped and fell back, reaching behind him. The girl puppet jerked away, a long blade wedged in her dead hands. The blade was dark with blood.

Gnide tried to close the gouting wound in his lower back. His knees gave and he fell. The girl swung in again and stuck the blade through his throat.

He fell, face down, soaking the carpet with his pumping blood.

'I am Vervunhive,' the girl said. The cherub and youth repeated it, dull and toneless.

Inside the iron tank, bathed in warm ichor and floating free, every organ and vessel connected by tubes to the life-bank, Salvador Sondar, High Master of Vervunhive… dreamed.

THE SALT GRASSES were ablaze. All along the scarp rise, Vervun Primary tanks were buckled and broken amid the rippling, grey grass, fire spilling out of them. The air was toxic with smoke.

Commissar Kowle dropped clear of the command tank as flames within consumed the shrieking Vegolain and his crew. Kowle's coat was on fire. He shed it.

Enemy fire pummelled down out of the smoke-black air. A Vervun tank a hundred metres away exploded and sent shockwaves of whickering shrapnel in all directions.

One shard grazed Kowle's temple and dropped him.

He got up again. Crews were bailing from burning tanks, some on fire, some trying to help their blazing fellows. Others ran.

Kowle walked back through the line of decimated hive armour, smelling the salt grass as it burned, thick and rancid in his nose.

He pulled out his pistol.

'Where is your courage?' he asked a tank gunner as he put a round through his head.

'Where is your strength?' he inquired of two loaders fleeing up the slope, as he shot them both.

He put his muzzle to the head of a screaming, half-burned tank captain and blew out his brains. 'Where is your conviction?' Kowle asked.

He swung round and pointed his pistol at a group of tank crewmen who were stumbling up the grassy rise towards him from their exploded tank.

'Well?' he asked. 'What are you doing? This is war. Do you run from it?'

They hesitated. Kowle shot one through the head to show he meant business.

'Turn! Face the foe!'

The remaining crewmen turned and fled towards the enemy positions. A tank round took them all apart a second later.

Missiles strafed in from the low, cloudlike meteorites and sundered twenty more tanks along the Vervun formation. The explosions were impossibly loud. Kowle was thrown flat in the grass.

He heard the clanking as he rolled over. On the far rise, battletanks and gun platforms painted in the ochre livery of Zoica rolled down towards him.

A thousand or more.

OUT OF NOWHERE, just before nightfall, about a half-hour after the klaxons had stopped yelping, the first shells fell, unexpected, hurled by long-range guns beyond the horizon.

Two fell short on the southern outer habs, kicking up plumes of wreckage from the worker homes.

Another six dented the Curtain Wall.

At Hass West, Daur yelled to his men and cranked the guns around. *A target… give me a target…* he prayed.

Dug-in Zoica armour and artillery, hidden out in the burning grasslands, found their range. Shells began to drop into the hive itself.

A gigantic salvo hit the railhead at Veyveyr Gate and set it ablaze. Several more bracketed the Vervun Primary barracks and atomised over a thousand troopers waiting for deployment.

Another scatter pounded the northern habs along the river. Derricks and quays exploded and shattered into the water. In mid-stream, Folik's over-laden ferry was showered with burning debris. Folik tried to turn in the current, yelling for Mincer. Another shell fell in the water nearby, drenching the screaming passengers with stinking river water. The ferry wallowed in the blast-wake.

Two more dropped beyond the *Magnificat*, exploding and sinking the ferry *Inscrutable*, which was crossing back over the tideway. The *Inscrutable* went up in a shockwave that peppered the water with debris. Diesel slicks burned on the choppy surface.

Folik pulled his wheel around and steered out into mid-channel. Mincer was screaming something at him, but the wail of shells drowned him out.

A STAGGERED SALVO rippled through the mining district, flattening wheel heads and pulley towers.

Deep below the earth, Gol Kolea tried to dig Trug Vereas out of the rock fall that had cascaded down the main lift chute of Number Seventeen Deep Working. All around, miners were screaming and dying.

Trug was dead, his head mashed.

Gol pulled back, his hands slick with his friend's blood. Lift cables whipped back down the shaft as cages smashed and fell. The central access had collapsed in on them.

'Livy!' he screamed up into the abyss. '*Livy!*'

VOR WAS OBLITERATED by the first shell that came through the roof of Vervun Smeltery One. Agun Soric was thrown flat and a chip of ore flying from the blistering shock took out his left eye forever.

Blood from cuts to the scalp streamed down his face. He rolled over in the wreckage and then was lifted off the floor by another impact that exploded the main conveyor. A piece of oily bracket, whizzing supersonically across the work-floor, decapitated one of the screaming workers nearby and embedded itself in the meat of Soric's thigh. He howled, but his cry was lost in the tumult and the klaxons as they started again.

LIVY KOLEA LOOKED around as the glass roof of the transit station fell in explosively and she tried to shield Yoncy and Dalin.

Glass shrapnel ripped her to pieces, her and another sixty civilians. The aftershock of hot air crisped the rest. Dalin was behind a pillar and remained miraculously unscathed. He got up, crunching over the broken glass, calling for his mother.

When he found what was left of her, he fell silent, too stunned for noise.

Tona Criid took him up in her arms.

'S'okay, kid. S'okay.' She pulled over the upturned cart and saw the healthy, beaming face of the baby smiling back at her. Tona took up the infant under one arm and dragged the boy behind her.

They were twenty metres from the south atrium when further shells levelled carriage station C4/a.

MENX AND TROOR escorted Guilder Worlin through the chaos of the Commercia. Several barter-houses to their west were ablaze and smoke clogged the marketways. The closest carriage station with links to the Main Spine was C4/a, but there was a vast smoke plume in that direction. Menx redirected their route through the abandoned Guild Fayk barter-house and headed instead for C7/d.

By the time they reached the funicular railway depot, Guilder Worlin was crying with rage. The bodyguard thought it was for fear of his life, but Worlin was despairing for purely mercantile reasons. Guild Worlin had no holdings in weaponshops, medical supplies, or food sources. War was on them and they had no suitable holdings to exploit.

They entered the carriage station, but the place was deserted. A few abandoned possessions – purse-bags, pictslates and the like – were scattered on the platform. The transit indicator plate overhead was blank.

'I want,' Worlin hissed through clenched teeth, 'to return to the Main Spine now. I want to be in the family house, to be inside the Spine hull. Now!'

Troor looked down the monotrack and turned back. 'I see lights, sir. A transit approaches.'

The carriage train pulled into the station and stopped on automatic for a moment. The twin cars were packed full of Low- and Mid-Spine citizens.

'Let me in!' Worlin banged on the nearest door-hatch. Terrified faces looked out at him silently.

Shells walloped into the Commercia behind him. Worlin pulled out his needle pistol and opened fire through the glass. The passengers, trapped like rats in a cage, screamed as they were slaughtered.

After a brief hesitation, Worlin's bodyguard joined him, slaughtering twenty or more with their unshrouded guns. Others fled the carriage, screaming. Pulling out bodies, the guards hauled Worlin into the carriage, just as the automatic rest period finished and the transit resumed. It engaged on the cog-track and slowly began to crank up into the hull of the main Spine.

'House Sondar, deliver us from evil,' hissed Worlin, sitting down on a gilt bench seat and rearranging his robes. Menx and Troor stood nearby, uneasy and unnerved.

Worlin gazed out of the window of the rising transit, apparently not seeing the smoke blooms and fireballs rising across the city below – just as he didn't seem to see the pools of blood that washed around his shoes.

VOLLEYS OF SHELLS and long-range missiles pounded into the southern face of the Main Spine. Despite the thick adamantine and ceramite sheath, some even punctured the skin of the great structure. A glassmaker's showrooms on the Mid-Spine Promenade took a direct hit and blew out, filling the air with whizzing splinters of lead-crystal and ceramite wall debris. Fifty house ordinary nobles and their retainers were shredded or burnt as they hurried in panic down the plush walkways.

Just a few steps beyond the glassmaker's, shielded from the out-blast by a row of pillars, Merity Chass continued to stride on, her weeping maids huddled behind her.

'This is not happening,' Merity Chass told herself. 'This is not happening.'

MULTIPLE SHELL HITS lit up the Curtain Wall around Hass West. An anti-aircraft post, the one that had been slow rising from its pit, was blown away and its ignited munitions tore a bite out of the wall.

Captain Daur traversed his guns and looked for an enemy. The grasslands were blank. Long-range weapons were reaching them, utterly beyond their power to resist.

If they even had the authority.

'Captain Daur to Marshal Gnide! Give us permission to arm! Give the order! Marshal, I'm begging you!'

IN THE DULL quiet of the audience chamber, Gnide's corpse was lifted away from the carpet by the slack puppets. The desperate voice of Daur and hundreds of other field commanders bayed unheard from his vox-plug.

THREE SHELLS HIT Hass West Fort in series. The first ignited the battery munitions. The second vaporised Corporal Bendace and sixteen other troopers. The third, a crippling shockwave, splintered the tower top and caused a vast chunk of rampart to slump away in a torrent of stone, dust and fire. Captain Daur fell with it, caught in the avalanche of rockcrete and ceramite. He had still not received the order to arm from the House Command.

IN THE IRON Tank, Salvador Sondar, High Master of Vervunhive, drifted and dreamed. The satisfaction he had gained from asserting his mastery over that fool Gnide was ebbing. There was something akin to pain creeping into him across the mind-impulse links that hooked his cortex into the datatides and production autoledgers of the hive. He rolled over in the warm suspension fluid and accessed the information currents of the Legislature and the guilds. The hive was... under attack.

He retuned his link to confirm. Even when the information was verified, it seemed wrong. There was a discrepancy that his mind could not resolve. Vervunhive was attacked. Yet this should not be.

He needed time to think.

Petulantly, he activated the Shield generators.

TWO
AN OCHRE WAVE

'Be it one man or one million, the enemy of the Imperium must be treated the same and denied with all diligence.'

— Pius Kowle, Imperial Commissar,
from his public education leaflets

DUSK CAME EARLY at the end of the first day. The darkening sky was stained darker still by the smoke plumes rising from the hive and its outer districts, and by the great ashen pall looming over the salt grasslands to the south. Thick, fire-swollen, black smoke boiled up from the mining district and the heavy industrial suburbs south of the Curtain Wall, and a murky brown flare of burning fuel rose from ruptured tanks and silos on the Hass docks to the north of the river. Other threads of white, grey and mauve smoke rose from hundreds of smaller, individual fires.

The bombardment continued, even though the Shield had been raised. A vast, translucent umbrella of field-energy extended out from the great Shield Pylon in the central district and unfurled itself in a dome that reached down to anchor substations inside the Curtain Wall. Thousands of shells and missiles burst against it every minute, dimpling the cloudy energy and making it ripple and wobble like green gelatine. From inside the Shield, it looked as if the green sky was blossoming with fire.

Observers on the southern wall, most of them soldiers of Vervun Primary, trained their scopes and magnoculars through the rising smoke and fires in the outer habs and saw the distant grass horizon flickering with a wall of flame seventy kilometres wide. The grass smoke – ash-grey but streaked with black from individual infernos down below the skyline – tarnished the southern sky in the dying light. Bright, brief flashes underlit the horizon smoke, hinting at the fierce armour battle taking place just out of sight. No communications had been received from General Vegolain's armoured column for two hours.

Now that the Shield was up to cover the main hive, the outer habs, the heavy industry sectors and the mining district south of the wall were taking the worst of it. Unprotected, they were raked mercilessly by long-range artillery, siege mortars and incendiary rockets. As the light faded, the southern out-hive suburb became a dark, mangled mass, busy with thousands of fires, drizzled by fresh rains of explosives. From the Wall, it was possible to see the shock waves radiating from each major strike, gusting the existing fires.

The population of the southern outer habs was in the order of nine million, plus another six million workers who dwelt in the main hive but travelled out to work the industrial district and the mines. They had little shelter. Some hid in cellars or underground storage bays and many died entombed in these places. Penetrator shells dug them out explosively like rats, opening the makeshift shelters to the sky. Others were sealed forever under thousands of tonnes of collapsed masonry.

There were a few deep-seated, hardpoint shelters in the southern habs, reserved for suburban officials and minor area legislators. These shelters had been dug ninety years before during the Trade War and few were in decent working order. One group of hab officials spent two hours trying to find the correct rune-code to let them into their assigned shelter and they were incinerated by a rocket before they could get the vault door open. Another group, a few blocks north, found themselves fighting off a terrified mob that wanted to gain access to a shelter too. A VPHC officer, leading the group, opened fire with his handgun to drive the frantic citizens away while the ranking official, a mill-boss with guild connections, opened the vault.

They sealed themselves in, twenty-three rank-privileged citizens of authority level three or less, in a bunker emplacement designed to shelter two hundred. They all died of suffocation by the following dawn. The air systems, long in need of overhaul and regular maintenance, failed the moment they were switched on.

By nightfall, millions of refugees were clogging the main arterial routes into the hive, bottled up at Sondar Gate, at the Hass West road entry and the ore works cargo route. They were even trying to gain access via the rail-link tunnel at Veyveyr Gate, but the terminal inside had been turned into an inferno in the first wave of bombing and the gate was blocked.

Others still, in desperate, slowly moving lines, many laden with possessions or injured family members, dared the Spoil and the mud flats, and some made it in through the as-yet-undamaged railhead at Croe Gate.

The Hass West Fort was still burning and the top of it was cascading debris down inside and outside the Wall. However, the Wall and the Hass Gate itself were still firm and streams of refugees made it into the hive via the Hass Road under supervision of Vervun Primary troopers manning the damaged emplacement. But access was still slow and a column of people, two kilometres long and growing, tailed back from the Hass Gate into the dark, vulnerable to the ceaseless onslaught pummelling the outer habs. Thousands died before they could pass into shelter, as shells landed in the thick queue. Just as many, perhaps eight or nine thousand, fled the traffic stream northwest and made progress into the river shores.

The last kinking stretch of shield wall north of Hass West Fort, known as the Dock Wall, reached out into the mid-waters and there was no way through. Some perished in the treacherous mud-flats; others tried to swim the Hass itself and were lost by the hundreds. Most cowered in the stinking slime under the dock wall, wailing plaintively up at the soldiers two hundred metres above them on the wall top, men who could do nothing to help them. Almost two thousand people remained penned in that filthy corner of the Wall through the first days of the conflict, too afraid to try the route back round the wall to Hass Gate. Starvation, disease and despair killed them all within four days.

The Sondar Gate was open and the main tide of refugees sought entry there. The Vervun Primary troops, focussed en masse to control the crowd, admitted the people as quickly as possible, but it was miserably slow going and the column of people stretched three kilometres back into the burning outer habs.

Many of the tail-enders, certain they would be dead before ever reaching the safety of the hive's Shield, turned around and headed out into the salt grasslands by the hundreds. None were ever seen alive again.

In the Square of Marshals, just inside the Heironymo Sondar Gate, the hive troopers struggled to manage the overwhelming influx of citizens. Forty percent of the arrivals were injured.

Captain Letro Cargin had been given charge of the operation and inside an hour he was close to despair. He had first tried to contain the refugees in the vast ceremonial square itself, but it quickly became filled to overflowing. Some family groups were climbing the pedestals of the statues around the square to find somewhere to crouch. There was group singing: work anthems of the hive or Imperial hymns. The massed, frail voices – set against the constant thunder of the bombardment and the crackle of the Shield above – unnerved his men.

The Vervun Primary barracks northwest of the square, which had taken hits in the first stage of the attack, was still blazing but under control. Cargin voxed House Command repeatedly until he was granted special permission from the guilds to open the Anko Chemical Plant west of the square and the guild manufactories to the east, to house the overspill. Quickly, these new areas became overfilled too. The guilds had issued particular instructions as to how much of those areas could be used or even entered. Cargin's men reported fights breaking out as they tried to deny access to certain areas. Shots were fired over the heads of the crowd. Compared to the onslaught they had weathered outside, the small arms of the troops were insignificant and the House Guard found themselves pushed back deeper into the industrial areas, trying to accommodate the intake. Most troopers were profoundly unwilling to shoot at their own citizens. In one instance, an angry junior officer actually fired into the encroaching crowd, killing two. He and his six man squad were torn apart by a pack of smoke-blackened textile workers.

Cargin voxed frantically for supplies and advice. By eight in the evening, new orders were being issued from House Command and the Legislature, designating refugee assembly areas, hastily arranged in the inner worker habs south of the Pylon and the Commercia. Asylum traffic from the Sondar Gate, Hass Gate and, to a lesser extent, the Croe Gate was now choking the southern sectors of the hive. Some of the House Legislature, meeting in extraordinary session in the Main Spine, argued that it was the hive's duty to house the outer hab population. Others were simply afraid that with the main southern arterials choked, they would never be able to mobilise their armies. Six noble houses also volunteered aid, which began to be shipped by carriage route down to the Square of Marshals and the main city landing field where the refugees from Hass Gate were also congregating.

It was a start, but not enough. Cargin began to wonder if the upper echelon of the hive really understood the scale of the problem. The Imperial mottoes, hive slogans and other messages of calming propaganda flashing up on the public-address plates did little to deaden the general panic. Cargin had angry, frightened citizens by the thousands, most stone-deaf from concussion shock, many burned naked by the blasts, many more dying and stretcher-bound. Short of closing the Gate itself, he had no way to stem the flow. His three thousand men were vastly outnumbered by the mass.

Cargin was voxed to the north corner of the square. There he found a field station had been set up by medics from some inner hab infirmary. Hundreds of the injured had been laid out on the stone paving. Doctors and orderlies dressed in crimson gowns and masks tended to them.

'Are you Cargin?'

Cargin looked round. A gowned and masked figure was addressing him. She pulled off her mask to reveal an appealing, heart-shaped face. The eyes, though, were hard and bewildered.

'Yes... doctor?'

'Surgeon Ana Curth, Inner Hab Collective Medical Hall 67/mv. I've been given authority here. We are trying to set up a triage station under the carriage stands over there, but the flow is too great.'

'I'm doing my best, surgeon,' he said flatly. He could see tractor units and trucks lining the barrack road, headlamps blazing and engines gunning, moving in to transport those in need of immediate surgery to the main infirmary facilities in the inner habs and Low Spine.

'Likewise,' said Curth without humour. The air smelled of blood and burned flesh and was full of piteous shrieking. 'The medical halls are already full of wounded from the inner city. There were huge casualties from the start of the raid, before the Shield was ignited.'

'I don't know what to say,' Cargin shrugged. 'I've followed my orders and allowed the incoming to flow out of the square into adjacent areas. There seems to be no end to them. My observers on the wall-top say the queue outside is still three kilometres long.'

The surgeon looked at the blood-spattered paving for a moment, her hands on her hips. 'I...' she began, then paused. 'Can you get me a vox link? I'll try sending to my superiors. The Commercia has been evacuated and there is vast floorspace inside it. I doubt they'll grant permission, but I'll do what I can.'

Cargin nodded. He called his vox-officer over and told him to attend the surgeon. 'Whatever you can do is better than nothing,' he told her.

THE TANK ROARED and bounced over the trampled grass hillocks, heading north at full throttle, its turret reversed to spit shells into the firefields behind it, into the invisible enemy at its heels.

The night sky was ablaze. Scorching trails of rockets and shrieking shells tore overhead, heading for the hive.

Commissar Kowle crouched in the turret of the running tank, shouting orders to fire to the gun-crew in the lit space below him. The vox-link was down. He couldn't reach House Command. He had forty-two tanks left out of the armoured column of more than four hundred and fifty that had left the Sondar Gate that afternoon. No ranking Vervun Primary armour officer was left alive. Cadet Fosker was also dead.

Kowle had command now. Using the VPHC Commissar Langana as his second officer, he had managed to regroup the shattered remnants of the tank force and swing it back towards the city. It felt like retreat, but Kowle knew it was a sound tactical decision. They were facing an ochre wave out there on the grass-flats, a stupendous Zoica armoured front, pushing in through three salients. Only in his days with the Imperial Guard, during major offensives like Balhaut and Cociaminus, had he seen anything like this scale of assault. And there were infantry regiments behind, thick like locusts, following the armour.

Kowle didn't even want to think about the size of the opposition just now. It was… unbelievable. It was impossible. An ochre wave – that's all he could see, the tide of ochre-painted machines rolling over his forces, crushing them.

He tried the vox again, but the enemy was jamming all bands. Shells rained down amongst the retreating Vervun tanks. At least two blew out as munitions ignited, sending tank hulls end-over-end in fireballs, spraying track segments out like shattered teeth.

The driver was calling him over the intercom. 'Ahead, sir!'

Kowle swivelled round. Vervunhive was in sight now, the great luminous blister of green energy flickering on the sky-line like a giant mushroom cloud, glowing in the night. Kowle grabbed his scope and saw the blackened, burning mass of the outer habs fast approaching. A persistent rain of explosives was still dropping into them.

'Kowle to column!' he spat into his inter-tank vox. 'Form up and follow me in down the Southern Highway. We will re-enter the city through the Sondar Gate. Let none shirk, for I will find them wanting and find them!'

He smiled at his last words. Even now, under a storm of fire, he could still turn a good, disciplinarian phrase.

THE HIGH-CEILINGED, gilt-ornamented Hall of the Legislature, high and secure in the upper sections of the Main Spine, was full of arguing voices.

Lord Heymlik Chass, noble patriarch of House Chass, sat back in his velvet-upholstered bench and glanced aside to his aides and chamberlains.

The Legislature was full tonight. All nine noble houses were in attendance, as well as the representatives of the other twenty-one houses ordinary, along with the drones of over three hundred guild associations and families in their flamboyant finery. And down in the commons pit, hundreds of habitat and work-clave representatives bayed for action.

As a scion of a noble house, Chass's bench was in the inner circle, just above the Legislator's dais. Vox/pict drones mumbled and hovered along the benches like bumblebees. The Legislature Choir, told to shut up some minutes before by Noble Croe, sat sullenly in their balcony, balling up pages of sheet music and throwing them down on the assembly beneath. Master Jehnik, of House Ordinary Jehnik, was on his feet in the middle circle, reading from a prepared slate and trying to get someone to listen to his fifty-five-point plan.

Chass pressed the geno-reader on the side of his hardwood stall and the plate slid open before him.

He keyed in his authority rating, touched the statement runes and wrote: *Master Legislator, are we going to debate or simply argue all night?*

The words flashed up on the central plate and six other noble houses, fifteen houses ordinary and the majority of the guild associations assented.

Silence fell.

The Master Legislator, Anophy, an ancient hunchback with a tricorn, ribboned hat, crawled to his feet from his dais throne and began the Litany of Enfranchisement. The assembly was quiet as it was intoned. Anophy stroked his long, silver moustache, smoothed the front of his opalescent robe and asked the assembly for points of order.

Around seventy holographic runes lit the plate display and glowed overhead via hovering repeater screens.

'Noble Anko has the floor.' There were moans from the commons pit.

Anko got up, or rather was helped up by his entourage. His raspy, vox-amplified voice rang around the hall.

'I deplore the attack on our city-hive by our erstwhile friends of Zoica. I press to vote we deny them and send them home, tails between their legs.'

No argument there, thought Chass. Typical Anko, going for the easy vote.

Anko went on. 'I wish the Legislature to back me on another matter. My plant is being overrun by indigents from the suburbs. House officers tell me that the plant is already overwhelmed and immediate production will be impossible. This hurts Vervunhive. I move that House Anko be allowed to eject the indigents from its premises.'

More squabbling and yelling from below.

'Noble Yetch?'

'Are we to disabuse our work population so, cousin Anko? You like them well enough when they raise your quotas. Do you hate them now they choke your factories?'

Commotion, louder than before. Several nobles and many guilders thumped their assent sirens vigorously. Anko sat down, his expression vile.

'Noble Chass?'

Chass rose. 'I fear my cousin Anko fails to read the larger story here. Ninety years have passed since we faced such a crisis. We face a Second Trade War. Reports are that the wave of enemy force is quite humbling to our own defences. We have all seen how the tumult today has wounded our hive. Why, my own dear daughter barely reached home alive.'

Sympathetic holograms flashed sycophantically from the tiers of some of the houses ordinary.

Chass continued. 'If this attack inconveniences our houses, I say: Let us be inconvenienced! We have a duty to the hive population and cousin Anko should put that bald fact before his production quota. I wish to frame more important questions to this Legislature. One: Why did this attack come as a surprise? Two: Should we signal the Imperium for assistance? Three: Where is the High Master, what did he know of this and why was the Shield ignited so late?'

Now the roaring grew. Assent sigils lit up all around. The Legislator screamed for order.

'Noble Chass,' a voice said, lilting through the huge hall. 'How would you wish me answer that?'

The place fell silent. Escorted by ten impassive, uniformed officers of the VPHC, High Master Salvador Sondar entered the Hall.

HE WAS BLIND in one eye and limping badly. His flesh was blistered and charred, and his clothes were tattered. But he was still plant supervisor.

Using an axe-rake as a crutch, Agun Soric bellowed as best his crisped lungs could manage, as he brought over three hundred smeltery workers out through the northern processing ramps of Vervun Smeltery One. Most were as soot-black as he was, the only things showing against the grime being the glistening red of wounds or the white of fresh dressings.

That and the workers' white, fear-filled eyes.

They carried their injured with them, some on makeshift stretchers, some in carriers made of tied sacking, some pushed in ore-barrows.

Soric stomped around and looked back with his one good eye. Vervun Smeltery One and parts of the surrounding ore plants were burning furiously. Chimney stacks collapsed in the heat, sending up white cinders against the yellow flames. The Veyveyr Rail Terminal, to the west, was also torching out.

He heard shouting and disputes from the concourse below him and he hobbled down, pushing his way through the rows of men and women from his plant.

A dozen Vervun Primary soldiers were stopping the survivors' advance down transit channel 456/k into the inner habs. A VPHC officer was leading them.

'We need to get in there,' Soric said, stomping up to the commissariat officer. Even with one eye, Soric could see the twitchy, frantic light in the young VPHCer's eyes.

'Orders from Main Spine, old man,' the Commissar told him. 'Low hab is choked with refugees. No more may be admitted. You camp here. Supplies will come in time.'

'What's your name?' Soric asked.

'Commissar Bownome.'

Soric paused, leaned awkwardly on his crutch, and wiped the ash from his supervisor's badge with a hawk of spit.

He held it up so the uniformed man could see. 'Soric, plant supervisor, Smeltery One. We've just been bombed to gak and my workers need access to cover and treatment. Now, not in time.'

'There is no way through. Access is denied. Make your people comfortable here.' The troopers behind Bownome raised their weapons as punctuation.

'Here? In a stinking street with the works burning behind us? I don't think so. Boy, Smeltery One is the property of Noble House Gavunda. We are all Lord Gavunda's souls. If he hears of this–'

'I answer only to House Sondar. As should you. Don't threaten me.'

'Where's the gakking threat, you idiot?' Soric asked, looking round at his massing workers and getting a spirited laugh in answer. 'A one-eyed cripple like me? Let us through.'

'Aye, let us through!' bellowed a worker beside Soric. Ozmac, probably, but it was impossible to tell under the soot. Other workers jeered and agreed.

'Do you understand what a State of Emergency is, old man?' Bownome asked.

'Understand? I'm gakking living it!' Soric blurted. 'Stand aside!' He tried to push past the VPHC officer, but Bownome pushed back and Soric fell off his crutch onto the debris-littered paving.

There were shouts of disbelief and anger. Workers surged forward. Bownome backed away, pulled out his autopistol and fired into the approaching mass.

Ozmac fell dead and another collapsed wounded.

'That's it! Enough! Be warned!' yelled the commissar. 'You will all stay where–'

Soric's axe-rake crutch shattered Bownome's skull and felled him to the ground. Before any of the troopers could react, the workers were on them like a tidal wave. All of the troopers were killed in a few seconds.

The smeltery workers gathered up their weapons. Worker Gannif handed the commissar's pistol to Soric.

'I'll see you right!' Soric barked. He waved for them to follow him down the transit channel. They cheered him and moved on, at his heels, into the city.

'MARSHAL GNIDE IS dead,' High Master Sondar told the Legislature. The hall had remained silent as the High Master's floating throne ascended to the main dais with its stone-faced VPHC vanguard. Sondar's throne had locked into place above the High Legislator's dais and the master of Vervunhive had spent a long moment looking out at the assembly before speaking. He was dressed in regal robes, his face masked with a turquoise ceramic janus.

'Dead,' Sondar repeated. 'Our hive faces a time of war – and you, noble houses, low houses, guilders, you decide it is time to usurp my position?'

Silence remained.

Sondar's masked visage turned to look around at the vast swoop of the tiered hall.

'We are one, or we are nothing.'

Still the nervous silence.

'I believe you think me weak. I am not weak. I believe you think me stupid. I am not that either. I believe that certain high houses see this as an opportunity to further their own destinies.'

The High Master allowed Noble Anko to rise with a wave of his hand.

'We never doubted you, High Lord. The Trade War fell upon us so suddenly.'

You witless weakling, Chass thought. Sondar has led us to this blind and you reconcile sweetly. Where is the fervour that had us vote to take executive action this afternoon?

'Zoica will be denied,' Sondar said. Chass watched the High Lord's movements and saw how jerky they were. It's not him, he thought. The wretch has sent another servitor puppet to represent him.

'We have sent word to the Northern Foundry Collectives and to Vannick Magna. They will bolster us with garrison troops. Our counterattack will begin in two days.'

There was delighted commotion from the commons pit and the guild tiers.

Chass rose and spoke. 'I believe it is in the interests of Verghast as a whole to send to the Imperium for assistance.'

'No,' responded Sondar quickly. 'We have beaten Zoica before; we will do it again. This is an internal matter.'

'No longer,' a voice said from below. The assembly looked down at the benches where the officials of the Administratum sat. Hooded and gowned, Intendant Banefail of the Imperial Administratum got to his feet. 'Astropathic messages have already been sent out, imploring Imperial assistance from Warmaster Macaroth. Vervunhive's production of ordnance and military vehicles is vital for the constant supply of the Sabbat Worlds Crusade. The warmaster will take our plight seriously. This is a greater matter than local planetary politics, High Lord Sondar.'

Sondar, or rather the being that represented him, seemed to quiver in his throne. Rage, Chass presumed. The balance between hive and Imperial authority had always been delicate in Vervunhive, indeed in all the nobilities of Verghast. It was rare for it to clash so profoundly and so visibly. Chass well knew the fundamental strategic import of Vervunhive and the other Verghast manufactory cities to the crusade, but still the magnitude of the intendant's actions amazed him. The Administratum was the bureaucratic right hand of the Emperor himself, but it usually bowed to the will of the local planetary governor.

Our plight must truly be serious, he realised, a sick feeling seeping into his heart.

HOLDING THE INFANT and pulling the small boy by the hand, Tona Criid ran through the burning northern section of the

Commercia. The boy was crying now. She couldn't help that. If they could make the docks, she could get them clear across the river and to safety. But the routes were packed. As fast as refugees came into the hive from the south, inhabitants were fleeing to the north.

'Where we going?' asked the boy, Dalin.

'Somewhere safe,' Tona told him.

'Who are you?'

'I'm your Aunt Tona.'

'I don't have an aunt.'

'You do now. And so does Yancy here.'

'He's Yoncy.'

'Yeah, whatever. Come on.' Tona tried to thread them through the massing crowds that filled the transit channels down to the docks, but they were jammed tight.

'Where are we going?' asked the kid again as they sheltered in a barter-house awning to avoid the press.

'Away. To the river.' That was the plan. But with the crowds this thick, she didn't know if it was going to be possible. Maybe they'd be safer in the city, under the Shield.

The baby began to cry.

HE COULDN'T BREATHE. The weight and blackness upon him were colossal. Something oily was dripping into his eyes. He tried to move, but no movement was possible. No, that wasn't true. He could grind his toes in his army boots. His mouth was full of rockcrete dust. He started to cough and found his lungs had no room to move. He was squashed.

There was a rattling, chinking sound above him. He could hear voices, distant and muffled. He tried to cry out, but the dust choked him and he had no room to choke.

Light. A chink of light, just above as rubble was moved away. Rubble moved and some pieces slumped heavier on him, vicing his legs and pelvis.

There was a face in the gap above him.

'Who's down there?' it called. 'Are you alive?'

Hoarse and dry, he answered. 'My name is Ban Daur – and yes, I am alive.'

* * *

HIS FAMILY HOUSE was deserted. Guilder Worlin strode inside, leaving a sticky tread of blood in his footprints. His clan was at the Legislature, he was sure. Let them go and bow and scrape to the High Lord.

He crossed the draped room to the teak trolley by the ornamental window and poured himself a triple shot of joiliq. Menx and Troor waited in the anteroom, whispering nervously.

'Bodyguard! To me!' Worlin called as the fire of the drink warmed his body. He waved an actuator wand at the wall plate and saw nothing but cycling scrolls of Imperium propaganda. He snapped the plate off and dropped the wand.

His bodyguard approached. They had both shrouded their weapons again, as was the custom inside guild households.

Worlin sat back on the suspensor couch and sipped his drink, smiling. Outside the window, the sprawl of Vervunhive spread out, many parts of it ablaze. The green, Shield-tinted sky contorted with the constant shelling.

'You have served me well tonight,' Worlin told them.

The bodyguards paused, uncertain.

'Menx! Troor! My friends! Fetch yourselves a drink from the cart and relax! Your master is proud of you!'

They hesitated and then turned. Troor raised a decanter as Menx found glasses. As soon as they had their backs to him, Worlin pulled the needle pistol from his robes and fired.

The first shot blew Menx's spine out and he was flung face first into the cart, which broke under him and shattered. Troor turned and the decanter in his hand was shattered by the second shot. The third exploded his face and he dropped backwards onto the cart wreckage.

Worlin got up and, drink in hand, fired thirty more needles into the twisted corpses, just to be sure. Then he sat back, sipping his drink, watching Vervunhive burn.

'THE ROAD IS blocked, sir!' the tank driver yelled through the intercom to Kowle. Chasing up the Southern Highway, through the wrecked outer habs, with shells still falling, Kowle's column had reached the rear of the queue of refugees tailing back from Sondar Gate.

Kowle sat up in the turret, looking ahead, taking in the sea of milling bodies before them.

Shells fell to the west and lit up the night.

Kowle dropped into the turret and said, 'Drive through.'

The driver looked back at him in amazement.

'But commissar–'

'Are you denying a direct order?' Kowle snapped.

'No, sir, commissar, sir, but–'

Kowle shot him through the throat and dragged his twitching body out of the driver's seat.

He settled into the blood-slick metal chair and keyed the intercom. 'Armour column. Follow me.'

Just outhab wretches… worthless, he decided, as he drove the tank down through the masses, crushing a path to the distant gates of Vervunhive.

THREE
A MIDNIGHT SUN

'After this, all battles will be easy, all victories simple, all glories hollow.'

— General Noches Sturm,
after his victory on Grimoyr

THE BOMBARDMENT CONTINUED, both day and night, for two and a half weeks. By the close of the twelfth day, day and night were barely distinguishable, so great was the atmospheric smoke-haze hanging around Vervunhive. The Shield held firm, but the southern outhabs and manufactories became a fire-blown wasteland, fifty kilometres square. Some shelling had also been deliberately ranged over the Shield, catastrophically wounding the unprotected northern districts and large sections of the Hass docklands.

On the afternoon of the sixth day, Marshal Edric Croe, the Legislature's appointed successor to Gnide, ordered the closing of the southern hive gates. The new marshal, brother of Lord Croe of that noble house, had been a serving major-colonel in Vervun Primary and his election was ratified by seven of the nine noble houses. Noble House Anko – who

46

were sponsoring their own General, Heskith Anko, for the post – voted to deny. Noble House Chass abstained.

Marshal Croe was a pale, white-haired giant, well over two metres tall. His fierce black eyes and hard gaze were the subject of barrack legend, but he was personally calm, quiet and inspirational, judicious in leadership and popular with the men. The majority vote of the noble houses reflected their confidence in him – and the fact they felt he would remain answerable to them in all circumstances. Heskith Anko, a plump, swarthy brute who approached war politically rather than tactically, was appointed Croe's chief of staff to appease House Anko. The two did not get on and their furious arguments in House Command became notorious.

Croe's decision to close the gates – at this stage there were still some half a million refugees streaming in from the southern districts seeking sanctuary at Hass West, Sondar and Croe Gates – surprised the houses and the Legislature as a whole. Many believed Croe had bowed to Anko's persistent pressure. House Chass, House Rodyin and seven houses ordinary raised a bill of disapproval and railed against the cruelty of the action. Half a million, left to die, the gates sealed against them. 'It defies humanity,' Lord Rodyin stated in the Hall of the Legislature.

In fact, Marshal Croe's decision had been far more deeply affected by the advice of Commissar Kowle, who had returned from the frontline with the tattered remnants of the tank divisions on the second night. Despite the losses suffered by Vegolain's forces, Kowle was hailed by many as a hero. He had single-handedly rallied more than thirty vehicles and crews and pulled them back, bringing first-hand details of the enemy home to the hive. The public-address plates spoke freely of his heroism and loyalty. His name was chanted in the refugee camps and in all gatherings of citizens and workers. The title 'People's Hero' was coined and stuck. It was popularly believed he would be decorated for his actions and many in the low classes saw him as a folk hero and a better choice for marshal than Croe. When, on the ninth day, food, water and energy rationing was imposed hive-wide by the Legislature, a speech by Kowle was published on the address plates, stating how he would not only be observing rationing strictly, but also rationing his rations. This astute piece of propaganda was Kowle's idea and the hive population almost universally embraced the restrictions, wishing to be 'true to the People's Hero and his selfless behaviour.'

Croe realised quickly that he should not underestimate Kowle's power as a popular figure. But that also meant he couldn't ignore Kowle's tactical suggestions out of hand.

Croe, Anko and the assembled officer elite spent most of the fifth day in conference. They filled the briefing hall of House Command in the Main Spine to capacity. An expectant hush fell on the assembled soldiers when Croe asked Kowle to give his assessment of the opposition. Kowle rose to his feet, the shrapnel wound in his forehead clearly and crudely sutured (another carefully judged move on Kowle's part).

'I cannot overstate the magnitude of the enemy,' Kowle said, his calm voice carried around the vast, domed hall by hovering drones. 'I have seldom seen a military force of such scale. Eighty or ninety thousand armoured vehicles, thousands of gun batteries and an infantry force behind them of several million.'

The hall was deadly quiet.

Marshal Croe asked the commissar to confirm what he had just said. During the Trade War, ninety years before, Vervunhive had faced a Zoican army of 900,000 and barely survived.

'Millions,' Kowle repeated simply. 'In all the confusion, I had little opportunity to make a head count, of course–'

General laughter welled from the officer cadre.

'But I am sure, by disposition alone, that at least five million troops were embarked in file behind the armour advance. And those were only the ones I could see.'

'Preposterous!' Vice Marshal Anko barked. 'Vervunhive supports over forty million inhabs and from that we raise half a million troops! Zoica is a third our size! How could they conceivably field five or more million troops?'

'I repeat only what I saw, general.' There was hubbub and murmuring in the officer ranks.

Croe had requested orbital pictures prior to the meeting, pictures he had hoped would confirm or deny these outlandish claims. But the smoke patterns from the continued bombardment were blanketing the continent and nothing

was discernible. He had to trust Kowle's estimation, an estimation supported by many of the armour crews he had
brought back with him.

Croe also had to consider the political and popular suicide
of contradicting the People's Hero.

Croe cleared his throat and his dark eyes fixed the
commissar across the central chart table. 'Your recommendations, commissar?'

'The south gates to the hive must be closed. Sooner or
later, the bombardment will stop. Then the Zoican legions
will descend on us in unprecedented force. Already they may
be approaching, cloaked by the barrage, entering the southern districts. We must make ourselves secure.'

Croe was silent. His gate officers had brought him updates
on the refugee intake, the miserable statistics of the dispossessed and wounded still pressing for entry after five days.
But Kowle's assessment was inarguable.

'The southern gates will close tomorrow at nine.' Croe
hoped he would not live to regret this callous act. As a matter of record, he would not.

While the magnitude of this decision soaked into the
stunned officers, Colonel Modile requested that the Wall
Artillery be raised and armed. At the first alarm, the rampart
defences had been manned and raised, but more potent heavy
guns, dormant since the Trade War, were still muzzled in
deployment silos in the Curtain Wall itself. Vice Marshal Anko
reported that this work was already underway. The hive's main
firepower would be ready in two more days and at last the city
would have long range artillery to answer the bombardment.

'What of the reinforcements High Master Sondar
promised?' asked an artillery officer on the front bench.

'Ten regiments of auxiliaries are moving south to us from
the Northern Foundry Collectives as we speak. Vannick Hive
has promised us nine regiments within a week.'

'And the request to the Imperium?' asked Commissar Tarrian, head of the VPHC.

Croe smiled. 'The will of the Emperor is with us. Warmaster Macaroth has already responded to our needs.
Ordinarily, his forces would be months away, but luck is on
our side. A troop convoy from Monthax, regrouping to

reinforce the warmaster's main crusade assault into the Cabal system, is just nine days away. It has been rerouted. Six regiments of Guard Infantry and three armour groups are moving to us directly.'

There was general noise and some cheers.

Croe rose and hushed them all. 'But that is still nine days away. We must be strong, we must be fast, we must be secure well before then. The south gates close at nine tomorrow.'

A PITIFUL SEMBLANCE of dawn was ebbing through the smoke cover when the Heironymo Sondar Gate shut the next morning. Dozens of refugees scrambled through in the last few moments. Dozens more were crushed by the slamming hydraulics. At West Hass and Croe Gates, the story was repeated. Veyveyr Gate had been immobilised by the first night's shelling, although the railhead fires were now out. Vervun Primary battalions, supervised by the VPHC, erected blockades of metal wreckage to close the gate, the commissariat officers ordering the troops to fire on any refugees still trying to gain access.

The piteous screaming and wailing of those shut outside was more than some Vervun Primary troopers could bear. Many wrote in letters or journals that it was the worst part of the whole campaign for them. Soldiers who had overseen the closing of the gates at the start of the sixth day, and who survived the entire ordeal, never forgot that moment. Years after, men woke in the night, or at grey daybreak, sweating and screaming, echoing the noises they heard from outside the walls. It was the most merciless act of the conflict so far and it would only be matched when the gates fell open again, over a month later.

THE VERVUNHIVE WALL Artillery began firing just before noon on the eighth day. The massive silos opened their ceramite shutters and volleyed shells back into the salt-grass hinterland where the enemy forces were massing. The salvoes were answered with redoubled bombardment from the still-unseen foe.

* * *

ON THE MORNING of the eleventh day, troop convoys began to thread down the motor routes north of the Hass. Twenty thousand men and nearly five thousand war machines sent out from the Northern Collectives to reinforce Vervunhive or, more particularly, the Hass crossing which protected them from the Zoican advance. Kicking dust, the troop carriers and tanks rumbled through the bombed outer habs and damaged manufactories, braving the bombardment that still fell across the river from far away. Thousands of citizens had fled across the river by ferry, some trying to reach their homes in the northern outer habs, many more seeking sanctuary in the Northern Collectives. In places, the mass of people on the roadways slowed the NorthCol advance, but VPHC details were sent across the river by Vice Marshal Anko to clear the way.

By the afternoon, the NorthCol regiments were moving freely down to the waiting ferries at the docks, all refugee columns driven into the roadside fields to allow the convoys to pass. Some three hundred refugees had been executed by the VPHC to force them to make way. The refugees jeered the NorthCol columns as they roared past. General Xance of the NorthCol 2nd Enforcers later wrote, 'This humiliating greeting did more to burn out the NorthCol morale than a month of bitter resistance at the Wall.'

Such was the size of the NorthCol deployment and such was the capacity of the ferries that estimates suggested it would take four days to cross them over the Hass into Vervunhive. When told of this, Marshal Croe ordered the Hass Viaduct reopened so that rail links could resume. The rail route had been closed at the start of the bombardment. Bypassing the ferry route, NorthCol got its forces into the hive in just under two days. Many tanks and armoured personnel carriers actually crossed the viaduct under their own power, trundling along the rail tracks. Two divisions of the NorthCol infantry also marched across the viaduct in a break between trains.

So far, nothing had been heard of the promised reinforcements from Vannick Hive, the great refinery collective three thousand kilometres away to the east. Vannick had undertaken to provide nine regiments, but thus far the only thing

that had come from them was the continued fuel-oil supplies carried by the eastern pipeline. Many in Vervunhive
wondered if the forces of Zoica had reached them too.

AT DAWN ON the fourteenth day, lights were seen in the upper
atmosphere. Flaring their braking jets, Imperial Guard dropships descended, diverted to the main lift-port at Kannak in
the Northern Collective Hives. With the Shield erected,
Vervunhive's central landing field could accept no ships.

The Imperial Guard disembarked at Kannak and then
marched south on the tail of the NorthCol forces. The simple sight of their high-orbit adjustments and blazing
descents lifted the morale of the battered hive. The Guard
was coming.

THE ROYAL VOLPONE 1st, 2nd and 4th deployed south from
Kannak Port swiftly, using the rail link to bring themselves
deep into the hive. Marshal Croe personally greeted General
Noches Sturm, the decorated victor of Grimoyr, on the rockcrete platform of the North Spine Terminus. A large crowd of
politically approved citizens cheered them, under the watch-
ful eyes of the VPHC.

Dressed in shimmering blue gowns, daughters of the
noble houses – Merity Chass, Alina Anko, Iona Gavunda
and Murdith Croe amongst them – were sent forward to dec-
orate Sturm and his second officers, Colonels Gilbear and
Corday, with silk floral wreathes.

Sturm was also greeted by the famous Commissar Kowle.
The image of their smiling handshake was repeated on a million public-address plates across the hive.

The 5th and 7th regiments of the Roane Deepers, under
General Nash, arrived by rail later that afternoon, amid
more pantomime celebrations. Vice Marshal Anko was
there to greet Nash and brass bands pomped and trum-
peted the arrival. Amid the jubilation, Nash was able to
confirm that three full regiments of Narmenian Armour
were off-loading from carriers at the Kannak Port landing
fields and would be en route south by dawn. The crowd
rose, cheering the news, hailing the honoured Guard
arrivals like they had already won the war.

The Tanith First-and-Only arrived by road, almost unnoticed, two nights later.

MORE THAN EIGHTY matt-black troop trucks rumbled down the NorthCol highway through the northern outhabs of Vervunhive. The canvas tilts had been removed and around thirty Tanith troopers rode in each, crouched down with their weapons, webbing, haversacks, musette bags and bedrolls gathered to them. The bouncing trucks – six-wheelers with large, snarling front grills and pop-eye headlamps – bore the quadruple chevron cab-marks of NorthCol Utility Transport Division Three. Jerry cans and spare wheels were slung to their sides on sponson fittings.

A dozen outriders astride black-drab motorcycles ran along their flanks, and behind the main column came thirty more high-cabbed eight-wheelers laden with ammunition crates and regimental supplies, as well as the numerous cooks, armourers, mechanics, servitors and other attendant hangers-on that followed a Guard regiment on the move. These freighters were dull yellow, the livery of the Kannak Port Cargo Union, and netting was draped over their payloads. NorthCol soldiers in pale blue overalls and forage caps drove all the trucks, but the outriders were Tanith, in their distinctive dark battledress. Twelve kilometres short of Vervunhive, they paused to trickle through a checkpoint on the highway and they gained a vanguard of two dark-blue staff cars crewed by VPHC officers to lead them in.

All the headlamps in the convoy were blazing. Night had fallen sometime, unnoticed in the thick wallow of smoke. The only sights were the battered districts to either side, the fuzzy green glow of the hive itself – partly obscured by the smoke – and the occasional flash and flare of long-range shells falling into the outer habs they raced through.

Brin Milo, the youngest Ghost, rode with the rest of number one platoon in the lead truck. A slender, pale youth just now filling out with adult bulk, he had been the only non-soldier saved from the ruins of Tanith when their homeworld was overrun and destroyed four years earlier. The commissar himself had saved his life and dragged him from the fires that burned Tanith away.

For a long while, he had been 'The Boy,' the company mascot, the piper, a little piece of Tanith innocence saved from hell, a reminder to all of the men of the place they had lost. But six months before, during the battle for Monthax, he had finally become a soldier too. He was proud of his issued equipment and lasgun, and he kept his pack in better order than any of the seasoned Tanith troopers.

He sat huddled in the cramped rear-bay of the rattling truck and polished the regimental crest on his black beret with a rag of gun-cloth.

'Milo.'

Brin looked up at Trooper Larkin opposite him. A wiry, taut-skinned man in his early fifties, Larkin was as well-known for his neurotic personality as his skill as the regiment's most able sniper. The long, specialised shape of his marksman's lasgun was sheathed in a canvas roll at his feet. Larkin had produced his gun-scope and was training it like a spyglass out of the truck. Larkin had once told Milo that he didn't trust anything he hadn't seen first through his beloved scope.

'Larkin?'

Larkin grinned and looked back, handing the delicate brass instrument to the youth, gently. From the tiny runes glowing on the setting dial, Milo noticed it was fixed to heat-see.

'Take a look. That way.'

Milo squinted into the scope, resting the rubberised cup to his eye-socket. He saw radiance and bewildering crosshair markers of floating red.

'What am I looking at?'

'The hive, boy, the hive.'

Milo looked again. He realised the radiance was the yellow dome of the Shield, a vast energy field that enveloped the unseen city-hive ahead.

'Looks big enough and ugly enough to look after itself,' he suggested.

'The same is said for so many of us,' Colonel Corbec said, holding on to the truck's iron tilt-hoops as he edged down to Milo and Larkin. 'Velvethive is in a pretty fix, so they say.'

'That's Vervunhive, chief,' Trooper Burun said from nearby.

'Feth you, clever-ass!' Corbec tossed back at the grinning soldier. 'Feth knows I can barely remember me own name most days, let alone where I'm supposed to be!'

First platoon laughed.

Milo held the scope up to Corbec, who waved it off with disinterest.

'I'll meet the place that'll kill me when I meet it. Don't need to look for it in advance.'

Milo gave the precious scope back to Larkin, who took a final look and then slid the instrument back into its drawstring bag.

'Seen enough, Larks?' Corbec asked, his vast arms gripping the overhead frame, his beard split by a toothy grin.

'Seen enough to know where to aim,' Larkin replied.

IN THE JUDDERING load-bay of the truck three vehicles back, Third Platoon were all wagering on cards. Trooper Feygor, a dangerous, lean man with hooded eyes, had bartered a full tarot pack from some Administratum fellow on the troop-ship and he was running a game of Hearts and Titans.

Trooper Brostin, big, heavyset and saturnine, had lost so much already he was ready to wager his flamer, with the fuel tanks, as his next lay-down.

Feygor, a thick cigar clenched between his sharp teeth, laughed at Brostin's discomfiture and shuffled the pack again. As he flicked the big pasteboard cards out into hands around the grilled deck, the men of the platoon produced coins, crumpled notes, rings and tobacco rations to add to the pot.

Trooper Caffran watched him deal. Short, young and determined, just a year older than Milo, Caffran had gained the respect of them all during the beach assault at Oskray about a year before. Caffran disliked cards, but in Rawne's platoon it paid to mix in.

Major Rawne sat at the end of the truck-bay, his back to the rear wall of the cab. The Tanith second officer, he was infamous for his anger, guile and pessimism. Corbec had likened him to a snake more than once, both physically and in character.

'Will you play, major?' Feygor asked, his hands hesitating on the deal. Rawne shook his head. He'd lost plenty to his adjutant in the last forty days of transit in the troopship.

Now he could smell war and idle gaming had lost its interest.

Feygor shrugged and finished the deal. Caffran picked up his hand and sighed. Brostin picked up his hand and sighed more deeply. He wondered if wool socks would count as a wager.

THE OUTRIDERS RACED around the speeding trucks, gunning for the destination. Sergeant Mkoll, head of the scout platoon, crossed his bike in between two of the troop vehicles and rode down the edge-gully so he could take a look at the hive emerging out of the smoke before them. It was big, bigger than any city he'd ever seen, bigger than the bastion towns of Tanith certainly.

He roared ahead, passing the staff cars of the local commissariat, until he was leading the column down the broken highway towards the docks.

A VOLLEY OF shells fell into the outhabs to the east. Dorden, the grizzled, elderly chief medic of the Tanith Regiment, heaved himself up to see. Conflagrations, bright and bitter-lemon in colour, sizzled out from the distant detonations. The truck sashayed into a pothole and Dorden was dropped on his arse.

'Why bother?' Bragg asked.

'Say again?' asked the doctor.

Bragg shifted his position in the flat-bed uncomfortably. He was huge, bigger than any other two Ghosts put together. 'We'll get there sooner or later; die there sooner or later. Why bother craning for a view of our doom?'

Dorden looked across at the giant. 'Is the cup half-full or half-empty, Bragg?' he asked.

'What cup?'

'It's hypothetical. Half-full or half-empty?'

'Yeah, but what cup are we talking about?'

'An imaginary cup.'

'What's in it?'

'That doesn't matter.'

'Does to me, doc,' Bragg shrugged.

'I, well, okay… it's got sacra in it. Half-full or half-empty?'

'How much sacra?' Bragg asked.

Dorden opened his mouth once, twice, then sat back again. 'Doesn't matter.'

Bragg pulled out a canvas bottle-flask. 'There's sacra in this,' he announced.

'Thanks, not just yet…' Dorden said, raising his hands as if in surrender.

Bragg, sat opposite him in the shuddering truck, nodded and took a long swig.

Shells wailed down, half a kilometre from the road, close enough to be uncomfortable. Dorden reached out for the flask. 'Ah well, if it's there…'

SERGEANT VARL, gripping the iron hand-loops of the truck's flatbed with his whirring mechanical limb, tried to rouse the spirits of his platoon by encouraging a song. A few of them joined unenthusiastically with a verse or two of 'Over the Sky and Far Away' but it soon faltered. When Varl tried another, he was told to shut up, to his face.

Sergeant Varl handled people better than most of the officers in the regiment and he knew when to reprimand and when to back off. He'd been a dog-soldier himself for long enough.

But the mood in his platoon was bad. And Varl knew why. No one wanted this. No one wanted to get in the middle of a hive-war.

THE MAGNIFICAT WAS waiting at the northern docks as the column rolled in out of the firelit night. All the Hass ferries were working full-stretch to keep the river open and convoy after convoy of military supplies and ammunition were arriving each hour from the Northern Collectives. Troops from Vervun Primary – in blue greatcoats, grey webbing and the distinctive spiked helmets – along with VPHC men, servitors and a good few red-robed clerks and overseers from the Administratum were now controlling the river freight, much to the fury of the regular longshoremen of the Dockmaster

Guild. Ecclesiarchy priests had also arrived on the third or fourth day, establishing a permanent prayer-vigil to protect the crossing and make the waterway and the viaduct safe. The hooded clergy were grouped around a brazier at a pier end, chanting and intoning. They were there each time Folik drew the *Magnificat* back to the northshore wharves. It seemed they never slept, never rested. He got into the habit of nodding to them every time he slid the ferry in past them. They never responded.

On this night run, Folik expected to take on more supply vehicles and crates, but the house troopers running the dockside had drawn the NorthCol freight trucks aside so that troop transports could move round them and roll down the landing stages.

Folik nursed the ancient turbines into station-keeping as Mincer dropped the ramp.

The first two trucks growled and bounced aboard. Mincer directed them to their deck spaces with a pair of dagger-lamps.

A tall, long-coated figure dropped from the cab of the first truck. He approached longshoreman Folik.

Folik was almost hypnotised by the commissar badge on the peaked cap. An awed smile creased his oil-spattered face and he took off his wool cap out of respect.

'Sir, it's an honour to have you aboard!'

'The pleasure's mine. What's your name?'

'Folik, Imperial hero, sir!'

'I... I had no idea my reputation preceded me this far. Greetings, Folik.'

'It's a true honour, sir, to be able to transport your reinforcement column to Vervunhive.'

'I appreciate the honour, Folik. My first vehicles are aboard. Shall we proceed?'

Folik nodded and shuffled away to get Mincer to unlap the rope coils.

'Commissar Kowle himself uses our boat!' gasped Folik to his crew mate.

'Kowle? Are you sure? The People's Hero?'

'It's him, I tell you, in the flesh, bold as all bastardy, right here on our tub!'

At the rail, Colonel-Commissar Ibram Gaunt gazed out from the deck of the *Magnificat* and smiled as he overheard the words.

THE MAGNIFICAT WAS in mid-stream when the eastern sky lit up brightly. There was a sucking shudder, like a wind-rush over the water. The eastern horizon blazed with a midnight sun.

'What was that?' Mincer cried. A commotion rose from the troops.

Gaunt raised his hand to shield his eyes from the glare as a heat-wash rolled down the river. He knew the blast-effects of a nuclear detonation when he saw it.

'That was the beginning of the end,' he said.

FOUR
HIVE DEATH

'Insanity! Insanity! What kind of war are we fighting?'
— Marshal Edric Croe, on hearing
the news from Vannick

KOWLE WENT DIRECTLY to House Command when the news
was voxed to him. He had been touring the South Curtain
and it took him almost an hour to cross the hive back to the
Main Spine.

The control auditorium was a chaotic mess. Munitorum
clerks, regimental aides and other junior personnel hurried
about, gabbling, panicking, relaying reports from the operators manning the main tactical cogitators banked around the
lower level of the large, circular chamber. Many Vervun Primary officers and even some VPHC troops were clogging the
place too, anxious to find out if the rumours were true.

Kowle pushed past the onlookers at the chamber door
and sent many back to their stations with curt words.
None argued. They saluted and backed off from him
quickly. He crossed the wide floor and then hurried up the
ironwork staircase onto the upper deck of the auditorium,

where the chiefs of staff were gathered around the vast, luminous chart table. Junior aides and technicians, many bearing important vox reports, made way for him without question.

Marshal Croe presided over the group at the chart table. His eyes were blacker than ever and he had removed his cap, as if the weight of it was too much now. His personal bodyguard, Isak, dressed in an armoured maroon body-glove and carrying a shrouded gun, hovered at his shoulder. Vice Marshal Anko, wearing a medal-heavy white ceremonial uniform, stood glowering nearby. He had been attending a formal dinner thrown by House Anko to welcome the Volpone. Sturm and his aides stood alongside him, clad in the impressive dress uniforms of the Volpone. Also present were Xance of North-Col – looking tired and drawn, along with several of his senior staff – the Narmenian Grizmund and his tank brigadiers, Nash of the Roane Deepers and his adjutants, and a dozen more senior Vervun Primary officers, as well as Commissar Tarrian of the VPHC.

'Is it true?' Kowle asked, removing his cap but making no other formal salute.

Croe nodded, but remained silent.

Tarrian coughed. 'Vannick Hive was destroyed ninety minutes ago.'

'Destroyed?'

'I'm sure you're familiar with the concept, Kowle,' Croe said flatly. 'It's gone.'

'Zoica has levelled it. We have no idea how. They got inside the Shield somehow and used a nuclear device–'

Croe cut Anko off mid-sentence. 'How is not the real issue here, vice marshal! There are any number of "hows" we might debate! The real question is why.'

'I agree, marshal,' General Sturm said. 'We must consider this may not have been deliberate. I've known emplacements destroyed accidentally by the over-ambitious actions of those attacking. Perhaps Zoica meant to take the hive and struck... too hard.'

'Is there any other way of striking when you use atomics?' a calm voice asked from the head of the stairs. The group turned.

'Gaunt...' Colonel Gilbear of the Volpone hissed under his breath.

The tall newcomer wore a commissar's cap and a long, black leather coat. He stepped towards them. His clothing was still flecked with dust from his journey. He saluted Marshal Croe smartly.

'Colonel-Commissar Gaunt, of the Tanith First. We arrived to reinforce you just as the event occurred.'

'I welcome you, Gaunt. I wish I was happier to see you,' the white-haired giant replied respectfully. 'Are your men billeted?'

'They were proceeding to their stations when I left them. I came here as soon as I could.'

'The famous Gaunt,' Anko whispered to Tarrian.

'You mean "notorious," surely?' Tarrian murmured back.

Gaunt stepped up to the chart table, pulling off his gloves and studying the display. Then he looked up and nodded a frank greeting to Nash.

'Well met, general.'

'Good to see you, commissar,' Nash replied. Their forces had served alongside each other on Monthax and there was a genuine, mutual admiration.

Gaunt greeted the Narmenian officers too, then looked over at Sturm, Gilbear and the other Volpone, who stared icily at him.

'General Sturm. Always a pleasure. And Major Gilbear.'

Gilbear was about to blurt out something but Sturm stepped forward, offering his hand to Gaunt.

'Gilbear's bravery on Monthax has earned him a colonel's pips, Gaunt.'

'Well done, Gilbear,' Gaunt smiled broadly. He shook the general's hand firmly.

'Good to know we have more brave, reliable Guard forces here with us, Gaunt. Welcome.'

Gaunt smiled to himself. The last time he had met Sturm in person, back on Voltemand, the pompous ass had been threatening him with court martial. Gaunt had not forgotten that Sturm's callous leadership had resulted in heavy losses in the Ghost ranks from friendly artillery.

You're only putting on this show of comradeship so you can look good in the eyes of the local grandees, Gaunt thought, returning Sturm's gaze with unblinking directness. You are an unspeakable wretch and I regret this place has the likes of you to look after it.

But Gaunt was a political animal as well as a combat leader, and he knew how to play this game as well as any runt general. He said, 'I'm sure our worthy brothers of the Volpone could handle this alone.'

Sturm nodded as the handshake broke, clearly trying to work out if there had been some cloaked insult in Gaunt's compliment.

'From your opening remark, may we presume you believe the loss of Vannick Hive is deliberate?' Kowle stepped forward to face Gaunt. The Imperial Commissars nodded a stiff greeting to each other.

'Commissar Kowle, the People's Hero. It's been a long time since Balhaut.'

'But the memories never fade,' Kowle replied.

Gaunt turned away from him. 'Kowle judges my words correctly. The enemy has destroyed Vannick Hive deliberately. Can there be any other explanation for a nuclear event?'

'Suicide,' Grizmund said. 'Overrun, overwhelmed, perhaps a last act of desperation in the face of a victorious foe. A detonation of the hive's power plant.'

Several Vervun officers expressed dismay.

'You are new to Verghast, general, so we will not think badly of your comment,' Tarrian said softly. 'But no Verghastite would be so craven as to self-destruct in the face of the enemy. The hives are everything, praise the Emperor. Through them and their output, we hallow and honour him. Vannick Hive would no more destroy itself than we would.'

Many around the chart table averred.

'Brave words,' Grizmund said. 'But if this hive was conquered, Emperor save us... Would you let it fall into the hands of the enemy?'

Various voices rose in anger, but Gaunt's words cut them to quiet. 'I'm sure the general here is not questioning any loyalties. And he may have a point, but I think it doubtful

Vannick Hive succumbed to anything other than an invader's wrath.'

'But why?' barked Croe. 'Again it comes back to this question! Invasion, conquest... I can understand those things! But to destroy what you have fought to take? Where is the sense?'

'Marshal, we must face the darkest truth,' said Gaunt. 'I have studied the data sent to me concerning this theatre. It seems that Commissar Kowle here has reported millions of foe, an assessment that beggars belief, given the proportional mustering capacity of a hive the size of Ferrozoica. The answer is there. Vervunhive can raise half a million from a forty million population. Zoica can only be raising millions from a population a third the size... if the entire population itself is being used.'

'What?' Anko barked, laughing at the idea.

'Go on, commissar,' Croe said.

'This is not a war of conquest. This is not a hive-war, a commercial spat, a new "Trade War", as you refer to it. Zoica is not massing, arming and rising to conquer and control the hive production of this planet or to subjugate its old rival Vervunhive. They are rising to exterminate it.'

'A taint,' murmured General Nash, slowly understanding.

'Quite so,' Gaunt said. 'To turn not just your potential fighting men into an army but your workers and hab families too, that takes a zealot mindset: an infection of insanity, a corruption, a taint. The vile forces of Chaos control Zoica, there can be no doubt. The poison of the warp has overrun your noble neighbour and set every man, woman and child in it on a frenzied path to obliterate the rest of this world and everything on it.'

FIVE
CLOSE QUARTERS

'In war, best know what enemies are around you in your own camp, before you step out to face the foe and wonder why you do so alone.'

— Warmaster Slaydo, from *A Treatise on the Nature of Warfare*

A PARTY OF local troops in blue greatcoats waited for them at the entrance to a dingy shed complex, under the stark-white light of sodium lamps. Their weapons were slung over their shoulders and they wore woollen caps, their spiked helmets dangling from their webbing. They flashed the convoy in through the chain-link gate with dagger-lamps.

Sergeant Mkoll was first into the compound, slewing up his motorbike on the greasy rockcrete skirt and heeling down the kickstand. The heavy machine leaned to the left and rested, its throaty purr cutting off. Mkoll dismounted as the Tanith troop trucks thundered into the yard after him.

Mkoll looked at the manufactory sheds around them. This was a dismal place, but the Tanith had billeted in worse. Despite the thunder of engines and shouts, he sensed a presence behind him and spun before the other could utter a word.

'Steady!' said the figure approaching behind him. He was a tall, well-made man in his twenties, dressed in the local uniform. A captain, his collar pins said. His right arm was bound up tight to his chest in a padded sling, so he wore his greatcoat on one side only, draping it like a cape over the other. Mkoll thought he was lucky that empty sleeve was not a permanent feature.

Mkoll made a brief salute. 'Sorry, you caught me by surprise. Sergeant Mkoll, 5th Platoon, Tanith First-and-Only.'

The captain saluted back stiffly with his left hand. Mkoll noticed he was also limping and there were sallow bruises along his forehead, cheek and around his eyes. 'Captain Ban Daur, Vervun Primary. Welcome to Vervunhive.'

Mkoll grunted a curt laugh. He'd never been personally welcomed to a warzone before.

'Can you introduce me to your commanding officer?' Daur asked. 'I've been given the job of supervising your billet. Not much good for anything else.' He said this with a rueful chuckle and a glance down at his slinged arm.

Mkoll fell in step beside him and they moved through a commotion of men, trucks, diesel fumes and unloading work. They made small, intense, flickering shadows under the harsh lighting gantries overhead.

'You've seen action already?' asked Mkoll.

'Nothing to get me a medal,' Daur said. 'I was on the ramparts on the first day when the shelling began. Didn't so much as even see what to shoot at before they took my position down and buried me in rubble. Be a few weeks yet till I'm fit, but I wanted to be useful, so I volunteered for liaison work.'

'So you've not even seen the enemy yet?'

Daur shook his head. 'Except for People's Hero Kowle and a few others who made it back from the grasslands, no one has.'

CORBEC WAS STANDING by his truck, smoking a cigar, gazing placidly around the place, oblivious to the frenzy of activity all about him. He turned slowly, taking in the sheer scale of the hive around him, beyond the glare of the sodium lamp rigs: the towering manufactories and smelteries, the steeples of the work habs beyond them, then the great crest of some Ecclesiarch basilica, and behind it all, the vast structure of the Main Spine, a mind-numbingly huge bulk illuminated by a million or more windows. Big as a fething mountain peak back home on...

On nowhere. He still forgot, sometimes.

His eyes were drawn to a vast pylon near the Main Spine which rose just as high as the hive-mountain. It seemed to mark the heart of the whole city-hub. Storms of crackling energy flared from its apex, spreading out to feed the flickering green shield that over-arched it all. Corbec had never seen a shield effect this big before. It was quite something. He gazed south and saw the rippling light flashes of shells falling across the Shield, deflecting and exploding harmlessly. Quite something indeed and it looked like it worked.

He took another drag on his cigar and the coal glowed red. The sheer size of this place was going to take a lot of getting used to. He had seen how most of his boys had been struck dumb as they entered the hive, gaping up at the monumental architecture. He knew he had to beat that awe out of them as quickly as possible, or they'd be too busy gazing dumbly to fight.

'Put that out!' a voice ordered crisply behind him.

Corbec turned and for a moment he thought it was Gaunt. But only for a moment. The commissar stalking towards him had nothing of Gaunt's presence. He had local insignia and his puffy face was pale and unhealthy. Corbec said nothing but simply took the cigar from his mouth and raised one eyebrow. He was a good twenty-five centimetres taller than the black-coated officer.

The man halted a few paces short, taking in the sheer size of Colm Corbec. 'Commissar Langana, VPHC. This is a secure area. Put that gakking light out!'

Corbec put the cigar back between his lips and, still silent, tapped the colonel's rank pins on his shoulder braid.

'I...' the man began. Then, thinking better of everything, turned and stalked away.

'Colonel?'

Mkoll was approaching with another local, thankfully regular army-issue rather than one of the tight-arsed political cadre.

'This is Captain Daur, our liaison officer.' Daur snapped his heels together as well as any man with a leg-wound could, and saluted with his left hand. He blinked in surprise when Corbec held out his own left hand without hesitation. Then he shook it. The grip was tight. Daur immediately warmed to this bearded, tattooed brute. He'd taken Daur's injury in at a glance and compensated without any comment.

'Welcome to Vervunhive, colonel,' Daur said.

'Can't say I'm glad to be here, captain, but a war's a war, and we go where the Emperor wills us. Did you arrange these billets?'

Daur glanced around at the mouldering sheds where the Tanith First were breaking out their kits and lighting lamps in neat platoon order.

'No, sir,' he replied sheepishly. 'I wanted better. But space is at a premium in the hive just now.'

Corbec chuckled. 'In a place this big?'

'We have been overrun with refugees and wounded from the south. All free areas such as the Commercia, the Landing Field and the manufactories have been opened to house them. I actually requested some superior space for your men in the lower Main Spine, but Vice Marshal Anko instructed that you should be barracked closer to the Curtain Wall. So this is it. Gavunda Chem Plant Storebarns/Southwest. For what it's worth.'

Corbec nodded. Lousy chem plant barns for the Tanith Ghosts. He was prepared to bet a month's pay the Volpone Bluebloods weren't bedding down in some sooty hangar this night.

'We've cleared seven thousand square metres in these sheds for you and I can annex more if you need room to stack supplies.'

'No need,' Corbec said. 'We're only one regiment. We won't take much space.'

Daur led them both into the main hangar space where most of the Ghosts were preparing their billets. Through an open shutter, Corbec could see into another wide shed where the rest were making camp.

'My men have dug latrines over there and there are a number of worker washrooms and facilities still operational in the sheds to the left.' Daur pointed these features out in turn. 'So far, the main water supplies are still on, so the showers work. But I took the liberty of setting up water and fuel bowsers in case the supplies go down.'

Corbec looked where Daur indicated and saw a row of tanker trucks with fuel clamps and standpipes grouped by the western fence.

'Sheds three, four and five are loaded with food and perishable supplies, and munitions orders will arrive by daybreak. House Command has requisitioned another barn over there from House Anko for use as your medical centre.'

Corbec gazed across at the rickety long-shed Daur pointed to. 'Get Dorden to check it out, Mkoll,' he said. Mkoll flagged down a passing trooper and sent him off to find the chief medic.

'I've also set up primary and secondary vox-links in the side offices here,' said Daur as he led them through a low door into what had once been the factory supervisor's suite. The rooms were thick with dust and cobwebs, but two deep-gain vox units were mounted on scrubbed benches along one wall, flickering and active, chattering with staccato dribbles of link-talk. There were even fresh paper rolls and lead-sticks laid out near the sets. The thoroughness made Corbec smile. Maybe it was the worker-mentality of the hive.

'I assumed you'd use this as your quarters,' Daur said. He showed Corbec a side office with a cot and a folding desk. Corbec glanced in, nodded and turned back to face the captain.

'I'd say you had made us welcome indeed, Daur, despite the facilities granted us by your hive-masters. Looks like you've thought of everything. I won't forget your trouble in a hurry.'

Daur nodded, pleased.

Corbec stepped out of the offices and raised his voice. 'Sergeant Varl!'

Varl stopped what he was doing and came across the hangar space double-time, threading between billeting Tanith. 'Colonel?'

'Rejoice. You've won the supplies duty. Those sheds there,' Corbec glanced at Daur for confirmation, 'are for storage. Raise a detail and get our stuff housed from the trucks.'

Varl nodded and strode off, calling up volunteers.

With Daur and Mkoll beside him, Corbec surveyed the activity in the billet. 'Looks like the Ghosts are making themselves at home,' he murmured to no one in particular.

'Ghosts? Why do you call them that? Where are you from?' Daur asked.

'Tanith,' Mkoll said.

Corbec smiled sadly and contradicted the sergeant. 'Nowhere, Captain Daur. We're from nowhere and that's why we're ghosts.'

'THIS IS THE only space available,' Commissar Langana said flatly.

'Not good enough,' Dorden said, looking around the dimly-lit hangar, taking in the shattered windows, the piles of refuse and the layers of dust. 'I can't make a field hospital in here. The filth will kill more of my regiment than the enemy.'

The VPHC officer looked round sourly at the doctor. 'The vice marshal's orders were quite specific. This area is designated for medical needs.'

'We could clean up,' Trooper Lesp suggested. A thin, hangdog man, Lesp was skulking to one side in the doorway with Chayker and Foskin. The three of them represented Dorden's medical orderlies, troopers who had been trained for field hospital work by the chief medic himself. Gherran and Mtane, the only other fully qualified medics in the unit, were looking around behind them.

'With what?' Dorden asked. 'By the time we've scoured this place clean, the war will be over.'

Lesp shrugged.

'You must make do. This is war,' Langana announced. 'War levels all stations and makes us work with the bravery in our limbs and the ingenuity in our minds.'

Dorden turned his grizzled face to look directly into the puffy visage of the political officer. 'Do you make that crap up yourself, or does someone write it down for you?'

The orderlies behind him tried to cover their sniggers. Gherran and Mtane laughed out loud.

'I could break you for such insolence!' Langana spat. Anger made his cheeks florid.

'Hmm?' Dorden replied, not seeming to hear. 'And deprive an Imperial Guard regiment of their chief medic? Your vice marshal wouldn't be too happy to hear about that, would he?'

Langana was about to retort when a strong, female voice echoed through the dirty space.

'I'm looking for the doctor! Hello?'

Dorden pushed past the seething commissar and went to the door. He was met by a short, slim, young woman in a form-fitting red uniform with embroidered cuffs. She carried a medical pack over one shoulder and was escorted by five more dressed like her: three men and two women.

'Dorden, chief medical officer, Tanith First.'

'Surgeon Ana Curth, Inner Hab Collective Medical Hall 67/mv,' she replied, nodding to him and glancing around the dingy hall. 'Captain Daur, your liaison officer, was troubled by the state of the facilities and called my hall for support.'

'As you can see, Ana, it is a long way short of adequate,' said Dorden with a gentle gesture that took in the decay.

She frowned at him briefly. His use of her forename surprised her. Such informalities were rare in the hive. It was discourteous, almost condescending. She'd worked for her status and position as hard as any other hiver.

'That's Surgeon Curth, medic.'

Dorden looked round at the woman, surprised, clearly hurt that he had offended her in any way. Behind Dorden, Langana smiled.

'My mistake. Surgeon Curth, indeed,' Dorden looked away. 'Well, as you can see, this is no place for wounded. Can you possibly… assist us?'

She looked him up and down, still bristling but calming a little. There was something in his tired, avuncular manner that made her almost regret her tone. This was not some bravo trooper trying to hit on her. This was an old man with slumping shoulders. There was a weariness in his manner that no amount of sleep could ease. His lined eyes had seen too much, she realised.

Ana Curth turned to Langana. 'I wouldn't treat cattle in a place like this. I'm issuing an M-notice on it at once.'

'You can't–' Langana began.

'Oh, yes I can, commissar! Fifth Bill of Rights, Amendment 457/hj: "In event of conflict, surgeon staff may commandeer all available resources for the furtherance of competent medical work." I want scrub teams from the hive sanitation department here by morning, with pressure hoses and steam scourers. I want disinfectant sluices. I want sixty cots, bedding, four theatre tables with lights, screens and instruments, flak-board lagging for the walls and windows, proper light-power, water and heat-links recoupled, and patches made to the gakking roof! Got it?'

'I–'

'Do you understand me, Political Officer Langana?'

Langana hesitated. 'I will have to call House Command for these requirements.'

'Do so!' barked Curth. Dorden looked on. He liked her already.

'Use my hive caste-code: 678/cu. Got it? That will give you the authority to process my request. And do it now, Langana!'

The commissar saluted briefly and then marched away out of the chamber. He had to push through the smirking Tanith orderlies to exit.

Dorden turned to the woman. 'My thanks, Surgeon Curth. The Tanith are in your debt.'

'Just do your job and we'll get on fine,' she replied bluntly. 'I have more wounded refugees in my hall now than I can deal with. I don't want your overspill submerging me when the fighting starts.'

'Of course you don't. I am grateful, surgeon.'

Dorden fixed her with an honest smile. She seemed about to soften and smile back, but she turned and led her team away out of the door. 'We'll return in two days to help you set up.'

'Surgeon?'

She stopped, turning back.

'How overrun are you? With the wounded, I mean?'

She sighed. 'To breaking point.'

'Could you use six more trained staff?' Dorden asked. He waved casually at his fellow medics and waiting orderlies. 'We have no wounded yet to treat, Emperor watch us. Until we have, we would be happy to assist.'

Curth glanced at her chief orderly. 'Thank you. Your offer is appreciated. Follow us, please.'

VARL SUPERVISED THE store detail, carrying more than his share thanks to the power of his artificial arm. With a team of thirty, he ordered the stacking and layout of the Tanith supplies. There was plenty of stuff in the barn already, well marked and identified by the triplicate manifest data-slates, but there was still more than enough room for the supplies and munitions they had brought with them.

Another truck backed up to the doorway, lights winking, and Domor, Cocoer and Brostin helped to shift the crates of perishables to their appointed stacks. Varl allocated another area for the munitions he had been told would arrive later.

Caffran looked up as the sergeant called to him. 'Sweep the back,' Varl ordered. 'Make sure the rear of the barn is secure.'

Caffran nodded, pulling his jacket and camo-cape from a nearby crate-pile and putting them back on. He was still sweat-hot from the work. Lifting his lasgun, he paced round the rear of the supply stacks, moving through the darkness and shadows, checking the rotting rear wall of the hangar for holes.

Something scurried in the dark.

He swung his gun round. Rodents?

There was no further movement. Caffran edged forward and noticed the edge of a crate that had been chewed away. The plastic-wrapped packets of dried biscuit inside had been invaded. Definitely rodents. There was a trail of crumbs and shreds of plastic seal. They'd have to set traps – and poison too probably.

He paused. The hole in the crate's side was far too high to be the work of rodents. Unless they bred something the size of a hound in the sewers of this place. That wouldn't surprise him, given the giant scale of everything else here in Vervunhive.

He armed his lasgun and slid around the edge of the next stack.

Something scurried again.

He hastened forward, gun raised, looking for a target. Feth, maybe the local vermin would be good eating. They'd had precious little fresh meat in the last forty days.

There was a movement to his left and he dropped to one knee, taking aim. Beyond the supply stacks, there was a pale, green slice of light, a jagged hole in the back of the barn through which the glow of the Shield high above leaked in.

Caffran shuffled forward.

A noise to the right.

He spun around. Nothing. He saw how several more crates had been clawed into.

Something flickered past the slice of light, something moving through it quickly, blocking out the glow.

Caffran ran forward, pulling himself sideways through the gap in the rotten fibre-planks of the hangar's rear wall and out into the tangled waste of debris and rubble behind the storage barn.

He crawled out, got down, raised his gun...

And saw the boy. A small boy, eight or nine years old it seemed to Caffran, scampering up a mound of rubble with a wrap of biscuits in his hand.

The boy reached the summit and another figure loomed out of the dark. A girl, older, in her late teens, clad in vulgar rags and decorated with piercings. She took the wrap from the boy and hugged him tightly.

Caffran got up, lowering his gun. 'Hey!' he called.

The child and the girl looked round at him sharply, like animals caught in a huntsman's light.

Caffran saw for just a moment the strong, fierce, beautiful face of the girl before the children ducked out of sight and vanished into the wasteland.

He ran up the slope after them, but they were gone.

* * *

IN A FOXHOLE a hundred metres away from the back of the storage barns, Tona Criid hugged Dalin to her and willed him to be quiet.

'Good boy, good boy,' she murmured. She took out the biscuits and tore the wrap open so he could have one.

Dalin wolfed it down. He was hungry. They were all hungry out here.

NUTRIENT CLOUDS PUMPED into the Iron Tank fed the dreaming High Master of Vervunhive. He rolled in his oily fluid womb, pulling at his link feeds, feet and hands twitching like a dreaming dog. He dreamed of the Trade War, before his birth. The images of his dream were informed by the pict-library he had studied in his youth. He dreamed of his illustrious predecessor, the great Heironymo, haughtily spurning the rivalry with Ferrozoica, arming for war. How wrong, how very foolish! Such a grossly physical stubbornness! And the hive held him in such esteem for his heroic leadership! Fools! Cattle! Unthinking chaff!

Commerce is always war. But the war of commerce may be fought in such subtle, exquisite ways. To raise arms, to mobilise bodies, to turn beautiful hive profits into war machines and guns, rations and ammunition...

What a pathetic mind, Heironymo! How blind of you to miss the real avenues of victory! House Clatch would have bowed to mercantile embargoes long before the brave boys of Vervun Primary had overturned the walls of Zoica! A concession here, a bargain there, a stifling of funds or supplies, a blockade...

Salvador Sondar floated upwards, his dreams now machine-language landscapes of autoledgers, contoured ziggurats of mounted interest values, rivers of exchange rates, terraces of production value outputs.

The mathematical vistas of mercantile triumph he adored more than any other place in the universe.

He twitched again in the warm soup, iridescent bubbles coating his shrunken limbs and fluttering to the roof of the Iron Tank. He was pleased now that he had killed the old man. Heironymo had ruled too long! A hundred and twenty years old, beloved by the stupid, vapid public, still unwilling to make way for his twenty year-old nephew and obvious successor! It had been a merciful act, Salvador dreamed to himself, though the guilt of it had plagued him for the last fifty years. His sleeping features winced.

Yes, it had been merciful... for the good of the hive and for the further prosperity of House Sondar, noble line! Had output not tripled during his reign? And now Gnide and Croe and Chass and the other weaklings told him that mercantile war was no longer an option! Fools!

Gnide...

Now... he was dead, wasn't he?

And Slaydo too? The great warmaster, dead of poison. No, that wasn't right. Stabbed on the carpet of the audience hall... no... no...

Why were his dreams so confused? It was the chatter. That was it. The chatter. He wished it would cease. It was a hindrance to reason. He was High Master of Vervunhive and he wanted his dream-mind clean and unpolluted so he could command his vast community to victory once more.

The Shield? What? What about the Shield?

The chatter was lisping something.

No! N-n–

Salvador Sondar's dreams were suddenly as suspended as the dreamer for a moment. Fugue state snarled his dream-mind. He floated in the tank as if dead.

Then the dreams resumed in a rush. To poison the servitor taster, that had been a stroke of genius! No one had ever suspected! And to use a neural toxin that left no trace. A stroke, they had said! A stroke had finally levelled old Heironymo! Salvador had been forced to inject his own tear glands with saline to make himself cry at the state funeral.

The weeping! The mass mourning! Fifty years ago, but still it gnawed at him! Why had the hivers loved the old bastard so dearly?

The chatter was there again, at the very boundary of his mind-impulse limit, like crows in a distant treeline at dawn, like insects in the grasslands at dusk.

Chattering...

The Shield? What are you saying about the Shield?

I am Salvador Sondar. Get out of my mind and–

The wasted body twitched and spasmed in the Iron Tank. Outside, the servitors jiggled and jerked in sympathy.

THE VAST RAILHEAD terminal at Veyveyr Gate was a dank, blackened mess. Clouds of steam rolled like fog off the cooling rubble and tangled metal where millions of litres of fluid retardant had been sprayed on the incendiary fires to get them under control.

Major Jun Racine of the Vervun Primary moved between the struggling work teams and tried to supervise the clearance work. Tried... it was a joke. He had two hundred bodies, mostly enlisted men, but some Administratum labourers, as well as trackwrights and rolling-stock stewards from the Rail Guild. It was barely enough even to make a dent in destruction of this scale.

Racine was no structural engineer. Even with fourteen heavy tractors fitted with dozer blades at his disposal, there was no way he was going to meet House Command's orders and get the railhead secure in three days. Great roof sections had slumped like collapsed egg-shell, and rockcrete pillars had crumpled and folded like soft candy-sticks. He was reluctant to instruct his men to dig out anything for fear of bringing more down. Already he had sent five men to the medical halls after a section of wall had toppled on them.

The air was wet and acrid, and water dripped down from every surface, pooling five centimetres deep on any open flooring.

Racine checked his data-slate again. The cold, basic schematics on its screen simply didn't match anything here in real life. He couldn't even locate the positions of the main power and gas-feed mains. Nearby, a rail tractor unit sat up-ended in a vast crater, its piston wheels dangling off its great black iron shape. What if fuel had leaked from it? Racine thought about leaked fuel, shorting electrics, spilling gas – even unexploded bombs – an awful lot. He did the maths and hated the answer he kept getting.

'Tough job, major,' said a voice from behind him.

Racine turned. The speaker was a short, bulky man in his fifties, black with grime and leaning on an axe-rack as a crutch. He had a serious eye-wound bandaged with a filthy strip of linen. But his clothes, as far as Racine could make out under the char and the dirt, were those of a smeltery gang boss.

'You shouldn't be here, friend,' Racine said with a patient smile.

'None of us should,' Agun Soric replied, stomping forward. He stood beside Racine and they both gazed dismally out over the tangled ruins of the railhead towards the vast, looming shape of the gate and the Curtain Wall. It was a sea of rubble and debris, and Racine's workforce moved like ants around the merest breakwaters of it.

'I didn't ask for this. I'm sure you didn't either,' Soric said.

'Gak, but that's right! You from the refuges?'

'Name's Soric, plant supervisor, Vervun Smeltery One.' Soric made a brief gesture over at the vast, ruined shell of the once-proud ore plant adjacent to the railhead. 'I was in there when the shells took it. Quite a show.'

'I'll bet. Get many out?'

Soric sucked air through his teeth and looked down, shaking his bullet-head. 'Not nearly enough. Three hundred, maybe. Got ourselves places in a refuge – eventually. It was all a bit confused.'

Racine looked round at him, taking in the set power and simmering anger inside the hive worker. 'What's it like? I hear the refuges are choked to capacity.'

'It's bad. Imagine this,' Soric pointed to the railhead destruction, 'but the ruins are human, not rockcrete and ceramite. Supplies are short: food, clean water, medical aid. They're doing their best, but you know – millions of homeless, most of them hurt, all of them scared.'

Racine shivered.

'I tried to get some aid for my workers, but they told me that all refugees were set on fourth-scale rations unless they were employed in the hive war effort. That might get them bumped up to third-scale, maybe even second.'

'Tough times...' Racine said and they fell silent.

'What if I could bring you close on three hundred eager workers? Willing types, I mean, workers who can haul and labour and who know a bit about shifting and managing loose debris?'

'To help out?'

'Gak, yes! My mob are sick of sitting on their arses in the refuge, doing nothing. We could help you make a job of this.'

Racine looked at him cautiously, trying to see if there was a trick. 'For the good of the hive?' he smiled, questioningly.

'Yeah, for the good of the hive. And for the good of my workers, before they go crazy and lose morale. And I figure if we help you, you could put in a word. Maybe get us a better ration scale.'

Racine hesitated. His vox link was beeping. It would be a call from House Command, he was sure, asking for a progress report.

'I need to get this cleared, or at least a path cleared through it. My regiment have the gate blocked temporarily, but if the enemy hits us there, we need to have a secure wall of defence dug in, with supply lines and troop access. You and your mob help me do that, I'll get your bloody ration scale for you.'

Soric smiled. He tucked the axe-rack crutch under his armpit so he could extend a dirty hand. Racine shook it.

'Vervun Smeltery One won't let you down, major.'

THE CHRONOMETER'S CHIME told him it was dawn, but even up here in the Mid Spine, there was little change in the light outside. The glow of the Shield and the smoke haze saw to that.

Amchanduste Worlin took breakfast in the observation bubble of his clan's palace. He had risen earlier than any of his kin, though junior Guild Worlin clerics and servitors were already about, preparing the day's work protocols.

In orange-silk night robes, he sat in a suspensor chair at the round mahogany table and consumed the breakfast his servants had brought him on a lacquered tray. The taster servitor had pronounced it safe and been dismissed. Worlin's attention oscillated between the panoramic view of the city outside and the data-plate built into the table top where the morning news and situation bulletins threaded and interwove in clusters of glowing runes.

An egg soufflé, smoked fish, fresh fruit, toasted wheatcakes and a jug of caffeine. Not recommended emergency rations,

Worlin knew, but what was the point of being a member of the privileged merchant elite if you couldn't draw on the stockpiles of your clan's resources once in a while?

He improved the caffeine with a shot of joiliq. Worlin felt a measure of contentment for the first time in days and it wasn't just the alcohol. There was one holding owned by House Worlin, one under his direct control, that gave them commercial leverage in this war: liquid fuel. He had quite forgotten it in his initial dismay and panic.

Last season, he had won the fuel concession from Guild Farnora, much to his clan's delight. Thirty percent of the fuel imports from Vannick Hive, three whole pipelines, were under the direct control of Guild Worlin. He looked at the megalitre input figures on his data-slate, then made a few calculations as to how the market price per barrel would soar exponentially with each day of conflict. He'd done the sums several times already, but they pleased him.

'Guild sire?' His private clerk, Magnal, entered the bubble.

'What is it?'

'I was just preparing your itinerary for the day. You have a bond-meeting with the Guild Council at eleven.'

'I know.'

Magnal paused.

'Something else?'

'I... I brought you the directive from the Legislature last night. The one that ordered all fuel pipelines from Vannick closed off now our kin-hive has fallen. You... you do not seem to have authorised the closure, guild sire.'

'The closure...'

'All guilds controlling fuel are ordered to blow the pipes on the north shore and block any remaining stretches with rockcrete.' Magnal tried to show a data slate to Worlin, but the guilder shrugged it away diffidently. 'Our work crews are standing by...'

'How much fuel have we stockpiled in our East Hass Storage facility?' Worlin asked.

Magnal muttered a considerable figure.

'And how much more is still coming through the pipe?'

Another murmur, a figure of magnitude.

Worlin nodded. 'I deplore the loss of our Vannick cousins. But the fuel still comes through. It is the duty Guild Worlin owes to Vervunhive that we keep the pipes open for as long as there is a resource to be collected. I'll shut the pipes the moment they run dry.'

'But the directive, guild sire…'

'Let me worry about that, Magnal. The flow may only last another day, another few hours. But if I close now, can you imagine the lost profits? Not good business, my friend. Not good at all.'

Magnal looked uncomfortable.

'They say there is a security issue here, guild sire…'

Worlin put down his caffeine cup. It hit the saucer a little too hard, making Magnal jump, though the kindly smile never left Worlin's face. 'I am not a stupid man, clerk. I take my responsibilities seriously, to the hive, to my clan. If I close the lines now, I would be derelict in my duties to both. Let the soldiery gain glory with their bravado at the war front. History will relate my bravery here, fighting for Vervunhive as only a merchant can.'

'Your name will be remembered, guild sire,' Magnal said and left the room.

Worlin sat for a while, tapping his silver sugar tongs on the edge of his saucer. There was no doubt about it.

He would have to kill Magnal too.

AT THE VERY southernmost edge of the outer habs and industry sectors, the great hive was a sky-filling dome of green light, pale in the morning sun, hazed by shell smoke.

Captain Olin Fencer of Vervun Primary crawled from his dugout and blinked into the cold morning air. That air was still thick with the mingled reeks of thermite and fycelene, burning fuel and burned flesh. But there was something different about this morning. He couldn't quite work out what it was.

Fencer's squad of fifty troopers had been stationed at Outhab Southwest when the whole thing began. Vox links had been lost in the first wave of shelling and they had been able to do nothing but dig in and ride it out, as day after day of systematic bombardment flattened and ruptured the industrial outer city behind them.

There was no chance to retreat back into the hive, though Fencer knew millions of habbers in the district had fled that way. He had a post to hold. He was stationed at it with the thirty-three men remaining to him when Vegolain's armoured column had rolled past down the Southern Highway, out into the grasslands. His squad had cheered them.

They'd been hiding in their bunkers, some weeping in rage or pain or dismay, that night when the broken remnants of the column had limped back in, heading for the city.

By then, he had twenty men left.

In the days that followed, Fencer had issued his own orders by necessity, as all links to House Command were broken. Indeed, he was sure no one in the hive believed there was anyone still alive out here. He had followed the edicts of the Vervun Primary emergency combat protocols to the letter, organising the digging of a series of trenches, supply lines and fortifications through the ruins of the outhabs, though the shelling still fell on them.

His first sergeant, Grosslyn, had mined the roadways and other teams had dug tank-traps and dead-snares. Despite the shelling, they had also raised a three hundred-metre bulwark of earth, filled an advance ditch with iron stakes and railing sections, and sandbagged three stubbers and two flamers into positions along the Highway.

All by the tenth day. By then, he had eighteen soldiers left.

Three more had died of wounds or disease by the fourteenth day, when the high-orbit flares of troopships told them Guard reinforcements were on their way planetside.

Now it was sunrise on the nineteenth day. Plastered in dust and blood, Fencer moved down the main trench position as his soldiers woke or took over guard duty from the weary night sentries.

But now he had sixty troops. Main Spine thought everything was levelled out here, everything dead, but they were wrong. Not everyone on the blasted outer habs had fled to the hive, though it must have seemed that way. Many stayed, too unwilling, too stubborn, or simply too frightened to move. As the days of bombardment continued, Fencer found men and women – and some children too – flocking to him from the ruins. He got the non-coms into any bunkers he had available and he set careful rationing. All able-bodied workers, of either sex, he recruited into his vanguard battalion.

They'd raised precious medical supplies from the infirmary unit of a bombed-out mine and they'd set up a field hospital in the ruins of a bakery, under the supervision of a teenage girl called Nessa who was a trainee nurse. They'd pilfered food supplies in the canteens of three ruined manufactories in the region. A VPHC Guard House on West Transit 567/kl had provided them with a stock of lasguns and small arms for the new recruits, as well as explosives and one of the flamers.

Fencer's recruits had come from everywhere. He had under his command clerks who'd never held a weapon, loom workers with poor eyesight and shell-shocked habbers who were deaf and could only take orders visually.

The core of his recruits, the best of them, were twenty-one miners from Number Seventeen Deep Working, who had literally dug their way out of the ground after the main lift shaft of their facility had fallen.

Fencer bent low and hurried down the trench line, passing through blown-out house structures, under fallen derricks, along short communication tunnels the miners had dug to link his defences. Their expertise had been a godsend.

He reached the second stub emplacement at 567/kk and nodded to the crew. Corporal Gannen was making soup in his mess tin over a burner stove, while his crewmate, a loomgirl called Calie, scanned the horizon. They were a perfect example of the way necessity had made heroes of them all. Gannen was a trained stub-gunner, but better at ammo feeding than firing. The girl had proven to be a natural at handling the gun itself. So they swapped, the corporal conceding no pride that he now fed ammo to a loom-girl half his age.

Fencer moved on, passing two more guard points and found Gol Kolea in the corner nest, overlooking the highway. Kolea, the natural leader of the miners, was a big man, with great power in his upper body. He was sipping hot water from a battered tin cup, his lasgun at his side. Fencer intended to give him a brevet rank soon. The man had earned it. He had led his miners out of the dark, formed them into a cohesive work duty and done everything Fencer could have asked of them. And more besides. Kolea was driven by grim, intense fury against the Zoican foe. He had family in the hive, though he didn't speak of them. Fencer was sure it was the thought of them that had galvanised Kolea to such efforts.

'Captain,' Kolea nodded as Fencer ducked in.

'Something's wrong, Gol,' Fencer said. 'Something's different.'

The powerfully built miner grinned at him. 'You haven't noticed?' he asked.

'Noticed?'

'The shelling has stopped.'

Fencer was stunned. It had been so much a part of their daily life for the last fortnight or more, he hadn't realised it had gone. Indeed, his ears were still ringing with remembered shockwaves.

'Emperor save us!' he gasped. 'I'm so stupid.'

He'd been awake for upwards of twenty minutes and it took a miner to tell him that they were no longer under fire.

'See anything?' Fencer asked, crawling up to the vigil slot in the sandbags next to Kolea for a look.

'No. Dust, smoke, haze... nothing much.'

Fencer was about to reach for his scope when Zoica began its land offensive.

A wave of las-fire peppered the entire defence line of the outhabs, like the flashes of a billion firecrackers. The sheer scale of the salvos was bewildering. Nine of Fencer's troops died instantly. Three more, all workers, fled, utterly unprepared for the fury of a land assault.

Grenades and rockets dropped in around them, blowing out two communication dug-outs. Another hit the mess hall and torched their precious food supplies.

Fencer's people began their resistance.

He'd ordered them all to set weapons for single fire to preserve ammunition and power cells. Even the stubbers had been ordered only to fire if they had a target. In response to the Zoican assault, their return seemed meagre and frail.

Fencer got up to the nest top and raised his lasgun. Five hundred metres ahead, through the smoke and the rubble, he saw the first shapes of the enemy, troopers in heavy, ochre-coloured battledress, advancing in steady ranks.

Fencer began firing. Below, Kolea opened up too.

They took thirteen down between them in the first five minutes.

Zoican tanks, mottled ochre and growling like beasts, bellied up the road and fanned out into the ruins, using the available open roadways and other aisles in the rubble sea. Mines took two of them out in huge vomits of flame and armour pieces, and the burning hulks blocked the advance of six more.

Rockets flailed into the bulwark and blew a fifteen-metre section out. Corporal Tanik and three other troops were disintegrated.

Another Zoican tank, covered with mesh netting, rumbled through the ruins and diverted down a dead-snare. Blocked in by rockcrete walls to either side and ahead, it tried to reverse and swing its turret as one of the Vervun flamer positions washed it with incandescent gusts of blowtorch fire and cooked it apart.

Sergeant Grosslyn, with two Vervun Primary regulars and six enlisted habbers, cut a crossfire down at Zoican troops trying to scramble a staked ditch on the eastern end of the file. Between them, they killed fifty or more, many impaled on the railings and wire. When Jada, the female worker next to him, was hit in the chest and dropped, screaming, Grosslyn turned to try and help her. A las-round from one of the dying Zoican assault troops impaled on the stakes took the back of his head off.

Gannen and Calie held the west transit for two hours, taking out dozens of the enemy and at least one armoured vehicle which ruptured and blew out as the loom-girl raked it with armour-piercing stub rounds.

Gannen was torn apart by shrapnel from a rocket when the enemy pushed around to the left.

Calie kept firing, feeding her own gun until a tank round blew her, her stub gun and twenty metres of the defence bulwark into the sky.

Overwhelmed, Fencer's force fell back into the ruins of the outhab. Some were crushed by the advancing armour. One enlisted clerk, dying of blood-loss from a boltwound, made a suicide run with a belt of grenades and took out a stationary tank. The explosion lit up the low clouds and scraps of tank metal rained down over the surrounding streets.

Others fought a last-ditch attempt as the sheer numbers of the advancing infantry overran them. There were insane pockets of close fighting, bayonet to bayonet, hand to hand. Not a metre of Vervunhive's outhab territory was given up without the most horrific effort.

Gol Kolea, his las weapon exhausted, met the enemy at the barricade and killed them one by one, to left and right, with savage swings of his axe-rake. He screamed his wife's name with every blow.

A las-round punctured Captain Olin Fencer's body at the hip and exited through his opposite shoulder. As he fell, weeping, he clicked his lasgun to autofire and sprayed his massing killers with laser rounds.

His hand was still squeezing the trigger when the pack ran out.

By then, he was already dead.

SIX
CHAINS OF COMMAND

'A war waged by committee is a war already lost.'
— Sebastian Thor, *Sermons*, vol. XV, ch. DIV

GAUNT FELT THE monumental bulk of the Curtain Wall around him actually vibrate. The shellfire falling against its outer skin was a dull roar.

Captain Daur and three other officers of the liaison staff led the oversight party up the stair-drum of a secondary tower in the wall just west of the massive Heironymo Sondar Gate. Gaunt had brought Rawne and Mkoll, with Trooper Milo as his adjutant. General Grizmund – with three of his senior Narmenians – and General Nash – with two of his regimental aides – made up the rest of the party, along with Tarrian of the VPHC. They had a bodyguard detail of thirty Vervun Primary troopers in full battledress.

The oversight party emerged onto the tower-top, where hot breezes, stifling with fycelene fumes, billowed over them. Three missile launchers were raised and ready here, their crews standing by, but additional awnings of flak-board had been erected in preparation for the visit of the dignitaries, and the launchers, with no safe room for their exhaust wash under this extra shelter, had fallen silent. The crews saluted the visitors smartly.

'These are for our benefit?' Gaunt asked Tarrian, indicating the freshly raised awnings.

'Of course.'

'You muzzle an entire defence tower so we can get a safe peek over the Wall?'

Tarrian frowned. 'General Sturm has made it a standing requirement every time he visits the Wall. I presumed you and the other eminent generals here would expect the same.'

'We've come to fight, not hide. Take them down and get these crews operational.'

Tarrian looked round at Nash and Grizmund. The Narmenian nodded briefly. 'Gaunt speaks for us all,' said Nash dryly. 'We don't need any soft-soap.'

Tarrian turned from the group and began issuing orders to the launcher crews.

The rest of the oversight party approached the rampart and took up magnoculars or used the available viewscopes on their tripod stands. Milo handed Gaunt his own scope from its pouch and the commissar dialled the magnification as he raised it and gazed out.

Below them, the miserable wasteland of the southern outer habs lay exposed and broken. There was no discernible sign of life, but a hateful storm of enemy shelling and missiles pounded in across it at the hive. A fair amount fell short into the habs, but a good percentage struck the Curtain Wall itself. Gaunt craned over for a moment, training his scope down the gentle slope of the Wall. Its adamantine surface was peppered and scarred like the face of a moon, as far as he could see. Every few seconds, batteries to either side of them on the Wall fired out, or the great siege guns in the emplacements below in the thickness of the Wall recoiled and volleyed again.

The vibration of the Wall continued.

'No way of knowing numbers or scale–' began Nash.

Grizmund shook his head. 'Not so, sir,' he replied, pointing out to the very edge of the vast, outer-hab waste. 'As we have been told, this is no longer the work of their long-range artillery out in the grasslands. This is ground assault from closer range – armour moving in through the outer habitations and factories.'

'Are you certain?' asked Gaunt.

'You can see the flashes of tank cannons as they fire. Four, five kilometres out, in the very skirts of the outer habs. Their weapons are on full elevation for maximum range, so the muzzle-flashes are high and exposed. It is a simple matter of observing, counting, estimating.'

Gaunt watched for flashes through his scope. Like Nash, he was an infantry commander, and he always appreciated technical insight from experienced officers with expertise in other schools of warfare. Grizmund had a fine reputation as an armour commander. Gaunt fully trusted the Narmenian's judgement in this. As he looked, he began to discern the flickering display of brief light points out in the hinterland.

'Your estimate?' asked Nash, also studying the scene and, like Gaunt, willing to listen to an expert opinion.

Grizmund glanced to his attending officers, who all looked up from their scopes.

'Nachin?'

The brigadier answered directly, his voice rich with the taut vowel sounds of the Narmenian accent. 'At a first estimate, armour to the magnitude of twenty thousand pieces. Straight-form advance, with perhaps a forced salient to the east, near those tall cooling towers still standing. Innumerable rockets and mortars, harder to trace, but all mobile. Forty, maybe forty-five thousand.'

The other Narmenians concurred. Grizmund turned back to Gaunt and Nash as Tarrian rejoined the group. 'Nachin knows his stuff as well as me. You heard his numbers. A multiple regiment-strength assault. Grand-scale armour attack. Yet – if what Commissar Kowle says is correct – not even a fraction of their numbers.'

'We can presume other army strengths are moving round through the mining district, the mud flats, perhaps the eastern outer habs and the Hass East river junction too,' said Nash dourly.

'I can make no estimates of troop strength, however,' Grizmund added.

'With permission, sir,' Rawne said, and Gaunt nodded for him to continue.

Rawne indicated the scene below with precise gestures of his nimble hands, his killer's hands. 'If you watch the armour flashes as General Grizmund has suggested, they form a rough line, like a contour. Compare that to the fall of shells. The edge of the shortest falling shells – you can see that from the explosions and from the smoke fires – approximately matches that line, with a break of perhaps a kilometre and a half between armour and line of fire. That is the space we might expect the infantry, advancing before the armour, to occupy.'

Nash nodded, impressed by the junior Tanith's insight.

'We can't judge their tactics by our own,' Rawne went on, 'Feth, I've seen the forces of the Chaos-scum perform many tactical aberrations on the fields of war, but assuming they are not intent on slaughtering their own troops, and assuming the widest margin of error, that shows us a clear belt of infantry advance. Even single line abreast, I'd say we were welcoming over half a million down there. Double the line, double the figure, triple it–'

'We may be senior cadre, but we follow your maths, major,' said Gaunt and the others laughed darkly. 'A fine assessment. Thank you.'

'At least a million,' said Mkoll, suddenly.

They all looked round at him.

'Scout-sergeant?'

'Listen, sir,' said Mkoll and they all did, hearing nothing more than the persistent wail and wail-echoes of the shelling and the crumps of explosions.

'Behind the impacts, a higher note, like a creaking, like the wind.'

Gaunt fought hard to screen out the sounds of the assault bombing. He heard vague whispers of the sound Mkoll described.

'Lasguns, sir. So many lasguns firing over each other that their individual sounds have become one shrieking note. You'd need a... a feth of a lot of lasguns to make that sound.'

At the back of the group, Daur noticed that Gaunt's adjutant, Milo, had crossed to the western lip of the tower and was gazing out. The adjutant was no more than a youth, his pale skin marked by a strange blue tattoo as seemed to be the custom with so many of the Ghosts.

Daur crossed to him, limping. 'What do you see?' he asked.

'What's that?' asked Milo, pointing down to the east. Far away, round the curve of the massive Curtain Wall, past the Sondar and Veyveyr Gates and the ruin of the Ore Works, a great, black slope extended down out of the hive, two kilometres wide and five deep. It looked like a tide of tar. The Curtain Wall broke in a gap fourteen hundred metres wide to let it out.

'The Spoil,' Daur replied. 'It's a... a mountain of rock refuse and processed ore waste from the smelteries and mine workings. One of the landmarks of Vervunhive,' he laughed.

'The Wall is broken there.'

'The Spoil's been there longer than the Wall. The Wall was built around it.'

'But still, it's a break in the defence.'

'Don't worry, it's well protected. The fifth division of my Regiment, the "Spoilers," are dedicated to guarding that area: twenty thousand men. They take their work seriously. Besides, the Spoil itself is bloody treacherous: steep, unsafe, constantly slipping. It's probably harder to get past than the Curtain Wall itself. An enemy would waste thousands trying a foolish gambit like that!'

Daur smiled encouragingly at Milo and then turned away and rejoined the oversight tour.

Milo felt sorry for him. Daur had no experience of the enemy, no knowledge of the way they expended and used their troops wholesale to gain their objectives. The soldiers of Vervunhive and the tactics they had evolved were too deeply focused upon the experience of fighting sane enemies.

In the main group, Gaunt looked to his fellow regiment commanders. 'Assessments?'

'Way too much armour for an infantry-based counterjab just now, but I'd as soon not let those bastards reach the walls,' said Nash.

'I'd like to deploy my tank divisions to engage them out there,' Grizmund said. 'Supported by whatever the NorthCol armour units can supply. We're not overwhelmed yet. If we can stop them in the outer habs clear of the main hive, we can push an advance spearhead right down into the heart of them. For all their infamous numbers, they are extended over a massive area. That's how I'd go. Armoured counter-assault, direct and sudden, take the ground out from under them, if only a section, then open a way to turn and flank them, cutting into their reserve lines. And dig a path for the infantry too.'

Nash agreed vehemently. 'I'll happily support an organised push of that sort.'

'So will I,' Gaunt said. 'They've taken more than enough ground. We should stop them dead, even if only in this west sector.'

Grizmund nodded. 'The gates this side of the hive must be opened. I'll gladly fight these bastards, no matter how many there are, but I need room for my machines to mobilise and manoeuvre. I'd rather do that out there in the habs than wait until they're at the Wall.'

'Or inside it,' Rawne added.

'Something of a first,' Gaunt smiled at his colleagues. 'Three regimental officers agreed on a tactical approach.'

There was more general laughter, cut short by the first shrieks of the missile launchers on the tower reopening fire now the awnings were down.

'That assessment does not jibe with General Sturm's strategy,' Tarrian said from the side.

Gaunt looked round at him. 'I feel uneasy whenever a political officer uses a vague word like "jibe", Commissar Tarrian. What do you mean?'

'I understand General Sturm's tactical recommendations for the prosecution of this conflict are already drawn up and under examination by Marshal Croe, the House Command Strategy Committee and representatives of the noble houses. I hear they have the full support of Vice Marshal Anko and Commissar Kowle.'

'It sounds like they're as good as decided!' Nash snarled, his heavy chin with its bristle of grey stubble set hard.

'Are we wasting our time up here? What good is this over-sight tour if they've already set on a course?' Grizmund asked.

'I have had past dealings with the general of the Volpone,' Gaunt remarked sourly. 'I have no doubt he feels himself to be the senior Guard officer in this theatre and the hive elders have lauded him as such. But he is not a man for personal confrontation. Better he gives us something to occupy our attentions while he makes his own decisions. Hence this... sight-seeing.'

Gaunt turned sharply to look at Tarrian. 'And you'd know what those decisions were, wouldn't you, Tarrian?'

'It is not my place to say, colonel-commissar,' Tarrian said flatly.

'To hold the Wall, to keep the gates sealed, to give up all territory outside and to dig in for a sustained siege, trusting the Shield, the Curtain Wall and the army strengths within Vervunhive to hold the enemy off forever, or at least until the winter breaks them.'

They all looked round. As he finished speaking, Captain Daur shrugged, ignoring the murderous look the VPHC commander was giving him. 'The plans were circulated this morning, with a magenta clearance rating. I have no reason to assume that clearance excluded senior echelon Guard officers.'

'Thank you, Daur,' Gaunt said. He looked back at Tarrian. 'The generals and I wish to see Sturm and the marshal. Immediately.'

QUIETLY, THE QUINTET of ochre-clad troops picked their way down the corridor of the bombed-out workshop, moving through the dust-filled air. Outside, a tank grated past down the river of debris that had once been Outhab Transit Street 287/fd.

The soldiers wore ochre battledress, shiny, black leather webbing straps, and polished, newly stamped lasguns. On their heads were full-face composite helmets with flared, sneering features like blurred skulls and the crest of Ferrozoica inlayed on the brow.

The squad checked each doorway and damage section they came to. Gol Kolea could hear the hollow crackle of their terse vox-signals barking back and forth.

He slid back into cover and made a hand gesture that his company could read. They moved back, swallowed by the shadows and the dust.

Gol let the five troopers advance down the corridor far enough until the last one was standing on the false flooring. Then he connected the bare end of the loose wire in his hand to the terminals of the battery pack.

The concussion mine tore out a length of the corridor and obliterated the last trooper where he stood, tearing the one directly in front of him into pieces with fragments of shrapnel and shards of bone from his exploded comrade.

The other three fell, then scrambled up, firing blind in the smoke. Bright, darting bars of las-fire pierced the smoke cover like reef fish scudding through cloudy water.

Gol smashed out his fake wall and came down on the first of them from the rear, swinging the hook-bill of his axe-rake down through helmet and skull.

Sergeant Haller dropped down from the ceiling joists where he had been crouching and felled another of them, killing him with point-blank shots from his autopistol as his bodyweight flattened the trooper.

The remaining Zoican bastard switched to full auto and swung wild. His withering close-range shots punched right through a flak-board wall partition and blew the guts and thighs out of Machinesmith Vidor, who had been waiting to spring out from behind it.

Nessa came out of cover under some loose sacking and slammed the rock-knife into the back of the Zoican's neck. She held on, screaming and yanking at the blood-slick knife-grip as the trooper bucked convulsively. By the time he dropped, his head was nearly sawn off.

Gol hurried forward, picking Nessa up and pulling her off the corpse. She handed the bloody rock knife to him, shaking.

'Keep it,' he mouthed. She nodded. Eardrums ruptured by a close shell on the seventh day, she would never hear again without expensive up-hive surgery and implants – which meant simply she would never hear again. She was a trainee medic from the outer habs. Not the lowest of the low, but way, way down in the hive class system.

'You did good,' Gol signed. She smiled, but the fear in her eyes and the blood on her face diffused the power of the expression and diluted the beauty of the young woman.

'Not so easy,' she signed back. She'd learned to sign her remarks early on. Captain Fencer, the Emperor save his soul, had trained her well and explained how she could not modulate the volume of her own voice now she was deaf.

Gol looked round. Haller and the other members of Gol's team had recovered four working lasguns, two laspistols and a bunch of ammunition webs from the dead by then.

'Go! Move!' Gol ordered, emphasising his words with expressive sign-gestures for the deaf. Of his company of nine, six were without hearing. He took a last look at Vidor's corpse and nodded a moment of respect. He had liked Vidor. He wished the brave machinesmith had found the chance to fight. Then he followed his company out.

They moved out of the workshop, circuiting back around through a side alley and into a burned-out Ecclesiarchy chapel. The bodies of the Ministorum brothers lay all around, venting swarms of flies. They had not abandoned their holy place, even when the shells began to fall.

Haller crossed to the altar, straightened the slightly skewed Imperial eagle and knelt in observance. Tears dripped down his face, but he still remembered to sign his anguish and his prayer to the Emperor rather than speak it. Gol noticed this, and was touched and impressed by the soldier's dual devotion to the Emperor and to their continued safety.

Gol got his company into the chapel, spreading them out to cover the openings and find the obvious escape routes.

The ground shook as tank rounds took out the workshop where they had sprung their trap.

In the cover of the explosions, he dared to speak, signing at the same time. 'Let's find the next ones to kill,' he said.

'A squad of six, moving in from the west,' hissed loom-girl Banda, setting down her lasgun and peering out of a half-broken lancet window.

'Drill form as before,' Gol Kolea signed to his company, 'Form on me. Let's set the next snare.'

* * *

LORD HEYMLIK CHASS sent his servitors and bodyguard away. The chief of the guard, Rudrec, his weapon dutifully shrouded, tried to refuse, but Chass was not in the mood for argument.

Alone in the cool, gloomy family chapel of House Chass, high up in the Main Spine upper sectors, the lord prayed diligently to the soul of the undying Emperor. The ghosts of his ancestors welled up around him, immortalised in statuary. Heymlik Chass believed in ghosts.

They spoke to him.

He unlocked the casket by the high altar between the family stasis-crypts with a geno-key that had been in his family for generations. He raised the velvet-padded lid, hearing the moan of ancient suspensor fields, and lifted out Heironymo's Amulet.

'What are you doing, father?' Merity Chass asked. His daughter's voice startled him and almost made him drop the precious thing.

'Merity! You shouldn't be here!' he murmured.

'What are you doing?' she asked again, striding forward under the flaming sconces of the chapel, her green velvet dress whispering as she moved.

'Is that…' Her voice trailed away. She could not utter the words.

'Yes. Given to our house by Great Heironymo himself.'

'You're not thinking of using it! Father!'

He stared down into her pained, beautiful face.

'Go away, my daughter. This is not for your eyes.'

'No!' she barked. She so reminded him of her mother when she turned angry that way. 'I am grown, I am the heir, female though I may be. Tell me what you are doing!'

Chass sighed and let the weight of the amulet play in his hands. 'What I must, what is good for the hive. There was a reason Old Heironymo bequeathed this to my father. Salvadore Sondar is a maniac. He will kill us all.'

'You have raised me to be respectful of the High House, father,' she said, a slight smile escaping her frown. That was her mother again, Heymlik noticed.

'It amounts to treason,' his daughter whispered.

He nodded and his head sank. 'I know what it amounts to. But we are on the very brink now. Heironymo always foretold this moment.'

He hugged her. She felt the weight of the amulet in his hands against her back.

'You must do what you must, father,' Merity said.

Like a slow, pollen-gathering insect, a vox drone hummed lazily in the chapel and crossed to the embracing figures. It bleeped insistently. Chass pulled away from his daughter, savouring the sweet smell of her hair.

'A vote is being taken in the Upper Legislature. I must go.'

Bumbling like a moth, the drone hovered in front of the Noble Lord, leading him out of the chamber.

'Father?'

Heymlik looked back at his beloved child, hunched and frightened by the cold, marble familial crypt.

'I will support you in whatever you do, but you must tell me what you decide. Don't keep me in the dark.'

'I promise,' he said.

THE PRIVY COUNCIL was a circular theatre set on the Spine-floor above the spectacular main hall of the Legislature, and it was reserved for the noble houses only. The domed roof was a painted frieze of the Emperor and the god-machines of Mars hovering in radiant clouds. Columns of warm, yellow light stabbed down from the edges of the circular ceiling and lit the velvet thrones of the high houses. Apart from Chass, they were all there: Gavunda, Yetch, Rodyn, Anko, Croe, Piidestro, Nompherenti and Vwik.

Marshal Croe stood by his brother, the old, wizened Lord Croe, in deep conference. Vice Marshal Anko, beaming and obsequious, was introducing General Sturm to his resplendently gowned cousin, Lord Anko. Commissar Kowle was diplomatically greeting Lords Gavunda and Nompherenti. Servants and house retainers thronged the place, running messages, fetching silver platters of refreshments, or simply guarding their noble masters with shrouded sidearms.

A gong sounded four strokes. The main gilt shutter at the east side of the room slid up into the ceiling with a hiss and

Master Legislator Anophy limped into the chamber, his opalescent robes glinting in the yellow light, his beribboned tricorn nodding with each heavy shuffle he took across the embroidered carpet. He was using the long, golden sceptre of his office as a stick. Child pages held his train and carried his gem-encrusted vox/pict drone and Book of Hive-law before him on tasselled cushions.

Anophy reached his place. He adjusted the silver arm of the vox-phone and spoke. 'Noble houses, your careful attention.' All looked round and quickly took their places. Kowle, Sturm and the other military men withdrew to one side.

Noble Chass's seat was vacant.

Anophy thumbed through the data on a slate held up by one of his pages and he set a palsy-trembling finger to his moist lips.

'A matter to vote. In all precision, before these houses, the ratification of the defence plans our noble friend, General Noches Sturm, has drawn up. The matter need not be lengthened further by discourse. The Hive, Emperor grant it wealth and longevity, awaits.'

Six assent runes, fizzling holograms, lit the air above Anophy. Rodyn and Piidestro houses voted against with dark-tinged, threatening lights.

'Carried,' said Anophy simply. The Privy Council began chattering and moving again.

A shutter of herring-bone steel to the west side of the chamber slid open and Noble Chass, accompanied by his bodyguard, entered the chamber. An awkward hush fell. It remained in place as Chass descended the steps, crossed the chamber and took his appointed seat. Once they had folded his great, silk train over the throne back, his bodyguard and servants stood away.

Chass gazed around the circular hall. Several of his fellow nobles did not meet his gaze.

'You have voted. I was not present.'

'You were summoned,' Lord Anko said. 'If you miss the given time, your vote is forfeit.'

'You know the rules, noble lord,' wheezed Anophy.

'I know when I have been... excluded.'

'Come now!' Anophy said. 'There is no exclusion in the upper parliament of Vervunhive. Given the extraordinary circumstances of this situation, I will allow you to vote now.'

Chass looked around again, very conscious of the way Lord Croe would not look at him.

'I see the matter has been voted six to two. My vote, whichever way I meant to cast it, would be useless now.'

'Cast it anyway, brother lord,' gurgled Gavunda through the silver-inlaid, wire-box augmentor that covered his mouth like an ornate, crouching spider.

Chass shook his head. 'I spoil my vote. There is no point to it.'

A group of figures was entering through the east hatch. Commissar Tarrian was trying to delay them, but they pushed past. It was Gaunt, Grizmund, Nash and their senior officers.

'I can scarce believe your guile, Sturm,' Nash spat, facing the other general. Gilbear moved forward to confront the Roane commander, but Sturm held him back with a curt snap of his fingers.

Gaunt crossed directly to the Master Legislator's place and took the data-slate from the hands of the surprised page. He reviewed it.

'So, it's true,' he said, looking up at Sturm and Marshal Croe.

'General Sturm's strategic suggestions have been agreed and ratified by the Upper Council,' Vice Marshal Anko said smoothly. 'And I strongly suggest you, and the other off-world commanders with you, show some order of respect and courtesy to the workings and customs of this high parliament. We will not have our ancient traditions flouted by–'

'You're all fools,' Gaunt said carelessly, setting the slate down and turning away, 'if you care more for ceremonial traditions than life. You've made a serious error here.'

'You've killed this hive and all of us with it!' Nash snapped, bristling with fury. Gaunt took the big Roane general by the shoulder and moved him away from confrontation.

'I am surprised at you, marshal,' Grizmund said, his stiff anger just held in check, like an attack dog on a choke chain, as he looked at Croe. 'From our meetings, I'd believed your grasp of tactics was better than this.'

Marshal Croe got up. 'I'm sorry at your unhappiness, General Grizmund. But General Sturm's plan seems sound to me. I have the hive to think of. And Commissar Kowle, who has – let's be fair – actually encountered our foe, concurs.'

Grizmund shook his head sadly.

'What would *you* have done?' Lord Chass asked.

There was a lot of shouting and protesting, all of it directed at Chass.

'Lord Chass has a right to know!' Ibram Gaunt's clear, hard voice cut the shouting away. Gaunt turned to face the nobleman. 'After due observation, Generals Nash, Grizmund and I would have opened the south-west gates and launched armour to meet them, infantry behind. A flanking gesture to front them outside of the Wall rather than give up all we have.'

'Would that have worked?' Chass asked.

'We'll never know,' Gaunt replied. 'But we do know this: if we wait until they reach the Wall, where do we have to fall back to after that?

'Nowhere.'

Noble Chass wanted to question further, but the Privy Council dissolved in uproar and Gaunt marched out, closely followed by the furious Grizmund and Nash.

'COMMISSAR? COMMISSAR-COLONEL?' In the crowded promenade hall outside the Privy Council, where parliamentary and house aides thronged back and forth with guilders and house ordinary delegates, Gaunt paused and turned. A tall, grim-looking man in ornate body armour was pushing through the crowds after him, a satin-cloth covering the weapon in his right hand. Gaunt sent his staff ahead with the other generals and turned to face the man. A household bodyguard, he was sure.

The man approached and made a dutiful salute. 'I am Rudrec, lifeguard of his excellency Lord Chass of Noble House Chass. My lord requests a meeting with you at your earliest convenience.'

The man handed Gaunt a small token-seal, with the Imperial eagle on one side and the Chass coat-of-arms on the other.

'With this, you may be admitted to House Chass at all times. My lord will await.'

Gaunt looked at the crest as the lifeguard bowed and departed, swallowed by the crowd.

Now what, he wondered?

SALVADOR SONDAR half-woke, a dream teetering on the edge of memory. The water around him was sweet and warm, and pink bio-luminescence glowed softly.

The chatter murmured at him, soft, soothing, compelling. It was there almost all the time now, asleep or awake.

Sondar listed in the water.

What? What is it? What do you want?

THE SOUTHERN outer habs were ablaze and ash-smog was being driven through the rubble-strewn streets by the cross-winds surging cyclonically from the hottest blazes.

Despite fierce pockets of guerrilla resistance, the Zoican forces pushed up through the ruins in spaced phalanxes of infantry and columns of armour – thousands of them – grinding ever north through the confusion.

The first of them were now just a kilometre from the Curtain Wall.

SEVEN
DEATH MACHINES

'Victory and Death are the twin sons of War.'

— Ancient proverb

THE BOMBARDMENT FROM the advancing Zoican land assault fell abruptly silent in the mid-morning of the twenty-fifth day. Hive observers had been carefully tracking the advance of the enemy legions through the outer habs, but by day twenty-two, the level of smoke and ash-clouds veiling the region made such a task impossible once again. Eerie silence now fell.

No one doubted that this cessation of shelling signalled an imminent storm-assault of the Curtain Wall and House Command ordered a swift redeployment to be made all along the southern defence sections. The Curtain Wall and gates were already fully manned by the Vervun Primary troops, and now significant portions of the Volpone, Roane and NorthCol armies were brought in to reinforce them. The Tanith Ghosts were also deployed to the frontline from their chem plant billet where they had been killing the hours in fretful indolence and frustration. Gaunt kept some platoons

102

in reserve at the billet, but five platoons under Major Rawne were sent to the Hass West Fortress, and another four under Colonel Corbec were moved to Veyveyr Gate in support of the three Vervun Primary and two NorthCol companies already stationed there.

Corbec saw the vulnerability of Veyveyr Gate the moment he and his men arrived by transit truck. Superhuman efforts had been made to clear sections of the ruined rail terminal and he and his troops rode in past pioneer teams still clearing rubble or shaping it into effective barricade lines. The gate itself, seventy metres wide and a hundred high, had been blockaded with wreckage, a lot of it burned-out rolling stock from the railhead. But there were no great blast doors to seal it like at the other main Wall gates.

Corbec met with Colonel Modile and Major Racine, the ranking Vervun officers in the sector, and with Colonel Bulwar of the NorthCol contingent. Modile was earnest and businesslike, though clearly very nervous about the prospect of seeing action for the first time in his career. Corbec didn't like the idea that the officer at the apex of the command pyramid at Veyveyr was a combat virgin. The major, Racine, was a more likeable fellow, but he was dead on his feet with fatigue. Corbec found out later that the Vervun Primary Officer had been awake for the best part of three days straight, supervising the preparation of the Veyveyr defence.

Bulwar at least was a combat veteran who had seen action during the years of rebellion wars in the NorthCol colonies on Verghast's main satellite moon. He was a thickset man who wore the same regular, evergreen flak-armour and fatigues as his men, though the braided cap and the crackling power claw marked him out instantly as a command officer. As the four officers met around the chart table in Modile's shelter, Corbec soon noticed the way Modile deferred to Bulwar's suggestions. Bulwar saw it too and in effect began to take command. All he had to do was hint and speculate, and Modile would quickly take up the ideas and turn them into tactical policy as if they were his own.

That's fine and good now, thought Corbec, but what happens when the shooting starts? Without direct, confident command, the defence would fall apart.

After the meeting, at which the Ghosts had been drawn to take position along the east flank, against the perimeter of the Ore Works and Smeltery ruins, Corbec took Bulwar to one side.

'With respect, Modile's a weak link.'

Bulwar nodded. 'Agreed. I think the same of most of the Vervun Primary units. No experience. At least my forces have had baptism enough in the moon war. But this is Vervunhive's show and their House Command has authority over us all, colonel.'

'We need a safeguard,' Corbec said flatly, scratching at his collar. There were damn lice in those chem barns. 'I'm not talking insubordination...'

'I know what you mean. My old call sign was "anvil." Let that be a signal to co-ordinate orders above Modile's head if it becomes necessary. I won't be hung out to dry by an inexperienced man. Even a well-meaning one like Modile.'

Corbec nodded. He liked Bulwar. He hoped it wouldn't come to that.

ANOTHER DAY PASSED, with only silence and smoke outside the Curtain Wall. Nerves began to fray. All the while the shelling had been going on, there had at least been the illusion that a war was being fought. Waiting, the common fighting man's worst foe, began to take its toll. Anxious minds had time to worry, to fear, to anticipate. Nearly three quarters of a million fighting men were in position at the southern Curtain Wall of Vervunhive, with nothing to do but doze, fidget, gaze up at the spectral flashes and crackles of the Shield far above, and distress themselves with their own imaginations.

The VPHC was busy. Sixty-seven deserters or suspected derelicts were executed in a twenty-four hour period.

ON THE AFTERNOON of the twenty-seventh day, troops on the Wall top began to detect ominous grinding and clanking noises emanating from the smoke cover below. Machine noises, vast servos, threshing gears, rattling transmissions, creaking metal. It seemed that at any moment, the storm would begin.

But the noises simply continued until after dark and more urgently through the night. They were alien and incomprehensible, like the calls of unseen creatures in some mechanical jungle.

THE TWENTY-EIGHTH day was silent. The machine noises ceased at dawn. By noon, the smoke had begun to clear, especially after a rising wind from the southwest brought rain squalls in from the coast. But still visibility was low and the light was poor. There was nothing to see but the grey blur of the mangled outhabs.

ON THE TWENTY-NINTH day, spotters on the Wall near Sondar Gate sighted a small group of Zoican tanks moving along a transit track adjacent to the Southern Highway, two kilometres out. With hurried permission from House Command in the Main Spine, they addressed six missile batteries and a trio of earthshaker guns and opened fire. There was jubilation all along the defence line, for no greater reasons than the soldiers finally had a visible enemy to target and the fighting drought was broken. The engagement lasted twelve minutes. No fire was returned from the enemy. When the shell-smoke cleared, there was no sign of the tanks that had been fired upon – not even wreckage.

During the evening of that day, the machine noises from outside grumbled and clanked again, sporadically. Marshal Croe made a morale-boosting speech to the population and the troops over the public-address plates. It helped ease the tension, but Gaunt knew Croe should have been making such speeches daily for the last week. Croe had only spoken now on the advice of Commissar Kowle. Despite his dislike of the man, Gaunt saw that Kowle truly understood the political necessities of war. He was enormously capable. Kowle issued a directive that evening urging all commissarial officers, both the VPHC and the regular Guard, to tour the lines and raise the mood. Gaunt had been doing just that since his units went into position, shuttling between Hass West and Veyveyr. On these tours, he had been impressed by the resolve and discipline of the Vervun Primary troopers who manned the defences alongside his men. He prayed dearly to the beloved Emperor that combat wouldn't sour that determination.

On that evening, riding his staff car down the inner transits to check on Rawne's units at Hass West, Gaunt found the seal Lord Chass's bodyguard had given to him in his coat pocket. There had been no time thus far to pay the noble a visit. Gaunt turned the token over in his gloved hand as the car roared down a colonnaded avenue. Perhaps tonight, after his inspection of Hass West.

He never got the chance. Just before midnight, as Gaunt was still climbing the stairs of the fort's main tower, the first Zoican storm began.

DESPITE THE MILITARY preparations, no one in the hive was really prepared for the onslaught. It fell so suddenly. Its herald was a simultaneous salvo from thousands of tanks and self-propelled guns prowling forward through the outer-hab wastes less than a kilometre from the Wall. The roar shook the hive and the explosive display lit the night sky. For the first time, the enemy was firing up at the Curtain Wall, point-blank in armour terms, hitting wall-top ramparts and fracturing them apart. Precision mortar bombardments were landing on the wall-top itself, finding the vulnerable slit between Wall and Shield. Other ferocious rains of explosive force hammered at the gates or chipped and flaked ceramite armour off the Wall's face.

The defenders reeled, stunned. Hundreds were already dead or seriously injured and the ramparts were significantly damaged in dozens of places. Officers rallied the dazed soldiery and the reply began. With its rocket towers, heavy guns, support-weapon emplacements, mortars and the thousands of individual troopers on the ramparts, that reply was monumental. Once they began to fight, a gleeful fury seized the men of Vervunhive. To address the enemy at last. To fire in anger. It felt good after all the waiting. It was absolving.

The Curtain Wall firepower decimated the Zoican forces now advancing towards the Wall-foot outside. Vervunhive laid down a killing field four hundred metres deep outside their Wall and obliterated tanks and men as they churned forward. It was later estimated that 40–50,000 Zoican troops and upwards of 6,000 fighting vehicles were lost to Vervun-hive fire in the first hour of attack.

But the sheer numbers of the enemy were overwhelming, both physically and psychologically. No matter how many hundreds were killed, thousands more moved forward relent-lessly to take their place, marching over the corpses of the slain. They were mindless and without fear in the face of the mass slaughter. Observing this from his trench position just inside Veyveyr Gate, Brin Milo reflected that this was precisely what he had been afraid of: the insane tactics of Chaos that Vervunhive's war plans simply did not take into account.

'You could fire a lasgun on full auto from the wall-top,' wrote General Xance of the NorthCol forces later, 'and kill dozens, only to see the hole you'd made in their ranks close in the time it took to change power cells. If war is measured by the number of casualties inflicted, then even in that first night, we had won. Sadly, that is not the case.'

'So many, so many…' were the last words spoken into his vox-set by a mind-numb Vervun Primary officer at Sondar Gate just before one of the VPHC shot him and took control of his frazzled forces.

At Hass West, Gaunt arrived on the main rampart just after a mortar round had taken out a section of wall-lip and blown the head off Colonel Frader, the commander of the area section. Gaunt took command, calling up a Vervun Pri-mary vox-officer and grabbing the handset from his pack. Gaunt was accompanied by Liaison Officer Daur, who confi-dently relayed vocal commands to the troops in earshot. Gaunt was glad of him. Daur knew the tower and knew the men from his time stationed here, and they responded bet-ter to an officer of their own. Many had seemed overawed by the Imperial commissar. Gaunt accepted that fear was a com-mand tool, but he loathed what the iron rule of the VPHC had done to the resolve of the local troops.

Gaunt reached Rawne on the vox-link. The major had the Tanith strength spread out along the lower towers and wall-line below the main fort.

'No casualties here,' the major reported, his voice punctu-ated by cracks and pops of static. 'We're pouring it on, but there are so many!'

'Stay as you are! Keep up the address! We know they won't break like a normal army, but you and I have faced this enemy before, Rawne. You know how to win this!'

'Kill them all, colonel-commissar?'

'Kill them all, Major Rawne!' And for all he personally trusted the man no further than he could throw him, Gaunt knew that was exactly what Rawne would do.

'WHAT'S THAT?' bellowed Feygor, firing over the buttress.

Rawne ducked along to him. 'What?'

Feygor pointed down. An armoured machine, three times the size of a main battle tank, was advancing towards the wall's skirt, a huge derrick of armour-plated scaffolding growing out of its top.

'Siege engine! For feth's sake! Get on the vox, tell Gaunt!' Feygor nodded.

Rawne scrambled closer to the lip and the las-storm below. 'Bragg! Bragg!'

The big trooper crawled over, hefting his missile launcher. 'Kill it!'

Bragg nodded and raised the launcher to his shoulder, then banged off three rockets that curled down towards the vast engine on plumes of blue smoke. They hit the superstructure and ignited, but no serious damage was done.

'Reload! Again!'

The monstrous siege engine reached the foot of the Wall and there was a shrieking sound as the metal tower scraped against the ceramite and stone facings. Gas-fired anchor ropes were shot into the Curtain Wall to hold the engine in place. Hydraulic feet extended beneath the armour skirts of the engine to steady it on the broken ground. With a wail of metal, the derrick tower began to telescope up, extending to match the height of the wall. Segmented armour, badged with the Zoican crest and other, less human insignias that made Rawne sick to see them, unfurled upwards to protect the rising throat of the siege tower.

At the same time, the base unit of the vast machine opened a well-protected hatch in its rear and Zoican troops began to pour into it.

The tower-top rose above the wall's lip, forty metres from Rawne. Hydraulic arms wheezed out and gripped the buttress, steel claws biting into the ceramite. The tower-top was an armoured structure with heavy flamer mounts positioned either side of a hatch opening.

'*Get down! Get down!*' Rawne bellowed.

The flamers drenched the top of the Wall with liquid fire, swivelling to rake the defences back and forth. Forty Vervun Primary troopers and nine Ghosts were incinerated as they fled back from the engine.

In addition to the shrieking flamers, automatic grenade launchers on the tower-top whirred and began to lob explosives out like hail. Multiple detonations exploded along the scorched wall.

Rawne fell into cover behind a bulwark with Bragg, Feygor and several other Ghosts. Feygor was firing his lasgun at the tower, but his shots were simply dinking off the armoured superstructure. Vervun troops, some on fire, fled past them.

'Bragg!'

'Got a blockage,' replied the giant, fighting with his launcher.

'Load him!' Rawne ordered Trooper Gyrd.

Gyrd, a grizzled Ghost in his forties, swung in behind Bragg as the big man got the launcher settled on his shoulder. The older Ghost fed fresh rockets into the load-cylinders of the massive weapon.

'Clear!' bawled Bragg as he sent a missile directly at the tower head. It blew the left-hand flamer mount clean off and ignited a huge fireball of venting prometheum. But the armoured delivery section remained unscathed.

'Wait, wait…' hissed Rawne. The skin on the left-hand side of his face was blackened and scorched by the flamer wash. If he lived till morning, he'd have what the Guard called a 'flamer-tan.'

'For what?' barked Feygor. 'Another moment and that hatch'll open. Then the bastards will be all over us!'

'For half a moment, then. We can't make a dent on this thing, so we wait for that hatch.'

The remaining flamer point raked back and forth, its white-hot fires beginning to blister the stone. Then it cut off and drips of fluid fire pooled out of its blackened snout. The grenade throwers stopped whirring.

The storm hatch opened with a shriek. For a scant second, the wall defenders saw the first of the ochre-armoured Zoican troops waiting to deploy out into Vervunhive.

Bragg fired three missiles, one of which went wide. The remaining pair disappeared into the hatchway. The tower-top blew out from within. Secondary explosions rippled down the tower structure and ablaze from inside, it toppled and crumpled with a tearing, metallic wail.

The defenders cheered wildly.

'Move back in! Cover the wall!' urged Rawne.

SIX MORE SIEGE engines had crawled forward towards the Curtain Wall in the time it had taken Rawne to repel the first.

Relentless fire from missile batteries had taken one apart before it could deploy, just short of the Sondar Gate. Another reached the Curtain Wall intact but positioned itself in front of an Earthshaker heavy battery in the Wall side. The massive, long-range cannons blew it apart point-blank, though the crews were fried by the flaming backwash that rushed into their silos.

A third reached Sondar Gate and deployed successfully, rising and clamping to the gatehouse top and then torching everything and everyone on the emplacement before opening its hatch and disgorging wave after wave of Zoican heavy troopers. The Vervun Primary forces were annihilated by this assault, but Volpone units from the neighbouring ramparts, under the command of Colonel Corday, scissored in to meet the invasion. Some of the fiercest fighting of the First Storm took place then, with twenty units of Volpone Bluebloods, including a detachment of the elite 10th Brigade under Major Culcis, undertaking a near hand-to-hand battlement fight with thousands of Zoican storm troops. The regular Bluebloods wore the grey and gold body armour of their regiment, with the distinctive low-brimmed bowl helmets. The elite 10th had carapace armour, matt-black hellguns and bright indigo eagle studs pinned into their armaplas collar sections. Culcis, who had won himself a valour medal on

Vandamaar, was young for a member of the tenth elite, but his superiors had rightly noticed his command qualities. Despite seventy per cent losses, he held Sondar Gate through nothing more than tactical surety and brute determination.

The top of Sondar Gate and the walls adjacent were thick with corpses. Culcis and his immediate inferior, Sergeant Mantes of the regular Volpone, tried to disable the siege engine with tank mines. Mantes died in the attempt, but the mines blew the support claws off the tower and it collapsed soon after under its own weight. Culcis, who had lost a hand in the detonation of the mines, reformed his forces and slaughtered all the remaining Zoicans who had made the wall-top. For the first of what would be three serious attempts, Sondar Gate resisted the enemy.

The fourth siege engine reached the Wall east of Sondar Gate, midway along the stretch that curved round to Veyveyr. Here Roane Deepers were in position, hard-nosed shock troops in tan fatigues and netted helmets. General Nash was in command in person and he mobilised the wall batteries to target the tower neck as it extended up towards them. The ripples of missiles didn't destroy it, but they damaged some internal mechanism and the tower jammed at half-mast, unable to reach the Wall top and engage. It raked upwards with its flamers and grenades spitefully, and Nash lost more than forty men. But it could not press its assault and remained hunched outside the Curtain Wall, broken and derelict, for the remainder of the war.

The other two siege engines assaulted Hass West Fort.

Gaunt saw then coming, slow and inexorable, and drew up his heavy weapons. He'd seen the system of assault through his scope watching Rawne's position, and he didn't want it duplicated here.

Under his voxed commands, the wall batteries strafed the nearest engine heavily and succeeded in blowing it apart. The upper section of the tower, beginning to telescope, snapped off to the left in a fireball, destroying the base unit as it collapsed.

But despite Gaunt's efforts, the second siege engine reached the western portions of the ramparts and engaged its clamps. The tower hoisted into position.

Gaunt ordered his men back from the surrounding area as the flamers retched and blasted and the grenades rained.

In cover next to him, Captain Daur pulled off his sling.

'Your arm?'

'Stuff that, commissar! Give me a gun!'

Gaunt handed the Vervun captain his bolt pistol and then cycled his chainsword. 'Prepare yourself, Daur. This is as bad as it ever gets.'

Zoican troops spilled out of the tower top, thousands of them. They were met by the Ghosts and the Vervun Primary. Another infamous episode of the First Storm began.

JUST BEFORE GAUNT's positions destroyed the first of the two engines, other Zoican death machines clanked out of the outhab wastes and assaulted the walls: a half-dozen tank-like vehicles, quickly dubbed the 'flat-crabs' by the Vervun troopers because of their resemblance to the edible crustaceans farmed in the Hass Estuary. They were the size of four or five tanks together, covered in a shell-like carapace of overlapped armour like huge beetles or horseshoe molluscs. A single, super-heavy weapon extended up from their dorsal mounts and they drummed the Wall with fast-cycle fire that shattered masonry and adamantine blocks.

The flat-crabs were siege-crackers, massive weapons designed to break open even the strongest fortifications. Two of them, with dorsal mounts slung to face forward and armed with massive rams, assaulted the gates at Hass West and Sondar. As they advanced, regular tanks, tiny by comparison, moved in beside them. The tidal wave of ochre-clad troops was undiminished.

Then it was the turn of the spiders, the largest and most fearsome of the Zoican siege weapons. A hundred metres long from nose to tail and propelled by eight vast, clawed cartwheels set on cantilever arms extending from the main bodies of their armoured structures, the spiders ground out of the smoke and rumbled towards the Wall. Gun and rocket batteries on their backs blazed up at the defences of Vervun-hive.

When they reached the Curtain Wall, the spiders didn't stop. The wheel claws dug into the ceramite and raised the death machines up the face of the defence, climbing like insects up the sheer face of the massive Wall. Of all the siege engines deployed at Vervunhive, the Zoican spiders came closer to taking the hive than anything else that night. There were five of them. One was destroyed by the Wall guns as it advanced. Another was immobilised by rocket fire twenty metres short of the Wall and then set on fire by further salvos.

The other three made it to the walls and hauled their immense bulks upwards, screeching into adamantium and ceramite as they dug with their wheeled claws. One was stopped by the VPHC Commissar Vokane, who got his troops to roll munitions from the launcher dumps to the Wall head and tip them over onto the rising beast, charges set for short fuse. The spider was blown off the wall and fell backwards, crushing hundreds of Zoican troops under it. It lay on its back and burned. Vokane and fifty-seven of his men didn't live to cheer. The explosive backwash of the spider's death engulfed them and burned them to bone scraps.

The second spider made it to Veyveyr Gate and began to claw at the barricades. Its mighty wheels sliced and crushed rail stock apart as it pulled itself in through the gate opening. Heavy artillery and NorthCol armour units met it with a pugnacious blitz of fire as it pushed its head through the gateway and they blew it apart. It settled sideways on its exploded wheels, half-blocking the entrance.

The remaining spider clawed its way over the Curtain Wall west of Hass West Fort. General Grizmund was waiting for it. As it scattered and burned the Wall defenders to left and right, Grizmund's Narmenian tanks, assembled in the open places of the House Anko chem works, elevated and fired, blasting the vast thing backwards off the Curtain Wall. The force of the salvo took part of the inner wall down too, but it was considered worthwhile. The spider was destroyed.

AT HASS WEST, Gaunt's men met the tide of Zoicans spilling from the engaged siege engine. In the narrow defiles of the ramparts, it became a match of determined close combat. Gaunt personally killed dozens with his chainsword and cut a flanking formation down towards the tower-top of the engine. Daur was with him, blasting with his borrowed bolt-gun, and so were a pack of more than sixty Ghosts and Vervun Primary troopers mixed together.

Squads under Varl and Mkoll joined them, and Gaunt was gratified that they seemed to be killing the storm troops as fast as the foes could stream out of the boarding tower.

Gaunt heard a yell through the confusion and looked up to see Commissar Kowle leading fifty or so Vervun Primary troops in an interception along the lower battlements.

Between them, Gaunt realised, they had the enemy pinned.

'I need explosives!' he hissed back to Daur. The captain called up a grenadier with fat pouches of tube mines and antipersonnel bombs.

'All of them!' spat Gaunt. 'Into the neck of that thing! Come with me!'

Gaunt advanced through the enemy waves, his chainsword biting blood, armour shards, hair and flesh from them. He cut a space to the tower head and then yelled for the grenadier to follow up. A las-shot tore through the grenadier's brow and he fell.

Gaunt caught him. 'Daur!'

Daur ran forward and helped the commissar. Together, they lifted the corpse, laden with its strings of explosives, and carried it to the open mouth of the tower. Gaunt pulled out a stick charge, set it, pushed it back into the corpse's webbing and together they flung the dead soldier down through the mouth of the siege tower.

The grenade went off a couple of seconds later. A bare millisecond after that, the rest of his munitions exploded as he fell, touched off by the first bomb.

The tower shuddered and broke, falling headlong into the sea of Zoicans milling at the foot of the Curtain Wall.

Kowle's forces moved in, killing the last of the Zoicans on the ramparts.

AT TWO IN the morning, just into the thirtieth day, the Zoican assault stopped and the Zoicans withdrew into the smouldering shadows of the outhabs. Flat-crabs wallowed backwards into the smoke, escorted by files of Zoican tanks and legions of ochre troops. An Imperial victory hymn was played at full volume from every broadcast speaker in the hive.

Vervunhive had lost 34,000 troops, twenty missile emplacements, fifty gun posts and ten heavy artillery silos. The Curtain Wall was scarred and wounded and, in several places, fractured to the point of weakness.

But the First Storm had been resisted.

EIGHT
HARM'S WAY

'The first trick a political officer of the Commissariat learns is: learn to lie. The second is: trust no one. The third: never get involved with local politics.'

— Commissar-General Delane Oktar,
from his *Epistles to the Hyrkans*

PROCESSIONS OF Ministorum Priests, the high faithful of the Imperial Cult, moved through the stone vaults of Inner Hab Collective Medical Hall 67/mv. They carried tapers and smoking censers, and chanted litanies of salvation and blessing for the wounded and dying now engulfing the place. Long, frail strips of parchment inscribed with the speeches of the Emperor trailed behind them like sloughs of snakeskin, dangling from the prayer boxes they carried.

Surgeon Ana Curth nodded respectfully to the clerics each time she encountered them in the wards and hallways of the medical facility, but privately she cursed them. They were in the way and they terrified some of the weaker or more critically injured who saw them as soul-catchers come to draw them from this life. Spiritual deliverance was all very well,

116

but there was a physical crisis at hand, one in which any able personnel would help more by tending the bodies rather than the spirits.

The Zoican assault had brought convoys of new casualties to all the inner hive medical halls, places already barely coping with the sick and injured refugees from the first phase of the conflict. Military field hospitals and medical stations were being set up to help, and the medical officers and staff that had arrived with the Imperial Guard forces were proving to be invaluable. Curth and her colleagues were community medics with vast experience in every walk of life – except combat injuries.

It was evening on the thirtieth day and Curth had been on duty for nearly twenty hours. After the nightmare of the storm assault the previous night, the fighting had slowed, with nothing more than random exchanges of shelling from both sides across the litter of Zoican dead outside the Wall.

Or so Curth had heard from passing soldiers and Administratum officials. She'd barely had time to raise her head above the endless work. She paused to scrub her hands in a water bath, partly to clean them but mainly to feel the refreshingly cold liquid on her fingers. She looked up to see groups of dirty Vervun Primary troopers wheeling a dozen or more of their wounded comrades down the hall on brass gurneys. Some of the wounded were whimpering.

'No! No!' she cried out. 'The west wards are full! Not that way!'

Several troopers protested.

'Weren't you briefed on admittance? Show me your paperwork.'

She checked the crumpled, mud- and blood-stained admission bills one trooper handed her.

'No, this is wrong,' she murmured, shaking her head as she read. 'They've filled out the wrong boxes. You'll have to go back to the main triage station.'

More protests. She took out her stylus and over-wrote the details of the bills, signing them and scorching her seal-mark on the paper with a brief flash of her signet ring.

'Back,' she told them with authority. 'Back that way and they'll look after you.'

The troopers retreated. Curth turned, now hearing raised voices in Ward 12/g nearby.

Ward 12/g had been filled with refugees from the outhabs, most of them fever-sick or undernourished. Days of careful feeding and anti-fever inoculations had improved things, and she was hoping to be able to discharge many of them back to the refugee camps in the next day or two. That would make some valuable space.

She entered the arch-ceilinged ward: a long, green-washed, stone chamber with seven hundred cots. Some were screened. Other cot spaces were crowded with the families of the patients who had refused to be separated from their kin. There was a warm, cloying smell of living bodies and dirt in the air.

The shouting was coming from a cot-space halfway down the ward. Two of her orderlies, distinct in their red gowns from the grimy patients, were trying to calm an outhab worker as gaggles of other outhabbers looked on. The worker was a large male with no obvious injuries but a wasted, pale complexion. He was yelling and making nervous, threatening gestures at the orderlies.

Curth sighed. This wasn't the first such incident. Like far too many of the impoverished underclass, the worker was an obscura addict, hooked on the sweet opiate as a relief from his miserable shift-life. Obscura was cheaper, hit for hit, than alcohol. He probably used a waterpipe or maybe an inhaler. When the invasion began, the workers had fled in-hive. Now many of them were regretting leaving their opiate stashes behind in their desperation. She'd had ninety or more admitted with what at first seemed like the symptoms of gastric fever. After a few days of support and food, this had turned out to be withdrawal cramps.

Strung out, some addicts demanded medicinal drugs to ease their agonies. Others got through the withdrawal phases. Still others became violent and unreasonable. For a few – the chronic, long-term users – she had been forced to prescribe ameliorating tranquillisers.

Curth stepped between her orderlies and faced the man, her hands raised in a gesture of calm.

'I'm chief surgeon,' she said softly. 'What's your name?'

The worker snarled something inarticulate, foam flecking his chin as his jaw worked. His eyes showed too much white.

'Your name? What's your name?'

'N-Norand.'

'How long have you been using obscura, Norand?'

Another squeal of not-words. A stammering.

'How long? It's important.'

'S-since I was a j-journeyman...'

Twenty years at least. A lifelong abuser. There could be no reasoning here. Curth doubted the worker would ever be able to kick the habit that was destroying his brain.

'I'll get something for you right now that will help you feel better, Norand. You just have to be calm. Can you do that?'

'D-drugs?' he muttered, chewing at his lips.

She nodded. 'Can you be calm now?'

The worker quivered his head and sat back on his cot, panting and raking the sheets with his fingers.

Curth turned to her orderlies. 'Get me two shots of lomitamol. Move it!' One of the orderlies hurried off. She sent the other away to encourage patients back to their cots.

There was a pause in the background noise of the ward, just for a second. Curth had her back to the worker and realised her oh-so-very-basic mistake. She turned in time to see him leaping at her, lips drawn back from his rotting teeth, a rusty clasp-knife in one hand.

Wondering stupidly how in the name of the Emperor he'd got that weapon into the hall unchecked, she managed to sidestep. The worker half-slammed into her and she went over backwards, overturning a water cart. The bottles smashed on the tiles. The worker, making a high-pitched whining sound, stepped over the mess while trying to keep his balance. He stabbed the knife at her and she cried out, rolling aside and cutting her arm on the broken glass. She scrabbled to rise, expecting to feel him plant the blade in her back at any moment.

Turning, she saw him choking and gagging, held in a firm choke-hold from behind. Dorden, the Tanith medical officer, had his left arm braced around the addict's neck, his right hand holding the knife-wrist tightly at full length away from them both. The addict gurgled. Dorden was completely tranquil. His hold was an expert move, just a millimetre or two of pressure away from clamping the carotid arteries, just a centimetre away from dislocating the neck. Only a brilliant medic or an Imperial assassin could be that precise.

'Drop it,' Dorden said into the worker's ear.

'N-n-nggnnh!'

'Drop. It,' the Ghost repeated emphatically.

Dorden dug his thumb into a pressure point at the base of the man's palm and the addict dropped his knife anyway. The rusty weapon clattered to the floor and Curth kicked it aside.

Dorden increased his chokehold for a fraction of a second, enough for the man to black out, and then dropped him facedown onto an empty cot. Orderlies hurried up.

'Restrain him. Give him the lomitamol, but restrain him all the same.'

He turned to Curth. 'This is a war now, you know. You should have guards in here. Things get dangerous during wars, even behind the lines.'

She nodded. She was shaking. 'Thank you, Dorden.'

'Glad to help. I was coming to find you. Come on.' He picked up a clutch of data-slates and paper forms he had dropped in order to engage the man, and he led her by the arm down the length of the ward to the exit.

In the cool of the corridor outside, she paused and leaned against the stone wall, taking deep breaths.

'How long have you been working? You need rest,' Dorden said.

'Is that a medical opinion?'

'No, a friend's.'

She looked up at him. She had still to get the measure of this off-worlder, but she liked him. And he and his Tanith medics had been the backbone of the combat triage station.

'You've been up as long as me. I saw you working at midnight last night.'

'I nap.'

'You what?'

'I *nap*. Useful skill. I'd rate it slightly higher than suturing. I know all the excuses about there being no time for sleep. I've used them myself. Hell, I've been a doctor for a lot of years. So I learned to nap. Ten minutes here, five there, in any lull. Keeps you fresh.'

She shook her head and smiled.

'Where do you nap?' she asked.

He shrugged. 'I've found there's a particularly comfortable linen cupboard on the third floor. You should try it. You won't be disturbed. They never change the beds in this place anyway.'

That made her laugh. 'I... thank you for that.'

He shrugged again. 'Learn the lessons, Surgeon Curth. Make time to nap. Trust your friends. And never turn your back on an obscura addict with a rusty knife.'

'I'll remember,' she said over-solemnly.

They walked down the hallway together, passing two crash-teams racing critical cases to the theatre.

'You were coming to find me?'

'Hmm,' he said, reminded, sheafing through the documents he was carrying. 'It's nothing, really. You'll think it stupid, but I have a thing about details. Another lesson, if you're in the mood for more. Take care of the details, or they'll bite you on the bloody arse.'

He stopped, looked at her and coloured. 'My apologies. I've been in the company of foul-mouthed soldiers for too long.'

'Accepted. Tell me about this detail.'

'I was in Intensive Ward 471/k, reviewing the situation. They are mostly inhab citizens up there, injured in the first raid. We've got blast wounds, shrapnel-hits, burn-cases, crush-injuries – a world of bad stuff, actually. They were all in the Commercia district when the bombs fell. Specifically,' he consulted the slates, 'Carriage Station C4/a and the eastern barter houses.'

She took the slate from him. 'Well?'

'I was checking to see if any could be discharged or at least moved to a non-intensive ward to make room. There are maybe twelve who could be shifted to the common wards.'

'Well?' she repeated. 'Was that it? An administrative suggestion?'

'No, no!' he said and leafed to another sheet. 'I told you the sort of injuries we were getting up there: mostly from the shelling, a few from panic stampedes. But there were two others, both in comas, critical. I... I was wondering why they had gunshot wounds?'

'What?' She snatched the slates and studied them closely.

'Small calibre, maybe a needle gun. Easy to mistake it for shrapnel wounding.'

'It says "glass lacerations" here. The station canopies all blew out and–'

'I know a needle-gun wound when I see it. And I'm seeing over a dozen shared between the two of them. They were shot at close range. I checked the records. Twelve others were brought in from the same site with identical wounds. But they were all dead on arrival.'

'This is the Commercia?'

'A subtransit station: C7/d. Not actually hit by direct shelling, so the records state. But there were at least twenty bodies recovered there.'

She read the forms again and then looked up at him.

'You're thinking what I'm thinking, aren't you?' he smiled. 'Hundreds of thousands, dead and dying, all needing us and I'm worried about just two of them. I shouldn't care how they were hurt, just that they need me.'

She paused. 'Yes, I am thinking that... but...'

'Ah: "but". Useful word. Why were they shot? Who was opening fire on helpless citizens in the middle of a raid?'

Despite her hours on duty, Ana Curth was suddenly awake again. Dorden was right: this was small compared to the scale of the general human misery in Vervunhive. But it could not go unmarked. The Scholam Medicalis had trained her to value every single life individually.

'Vervunhive is being murdered,' she said. 'Most of the murderers are out there, wearing ochre armour. Some, I have to say, are sitting pretty around the chart tables in House Command. But there is another – and we will find him.'

GAUNT STRAIGHTENED HIS cap, smoothed the folds of a clean leather jacket and left his escort of six Tanith troops at the elevator assembly. The escort, led by Caffran, stood easy, gazing around themselves at the lofty, gleaming architecture of the upper Spine. None of them had ever expected to see the inside of a hive's noble level.

'Even the fething lift has a carpet!' Trooper Cocoer hissed.

Gaunt looked round. 'Stay here. Behave yourselves.'

The Ghosts nodded, then congregated around an ornamental fountain where foamy water bubbled from conches held by gilt nymphs into a lily-skinned, green pool. Some of the Ghost guard rested their lasguns against the marble lip. Gaunt smiled to see Caffran check that the seat of his pants was clean before sitting on the marble.

So out of place, he thought as he left them with a last look, six dirty dog-soldiers, fresh from battle, in the middle of the serene vaults of the worthy and powerful.

He paced down the length of the promenade, his shiny boots hushing into the blue carpeting. The air was perfumed and gentle plainsong echoed from hidden speakers. The vault above was glass, supported by thin traceries of iron. Trees, real trees, grew in the centre beds of the long hall and small, bright songbirds fluttered through the branches. This is the privilege of power, Gaunt thought.

The great doors, crafted from single pieces of some vast tree, stood before him, the crest of House Chass raised in varnished bas-relief on their front. Ivy traces clad the walls to either side and small, blue flowers budded from fruit trees in the avenue that led to the doorway. He took out the token-seal and fitted it into a knurled slot in the door lock.

The great doors swung inwards silently. There was a fanfare of choral voices. He stepped inside, entering a high vault that was lit blue by the light falling through stained-glass oriels high above. The walls were mosaics, depicting incidents and histories that were unknown to him. The Chass crest was repeated at intervals in the mosaic.

'Welcome, honoured visitor, to the enclave of House Chass. Your use of a token emblem signifies you to be an invited and worthy guest. Please wait in the anteroom and refreshments will be sent while his lordship is informed of your arrival.'

The servitor's voice was smooth and warm, and it issued from the air itself. The great doors hushed closed behind

Gaunt. He removed his cap and gloves and set them on a teak side table.

A second later, the inner doors opened and three figures entered. Two were house guards dressed in body armour identical to that of the one who had accosted Gaunt outside the Privy Council. They had satin shrouds over their handweapons and nodded to him stiffly. The third, a female servitor, her enhancement implants and plugs made of inlaid gold, carried a tray of refreshments on long, silver, jointed arms which supplemented her natural limbs.

She stopped before Gaunt. 'Water, joiliq, berry wine, sweetmeats. Please help yourself, worthy guest. Or if nothing pleases you, tell me, and I will attend your special needs.'

'This is fine,' Gaunt said. 'A measure of that local liquor.'

Holding the salver with her extra arms, the female servitor gracefully poured Gaunt a shot of joiliq into a crystal glass and handed it to him.

He took it with a nod and the servitor withdrew to the side of the room. Gaunt sipped the drink thoughtfully. He was beginning to wonder why he had come. It was clear there was a universe of difference between himself and Chass. What could they have in common?

'To be here you must have been invited, but I do not know you.'

Gaunt turned and faced a young noblewoman who had entered from the far side of the anteroom. She wore a long gown of yellow silk, with a fur stole and an ornate headdress of silver wire and jewels. She was almost painfully beautiful and Gaunt saw cunning intelligence in her perfect face.

He nodded respectfully, with a click of his heels.

'I am Gaunt, lady.'

'The off-world commissar?'

'One of them. Several of my stripe arrived with the Guard.'

'But you're the famous one: Ibram Gaunt. They say the People's Hero Kowle was beside himself with rage when he heard the famous Gaunt was coming to Vervunhive.'

'Do they?'

The girl circled him. Gaunt remained facing the way he was.

'Indeed they do. War heroes Kowle can manage to stomach, so they report, but a commissar war hero? Famous for his actions on Balhaut, Fortis Binary, the Menazoid Clasp, Monthax? Too much for Kowle. You might eclipse him. Vervunhive is large, but there can be only one famous, dashing commissar hero, can't there?'

'Perhaps. I'm not interested in rivalry. So… you're versed in recent military history, lady?'

'No, but my maids are.' She smiled dangerously.

'Your maids have taken an interest in my record?'

'Deeply, you and your – what was it they said? Your "scruffy, courageous Ghost warriors". Apparently, they are so much more exciting than the starchy Volpone Bluebloods.'

'That I can vouch for,' he replied. Though she was lovely, he had already had enough of her superior manner and courtly flirting. Responding to such things could get a man shot.

'I've six scruffy, courageous Ghost warriors right outside if you'd like me to introduce them to your maids,' he smiled, 'or to you.'

She paused. Outrage tried to escape her composed expression. She contained it well. 'What do you want, Gaunt?' she asked instead, her tone harder.

'Lord Chass summoned me.'

'My father.'

'I thought so. That would make you…'

'Merity Chass, of House Chass.'

Gaunt bowed gently again. He took another sip of the drink.

'What do you know of my father?' she asked crisply, still circling like a gaud-cock in a mating ritual.

'Master of one of the nine noble houses of Vervunhive. One of the three who opposed General Sturm's tactical policy. One who took an interest in my counterproposals. An ally, I suppose.'

'Don't use him. Don't dare use him!' she said fiercely.

'Use him? Lady–'

'Don't play games! Chass is one of the most powerful noble houses and one of the oldest, but it is part of the minority. Croe and Anko hold power and opposition. Anko especially. My father is what they call a liberal. He has… lofty ideals and is a generous and honest man. But he is also guileless, vulnerable. A crafty political agent could use his honesty and betray him. It has happened before.'

'Lady Chass, I have no designs on your father's position. He summoned me here. I have no idea what he wants. I am a warmaker, a leader of soldiers. I'd rather cut off my right arm than get involved in house politics.'

She thought about this. 'Promise me, Gaunt. Promise me you won't use him. Lord Anko would love to see my noble house and its illustrious lineage overthrown.'

He studied her face. She was serious about this – guileless, to use her own word.

'I'm no intriguer. Leave that to Kowle. Simple, honest promises are something I can do. They are what soldiers live by. So I promise you, lady.'

'Swear it!'

'I swear it on the life of the beloved Emperor and the light of the Ray of Hope.'

She swallowed, looked away, and then said, 'Come with me.'

WITH HER BODYGUARDS trailing at a respectful distance, she led Gaunt out of the anteroom, along a hallway where soft, gauzy draperies billowed in a cool breeze and out onto a terrace.

The terrace projected from the outer wall of the Main Spine and was covered by a dedicated refractor shield. They were about a kilometre up. Below, the vast sprawl of Vervunhive spread out to the distant bulk of the Curtain Wall. Above them rose the peak of the Spine, glossed in ice, overarched by the huge bowl of the crackling Shield.

The terrace was an ornamental cybernetic garden. Mechanical leaf-forms grew and sprouted in the ordered beds, and bionic vines self-replicated in zigzag patterns of branches to form a dwarf orchard. Metal bees and delicate paper-winged butterflies whirred through the silvery stems and iron branches. Oil-ripe fruit, black like sloes, swung from blossom-joints on the swaying mechanical-tree limbs.

Lord Heymlik Chass, dressed in a gardener's robes, slight marks of oil-sap on his cuffs and apron, moved down the rows of artificial plants, dead-heading brass-petalled flowerheads with a pair of laser secateurs and pruning back the sprays of aluminium roses.

He looked up as his daughter led the commissar over.

'I was hoping you would come,' Lord Chass said.

'I was delayed by events,' Gaunt said.

'Of course.' Chass nodded and gazed out at the south Curtain for a moment. 'A bad night. Your men… survived?'

'Most of them. War is war.'

'I was informed of your actions at Hass West. Vervunhive owes you already, commissar.'

Gaunt shrugged. He looked around the metal garden.

'I have never seen anything like this,' he said honestly.

'A private indulgence. House Chass built its success on servitors, cogitators and mechanical development. I make working machines for the Imperium. It pleases me to let them evolve in natural forms here, with no purpose other than their own life.'

Merity stood back from the pair. 'I'll leave you alone, then,' she said.

Chass nodded and the girl stalked away between the wire-vines and the tin blooms.

'You have a fine daughter, lord.'

'Yes, I have. My heir. No sons. She has a gift for mechanical structures that quite dazzles me. She will lead House Chass into the next century.'

He paused, snicked a rusting flowerhead off into his waist-slung sack and sighed. 'If there is a next century for Vervunhive.'

'This war will be won by the Imperial force, lord. I have no doubt.'

Chass smiled round at the commissar. 'Spoken like a true political animal, Commissar Gaunt.'

'It wasn't meant to be a platitude.'

'Nor did I take it as one. But you are a political animal, aren't you, Gaunt?'

'I am a colonel of the Imperial Guard. A warrior for the almighty Emperor, praise His name. My politics extend as far as raising troop morale, no further.'

Chass nodded. 'Walk with me,' he said.

They moved through a grove of platinum trees heavy with brass oranges. Frills of wire-lace creepers were soldered to the burnished trunks. Beyond the grove, crossing iron lawns that creaked under their footsteps, they walked down a row of bushes with broad, inlaid leaves of soft bronze.

'I suppose my daughter has been bending your ear with warnings about my liberal ways?'

'You are correct, lord.'

Chass laughed. 'She is hugely protective of me. She thinks I'm vulnerable.'

'She said as much.'

'Indeed. Let me show you this.' Chass led Gaunt into a maze of hedges. The hedgerows crackled with energised life, like veils of illusions.

'Fractal topiary,' Chass said proudly. 'Mathematical structures generated by the stem-forms of the cogitators planted here.'

'It is a wonder.'

Lord Chass looked around at Gaunt. 'It leaves you cold, doesn't it, Gaunt?'

'Cold is too strong a word. It leaves me… puzzled. Why am I here?'

'You are an unusual officer, Gaunt. I have studied your record files carefully.'

'So have the housemaids,' Gaunt said.

Chass snorted, taking a cropping wand from his belt. He began to use it to shape the glowing, fractal hedges nearby. 'For different reasons, I assure you. The maids want husbands. I want friends. Your record shows me that you are a surprisingly moral creature.'

'Does it?' Gaunt watched the noble trim the light-buds of the bush, disinclined to speak further.

'True to the Imperial Cause, to the crusade, but not always true to your direct superiors when those motives clash. With Dravere on Menazoid Epsilon, for example. With our own General Sturm on Voltemand. You seek your own way, and like a true commissar you are never negligent in punishing those of your own side who counter the common good.'

Gaunt looked out across the vast hive below them. 'Another sentence or two and you'll be speaking treason, Lord Chass.'

'And who will hear me? A man who roots out treason professionally? If I speak treason, Gaunt, you can kill me here.'

'I hope we can avoid that, lord,' Gaunt said quietly.

'So do I. From the incident in the Privy Council the other day, I understand you do not agree with General Sturm's tactical plan?'

Gaunt's measured nod spoke for him.

'We have something in common then. I don't agree with House Sondar's leadership either. Sondar controls Croe and Anko is its lapdog. They will lead us to annihilation.'

'Such machinations are far above me, Lord Chass,' Gaunt pointed out diplomatically.

Chass wanded the hedge again. He was forming a perfect Imperial eagle from the blister-tendrils of light. 'But we are both affected. Bad policy and bad leadership will destroy this hive. You and I will suffer then.'

Gaunt cleared his throat. 'With respect, is there a point to this, Lord Chass?'

'Perhaps, perhaps not. I wanted to speak with you, Gaunt, get the measure of you. I wanted to understand your inner mind and see if there was any kindred flame there. I have a great responsibility to Vervunhive, greater than the leadership of this noble house. You wouldn't understand and I'm not about to explain it. Trust me.'

Gaunt said nothing.

'I will preserve the life of this hive to my dying breath – and beyond it if necessary. I need to know who I can count on. You may go now. I will send for you again in time. Perhaps.'

Gaunt nodded and turned away. The Imperial eagle in the fractal topiary was now complete.

'Gaunt?'

He turned back. Lord Chass reached into his waist-sack and pulled out a rose. It was perfect, made of steel, just budding and faintly edged with rust. The silver stem was stiff and aluminium thorns split out of it.

Chass held it out.

'Wear this for honour.'

Gaunt took the metal rose and hooked it into the lapel of his jacket, over his heart.

He nodded. 'For honour, I'll wear anything.'

Chass stood alone as Gaunt threaded his way out of the metal garden and departed. Chass remained stationary in thought for a long time.

'Father?' Merity appeared out of the brass-orange grove.

'What did you make of him?'

'An honourable man. Slightly stiff, but not shy. He has spirit and courage.'

'Undoubtedly.'

'Can we trust him?'

'What do you think?'

Merity paused, stroking the fractal blooms absently.

'It's your choice, master of our house.'

Heymlick Chass laughed. 'It is. But you like him? That's important. You asked me to keep you informed.'

'I like him. Yes.'

Chass nodded. He took the amulet from the waist sack where it had been all the time, buried in the garden scraps.

He turned it over in his hands. It writhed and clicked.

'We'll know soon enough,' he told his daughter.

DAY THIRTY-ONE passed without major incident. Shelling whined back and forth between the wall defenders and the waiting Zoican army.

At dawn on the thirty-second day, the second Zoican assault began.

NINE
VEYVEYR GATE

*'Do not ask how you may give your life for the Emperor.
Ask instead how you may give your death.'*

— Warmaster Slaydo, on his deathbed

IT WAS A dismal, hollow dawn. The early daylight was diffused by cliffs of grey cloud that prolonged the night. Rain began to fall: spots at first for a half hour, then heavier, sheeting across the vastness of the hive and the wastelands beyond. Visibility dropped to a few hundred metres. The torrential downpour made the Shield crackle and short in edgy, disturbing patterns.

At the Veyveyr position, in the first hour of light, Colm Corbec walked the Tanith line, the eastern positions of the ruined railhead. His piebald camo-cloak, the distinctive garb of the Tanith, was pulled around him like a shroud, and he had acquired a wide-brimmed bowl helmet from somewhere – the NorthCol troops most likely – which made more than a few of his Ghosts chuckle at the sight of it. It was cold, but at least the Shield high above was keeping the rain off.

Corbec had surveyed the Ghost positions a dozen times and liked them less each time he did. There was a group of engine sheds and cargo halls through which sidings ran, all of them bombed-out, and then a forest of rubble and exploded fuel tanks leading down to the vast main gate, the white stone of its great mouth scorched black. Beyond the rear extremity of the railyard's eastern border rose the burned-out smelteries. A regiment of Vervun Primary troops – called the Spoilers, Corbec had been told – held that position and watched the approach up the treacherous slag-mountain. Corbec had around two hundred Ghosts dug in through the engine sheds and the rubble beyond, with forward scout teams at the leading edge towards the gate.

Colonel Modile's Vervun Primary units, almost five thousand strong, manned the main trenches and rubble glacis in the central sector of the wide railyard. Bulwar's NorthCol troops, two thousand or more, were positioned along the west, towards proud and grimy rows of as yet undamaged manufactories. Fifty units of NorthCol armour waited at the north end of the railhead in access roads and marshalling yards, ready to drive forward in the event of a breakthrough.

Corbec crossed between fire-blackened, roofless engine sheds, his hefty boots crunching into the thick crust of ash and rubble that littered the place despite the pioneer teams' clearance work.

In the shed, twenty Ghosts were standing easy, all except their spotters at blast-holes and windows, looking south. The roof was bare ribs and tangles of reinforcing metal strands poked from broken rockcrete.

Corbec crossed to where Scout MkVenner and Trooper Mochran squatted on a makeshift firestep of oil drums, gazing out through holes in the brickwork.

'You've a good angle here, boys,' Corbec said, pulling himself up onto the rusty drums and taking a look.

'Good for dying, sir,' MkVenner muttered dryly. He was a scout in the true mould of Scout Sergeant Mkoll, dour and terse. Mkoll had trained most of them personally. MkVenner was a tall man in his thirties with a blue, half-moon tattoo under his right eye.

'How's that, MkVenner?'

MkVenner pointed out at the gates. 'We're square on if they make a frontal, us and the locals in the main yard.'

'And our angles have been cut and blinded since that thing fell in,' Mochran added in a tired voice.

The 'thing' he referred to was the gigantic wreck of the spider siege engine which the NorthCol batteries had brought down during the First Storm three days before. Its massive bulk, slumped across the gatemouth barricades, half blocked the entrance and had proved impossible to shift, despite the efforts of pioneer teams and sappers with dozers and heavy lifters.

Corbec saw the trooper was right. Enemy infantry could come worming in around the bulk and be inside before they were visible. The war machine gave the enemy a bridge right in through the tangled, rusting hulks of the gate barricade.

Corbec told them something reassuring and light that made them both laugh.

Afterwards, though he tried, he could not recall what it was.

He sauntered southwards, skirting through a trenchline and entered the rubble scarps closer to the gate. He had eleven heavy weapon teams tied in here at intervals behind flakboards and bagging. Six heavy stubbers on tripod mounts, two autoguns on bipods with ammo feeders sprawled on their bellies next to the gunners, and three missile launchers. Between the weapon positions, Tanith troopers were spread in lines along the embrasures. Walking amongst them, Corbec sensed their vulnerability. There was nothing to their rear and east flank but the ruined smelteries and the Spoil. They had to trust the abilities of the unseen 'Spoilers' to keep them from surprises.

Corbec opened his vox-link and called up three flamer-parties from the reserves behind the engine sheds. Now he was out here, with dawn upon them, he could see how raw and open the scene was, and he wanted it secured.

He found Larkin in a foxhole close to the gates. The wiry sniper was breaking down his specialised lasgun and cleaning it.

'Any movement, Larks?'

'Not a fething hint.' Larkin clacked a fresh, reinforced barrel into place and then stroked a film of gun-oil off the exchanger before sliding one of the hefty charge packs into its slot.

Corbec sat down beside Larkin and took a moment to check his own lasgun. Standard issue, with a skeleton metal stock, it was shorter and rougher than the sniper's gun and lacked the polished nalwood grips and shoulder block.

'Gotta get myself one of those one day,' said Corbec lightly, nodding at Larkin's precious gun.

Larkin snorted and clicked his scope gently into place on the top of the weapon. 'They only give sniper-pattern M-G's to men who can shoot. You wouldn't know how to use it.'

Corbec had a retort ready to go when his vox-link chirped. 'Modile to all sections. Observers on the Curtain Wall have detected movement in the rain. Could be nothing, but go to standby.'

Corbec acknowledged. He looked up at the huge wall and the towering top of the gatehouse. He often forgot that they had men and positions up there, thousands of them, a hundred metres up, blessed with oversight and a commanding position of fire.

He nodded across at Larkin, who slid the long flash-suppresser onto his muzzle with a hollow clack.

'Ready?'

'Never. But that's usual. Bring 'em on. I'm tired of waiting.'

'That's the spirit,' Corbec said.

That was what his mouth said, anyway. The sound was utterly stolen by a marrow-pulping impact of shells and las-fire that bracketed the gatehouse and shook the wall. Billows of flame belched in over the ruined death machine and the barricade and swirled up above the railyard. Parts of the barricade, sections of rolling stock, fifty tonnes apiece, shredded and blew inwards.

Corbec dropped. Billions of zinging shards of shrapnel, many white-hot, whickered down over the Tanith lines. Already, he could hear urgent calls over his link for medics coming from the Vervun Primary positions in the centre of the yard. He swung round and saw shells falling in the Spoil behind the Tanith position, blowing up fierce spumes of rock-waste. The Second Storm had started.

Ferrozoica changed tactics for its second assault. The First Storm had been an all-out, comprehensive attack along the southern Curtain Wall. This time they began a sustained bombardment of the wall length to keep Vervunhive reeling and they focussed their invasion to three point-assaults. One, an armoured formation led by two of the fearsome 'flat-crabs,' hit Sondar Gate and pummelled at it for over two hours before being driven back by the wall-guns. Another slid west along the eastern rail-lines and struck at Croe Gate and the railhead behind it with battalion-strength force. The fighting in that sector, fronted by Vervun Primary and Roane Deeper regiments, lasted until the early afternoon.

The third attack went straight in for the vulnerable Veyveyr Gate.

In the first ten minutes of the Second Storm, flat-crabs and other heavy artillery siege-crackers brought down the barricade and blasted apart the corpse of the spider. The first flat-crab rolled right in through the gate, squashing metal and splintering rubble, driving down into the Vervun Primary positions in the main yard. Further artillery obliterated all defences along the bastions of the gateway and the walls nearby, and Veyveyr found itself shorn of its precious raised gunnery positions.

There were a few, desperate minutes of confusion as Colonel Modile tried to rally his splintered ground forces in the main area of the yard. They were falling back in droves before the armour attack, stampeding down the trenchways to escape the insurmountable power of the Zoican death machine. A second flat-crab began to grind in behind the first, searing shells to the right into the Tanith positions.

Modile fabricated a clumsy counter-assault and withdrew his infantry in a V-shape, allowing the NorthCol armour to press forward to meet the siege engines. The railhead air was full of clanking tracks and whinnying shells as the formations moved in. NorthCol tanks were blown apart by the heavy dorsal cannons of the flat-crabs, and other tanks and Chimeras were crushed flat under the siege engine's tracks.

All the infantry, Ghosts included, could do little but cower in the face of this monumental clash. The noise level was physically painful and the ground trembled.

There was a vast detonation and a cheer went up all along the infantry lines. Sustained fire from three dozen NorthCol tanks had finally crippled the first flat-crab and blown it apart. The second, grinding through the gate, was blocked by the wreck.

Corbec scurried round in his cover and started to break towards the flank of the second crab.

Larkin caught him by the arm.

'What the feth are you doing, Colm?'

'We have to hit that thing! Maybe a man on foot can get close enough to st–'

A close shell blast threw them into the ash-cover.

'You're mad!' cried Larkin, getting up. He found the brim of the defence and trained his gun out.

'Let the fething armour worry about the crabs! Here's our problem!'

Corbec crawled up alongside him.

Zoican infantry, hundreds of them, were charging through the breach the flat-crabs had gouged, pouring through Veyveyr Gate itself.

Corbec began to fire. The thin crack of his lasgun was quickly joined by the heavier whine of Larkin's sniper weapon. The support weapons along the Tanith lines opened up behind them.

MISSILES FROM THE heavy weapon positions hissed above his head as Brin Milo bellied forward through the rubble and began to scope for enemy infantry. Colonel Corbec's hasty orders were crackling over the vox-link. Hell was erupting around them.

Milo saw a few ochre shapes clambering across the dead zone in the gate mouth and took aim. His first shot went wide, but he adjusted and dropped a Zoican with his second and his third.

Trooper Baffels and Trooper Yarch flung themselves down beside him and started firing too. Las-fire slashed back and forth across the railyard, flickering in multicoloured, searing lines. Someone a few metres away was screaming.

Milo tried to shut it out. He aimed his weapon as Larkin had taught him, kept his breathing slow, squeezed. A blurt of las-fire. An ochre warrior spun off his feet.

Yarch crawled up to the lip of the embrasure and primed a grenade. He tossed it and a crumping vortex of wind blew grit back onto them.

'If we–' Yarch began.

Milo and Baffels never found out what Yarch was planning. A las-round entered his skull though his nose-bone, blowing out the back of his head. As he rose weightlessly and jerked back, two more lasrounds hit him, one through the throat and the other through the eye. He tumbled down the rubble. Another lost man lost.

Baffels, a bearded man in his early forties with a barrel chest and a blue tattoo claw that lined his cheek, pulled Milo back into cover as tremendous las-fire exploded along their trench top.

Together, they crawled down into the trench bottom and found Fulch, MkFeyd and Dremmond trying to edge round south.

A light-storm of las-fire drummed around them. A ricochet hit Fulch in the buttock and dropped him to his knees. MkFeyd tried to rise to the fire step, but las-fire walked along its edge, exploding the fore-grip of his weapon and taking off the tops of two fingers of his left hand. He fell back, cursing his luck and jetting the others with bright, red blood.

Milo started to bind MkFeyd's fingers with strips of field bandage, keeping his head low. Baffels was trying to patch the oozing wound in Fulch's hindquarters and was calling for a medic over his vox-link.

Dremmond, who was bringing one of the flamers Corbec had requested forward, crawled up to the lip and sent withering blasts of incendiary death over the top. He was already boasting a flamer-tan from the First Storm, in which he had fought at Hass West.

More troopers battled along to join them. Some, led by Sergeant Fols, went ahead down the zag in the trench line to create an enfilade.

Milo looked up from his work with MkFeyd's hand, his face smeared and dripping with blood, as a trooper nearby was cut in two. Dremmond kept firing with his flamer and three more Ghosts joined him at the firestep, opening up with their lasguns.

'Best I can do!' Milo said to the injured man, then crawled up to take his place at the firestep too. MkFeyd was working on pure adrenaline now and he crawled up alongside the boy. He managed to brace his gun with his bandaged hand and began firing. The line of Ghost lasguns barked and flashed down the length of the eastern position.

MKVENNER MOVED his team out of the engine shed just as shelling from the second flat-crab blew it out. Mochran was already dead, punctured apart by a series of stub-rounds that had perforated the shed wall.

MkVenner had ordered his unit to fix bayonets – the long silver daggers of the Tanith – at some point early in the assault, and now he was glad of it. Zoican infantry, their faces hidden by those sculpted ochre masks, were pouring into the Tanith trench lines from the south. With no more than fifteen men around him, MkVenner engaged them, stabbing and slicing, firing weapons point-blank. The Zoicans were overrunning them. There seemed no end to the numbers of ochre enemy. As fast as MkVenner could kill them, there were more. It was like fighting the ocean tide.

MAJOR RACINE, of the Vervun Primary, had been out inspecting the forward arrays of his Veyveyr positions when the storm came down. He had tried to control the retreat and he debated fiercely with Colonel Modile about how best to counter the Zoican push. After a few bitter returns over the vox-line, it had gone dead. Modile clearly didn't want to argue with his subaltern any more.

Racine had five hundred men behind a glacis of rubble in the main yard, facing the encroachment of the second flat-crab. He called up his bombardier and took three satchels full of mine charges and grenades.

Then he hauled himself over the lip and ran towards the siege engine.

A raging storm of las- and bolt-rounds whipped around him. Not one touched him. All that saw it regarded it as a miracle. Racine was ten metres from the vast supertank, with its grinding segmented armour, when a las-round went through his ear into his brain and killed him. He dropped.

There was a dreadful hiss of wronged valour and injustice from his watching troops. He had got so close.

The flat-crab ground forward, crushing Racine's corpse into the ash.

The pressure set off the charges looped around him.

The vast cannonade of explosions flipped the crab up and over on its rear end. Quick-thinking gunners in the North-Col armour hit its exposed belly hard. One shell touched off its magazine and it vaporised in a colossal jet of fire that blew out the top of Veyveyr Gate itself.

The Vervun Primary troops, wilting and shattered in the aftershock, swore that Racine would be remembered.

THE ZOICAN TROOPS were all over them. Corbec edged down a gully that had once been a side street in the railyard, the walls still standing, scarred and crater-peppered, around him. He had sixteen men with him, including Larkin and Trooper Genx, who carried a bipod autocannon.

Corbec's first thought was to order his men to hug the walls, but the streets seemed to funnel and corral the enemy fire, and las- and bolt-rounds ricocheted along them. He'd already lost three men who had kept to the walls and been blown down by the fire sliding down them. It was safer to stand out in the middle of the street.

They pushed ahead and met a detachment of Zoican storm troops, at least fifty of them, pouring into the eastern positions. Fire walloped back at them and Corbec marvelled at the way the las-rounds kissed and followed the stone walls. Trooper Fanck dropped, his chest gone. Trooper Manik was hit in the groin and his screams echoed around them.

Genx opened fire and his heavy cannon made a distinctive 'whuk-whuk-whuk' in the closed space. An enemy round took off his hand at the wrist and Corbec scooped up the autocannon and fired it himself. Genx, his stump instantly cauterised by the las-fire, got up without comment and began to feed his colonel's weapon.

Larkin took his targets as they came, blowing off heads or blowing out chests with the powerful kick of his sniper gun. The las-fire of the normal weapons was superhot but lacked stopping power. Larkin blanched as men beside him hit enemy troops who kept going despite precise hits which had passed through them cleanly. Only Larkin's sniper gun and Corbec's autocannon were actually dropping the foe first time so they wouldn't get up again.

THE NORTHCOL were almost overrun. Colonel Bulwar called to Colonel Modine, but the Vervun Primary officer had apparently shut his vox link down.

'Anvil!' Bulwar signalled to Corbec, the only officer in this hell-fight he trusted. *'Anvil!'*

MORNING ITSELF WAS rising above it all, unnoticed. At Sondar Gate, after more than two hours of intense fighting, the Zoican attack was driven off. Grizmund's Narmenian tanks had assembled in the Square of Marshals just inside the gate ready to face any force that broke in. They stood in rumbling lines just like Vegolain's had done in the first hours of the war, over a month before.

When the push at Sondar was repulsed, House Command signalled Grizmund to pull out and deploy along the southern manufactory highway to reinforce Veyveyr Gate. Two regiments of Vervun Primary Mechanised and a Volpone battlegroup were also directed to support Veyveyr, but the orders, handed down by Vice Marshal Anko, were imprecise and the reinforcement elements became throttled in queues on the arterial routes. Grizmund, frustrated and unable to get clear direction from House Command, moved his armour column off the highway and tried to approach Veyveyr via stock yards behind the manufactories. Proper authorisation for this was impossible as the vox-links were jammed with chatter from the chaos at the railhead. Grizmund had gone about two kilometres, forcing his tanks through chainlink fences and razorwire barricades, when VPHC units bellowing curses and orders through loudhailers headed them off and demanded they return to the highway.

The confrontation grew ugly. Grizmund himself descended from his tank and approached the VPHC troops directly, arguing that his unorthodox route was necessary. Tempers flew and when one of the VPHC commissars drew a pistol, Grizmund knocked him down. There was a brief brawl and the astonished Grizmund found himself and four of his senior commanders arrested at gunpoint. The VPHC dragged them off to House Command, leaving the Narmenian tank force leaderless and stymied, under the close watch of a growing force of VPHC.

The lack of concerted direction from House Command caused other disasters that made a bad day worse. The Vervun Primary and Volpone reinforcements were stalled all along the southern access. One group of Vervun motortroops riding half-tracks with Hydra batteries mounted on the flatbeds were trapped in a side transit rout. In their agitation, they mistook a unit of Volpone Chimeras advancing behind them for an enemy force. By that stage, with nothing coming over the vox-links but undisciplined terror and panic from Veyveyr Gate, there was a general impression that the Zoicans had forced entry into the Hive and were sacking the southern quarters. The Hydra batteries opened fire, briefly, until the mistake was discovered. By then, thirteen Volpone troops were dead.

The Second Storm was showing up a great weakness in the Vervunhive command structure. Vervun Primary, House Command and the VHPC had communication protocols and designated channels which worked efficiently during peace time or practice drills, but which were incapable of handling the sudden spikes in vox-traffic that accompanied heavy fighting. Worse still, the House Command vox-system, modelled on Imperial standard, used the same channel bands as the Imperial Guard and the NorthCol. Within an hour of the assault starting, it was virtually impossible for any unit commander to talk long range to his troops or for any order signals from House Command to reach the ground. It was even impossible to vox House Command for clarification. Only short-range vox-links between troops and officers in the field ground were still functioning. Some commanders tried to switch channels, hoping their men would have the same idea, but there was little chance of officers and men guessing the same new channel simultaneously.

At Croe Gate, General Nash had a measure of success. He switched to a wideband his Roane Deepers had famously been forced to use once on Kroxis and his vox-staffers on the ground had the same idea. For most of the day, Nash was the only senior commander in the field to have a direct open link to his forces.

A Volpone force under Corday also managed to resume contact with its distant elements. Corday adroitly used his short-range micro-beads to relay the new channel setting from man to man through the field. Unfortunately, he had chosen a channel that was crippled by interference from the Shield harmonics.

At Veyveyr, matters were made worse by the fact that Modile had shut down the main channel to cut off the demands of his officers – men like the late Racine – who were now questioning Modile's orders. Corbec received Bulwar's 'Anvil' code over the short-range and was able to co-ordinate his resistance with the NorthCol commander, but they found their forces conflicting with Vervun Primary troops following Modile's increasingly knee-jerk commands.

Gaunt, who had been at Hass West when the storm began, immediately headed for Veyveyr with Daur and a platoon of Tanith. Their troop-truck convoy found the back end of the reinforcement columns jammed fast and they struggled to find a way around or through. Gaunt tried Raglon's vox-set frantically to get House Command to rectify the growing logistical disaster, but he found the lines as jammed as the other commanders had before him.

He handed the speaker horn back to Raglon and looked down at the pale-faced Daur. The rumble and roar of the nightmarish Veyveyr battle backlit the buildings and habs ahead of them.

'How far to Veyveyr from here?' Gaunt snapped.

'Four, maybe five kilometres,' replied the Vervun Primary liaison.

Gaunt eyed the solid wall of troops and troop carriers choking the highway ahead and cursed quietly. Establishing proper and workable vox-protocols would be his priority once this day was done. The Vervun Primary were brave men and the noble houses were honourable institutions, but in war they were rank amateurs.

'Dismount!' Gaunt yelled back down his force and leaped out of the lead truck. Daur joined him, prepping the lasrifle he had drawn from stores after the First Storm. His arm still hurt and wasn't mended, but it worked well enough for him to carry a weapon and he'd be damned if he was going to follow the commissar into action again and have to ask to borrow a gun. He gulped down a couple of painkiller tablets to soothe the ache.

The fifty Tanith Ghosts had assembled on the road beside the trucks.

Gaunt walked down the rank, speaking directly and briefly. 'We're advancing on foot. It's five or so kilometres and we need to move fast, so ditch any extra weight – just carry weapons and ammunition, bayonets. Get rid of anything that'll slow you down or wear you out by the time we get there. Daur will lead.'

He looked round at Daur. 'Captain? Find a way.'

Daur nodded, confidently. Though a hiver born and bred, he knew the vast complexities of the southern manufactory district no better than the off-worlders. He pulled a chart-plate out of a thigh-pouch and deftly cycled through the map-patterns until he found the area they were in. With a stylus, he worked out a possible route. He was determined not to fail the Ghosts – and, more particularly, Gaunt.

'Follow me,' he said and headed off the road at a trot, pushing through a flak-board fence and into the service yard of a machinesmithy.

Gaunt and the Ghosts hurried after him.

AT CROE GATE, the Zoican push was hitting the adamantine gates so hard and so frequently that they were denting and starting to glow with heat. Nash brought what mechanised forces he had into place inside the gates, in case they fell.

Outside, a line of enemy tanks and armoured fighting vehicles perhaps five hundred strong, stretched out down the cuttings of the rail tracks and the rockcrete supports of the elevated express line. Some Zoican infantry strengths were visible too, but so far it was entirely a war of cannon, rocket, mortar and wall-gun against tank and artillery. If the Vervun-hive forces could only keep them out and keep the mighty gates sealed tight, the battle might never descend to the level of infantry mayhem that was occurring at Veyveyr.

If two such infantry fronts opened – if Croe Gate broke – Nash knew it could signal the start of an inexorable defeat for Vervunhive. He prayed to the holy Emperor of Terra that the Zoicans had no more death machines left to unleash.

VEYVEYR WAS TRULY a nightmare. The air across the vast yard was thick with las-fire and tracers, gouts from flamers, whooping rockets and dense palls of smoke. Despite the volatile highlights of his combat career, Corbec had seldom seen anything so fierce or intense. Ducking into cover and try-ing to clear a feed-jam in the autocannon with Genx crouched next to him, Corbec wondered if it was because the fight was so enclosed: the Curtain Wall on one side, the man-ufactories around, the Shield above. It was as if this hellish firefight was being conducted in a box that concentrated the fury and amplified the noise.

Bulwar signalled him again and Corbec had to strain to hear. The NorthCol Commander was driving forward in a wedge from the west, bringing his armour in as well as his ground troops and several units of Vervun Primary that he had been able to pry away from the useless Modile. He wanted Corbec to support with his Ghosts from the east.

Corbec acknowledged. He sent the word down, from man to man, trying to unify them into a co-ordinated effort. But the Zoicans were everywhere and Corbec knew at least three parts of his force were bottled in behind him and fighting for their lives.

He took a look eastwards at the dank slopes of the Spoil. Enemy shelling still whooshed down into it and he could see the sparks of las-fire exchanged up and down the ore-slag. The Spoilers were engaging hostiles coming up the Spoil. He hoped the Zoicans would continue their push up at the well-defended Spoilers. If they turned west, they would flow in on his meagre force from the rear and–

He shut off the thought.

'How much?' he shouted at Genx.

With his one good hand, Genx indicated they had about three thousand rounds left for the autocannon, in loops around his body or in the panniers of ammo-drums he had collected. About two minutes' sustained fire, Corbec thought.

He voxed his men to present and move west. They rose, then immediately ducked back as a heavy rake of las-fire swept in from the northwest.

Corbec screamed a curse. The fething Vervun Primary, effectively leaderless and alone in the mid-yard, were firing at anything that moved and had flanked the Ghosts as well as if they'd planned it.

Corbec tried to raise Modile on the vox. All he got was Modile's adjutant screaming obscenities down the link, demanding that the NorthCol and the Tanith regroup as per battle orders.

Modile's dead. Gonna kill him myself, Corbec decided.

He rose and set the autocannon chugging a blurt of fire down the rubble line at Zoican movement.

A bolt-round slammed into the stone beside him and glanced off, hitting him in the thigh.

Corbec tumbled down with the impact and tried to claw the smouldering shell-case fragments out of his tunic pants. The cloth was punctured and there was blood. He found the round had been spent on impact with the stone and just the case had spun off into him, peppering his leg with dozens of metal scraps. He flexed the limb. It hurt and was bleeding freely, but he could use it.

Modile was definitely going to die.

There was no going west, not directly. He pulled his units after him and headed towards the gate under cover of the eastern trenches and barricades. They might be able to break west further down, beyond the range of the hopeless Vervun Primary.

Shells roared overhead and there were a great many more rockets banging in through the gate mouth now.

Corbec's force had gone a hundred metres when they met a battlegroup of Zoican shock troops head on.

* * *

Milo reached the end of a shattered stretch of wall and tossed a grenade around the corner. As soon as the blast thumped out, vibrating his chest and spilling brick dust and plaster from the wall-section, he raced across the gap and took up station at the next las-chewed corner, kneeling, sweeping his lasgun around in the grenade smoke to cover Baffels, who crossed behind him.

A few enemy shots rang over their heads, higher than the wall, cracking the air.

Neskon and Rhys came up after, darting across the gap as Baffels and Milo fired cover.

'Where's Dremmond?' shouted Neskon over the roar. He was plastered in blood, but it wasn't his own.

'Ahead, I think!' yelled Milo. He tried his micro-bead link, but it just ground out static.

The platoon had been advancing down the ditchlines between the buildings towards the gate, in support of Colonel Corbec's brave push and for a while Dremmond's flamer had been clearing the way. But a trio of rockets had slammed into the ditch and broken the advance, and now the forward section of the platoon format, with Dremmond and Sergeant Fols in it, had advanced out of sight in the smoke.

Milo, Baffels and Rhys pushed on down the side of the next bombed-out storeblock as Neskon covered the gap for the next group of Ghosts: Domor, Filain and Tokar, followed by the vox-officer, Wheln, and Troopers Caill and Venar. Neskon and Domor then advanced, leaving Filain and Tokar to cover the overlap for the three following.

At the front of the group, Milo, Baffels and Rhys pushed forward again, grenading a break in the wall and sprinting across it to lay cover for the parties behind.

There was ferocious fighting from a hundred metres ahead. Milo's micro-bead squawked and he heard flashes of Corbec's commanding voice.

Domor and Neskon moved up to them and Domor probed the smoke cover ahead with the optic implants he had acquired after an injury on Menazoid Epsilon.

The focus rings hummed and whirred around the blank lenses. 'I read heat – lots of it. A flamer, pouring it on.'

Milo nodded. He could smell prometheum.

'Dremmond,' Baffels suggested.

Encouraged that they might be closing on their forward element, the platoon rallied and pushed forward. Milo realised that they seemed to be following him, looking to him for leadership, with Sergeant Fols absent. It was mad – they all had more combat experience than him, and all were older.

It was as if the gloss of Gaunt was on him, as if he represented some kind of natural authority simply by association with the commissar.

The cover ahead broke into a series of low-dug ditches punctuated with shell-craters. Enemy fire was sheeting across it, making it impassable. Milo saw at least two dead Ghosts twisted and broken in the ditch-line.

'Round! We go round!' he urged and Baffels nodded. The men liked Baffels too, and he seemed to be readily adopting the role of second to Milo's lead, like Corbec to Gaunt. Milo marvelled at the way structures simply evolved organically in combat, without question or spoken decision. With focus, fear and adrenaline that high, right on the tightrope of life and death, men made simple, natural decisions.

Or a well-trained, motivated unit like the Ghosts did at any rate. Milo was sure the Vervun Primary troops were collapsing simply because they lacked that resolve and that organic spontaneity.

He took his fellows left, towards the edge of the Spoil, through a series of drumlike scrap stores where greasy rail bogeys and axle blocks were stacked. Venar had an autocannon and several cans of ammo still strapped to his load-bearing harness, so Milo gave him point to clear the way. The rattle of short cannon bursts echoed through the stores as Venar picked the way ahead clean.

The stores opened out into a hectare or so of stockyard that was miraculously unscathed. Flatbed wagons and pipe-trucks sat in linked trains along six parallel sidings. There was a burned-out diesel locomotive at one buffer-end.

The platoon edged forward, through and around the dormant wagons, sometimes sliding under or between trucks, or clambering over hook assemblies thick with sooty oil.

Las-shots began to hammer into the wagons near Milo. They blew out sections on the wooden sideboarding, and Baffels and Milo were showered with splinters.

The men dropped into cover, spread out through the wagon yard. Curt assessments as to the angle and position of the shooters flicked back and forth through the micro-bead link. Venar fired a few bursts of cannon under the wagon he was sheltering behind, and Milo heard shots ping and ricochet off the ironwork of the bogeys.

The enemy fire increased.

Milo moved them forward. He saw Filain scoot out from between wagons and then duck back into cover as las-fire scooped up the gravel and stone around him. One shot severed a piece of track and the metal section broke with an almost musical chime.

Domor and Neskon also tried to move forward. They skirted back a few trucks and came out around a high-sided freight wagon. Las-shots spanged off the thin metal sides of the wagon. Neskon dropped, but Domor dragged him up and they fell into cover along the next truck line. Neskon wasn't hit. He had simply stumbled.

Milo and Baffels, with Rhys and Tokar just behind them, were pinned. Milo tried to creep around the end of the nearest wagon, but more firing erupted and he hit the ground, winded.

'You're hit!' he heard Baffels call.

'No, I'm fine–' Milo said.

'You're fething hit!' Baffels repeated.

Milo reached around and felt a wet hole in the left shoulder of his tunic. It was sore, but there was no real pain. He had been hit. He hadn't even felt it.

Milo got to his feet and then paused, lowering himself again and carefully looking out under the wagons. When he had dropped, he'd glimpsed something that his mind was only just identifying.

Three trains away, under the trucks, he could see feet. Armoured, heavy booted feet in distinctive ochre armour.

He waved the others down to look.

A dozen, maybe more.

Zoicans.

The punishing fire that had pinned them slowed. The Zoicans were evidently moving too, pushing in and around the trucks just as the Ghosts were, but from the other side.

Milo counted off the men and sent them wide, using the concealment of the trucks. Few in the Imperial Guard moved as stealthily as the Tanith.

There was a burst of cannon fire twenty metres south of Milo. Then two more, a few answering las-shots. Venar had engaged.

More firing, brief and fierce, came from the next lane of wagons. Over the link, he heard Wheln curse, then laugh.

Baffels crawled ahead of Milo, down the length of a flatbed wagon. The Ghosts were all grey with gravel dust now, and their hands and knees were thick with oil.

Milo heard a dull sound from the body of the truck.

He yelled a warning and swung upwards as the Zoican storm-trooper appeared over the lip of the wagonbed and fired down. Baffels had rolled instinctively in under the side of the truck and slammed against the wheels and the sleepers as the Zoican's fire exploded the grit where he had been crawling.

Milo fired a burst upwards, punching three las-rounds through the aluminium siding of the wagon and the Zoican behind. The ochre-armoured figure convulsed and toppled clumsily out of the wagon. He landed next to the cowering Baffels, who automatically turned and shot the corpse through the head, point-blank.

Neskon, Rhys and Tokar were firing out between wagons, scoping for Zoicans just the other side of the track. Zoican las-fire and hard rounds came back between and under the wagons and forced Tokar to scramble on his arse back behind a slumped fuel drum. Neskon used the heavy bogey assembly of a wagon as cover and shuddered as persistent fire whipped under the cart-body and slammed into the huge iron wheels against his back.

Rhys rose, a las-round just missing his head, and lobbed a grenade over the wagon so that it fell neatly on the Zoican side of the rolling stock and vaporised them. A cracked Zoican helmet, split across the sneering, emotionless sculpture of the face, tumbled through the air and bounced near to his feet. He thought about taking it as a trophy until he realised there was the best part of a head left in it.

Milo heard Wheln cry out. The man was down. He could hear him moaning just a few paces away on the other side of the wagon.

'My leg… my leg…'

'Shut up!' Milo yelled, then dove over the hook-lock between wagons to roll clear on the other side of the track. Wheln was sprawled in the open between siding tracks, his left leg below the knee a ruin of blood, bone and tattered cloth.

Milo ran low to him, grabbed him under the arms and began to drag him into cover. Shots stitched the gravel around them. Two Zoicans appeared on the top of the next wagon over and another two edged out from between trucks. A las-shot cracked past Milo's nose, and then two more ripped through the loose folds of his camo-cape.

There was a bark of cannon fire, and the two Zoicans on the truck top came apart and fell. The others dropped back into cover. Milo got Wheln into the shelter of the back end of the wagon, pulling him in between the tracks. There was a group of Zoicans at the other end of the same truck, firing around it. Some fired under, but the shots were deflected by the axles. Milo looked frantically to each side for help. He saw Baffels in position behind a cart on the adjacent train, the one Milo had just scrambled from to reach Wheln. Baffels was too pinned with fire to make a shot.

Milo looked up, trying to ignore Wheln's moaning, and studied the hook-clamp that linked the wagon they were using as cover to the one behind them. It took him a few moments to figure out how to disengage it, his hands slipping on the greased iron.

When it was free, Milo hooked a grenade over a brake cable and pulled the pin. Then he yanked Wheln out from behind the truck and they fell down a slope the other side, Wheln shrieking with pain.

The grenade detonated and the force cannoned the freed truck, all eighteen tonnes of it, down the trackway, crushing the Zoicans sheltering at the far end between it and the next wagon on the rail. The entire length of rolling stock slammed and rattled into itself.

Rhys, Neskon and Baffels crossed over to cover Milo as the boy struggled to tie off Wheln's ruined limb and stop him bleeding out.

Wheln wouldn't stop screaming. Milo wanted to call for a medic, but he knew the vox-lines were useless and besides, Wheln had smashed the voxcaster when he fell. That was even supposing there was a medic anywhere near.

Baffels led Venar and the others and proceeded to clear the rest of the yard. A few brief exchanges with retreating Zoicans left more ochre bodies lying on or between the rails.

Milo could hear something else now, over the shooting and Wheln's shrieking and the constant thunder of the main battle.

Voices. Chanting voices, low and slick and evil.

THE AMMO-CAN clacked dry and the autocannon was useless. Corbec threw it aside and pulled his lasrifle off his shoulder, opening up again. His unit was right at the gate now, embroiled in an entirely structureless fight with the main force of the Zoican shock-troops. The fight blasted through the ruined outbuildings of the gatehouse complex and across the rubble-thick ground in the gate-mouth itself.

There were Zoicans everywhere.

Corbec had ceased to be a commander. There was nothing to command. He was simply a man fighting with every iota of strength and stamina left in him. He fought to stay alive and to kill the ochre shapes that drove at him from all sides.

It was the same for all the Ghosts in that engagement. The only thing that slowed the tide of Zoican invasion was the width of the blasted gate. In an open field, the forty or so Ghosts with Corbec would have been overrun long since.

Corbec was bleeding from a dozen light wounds. Those enemies he didn't kill outright with las-fire he demolished with blows from his rifle-stock and stabs of his bayonet.

Dremmond was suddenly alongside him, swathing the enemy in a wide cone of flames. The flamer pack on his back stuttered. Corbec knew that sound. The tanks were almost dry.

He yelled at Dremmond to wash the gates. What little flame they had left could best be used burning the entrance out.

Dremmond swung around, his spurting fire twisting like a whip. A dozen Zoicans crumpled, armour burning and melting off them. Some became torches that stumbled a few paces before they fell.

Dremmond bought Corbec a moment to think.

Corbec crossed, firing still, towards the wound-peppered wall of an outbuilding, glad he had jammed all the energy clips he could find into his jacket pockets that dawn.

Genx was in cover by the wall. By now the pain was beginning to trickle through and Genx was pale with trauma. Without his hand, he couldn't handle a lasrifle, although there were several fallen nearby, dropped by dead Zoicans and Tanith alike.

Corbec handed Genx his laspistol and the lad – Genx was no more than twenty, though built like a ox – began to crack away at any target in sight.

Supported by a trio of men, Sergeant Fols covered the entrance to a stairwell in the gatehouse, its roof blown off by the advance of the first flat-crab earlier. The blackened corpses of Vervun Primary gunners from the upper ramparts lay all around, amid the twisted wreckage of their fallen guns and piles of ceramite chunks.

Fols looked up at the mighty gate that they fought to protect. It was almost painful to see it with the top blown away, just two great gate towers adjoining the splintered Curtain Wall. The fort on top had fallen in and its debris made up the ground they fought over.

Fols also noticed how the Shield above them was rough-edged and intermittent. The death of the flat-crab which had blown out the arch of the massive gate had also taken down a relay station, and the Shield canopy was fraying and sparking out over them.

Fols felt wet and realised it was rain. The torrential downpour outside was still hammering and now, with the Shield ripped back for a hundred metres or so, it was falling on them too.

The ground was turning to mush as the rain made gluey soup out of the ankle-deep ash.

The Ghost next to Fols dropped wordlessly, his jaw vaporised. Streams of rain ran down them all, colouring with blood and dirt.

Fols rounded his two remaining men into the staircase, firing across the gate. The rain and smoke was killing visibility.

Fols saw the bright blurt of Dremmond's flamer a little way off, saw how the rain made steam off the white-hot blasts and heated stones.

The man next to him yelled something and Fols realised there were Zoican shock troops spilling over the side walls behind them by the dozen.

He turned, killed three. A welter of las-shots cut his men apart and splashed the wall they had just been using for cover with their blood. Fols lost a knee, an eye, an elbow and a fourth shot tore through his belly.

He was still firing when a Zoican bayonet impaled him to the wall.

THE CHANTING CONTINUED. The Zoican shock forces were pushing through Veyveyr Gate holding banner-poles aloft, the whipping flags marked with the symbol of Ferrozoica and with other emblems that stung the eyes and nauseated the gut: the runes and badges of the Chaos pestilence that had overwhelmed them.

Some of the Zoicans had loudhailers wired and bolted to their helmet fronts and were broadcasting abominable hymns of filth and whining prayers of destruction.

From his position, Corbec knew the Zoicans believed their victory was assured.

He wished he could deny it, but with the pitiful numbers left to him, he didn't stand a chance.

He changed clips again, throwing the dead one away into the rubble. Next to him, Genx and two other troopers reloaded.

They would kill as many as they could. In the name of the Emperor, there was no more they could do.

DATA-PULSES TOLD him the fighting was intense, bestial. But it was so very far away. It came to him only as unemphatic bursts of information, unemotional cascades of facts.

Salvador Sondar drifted in his Iron Tank. He was becoming increasingly disinterested in the trials of the hive soldiers. What was happening at Croe Gate and, more vitally, at Veyveyr was an inconsequential dream to him.

All that really mattered now to the High Master of Vervunhive was the chatter.

A ROCKET CREMATED Trooper Feax and threw Larkin into the air. He came down hard amid the rubble and the bodies, ears dead, vision swimming and his beloved rifle nowhere in sight.

He clambered up. He had been with Corbec's unit at the gate. That was the last thing he remembered.

His hearing began to return. He heard the wretched chanting of the Zoican advance as from underwater. He saw the las-fire and banner poles as dancing bright colours in the smoke.

A Zoican was right on top of him, glaring down out of that fearsome mask-visor, stabbing with his bayonet.

Larkin lurched aside and fell off a length of wall, two metres down to a bed of debris below. Ignoring his spasming back, he yanked out his silver Tanith knife and leapt at the Zoican the moment he reappeared over the gully-lip.

The Zoican bayonet cut through Larkin's sleeve. He slammed the brute back over into the rubble and pushed his blade in, trying to find a space between the ochre armour plating.

It went in, just below the neck seal of the battle-suit. Foul-smelling blood began to spurt out over Larkin's arm and hand, and it stung like acid.

The Zoican thrashed and spasmed. Larkin fought back, clawing, kicking and wrenching on his blade's grip.

He and the Zoican rolled twenty metres down the rubble slope. At the foot, Larkin's frantic efforts ripped the Zoican's helmet off.

He was the first person in Vervunhive to see the face of the enemy, square on, naked, shorn of armour or mask or visor.

Larkin screamed.

And then stabbed and stabbed and stabbed.

* * *

A TORRENT OF las-fire cut across the gate from the west. Zoicans crumpled, falling on their banner poles, loudspeakers exploding as they died. Corbec and his men, amazed, pushed around to support, hammering into the halted storm force with renewed vigour.

Nine platoons of Vervun Primary troops funnelled in across the open gate from the west with Commissar Kowle at the head.

Kowle had headed for Veyveyr Gate from House Command the moment the action began at dawn and it had taken him until now – almost noon – to reach the front. Unable to reach Modile or any Vervun command group, he had grabbed Vervun troops by force of authority and personality alone and led them towards the gate flanked by Bulwar's men and armour.

Kowle was singing an Imperial hymn at the top of his lungs and firing with a storm bolter.

Bulwar's NorthCol units pressed in behind, and Bulwar had the sense to spread them east to reinforce the failing Tanith line.

Corbec couldn't believe his eyes. At last, a co-ordinated effort. He rallied his remaining men and scoured the eastern flank of the gate for signs of Zoicans. His support helped Kowle reach the gate itself, a gate that had been held by the Tanith alone for more than an hour.

The three prongs – Tanith, Vervun and NorthCol – pushed the Zoicans back out into the outer habs and the torrential rain. Kowle moved his units aside to allow Bulwar's armour to finish the job and block the gate, though not before the commissar had posed for propaganda shots that were quickly relayed across the entire public-address system of the hive: Kowle, victorious in the blasted mouth of Veyveyr; Kowle, blasting at the enemy; Kowle, holding the Vervun banner aloft on a heap of rubble as Vervun Primary troops mobbed to help him plant the flag-spike in the ground.

By early afternoon, the gate was held fast by fifty tanks of the NorthCol armoured. Kowle was once more the People's Hero. The battle for Veyveyr Gate was over.

At Croe Gate, as news of the overturn reached the Zoican elements, the fighting diminished. Nash sighed in relief as the enemy withdrew from the smouldering gate-hatches. He ordered the wall guns to punish them anyway.

NONE OF THE victorious public-address messages mentioned the losses: 440 Vervun Primary and 200 Roane Deepers at Croe Gate, 500 Vervun 'Spoilers' along the Spoil, 3,500 Vervun Primary, 900 NorthCol and almost a hundred Tanith at Veyveyr.

They had a victory and a hero, and that was all that mattered.

GAUNT AND HIS small reinforcement group reached Veyveyr just as the battle was ending. Gaunt was hot with anger and determination.

Daur led him down a trench to the Vervun Primary Command post where Colonel Modile was rallying men and directing vox-links.

Modile looked around as Gaunt strode into the culvert shelter, stony-faced.

'The battle is over. We have won. Vervunhive is victorious,' Modile said blankly into Gaunt's face.

'I've been listening to the vox. I know what occurred here. You balked, Modile. You lost control. You hid. You shut down the vox-channels when you didn't like what you heard.'

Modile shrugged vacuously at Gaunt. 'But we won…'

The Tanith troops stepped into the command post around Gaunt. Even Daur, grim-faced, had a weapon drawn.

'Round up all the officers and detain them. I want a transcript of all vox-traffic,' Gaunt ordered. The Ghosts fanned out to do so and the Vervun Primary staffers blinked in confusion as they were jostled around.

'What are you doing?' Modile asked haughtily. 'This is my gakking command area!'

'And you've commanded what, exactly? A bloodbath. You dismay me, Modile. Men were shrieking for orders and support, and you ignored them. I heard it all.'

'It was a difficult incident,' Modile said.

'I have a reputation, Modile,' Gaunt said, 'a reputation as a fair, honest man who treats his soldiers well and supports them in the face of darkness. Potentially, that reputation makes me soft. It seems I understand failure and forgive it.

'Some, like Kowle, believe me to be a weak commissar, not prepared to take the action my rank demands. Not prepared to enforce field discipline where I see it failing.'

Gaunt removed his cap and handed it to Daur. He stared at Modile, who still wasn't sure what was going on.

'I am an Imperial commissar. I will enflame the weak, support the wavering, guide the lost. I will be all things to all men who need me. But I will also punish without hesitation the incompetent, the cowardly and the treasonous.'

'Gaunt, I–' Modile began.

'*Commissar* Gaunt. Do not speak further. You have cost lives this day.'

Modile backed away, suddenly, horribly realising what was happening.

Gaunt took his bolt pistol from his holster. 'For courtesy, choose: a firing squad of your own men or a summary execution.'

Modile stammered, lost control of his bowels and turned to run.

Gaunt shot him through the head.

'Have it your own way,' he said sadly.

TEN
CASUALTIES

*'There came a point, a few years into my career, when I knew
I had seen enough. Since then, I have seen a lot more, but I
have blocked it out. The soul stands only so much.'*

— Surgeon Master Goleca, after the
Exsanguination of Augustus IX

FROM THE SOUND of it, there was a hell of a brawl going on at
Veyveyr Gate. The sky under the Shield blazed up at intervals
with explosive light, and sound drummed across the hive. It
had been going on since daybreak.

The baby, Yoncy, was crying plaintively and making sobbing, sucking noises. It had been doing it all night. Tona
wasn't sure what to do. Dalin was sullen and quiet, and he
slept in the back of the trash-cave most of the time.

Tona crawled forward out of her dugout and looked across
the shell-ruined slopes. Below, half a kilometre away, lay the
fenced and razor-wired troop billet of Gavunda Chem Plant
Storebarns/Southwest.

That was where the off-world soldiers lived, the pale-
skinned, dark-haired ones with their black costumes and

blue tattoos. Tona wondered if they came from a hiveworld too, if the blue tats were gang badges or rank marks.

She dreamed of their food. There was a banquet fit for the Emperor secured down there in the back sheds. She'd sent Dalin in to scrounge and steal a few times, but it was getting dangerous.

Tona knew it was up to her now. The baby was weak and crying. She needed milk powder and basic nutrient paste.

There were over a thousand other refugees hiding in the trash slopes and crater-plains in the shell-flattened manufactories near to her, but she never thought to ask any for help. Everyone in Vervunhive was on their own now.

A particularly fierce airburst cracked the sky above Veyveyr, and Tona turned to look. She'd been to Veyveyr railhead a few times and had stood in the glass hall of the main station, now long gone, watching the snooty up-Spine travellers move to and fro from platforms. Her twice-uncle Rika had run a snack-stall there, and she'd also been a part of a pocket-prey team for a few months.

The Grand Terminus had awed her, even as she worked it. It had seemed to her a doorway to anywhere. If she'd had the credit, she'd have jumped a train south to the tropical hives, to the archipelago, maybe even to Verghast Badport where, so they said, it was possible to buy a route to anywhere, including off-world.

Veyveyr Gate had always seemed to her a way off this rock. A possible future. A promise.

Now it was dead and burned out, and callous, off-world soldiers dirtied it with brutal war.

The baby was squalling again. Tona edged out of her bunker and looked back at Dalin. 'Stay with him. I'll be back soon with food.'

Tona slid down the rubble stacks and moved towards the wire fence of the troop compound.

Tona crossed the ruinscape of the manufactories, industrial areas that had been levelled on that first day before the Shield lit up. Shattered rockcrete buildings flanked the lips of craters twenty metres across or more. Ruptured metal sheeting and snapped pipes poked from the brick dust.

Unrecognisable pieces of burnt machinery scattered the ground.

Bodies lay where they had fallen and after a month these were nothing more than loose husks of shrivelled bone and ragged clothing. The rescue teams had taken away most of the wounded in the initial recovery and habbers had carried their own dead out. But still bodies remained, crumpled and half-buried in the wide ruin. Carrion-dogs, lean, diseased and mangy, haunted the rubble, scavenging what they could – like her, she supposed, though unlike the hounds, she drew the line at feeding off corpses. There was a stagnant, rotten smell to the place and sickness lingered. Thousands like her, mostly low-caste or the dispossessed from the outer habs, had made this place a temporary home when the main refuge camps had over-spilled. Tona Criid, like many of Vervunhive's base-level citizens, avoided the refuges, for though they offered food and medical rations, they also represented authority and prejudice. The VPHC controlled most refuges brutally.

She saw others prowling the ruins. Adults mostly, a few children, all thin and dark with filth, their clothes wretched and ragged. Some stared at her as she passed; some ignored her. None spoke.

She passed a store block where parts of the side windows were intact and she saw her own reflection. It shocked her. A straggly, pale thing with dirty clothes and sunken eyes looked back at her. She had expected to see the bright-eyed, cocky hab-girl with the flashy piercings and snarling smile.

Seeing the leanness of her own face, she realised how hungry she was. She'd been blocking the feeling. Her empty belly knotted and ached with such sudden fury that she dropped to the ground for a moment, sitting on a cinder block until the pain eased enough for her to stand without cramps or wooziness.

She took the flask from her belt and sipped a few, precious mouthfuls from the drink-spout. Half full, it was the last of a box of electrolyte fluid bottles she'd recovered from a mining store near Vervun Smeltery One. She was sure that the fluid-packs were the main reason she'd kept herself and the children alive for the last month.

She hooked the flask back onto her belt and then took out her blade. The back fence of the military compound was just a few metres away now. It seemed deserted. Maybe they were all fighting at the gate. It sounded like it.

Her brother Nake had given her the blade on her tenth year-day, just a few weeks before he was killed in a gangfight in Down-Reach under the Main Spine. Nake Criid had been a member of the Verves, one of the key undergangs, and the knife's handle was decorated with a carefully carved Verve crest: a laughing skull resting in the dip of a gothic V. Tona sported a few gang badges herself – an ear-stud, a buckle, a small snake-tat on her shoulder – but she'd never been properly blooded into any gang to speak of. She had run with a few gang crowds and known a boy or two who'd been gang-blooded. While she was with them, they'd each tried to induct her, but she'd resisted. The one thing Tona Criid had always known, ever since Nake had died of stab wounds in an unlit, Down-Reach sewer seven years ago, was that ganger life was dumb and pointless and short. She'd make her own way in life, be her own master, or get nowhere at all.

The blade was a compact chain-form: a thick, decorated grip with an extending blade of steel fifteen centimetres long. A flick of the rubberised stud on the index-finger ridge activated an internal power-cell that made the blade-edge vibrate so fast it looked still. But, gak, could it cut!

She touched the stud and the blade purred. She switched it off and crawled towards the flak-board fence.

THE SUPPLY BARN was dark and as stacked with supplies as she remembered it. She couldn't read many of the labels on the crate stacks, so it was a matter of cutting them open and sampling them. The first she tried was full of small flat boxes packed with bootlaces.

The second had cartons of stoppered metal tubes. Hoping they might be food-paste, she squeezed a coil of black matter out into her palm and licked it.

She spat, retching. If this is what the off-world fighters ate, they were truly from another world. She moved on, leaving the half-squeezed tube of camo-paint on the floor behind her.

Ear-pieces with wires and plugs. Powercells. Rolls of gauze in paper wraps that smelled of disinfectant.

In the next crate-stack, foil-packs of freeze-dried buck-wheat porridge. Better. She dropped half a dozen into her bag, then added a handful more. She'd eat them dry if she couldn't find water. Then she found chemical blocks for firelighting and a pile went into her bag. Next, metal beakers. She prised one out of its packing, then another. Dalin would want his own.

In the next row, pay dirt: corn crackers in long, plastic tubes, soya bars in vacuum-packets. She pushed a dozen or more into her bag and bladed one open, cramming the soft, wet food into her mouth and gulping it down, brine drib-bling down her chin and pattering on the floor.

Tona froze, mid-swallow, her cheeks bulging, her stomach gnawing at her with the sudden input of food. A noise, behind her, to the right, a noise her wolfish chewing had half-hidden. She ducked into cover.

A flashlight flickered between supply stacks, three rows away. She willed herself invisible and huddled behind a tower of mess-tin crates, the blade in her hand. The beam of light jiggled around and she heard a voice, uttering a snarl. The sudden crack and flash of a lasweapon made her jump out of her boots. A carrion-dog went racing past her, yelping and trailing a burned hind leg.

She relaxed a little. The voice said something in an accent she couldn't work out. The flashlight wavered, then moved off and away.

She darted across the aisle into the next bank of crates. A few slices of her knife, all the while listening to the darkness around her. Nutrient packs for first aid. Tins of soup that heated themselves when the foil strip was pulled out. Jars of air-dried vegetables in oil. Small, flat cans of preserved fish. Cartons of heat-treated milk.

She took a handful of them all. Her pack was heavy now and she was pushing her luck. Time to go.

Light jabbed down into her face, making her cry out, and a hand grabbed her shoulder.

Tona Criid had been taught to fight by her brothers, all of them gangers. Instinctively, she pivoted back into the grip and shoulder-threw the owner of the hand. The flash-light bounced away across the rockcrete barn floor and the heavy male form bounced after it, barking out an oath and most of its breath.

But it had her still, and even as it went over her, it twisted her round in combat-trained hands and threw her sideways into the crate stack.

The impact stunned her. She tried to rise, hearing the other moving too. A few more oaths, a harsh question she didn't understand.

She rose and delivered a spin-kick into the darkness. It would be the VPHC, she was sure. She braced for the las-shot, the bolt-round, the mindset that would treat her no better than a carrion-dog.

Her spinning foot connected and the figure went down with a bone-crack. More rampant cursing.

Tona ran for the crack in the barn wall.

A much larger form tackled her from behind in the dark and brought her down on her belly on the rockcrete floor. She was frantic now, kicking and thrashing.

Her assailant had her pinned by way of superior strength and technique. His weight slumped on top of her and the flashlight winked on again, probing down at her wincing eyes.

'It's all right, it's all right,' said a hoarse voice in tunefully accented Low Gothic. 'Don't fight me.'

She looked up, fighting still. She saw the face of the off-world soldier, the young one, the man who had chased Dalin out of the barn weeks before.

The blade purred in her hand and she sliced it upwards.

CAFFRAN SAW THE vibro-blade coming and threw himself aside, releasing his captive. It was the gang girl, the beautiful one he had glimpsed across the rubble when he had gone chasing the boy.

She was on her feet now, menacing with the buzzing blade, head down. Knife-combat stance, thought Caffran, good enough to be a Ghost.

'Put it down,' he said carefully. 'I can help you.'

She turned and ran, heading for the slit in the fibre-board back wall of the barn.

Caffran pulled out his laspistol, braced his aiming hand and fired three times, blowing a ring of holes in the back wall of the shed around her. Daylight streamed in through the punctures. She skidded to a halt, frozen, as if expecting the next one to let the light shine through her too.

Caffran got to his feet, gun raised. 'I can help you,' he repeated. 'I don't want to see you live like that. You've got children, right, a boy at least? What do you need?'

She turned slowly to face him and his light, blade in one hand, the other raised against the stabbing beam. Caffran lowered it so it wouldn't blind her.

'Trick,' she said.

'What?'

'This is a trick. Just shoot me, you gak.'

'No trick.' He stepped forward and holstered his pistol. 'No trick.'

She flew at him, blade slicing the air. He flinched and grabbed her arms, rolling backwards to deposit her flat on her own back. The impact knocked her out for a moment.

Caffran kicked the purring blade away.

He pulled her up. She was coughing and gasping. She felt so thin and fragile in his hands, though he knew she was mean and tough enough to hurt him.

'What's your name?' he asked.

Her jabbing fingers punched into his eyes and he bellowed, rolling back and clutching his face.

By the time he struggled up again, she was pushing through the back wall to freedom. Caffran noticed she had been mindful enough to recover her blade.

He ran after her.

'Feth you, stop! I want to help! Stop!'

She looked back at him, her eyes as wild and mad as an animal. Her bulging pack was caught on a fork of fibreboards, preventing her from squeezing through the hole.

'Get away! Get away!' she shrilled.

He approached her, hands held wide and empty, trying to look unthreatening.

'I won't hurt you... please... my name is Caffran. My friends call me Caff. I'm a lost soul like you. Just a Ghost without a home. I didn't ask for this and I know you fething didn't. Please…'

He was a hand's reach away from her now, hating the fear in her face. She spat and howled, then jabbed her blade round and cut the strap of her pack. It dropped to the ground, but she was free. Abandoning it, she flew out of the barn and sprinted away across the rubble.

Caffran pushed out after her, straining to get his greater bulk through the slit.

He got a glimpse of her looking back and terrified, darting over the splintered mounds of wreckage before dropping out of sight.

TONA LAY IN cover for a few minutes, buried in the soot of a crater, stinking corpses around her. When it seemed the soldier was not following, she crawled out and ran a few metres to a slumped wall and hid behind it.

Then she heard a crunch of boots on rubble and froze.

Twenty metres away, looking in the wrong direction, the black-uniformed soldier was walking up through the ruins, her pack dangling from his hand.

'Hello?' he was calling. 'Hello? You need this. You really do. Hello?'

He stood for a long while, maybe ten minutes, looking around. Tona remained in hiding. Finally, the soldier put the pack down.

'It's here if you want it,' he said. A long pause.

Then he walked back down the ruin slope and clambered back into the barn.

Tona waited a full fifteen minutes more before she moved. She ran from cover, scooped up the pack and leapt away into the confused maze of the ruins.

The soldier didn't reappear or follow.

In a foxhole, she hunched and opened the pack, studying the contents. Everything she had taken was there, everything – as well as three flasks of sterilised water, a field-dressing kit, a pack of one-shot antibiotic jabs, some net-wrapped dry sausage… and a laspistol, the very laspistol she was sure he had fired after her in the barn. The charge pack was almost full.

She was dazed for a while, then she laughed. Gleeful, she took up the sack of trophies and ran back to her shelter, taking a wide route so she wouldn't be followed.

It was only later, after she and Dalin had eaten their first good meal in a month and Yoncy was sleeping and content on milk-broth, that she found the cap-pin at the bottom of the pack: silver, clean, an Imperial eagle with the double head and the inscription *Tanith First, by the Grace of the God-Emperor of Terra* on the scroll held in the clawed feet.

In the gloomy dugout, her belly full, her wards fed and content, Tona Criid sat back by the light of a fire kindled from Guard-issue chemical blocks and wondered where she would pin the crest. As gang-badges went, it was better than most.

BEHIND VEYVEYR GATE, the dead dominated the streets and squares.

Teams of Vervun Primary, work militia and Munitorum labourers, their faces masked by breathers or strips of torn cloth, carried the dead from the battle away from the smouldering railhead and laid them out in the open places north of Veyveyr for identification and disposal.

Agun Soric had brought his workforce in from the Commercia Refuge after the fighting had died down, and he had put them to work assisting the morbid but necessary duty.

He wanted to fight. Gak, but that brave Vervun Primary officer – what was his name? Racine! The one who'd given them the chance to pull their weight preparing the defence. He'd given Soric the taste of it. But for want of proper weapons, Soric and his people would have been at the front that morning. Let Ferrozoica tremble to face the wrath of smeltery workers from Vervun One with the blood up!

From what he'd been able to learn from those milling about him – some off-world Guard, some NorthCol – Soric knew the ferocious battle had ended with Zoica pushed out against all odds. He hoped to see Racine soon and slap the man's back and hear how the pioneer efforts his workers had put in had helped to win the day by building defences the enemy couldn't overrun.

There was time enough. With smeltery workers Gannif, Fafenge and Modj, Soric began loading corpses onto a hand-cart. It was filthy, bestial work. They tried to wrap each body in a skein of linen and they'd been told to take tags and mark the identity of each on a data-slate. But some bodies didn't come up in one piece. Some were only parts. Some parts didn't match up obviously with others.

Some were still alive.

The place was a charnel house. Bodycarts moved all around them, medical and clearance personnel milled around and the wounded shuffled in slow, weary lines away from the gate railhead, many exhibiting awful injuries. Every now and then, they made way for a truck or a trundling med-ical Chimera, speeding away to the medical halls.

Soric, his hip braced on his axe-rake crutch, leaned down and slid his paper-gloved hands under the armpits of a blackened, legless corpse.

As he raised the cadaver, it groaned.

'Medic! Medic!' he cried out, pulling back from the ruined thing he had been touching.

A thickset medical officer pushed through the milling crowd, a man in his fifties with a silver beard and the look of an off-worlder about him. Under his hall-issue crimson apron he wore black fatigues and Guard-issue boots.

'Alive?' the medic asked Soric.

'Gak me, I suppose so. Tried to move him.'

The medic took out a flexible tube, put one end to his ear and the other to the blackened torso.

'Dead. You must have squeezed air out of the lungs when you lifted him.'

Soric nodded as the medic stood up, folding his scope-tube away into his shoulder-slung pack.

'You're off-world, right?' asked Soric.

'What?' asked the medic, distracted.

'Off-worlder?'

The medic nodded curtly. 'Tanith First. Chief medic.'

Soric stuck out a hand, then pulled the paper glove off it. 'Thank you,' he said.

The medic paused, surprised, then took the hand and shook it.

'Dorden, Gaunt's First-and-Only.'

'Soric. I used to run that place.' Soric gestured over his shoulder at the ruin of Vervun Smeltery One east of the railhead.

'This is a bad time for all of us,' Dorden said, studying the bullish, noble man who leaned on his crutch, black with ash.

Soric nodded.

'That eye wound… has it been treated?' asked Dorden, stepping forward.

Soric held up his hand. 'Old news, friend, weeks old. There are others more needy of your skills.'

As if on cue, VPHC troops wheeled past a cart carrying a screaming, blood-soaked NorthCol soldier.

Mtane and one of Curth's people hurried to it.

Dorden looked round at Soric. 'You thanked me. Why?'

Soric shrugged. 'I've been through this from the start. We were left to die. You didn't have to come here but you did and I thank you for it.'

Dorden shook his head. 'Warmaster Macaroth sends us where he wills. I'm glad to be able to help, however.'

'Without you off-worlders, Vervunhive would be dead. That's why I thank you.'

'I appreciate it. Mine is often a thankless task.'

'Have you seen Major Racine? Vervun Primary? He's a good man…'

Dorden shook his head and turned to where stretcher-bearers were beginning to bring the Tanith wounded out of the warzone. Troopers Milo and Baffels were carrying Manik, howling from the wound to his groin, blood dribbling over the edges of the stretcher.

Dorden moved in to deal with Manik. He was sure the young trooper was going to bleed out any moment.

He looked around at Baffels and Milo as he worked. 'Racine? You know what happened to him?'

Dorden's hands were already slippery with Manik's blood. The groin artery had burst and he couldn't tie it. It was pulling back into the body cavity and Dorden bellowed for Lesp to bring clean blades.

'Major Racine?' Milo said, standing back from Manik's stretcher, adjusting the dressing on his shoulder wound. 'He died. Under a flat-crab. He killed it, but he died.'

Soric listened to the off-world boy and shook his head sadly.

Lesp stumbled over the rubble and brought Dorden a scalpel. Dorden used it to try and open the screaming Manik's groin wide enough so he could push his fingers in and pull the severed artery down to clamp it. It was too late. Manik bled out through his body cavity and died with Dorden's hand still inside him.

'Let me take him,' Soric said and, with his men, he gently lifted Manik's body onto his wheel-cart. Dorden was almost shocked by the reverence.

'Every soul for the hive, and the hive for every soul,' Soric said over his shoulder to the blood-soaked Dorden as he wheeled the dead Ghost away.

ANA CURTH MOVED her orderlies through the confusion of Veyveyr Gate. There were more dead to recover than living.

She checked each corpse in turn, pulled off the tags and then left them for the recovery units.

She hesitated slightly when she found the corpses of Tanith. These were all Dorden's friends. She took off their tags carefully and entered all the names in her dataslate.

In the gateway of Veyveyr, she paused. She checked the latest set of tags three times to be sure.

Tears welled in her eyes and she pushed the bloody tags into her apron-front.

THE THIRTY-SECOND day drew to a close. It was a day the citizens of Vervunhive would remember perhaps more keenly than anything that had taken place so far. Despite the success of driving back the First Storm three days before, this seemed much more of a victory. Scant hours after the battle, the defence of Veyveyr began to take on a mythical flavour. In the Spine, the habs and the refuges alike, Vervunhivers spoke of it as a turning point, as the start of deliverance.

Public-address plates across the hive broadcast triumphant slogans, sanitised accounts of the battle and pictures from the glorious front, mainly those showing the People's Hero raising the flag in the shattered gate-mouth, surrounded by jubilant Vervun Primary troopers. In the

Basilica of the Ecclesiarchy, a victory mass was organised, featuring a choir of over ten thousand and long liturgical readings from the Codex Imperialis. Loudspeakers broadcast the worship across all the hive levels.

Spontaneous celebrations began in different areas and some revels – amongst Vervun Primary troops heady with relief – were broken up by the VPHC.

But the mood was impossible to suppress in the highest and lowest quarters of the hive. Oilcan fires were lit along the wharves and in the refuges, and drums, many homemade or improvised, thundered into the night. There were many reports of decadent banqueting in the High Spine, as merchants and house ordinary families abandoned the rationing restrictions and indulged in sumptuous private dinners of unstinting debauchery.

When Gaunt heard about them, he sighed. These were either gestures of ignorance or acts of denial against what must surely still await.

But let them have their delights, he decided. They may be their last.

In a grim mood, he'd stayed on at Veyveyr as the light failed, touring his men, noting those lost, restructuring squads around those losses. He gave Trooper Baffels a field promotion to sergeant and placed him in charge of Fols's unit. The stocky, bearded trooper was almost overcome with emotion as Neskon, Domor, Milo and the others cheered him. He shook Gaunt's hand and wiped away a tear that trickled down over his blue claw tattoo. There had been a brief rumour that Gaunt would award the sergeant pin to Milo, but that was absurd. He was barely a trooper and it wouldn't look right, though Milo's actions and improvised leadership at Veyveyr had won him a considerable respect that sat well with his reputation as the avatar of Gaunt.

Under Corbec's command, the Tanith units who had seen action at Veyveyr pulled out to a mustering yard north of the Spoil, and fresh units under Rawne, partnered with Volpone forces commanded by Colonel Corday, moved in to hold the gate position. Stonemasons, metalworkers and engineers from the hab workforce were called up to assist the sapper units in defending the gate. Using fallen stone from the gate top, the masons erected two well-finished dyke walls just outside the gate, and the incandescent glare of oxylene torches fizzled in the night rain as the metal-wrights crafted pavises and hoardings from broken tank plates. Sections of rail – and there were kilometres of it scattered throughout the railhead – were broken up and welded into cross-frames to carry barbed wire and razor-wire strings. In an intensive twelve-hour period, with work continuing throughout the night under lamp-rigs, the workforce raised impressive concentric rings of well-built defences both inside and outside the broken gate. There were ramps along the eastern edge to allow forward access for the NorthCol tank files marshalled behind the troop lines. A forest of howitzers, barrels raised almost upright like slightly leaning trees, was established on the site of the main terminus, with a clear field of fire to bombard up and beyond the gate.

In the mustering yard, weary Tanith and NorthCol units from the front sprawled on rolled up jackets or on the hard-pan itself, many falling asleep as soon as they got off their feet. Mess trucks with tureens of soup, baskets of bread and crates of weak beer arrived to tend them. It was estimated that they would be there until dawn, when the arterial routes would be finally clear enough for transports to carry them back to their billets.

In the gloomy rear section of a NorthCol Chimera, Corbec and Bulwar shared a bottle and dissected the day. The performance of the Vervun troops and of Modile especially was cursed frequently. The bottle was vintage sacra from Corbec's own stock and he broke the wax-foil stamp with relish. Bulwar had set his power-claw on a metal rack and, flexing fingers stiff from the glove, produced two shot glasses from a leather box, and a tin of fat smokes, the best brand the Northern Collective hives produced.

Bulwar had never tasted the Tanith liquor before, but he didn't flinch and Corbec wasn't surprised. Bulwar was as grizzled and hardened a soldier as any Corbec had met in his career. They clinked glasses again.

'Anvil,' Corbec toasted, letting blue smoke curl out of his mouth to wreath his face.

Bulwar nodded. 'Let's hope we don't need it again. But I have an ache in my leg that says there's a measure left before us.'

'Your leg?'

Bulwar tapped his right thigh. 'Metal hip. A stub round during the moon war. Hurts like buggery when it's damp – and worse when trouble's coming.'

'Weather's changing. More rain on the way.'

'That's not why it's aching.'

Corbec refilled their glasses.

'But for this moon war, you've never been off this place?'

'No,' replied Bulwar. 'Wanted to muster for the Guard at the last founding, but I was a major by then and my path was set. Planetary Defence, like my father and his before him.'

'It's a noble calling. I could have wished for it myself, commanding the garrison of a city back home.'

'Where is that again? Tanith?'

Corbec toyed with the tiny glass in his paw. He pursed his lips. 'Dead and gone. We're the last of it.'

'How?'

'We were founding, the first founding Tanith had made. Three regiments assembled to join the warmaster's crusade. This was just after Balhaut, you understand. Gaunt had been sent to knock us into shape. There was a… a miscalculation. A Chaos fleet slipped through the interdiction set up by the advancing Segmentum Pacificus navy and assaulted Tanith. Gaunt had a choice: Get out with those troop elements he could save, or stay and die with the planet.'

'And he chose the former…'

'Like any good commander would. I like old Ibram Gaunt, but he's a commissar at heart. Hardline, worships the Emperor above his own life, dedicated to discipline. He took us out, about two thousand of us, and Tanith burned as we left it behind. We've been paying back the enemy ever since.'

Bulwar nodded. 'That's why you're called Ghosts, I suppose?'

Corbec chuckled and poured some more sacra for them both.

Bulwar was silent for a while. 'I can't imagine what it's like to lose your homeworld.' Corbec didn't make the reply that flashed into his mind, but Bulwar saw the logic of his own words and spoke the unspoken anyway. 'I hope I don't find out.'

Corbec raised his glass. 'By the spirit of my lost world,' he said mischievously, glancing at the sacra, 'may we Ghosts ensure there are never any Verghast ghosts.'

They downed their drinks with heartfelt gulps. Bulwar got up and began to rummage in a footlocker bolted to the carrier's hull. He pulled out map-cases, ammo-cans and a sheaf of signal flags before finding what he was looking for: a tall-shouldered bottle of brown glass. 'We've toasted with your Tanith brew, which I commend for its fine qualities, but it's only fair we toast now with a Verghast vintage. Joiliq. Ten year old, cask-fermented.'

Corbec smiled. 'I'll try anything once.' He knocked it back, savoured it, smiled again. 'Or twice,' he said, proffering his glass.

BY A ROARING oil-drum fire, Baffels sat with Milo, Venar, Filain and Domor. Filain and Venar were snoring, propped against each other. Domor was spooning soup into his mouth with weary, almost mechanical motions.

'I want you with me,' Baffels said quietly to Milo.

'Sergeant?'

'Oh, stop it with that crap! These pins should have been yours.'

Milo laughed and Filain looked up at the noise for a moment before slumping and snoring again.

'I've been a trooper for all of ten seconds. And I'm the youngest Tanith in the regiment. Gaunt would never have been crazy enough to make me sergeant. You deserve it, Baffels. No one denies it should be yours.'

Baffels shrugged. 'You led us today. No one denied that either. You're trusted.'

'So are you and we worked as a team. If they followed me at all it's only because you did. They may think of me as some lucky fething charm, touched by the commissar himself, but it's you they respect.'

'We did okay though, didn't we?'

Milo nodded.

'Whatever you say, I want you at point, right up near me, okay?'

'You're the sergeant.'

'And I'm making a command decision. The men respect you, so if you're near me and with me, they'll follow me too.'

Milo looked into the fire. He could sense Baffels was scared by his new responsibilities. The man was a great soldier, but he'd never expected unit command. He didn't want to fail and Milo knew he wouldn't, just as Gaunt had known when he'd made the promotion. But if it helped Baffels's confidence, Milo would do as he was asked. Certainly, through that strange, organic process Milo had observed in the firefight that morning, soldiers chose their own leaders in extremis, and Baffels and Milo had been chosen.

'Where's Tanith, d'you think?'

Milo glanced round, initially assuming Baffels had asked a rhetorical question. But the older man was looking up at the sky.

'Tanith?'

'Which of those stars did we come from?'

Milo gazed up. The Shield was a glowing aura of green light, fizzing with rain that fell outside. But even so, they could just glimpse the starfields pricking the blackness.

Milo chose one at random.

'That one,' he said.

'You sure?'

'Absolutely.'

It seemed to please Baffels and he stared at the winking light for a long time.

'D'you still have your pipes?'

Milo had been a musician back on Tanith and before he'd made trooper he'd played the pipes into battle.

'Yes,' he said. 'Never go anywhere without them.'

'Play up, eh?'

'Now?'

'My first order as sergeant.'

Milo pulled the tight roll of pipes and bellows from his knapsack. He cleared the mouth-spout and then puffed the bag alive, making it whine and wail quietly. The hum of conversation died down at fires all around at the first sound.

Pumping his arm, he got the bellows breathing and the drone began, rising up in a clear, keening note. 'What shall I play?' he asked, his fingers ready on the chanter.

'My Love Waits in the Nalwoods Green,' Domor said suddenly from beside him.

Milo nodded. The tune was the unofficial anthem of Tanith, more sprightly than the actual planetary anthem, yet melancholy and almost painful for any man of Tanith to hear.

He began to play. The tune rose above the yard, above the flurries of sparks rising from the oil drums. One by one, the men began to sing.

'WHAT IS THAT?' asked Bulwar hoarsely as Corbec sang softly. Across the yard, the NorthCol men were silent as the bitter, haunting melody filled the air.

'A song sung by ghosts,' Corbec said as he reached for the sacra.

THE MAIN SPINE rang with the sound of massed voices. In the halls of the Legislature and the grand regimental chapel of House Command, victory choirs thousands strong sang victory masses and hymns of deliverance.

Crossing a marble colonnade with Captain Daur and several officers on the approach to House Command, Gaunt paused on a balcony and looked down into the regimental chapel auditorium. He sent his contingent on ahead and stood watching the mass for a while. Twelve hundred singers in golden robes, red-bound hymnals raised to their chests, gave voice to the hymn 'Behold! The Triumph of Terra' in perfect harmony, and the air vibrated.

The auditorium's high, arched roof was adorned with company banners and house flags, and censer smoke billowed into the candlelit air. A procession of Ministorum clerics carrying gilt standards and reliquary boxes, their long ceremonial trains supported by child servitors, shuffled down the main aisle towards the Imperial Shrine, where Intendant Banefail and Master Legislator Anophy waited. There were hooded Administratum officials in the procession and three astropaths from the guild, their satin-wrapped bulks bulging with tubes and pipes and feed-links. The astropaths were carried on litters by adult servitors, and many of the tubes and pipes issuing from the folds of their cloaks were plugged to cogitator systems built into the silver-plated litter-pallets.

'It lifts the heart, does it not?' a voice from behind Gaunt asked.

Gaunt turned. It was Kowle.

'If it lifts the morale of Vervunhive, so be it. In truth, it is premature.'

'Indeed?' Kowle frowned, as if not convinced. 'I am going to House Command. Will you walk with me?'

Gaunt nodded and the two grim, black figures in peaked caps strode together down the marble colonnade under the flickering ball-lamps strung along the walls.

'This day has seen victory, yet you seem low in spirit.'

Gaunt grunted. 'We drove them off. Call it a victory. It was bought too costly and the cost was unnecessary.'

'May I ask on what you base that assessment, colonel-commissar?'

They strode under a high arch where banners flapped in the cool air. The choir echoed after them.

'Vervunhive's command and control systems are inadequate for a military endeavour of this magnitude. The system broke down. Deployment was crippled behind the front and devastated at the sharp end. There is much to be criticised in the command structure of the Vervun Primary itself.'

Kowle stopped short. 'I would take such criticisms personally. I am, after all, the chief disciplinary officer of this hive.'

Gaunt stopped as well and turned back to face Kowle. There was an immoderate darkness in the man's face. 'You seem to excel in your duties, Commissar Kowle. You understand, better than any man I have ever met, the uses of propaganda and persuasion. But I wonder if you hold the officer ranks in place by force of will and fear rather than sound tactical order. The commanders of Vervun Primary have no experience of war on this scale. They know what they know from texts and treatises. They must be made to acknowledge the experience of active field officers.'

'Such as yourself and the other Guard commanders like General Grizmund?'

'Just so. I trust I can count on your support in this when we meet with House Command. I want you with me, Kowle. We can't be pushing from different angles.'

'Of course. I am of one mind with you on this, colonel-commissar.'

They walked on. Gaunt could read Kowle's soothing tone – and he despised it. He was well aware of the two dozen requests for transfer back into the active Guard which Kowle had made in the past three years. A master politico, Kowle was clearly courting Gaunt's favour, assuming Gaunt could make a good report and effect him that transfer.

'I understand you executed Modile,' Kowle said matter-of-factly.

'A necessary measure. His negligence was criminal.'

'It was, as you described, his inexperience, that let him down. Was summary execution too harsh for a man who might yet learn?'

'I hope you would have done the same, Kowle. Modile caused many deaths by his inaction and fear. That cannot be conscienced. He ignored both pre-orders and direct commands from above.'

Kowle nodded. 'Where a seasoned Guard commander would have held fast to the chain of command.'

'Indeed.'

Kowle smiled. It was an alarming expression on such a cruel face. 'Actually, I applaud your action. Decisive, forceful, true to the spirit of the Commissariat. Many have feared the great Gaunt has grown soft now he has a command of his own, that his commissarial instinct might have been diluted. But you disabused that notion today with Modile.'

'I'm glad to hear it.'

They had arrived at a set of great doors ornate with golden bas-relief. Vervun Elite troops in dress uniforms crusted with brocade, with plumes sprouting from their helmet spikes, opened the doors to admit them.

Beyond the doors, the audience theatre of House Command was seething with voices and commotion.

GENERAL NASH WAS at the lectern, trying to speak, but the noble houses were shouting him down. Junior Vervun

Primary officers were stamping in their tiered seats and jeering, and Roane Deeper adjutants were yelling back at them, urged on by officers from NorthCol, the Narmenians and the Volpone.

Vice Marshal Anko rose to his feet, slamming his white-gloved hand into the bench-head for silence.

'While I welcome the aid our off-world kin have rendered us, I find this an affront. General Nash condemns our military organisations and says we are ill-equipped to deal with this fight. An insult, no less, no more! Does his highness General Sturm share this view?'

Sturm rose. 'War, honoured gentlemen,' he began in soothing, mellow tones, 'is a confusion. Emotions run high. It is hard to say if a system is right or wrong until it is found wanting in the fire of battle. The Vervun Primary are exemplary soldiers, well-drilled and highly motivated. Their bravery is beyond question. That our command channels clashed during today's engagement is simply unfortunate. It is not the fault of Vervun officers. I have already issued standing orders to range the vox-channels so that there will be no further overlap. Any deaths that have resulted from this misfortune are greatly regretted. Such incidents will not recur.'

'What about discipline?' Gaunt's voice cut across the great hall and all the faces turned to look. Gaunt walked to the end of the chamber and stepped up to the lectern. Kowle took his place on the front bench next to Anko.

'Colonel-commissar?' Marshal Croe rose and looked down the vast hall into Gaunt's eyes. 'Is there another matter? General Nash has already been unkind enough to reprimand Vervunhive for its weakness in command. Do you share that view?'

'In part, marshal. The communication problems General Sturm has referred to were only a piece of the crisis we faced today. We were lucky to survive the Veyveyr assault.'

Anko jumped to his feet. 'And have we not our own hero, Commissar Kowle, to thank for turning that crisis around?'

The hall broke out in ripples of applause and cheers, mainly from the Vervun majority. Kowle accepted the applause with a gracious, modest nod. Gaunt knew better than to point out the cosmetic nature of Kowle's involvement.

'Commissar Kowle's actions are a matter of record. History will record the nature of his contribution to the Vervunhive war.' Gaunt couched his response carefully. 'But the line of command failed severely during Veyveyr. Field commanders of the Vervun Primary, whose bravery is beyond question, failed to relay strategic orders or were unable – or unwilling – to redirect their forces in the face of the assault.'

Jeers and boos thundered down at Gaunt.

'I understand you have already exacted discipline, colonel-commissar,' Anko said stiffly.

'And I will do so again,' Gaunt raised his voice above the background roar. 'But that simply punishes the symptoms of the problem. It does not address the heart of it.'

'That problem being a failure to obey direct orders?' Kowle asked, rising to his feet amid more cheers.

Gaunt nodded. 'Chain of command must be observed at all times. Any who break it must do so knowing they risk the highest penalty. Without such order and control, this war will be lost. I trust Vervun Primary will respect this philosophy from now on.'

'So all who transgress must be punished?' Kowle asked.

He wants his transfer badly, Gaunt thought. He's supporting me every step of the way.

'Of course. Without the threat of sanction, insubordination will continue.'

'Then you will support the punishment of General Grizmund?' asked Vice Marshal Anko.

'What?'

'General Grizmund – who broke orders this day and began his own deployment of the Narmenian armour?' Now the Narmenian staff booed and heckled.

Gaunt faltered. 'I... I was not aware of this. It must have been a mistake. General Grizmund has my complete confidence and–'

'So, one rule for the locals, another for the Guard?' sneered Anko.

'I didn't say that. I–'

'General Grizmund defied direct orders from House Command and redeployed his tanks through noble house territory. Forgetting the collateral damage he caused, is not his action worthy of the most severe censure?' Tarrian of the VPHC looked across at Gaunt. 'That was the philosophy you were advocating, wasn't it?'

Gaunt looked away from the hooded eyes of the VPHC commandant and found Kowle's face in the throng. Kowle smiled back at him, unblinking, soulless.

He knew. He had known about Grizmund even before they had reached the chamber. He had manoeuvred Gaunt right into this trap.

Gaunt realised in an instant he had underestimated Kowle's ambition. The man was after more than a simple transfer off Verghast. He was after glory and command.

'Well, colonel-commissar? What do we do with Grizmund?' asked Anko.

Gaunt stepped away from the lectern and strode down the hall to the exit, yells and cat-calls showering over him.

OUTSIDE, HE GRABBED one of the Vervun Elite minding the door by the brocade and slammed him into the wall.

'Grizmund! Where is he?'

'In the s-stockade, sir! Level S-sub-40!'

Gaunt released him and strode away.

The rousing hymns of the great choirs shivered the air around him. Their sentiments sounded all too hollow.

THE SUNRISE WAS an hour away.

A file of Ghosts moved up from trucks parked on the eastern hab expressway and entered the manufactory depots that backed on to the Spoil.

Thirty men, the cream of the Tanith scout cadre. The Vervun troops occupying the location, soldiers of the so-called Spoilers unit, greeted them in the undercroft of an ore barn. The air was thick with rock-dust and the light was poor, issuing from a few hooded lamps nailed to the wall.

'Gak' Ormon, the major in command of the Spoilers, saluted as Mkoll led his men in. He was a big, bulky man with bloodshot eyes and a flamer-burned throat.

'I understand you have good snipers and stealthers,' Ormon said to Mkoll as he walked over to a chart table with him.

Mkoll nodded. He surveyed the chart. The Spoil, a vast heap of slag, was a real vulnerability for Vervunhive. They knew as much, otherwise they wouldn't have formed a dedicated defence force, but the battle of the day before had decimated the Spoiler unit.

'General Sturm has acknowledged the Tanith ability in such endeavours. We're here to support you.'

'Gak' Ormon's great bulk was clad in the blue greatcoat and spiked helmet of the Vervun Primary. He looked down at the wiry off-worlder with his faded black fatigues and curious piebald cape. He was not impressed.

All of the Spoilers present, including Ormon, carried long-barrelled autoguns with scopes dedicated to sniping. Their faces were striped with bars of black camo-paint. Several had fresh wounds bound tightly.

Sergeant Mkoll called up his men so they could all study the chart. The Ghosts grouped around the table, making comments, pointing.

'Why don't you just give them orders?' Ormon asked disdainfully.

'Because I want them to know the situation and understand the terrain. How can they defend an area effectively otherwise? Don't you do the same?'

Ormon said nothing.

Mkoll broke his men into work-teams and sent them away in different directions, though not before checking they had set their micro-beads to the same channel.

Ormon joined Mkoll as the sergeant led his group of MkVenner, Domor, Larkin and Rilke up shattered internal stairways to the third storey overlooking the slag heap. Nine Spoilers were stationed at the shattered windows up here, using scopes to watch the sleek slopes of the Spoil.

The Ghosts took position amongst them.

Larkin and Rilke, both armed with sniper-variant lasguns, set themselves up carefully. Rilke used a length of pipe to disguise the end of his gun as it protruded from the wall. Larkin covered his own gun down to the muzzle under loose sacks.

Domor took Mkoll's scope, set it up on a tripod stand in the shadow of a window and linked his mechanical eyes to the sight. He could now see further and clearer than anyone in the fortification.

Ormon was about to ask Mkoll a question when he realised he and the Ghost called MkVenner had vanished.

MKOLL AND MKVENNER moved invisibly down the Spoil slope, their capes spread over them. The coal-like ore-refuse was wet and slimy underfoot. They were outside the protection of the Shield and the night rain fell around them, making puddles amongst the rock waste.

They raised their scopes. Beyond the Spoil, two kilometres away, they saw the open, flat land and the blasted habs beyond. The heavy rain was creating standing water on the flat soil and the water was rippling like dimpled tin with the rainfall. Visibility was down and cloud cover was descending.

There was a sound. MkVenner armed his lasgun and Mkoll crawled forward.

It was singing. Chanting. From out in the enemy positions, via loudhailers and speakers, a foul hymn of Chaos was ringing out to answer the triumph hymns of the hive.

It grew louder.

Mkoll and MkVenner shuddered.

In the ore-works behind them, Ormon felt his bladder vice and hurried away.

At his position, Larkin tensed. He was weary from the day's nerve-shredding battle and had only been sent in with Mkoll's men because of his skills as a sniper.

Every time he closed his eyes, he saw the face, the face of the Zoican.

Now, from below, down the length of the Spoil, he could hear them.

The Zoican filth were singing a name over and over, in a canon repeat.

Heritor Asphodel… Heritor Asphodel…

ELEVEN
THE HERITOR

'Kill us! Kill us all! In the name of Terra, before he–'
— Transcript of last broadcast from Ryxus V,
the first 'inherited' world

LEVEL SUB-40 was almost a kilometre underground, deep in the foundation structure of the Main Spine. An armoured lift cage with grilled sides transported Gaunt down the last three hundred metres, lowering him into an underworld of dark, damp stone, stale air and caged sodium lamps.

He entered an underground concourse where ground water dripped from the pipework roof onto the concrete floor and rusting chains dangled over piles of mildewed refuse. Along one side was a row of wooden posts with shackle-loops at wrist height. The wall behind the posts was stippled with bullet pocks and darkly stained.

Gaunt approached an adamantine shutter marked with yellow chevrons. Rockcrete bunkers stood on either side of the shutter, blank except for letterbox slits set high up.

As he moved forward, automatic spotlights mounted above the hatch snapped on and bathed him with blue-white light.

'Identify!' a voice crackled out of a vox-relay.

'Colonel-Commissar Ibram Gaunt,' Gaunt replied curtly, reeling off his serial number afterwards.

'Your business?'

'Just open the shutter.'

There was a brief pause, then the great metal hatch screeched open. Gaunt stepped through and found himself facing a second shutter. The one behind him slammed shut before the inner one would open.

Inside the stockade, a caged walkway led down into a dispatch area with an open-sided shower stall and low tables for searching through personal effects. The sodium lamps gave the foetid, recirculated air a frosty hue.

Guards moved out of side bunkers to meet him. They were all VPHC troopers dressed in black shirts, black, peaked caps, graphite-grey breeches and black boots. Each one wore orange arm-bands and wide, black, leather belts with riot-batons and cuffs dangling from them. Three carried pump-action shotguns.

'Grizmund,' Gaunt told them briefly. He allowed himself to be frisked and handed over his bolt pistol. Two of the guards then led him through a series of cage doors with remotely activated electric locks, down the austere, red-washed hallways of the cell-block. There was an astringent ammonia stink of open drains, with a mouldering aftertaste of deep rock and soil. Every sound rang out and echoed.

Grizmund and the four officers arrested with him were sharing a large communal holding tank. They still wore their mustard-brown Narmenian uniforms, but caps, belts, laces and all rank pins had been removed.

Grizmund met Gaunt at the cage door. The VPHC guards refused to open it, so they were forced to talk through the bars.

'I'm glad to see you,' Grizmund said. He was pale, and there was a dark look of anger in his eyes. 'Get us out of this.'

'Tell me what happened. In your own words,' Gaunt said.

Grizmund paused, then shrugged. 'We were ordered to Veyveyr. Thanks to the gross idiocy of House Command organisation, the routes were blocked. I took my column off the roadway and headed on to the gate through an industrial sector. Next thing I knew, the VPHC were heading me off.'

'Did you disobey any direct order?'

'I was ordered to Veyveyr,' the man repeated. 'I was told to take Arterial Route GH/7m. When I couldn't get through, I tried to achieve my primary order to reach the appointed frontline.'

'Did you strike a VPHC officer?'

'Yes. He drew a gun on me first, without provocation.'

Gaunt was quiet for a moment.

'You'd think these bastards didn't want us to fight for them,' growled Grizmund.

'Their pride is hurt. The inadequacies of their command systems were shown up clearly today. They're looking for others to blame.'

'Screw them if they try to pin anything on me! This is crazy! Won't Sturm back you up?'

'Sturm is too busy trying to please both sides. Don't worry. I won't let this continue a moment longer than it has to.'

Grizmund nodded. Loud footsteps, unpaced and overlapping, reverberated down the dank cell-block behind them. Gaunt turned to see Commissar Tarrian enter with an escort of VPHC troops.

'Commissar Gaunt. You shouldn't be here. The Narmenian insubordination is a matter for the VPHC Disciplinary Review. You will not interfere with Verghastian military justice. You will not confer with the prisoners. My men will escort you back to the elevator.'

Gaunt nodded to Grizmund and walked over to the VPHC group, facing Tarrian for a moment. 'You are making a mistake both you and your cadre will regret, Tarrian.'

'Is that some kind of threat, Gaunt?'

'You're a commissar, Tarrian, or at least you're supposed to be. You must know commissars never issue threats. Only facts.'

Gaunt allowed himself to be marched out of the stockade.

THE THIRTY-THIRD DAWN was already on them, with heavy rain falling across the entire hive, the outer habs and the grasslands beyond. Marshal Croe was taking breakfast in his retiring chamber off the war-room when Gaunt entered.

The room was long, gloomy and wood-panelled with gilt-framed oil paintings of past marshals lining the walls. Croe sat at the head of a long, varnished mahogany table, picking at food laid out on a salver as he read through a pile of data-slates. Behind him, the end wall of the room was armoured glass and overlooked the Commercia and Shield Pylon. Backlit by the great window and the grey morning glare, Croe was a dark, brooding shape.

'Commissar.'

Gaunt saluted. 'Marshal. The charges against the Narmenian officers must be dropped at once.'

Croe looked up, his noble, white-haired head inclining towards Gaunt like an eagle considering a lamb. 'Because?'

'Because they are utterly foolish and counterproductive. Because we need officers of Grizmund's standing. Because any punishment will send a negative message to the Narmenian units and to all Guard units as a whole: that Vervunhive values the efforts of the off-world forces very little.'

'And what of the other view? You heard it yourself: one rule for Vervun, one for the Guard?'

'We both know that's not true. Grizmund's actions are hardly capital in nature, yet the VPHC seems hell-bent on prosecuting them to the extreme. I'm not even sure this so-called "insubordination" was even that. A tribunal would throw it out, but to even get to a tribunal would be damaging. Narmenian and Guard honour would be slighted, and the VPHC would be made to look stupid.' At the last minute, Gaunt managed to prevent himself from saying 'even more stupid.'

'Tarrian's staff is very thorough. They would not undertake a tribunal if they thought it would collapse.'

'I am familiar with such "courts", marshal. However, that will only happen if the VPHC are allowed to run the hearing themselves.'

'It is their purview. Military discipline. It's Tarrian's job.'

'I will not allow the VPHC to conduct any hearing.'

Croe put down his fork and stared at Gaunt as if he had just insulted Croe's own mother. He rose to his feet, dabbing his mouth with a napkin.

'You won't... allow it?'

Gaunt stood his ground. 'Imperial Commissariat edict 4378b states that any activity concerning the discipline of Imperial Guardsmen must be conducted by the Imperial Commissariat itself. Not by planetary bodies. It is not Tarrian's responsibility. It should not be a matter for the VPHC.'

'And you will enforce this ruling?'

'If I have to. I am the ranking Imperial commissar on Verghast.'

'The interpretation of law will be murderous. Any conflicts between Imperial and Planetary rules will be argued over and over. Do not pursue this, Gaunt.'

'I'm afraid I have to, marshal. I am not a stranger to martial hearings. I will personally resource and provide all the legal precedents I need to throw Tarrian, his thugs and his pitiful case to the wolves.'

A Vervun Primary adjutant hurried into the retiring room behind Gaunt.

'Not now!' barked Croe, but the man didn't withdraw. He held out a data-slate to the fuming marshal.

'You – you need to see this, sir,' he stammered.

Croe snatched the slate out of the man's hands and read it quickly. What he read arrested his attention, and he went back and re-read slowly, his eyes narrowing.

Croe thrust the slate to Gaunt. 'Read it yourself,' he said. 'Our observers along the South Curtain have been picking it up since daybreak.'

Gaunt looked through the transcripts recorded by the wall-guards as they scrolled across the glowing screen.

'Heritor Asphodel,' he murmured. He looked round at Croe. 'I suggest you release Grizmund now. We're going to need all the men we can get.'

GAUNT AND CROE left the retiring room together and strode down the short hall into the great control auditorium of House Command. Both the lower level and the wrought-iron upper deck of the place were jostling with activity. Hololithic

projections of the warfront glowed upwards into the air from
crenellated lens-pits in the floor, and the air throbbed with
vox-caster traffic, astropaths' chants and the clack of the cogitator banks.

A gaggle of Munitorum staffers, Vervun Primary aides and
technical operators hastened forward around the marshal as
he entered, but he waved them all away, crossing to the ironwork upperdeck, his boots clanging up the metal steps. Vice
Marshal Anko, General Sturm, Commissar Kowle and General Xance of the NorthCol were already assembled by the
great chart table. Silent servitors, encrusted with bionics, and
poised regimental aides waited behind them. An occasional
vox/pict drone bumbled across the command space. Gaunt
hung back at the head of the stairs, observing.

'Kowle?' asked Croe, approaching the chart table.

'No confirmation. It is impossible to confirm, lord marshal.'

Croe held up the data-slate. 'But this is an accurate transcript of the enemy broadcasts? They're chanting this at the
gates?'

'Since dawn,' replied Sturm. He looked bleary-eyed, and
his grey and gold Volpone dress uniform was crumpled, as if
he had been roused hurriedly. 'And not just chanting.'

He nodded and a servitor opened a vox-channel. A chatter
of almost unintelligible noise rolled from the speaker.

'Vox-central has washed the signal clean. The name repeats
on all bandwidths as a voice pattern and also as machine
code, arithmetical sequence and compressed pict-representa-
tion.' Sturm fell silent. He reached for a cup of caffeine on
the edge of the chart table, his hand trembling.

'A blanket broadcast. They certainly want us to know,'
Gaunt said.

Kowle looked round at him. 'They want us to be scared,' he
said snidely. 'Just hours ago, you complimented me on my
ability to control information. We can presume the enemy
are similarly efficient. This could be propaganda. Demoral-
ising broadcasts. They may simply be using the name as a
terror device.'

'Possibly... but we agreed it would take a force of great
charisma to turn a hive the size of Ferrozoica. Heritor

Asphodel is just such a force. His fate and whereabouts since Balhaut are unknown.'

Anko looked away from Gaunt deliberately and turned to Kowle. 'You were on Balhaut, Kowle. What is this creature?'

Kowle was about to speak when Gaunt cut across. 'Both Kowle and I served on Balhaut. I believe the commissar was deployed on the south-west continent, away from the main battle for the Oligarchy. I encountered the Heritor's forces personally.'

Kowle conceded. He could barely hide his bitterness at the memory. 'The colonel-commissar may... have more experience than me.'

Croe turned his hooded eyes back to Gaunt. 'Well?'

'The Heritor was one of Archon Nadzybar's foremost lieutenants, a warlord in his own right, personally commanding a force of over a million. He was one of the chief commanders Nadzybar gathered in his great retinue to form the vast enemy force which overran the Sabbat Worlds, Emperor damn him. Despite the notoriety of the other warlords – filth like Sholen Skara, Nokad the Blighted, Anakwanar Sek, Qux of the Eyeless – Heritor Asphodel remains the most notorious. His sworn aim, both before and after Archon Nadzybar co-opted him into the pact, was to "inherit" Imperium world after Imperium world and return them to what he saw as the "true state" of Chaos. His ruthlessness is immeasurable, his brutality staggering and the charismatic force of his personality as a leader cannot be underestimated. And with the possible exception of Sek, he is probably the most tactically brilliant of all Nadzybar's commanders.'

'It almost sounds like you admire the bastard,' sniffed Sturm.

'I do not underestimate him, general,' Gaunt said coldly. 'That is different.'

'And he could be here? It could be more than an enemy lie?' Anko asked, failing to disguise the wobble in his voice.

'The Heritor fled Balhaut along with all the surviving warlords after Warmaster Slaydo slew the Archon. This may be his first reappearance. The Zoican forces have encircled us well and swiftly, and they have used both waiting and surprise to great effect. Both are tactics I know the Heritor favours. Furthermore, he delights in war machines. With access to Ferrozoica hive's fabricating plants, the baroque war machines we have seen are precisely the sort of things I would expect him to send out at us.'

Croe said nothing as he took it in. 'Suggestions? Gaunt?'

Astutely, Gaunt deferred to Kowle, aware of how the commissar was bristling at what he would no doubt see as the colonel-commissar's grandstanding. 'I would invite Commissar Kowle's ideas on how to deal with this information.'

Kowle greedily accepted the scrap thrown to him. 'We can't shut out blanket broadcasts, so we must refute them. All military, municipal and guilder institutions in Vervunhive, along with select representatives of the citizenry and the Legislature, must be clearly and emphatically briefed that this is hollow propaganda. We should prepare statements for the public address plates to repeat denials of this. I also urge we counter with broadcasts of our own. Simple repeats of the statement "the Heritor is dead" should suffice for now.'

'Begin the work. I want regular updates.' Croe waited as Kowle saluted and left, then faced Sturm and Xance. 'Battle standby remains in force, but I want all military resources moved into position now. No reserves. We must meet the next thrust with absolute power.'

Both generals nodded.

'I trust the revisions you ordered to the communications net have been affected, General Sturm?'

'New channel settings and new codes have been issued to our forces. The confusions of the last storm should not recur.'

Gaunt hoped Sturm was correct. He had reviewed the general's revisions and they seemed sound, though they favoured the Volpone Bluebloods and the Vervun Primary with the most accessible bands.

'Have you yet considered my proposal to engage them outside the Wall?' asked Xance.

'Impractical, general,' replied Croe.

'We saw how the Vervun Mechanised were destroyed in the grasslands,' Sturm added.

'But now they are dug in and restricted by the streets of the outer habs. The policy vouched by Nash, Grizmund and Gaunt early on would seem more attractive now. The North-Col and Narmenian armour could sally out with infantry support and shake them from their forward line.'

Gaunt listened, fascinated. This was the first he had heard of Xance's plan. Clearly Sturm, Anko and Croe had made efforts to suppress it. It could not be coincidence that Xance was voicing it now in Gaunt's presence.

'No!' barked Sturm, anger getting the better of him for a moment. 'We will not dilute our resistance here by wasting manpower and machines in an external raid.'

Xance shook his head and left the upper auditorium without saluting.

Sturm looked over at Gaunt with a scowl. 'Don't even begin to think about supporting Xance, Gaunt. The Imperial Forces here at Vervunhive will not go on the offensive now or in the foreseeable future.'

Gaunt nodded, saluted and left. He knew when it was time to argue, and he'd been sticking his neck out more than enough in the last few days.

THE ZOICANS RECOMMENCED sporadic bombardment at dusk, throwing shells and rockets up at the Curtain Wall at a list-less rate, more to annoy than to do any real damage. The Wall positions returned fire intermittently, whenever a target was designated by the spotters.

Zoican ground forces, edging closer to the Wall, fired las- and bolt rounds at the gates from foxhole cover and ditches. At Sondar Gate, Vervun Primary corps under Captain Cargin elevated the armoured domes of the electric rotating turrets and peppered the ground in range outside with torrents of heavy autofire.

The new defences at Veyveyr Gate took their first battering. There was the *punk! punk!* of mortars dropping shells close to the skirts of the stone siege walls and dirt clouds drifted back across the troops at the parapet.

Feygor swivelled his scope, hunting for a target in the hab waste beyond, and he quickly identified the rising tendrils of smoke from the concealed mortars.

He ordered Bragg up to the wall-line and spotted for him
as Bragg loaded rocket grenades into his shoulder launcher.
Then Feygor voxed to Rawne for permission to fire.

Rawne was crossing the inner trenches below the gate
when he received the request and told Feygor to hold fire.

He hurried down a dugout towards the Volpone command
section, a half-smashed rail carriage buried to the axles in ash
and rubble and shielded along its length with flak-board,
sandbags and piled stone. Rawne had been ordered to co-
ordinate the defence with his Volpone opposite number, but
despite Sturm's communication review – or because of it,
Rawne grimly suspected – the inter-unit vox links seemed
stilted and slow.

Two Bluebloods of the elite 10th Brigade stood guard at
the gas-curtained entrance. They were giants in their carapace battledress, the grey and gold of their segmented
armaplas and fatigues spotless and austere. Each carried a
gleaming black hellgun with a sawn-off pump-gun attached
to the bayonet lug under the main barrel.

They blocked his advance.

'Major Rawne, Tanith area commander,' he said briskly
and they stood aside to let him enter.

Colonel Nikolaas Taschen DeHante Corday was a true
Blueblood: massive, powerful and square-jawed with
hooded eyes. He was sitting at his chart desk in the carriage
as Rawne entered and he looked the Tanith over like he was
something he'd found adhering to his boot.

Rawne nodded. 'I wish to commence discriminate
return of fire. There are mortars trying to range my positions.'

Corday looked at his chart again and then nodded. 'Do
you want support?'

'They're simply harrying, biding their time. But I'd rather
not sit my men there while they find their true range.'

'Is it worth drawing up the artillery?

Rawne shook his head. 'Not yet. Let me silence the mortars and see what they try next.'

'Very good.'

Rawne turned to leave.

'Major? Rawne, isn't it?'

Rawne turned back to see that Corday had risen to his feet. 'I am anxious that the Volpone and the Tanith can complement each other in this position,' he said.

'I share your hope.'

'There is not a good record between our regiments.'

Rawne was surprised by the frankness.

'No. No, there isn't. May I ask… do you know why?'

Corday sighed. 'Voltemand. I was not part of that action, but I have reviewed the records. A miscalculation on General Sturm's part caused artillery to injure your units in the field.'

Rawne coughed gently. It was a polite and rather inaccurate appraisal, but he didn't want to antagonise the Blueblood officer.

'I don't believe the Volpone have ever formally apologised to the Tanith for it. For what it's worth, I make that apology now.'

'Is there a reason?' Rawne asked guardedly.

'One of my men, Culcis, speaks highly of the Ghosts, of your Colonel Corbec in particular. He fought with them on Nacedon. Others have praised Gaunt's leadership on Monthax.' Corday smiled. The smile seemed genuine, despite the aristocratic languor of the face. Rawne thought it would not be impossible to like Corday.

'Sturm, Emperor honour him… Gilbear… many of the upper echelon will of course despise the Tanith for eternity!' They both laughed. 'But you'll find me a fair man, Rawne. We Bluebloods have prided ourselves on our superiority for a long time. It is time we learned from others and realised that the Imperial Guard has other fine regiments within it that we might be honoured and educated to serve alongside.'

Rawne was quietly astonished. Like all the Ghosts, he had come to loathe the Bluebloods, and for a damaged, hating soul like Rawne that loathing came easy. He could never have believed he would hear such comradeship from one of them, especially a senior officer.

'I appreciate your words, colonel. I will bear them in mind and circulate your thoughts amongst my own men. It's fair to say that unless we learn to fight together, we will die here. In the spirit of co-operation, may I note that our inter-unit vox-links are still unreliable?'

Corday nodded and made a note on his data-slate with a stylus. 'Select band pi as a working link, with band kappa as reserve. I think I'll send one of my subalterns with a vox-set to work as liaison. I suggest you reciprocate.'

Rawne nodded, saluted and left the carriage.

Corday called his bodyguard in to join him. 'Send Graven to the Tanith position with a vox-set. Tell him to act as intermediary. I want these disgusting Ghost scum kept sweet, make that clear to him. We don't want them hanging our arses out to dry when the fighting starts.'

RETURNING DOWN the trench, Rawne sent a confirmation to Feygor at the leading wall. Bragg's launcher thumped and the mortar position erupted in a sheet of flame and debris as its munitions were hit.

After a while, las-fire began to pepper back from the Zoican lines. The Ghosts kept their heads down and waited.

AT HASS EAST FORT, overlooking the estuary inlet, it was deathly quiet. Hass East had been spared all the fighting so far, but the position was still vital, as it watched the Vannick Highway and guarded the Ontabi Gate entrance to the hive, the only one of the five great city gates not yet assaulted.

On the high top of the tower, Sergeant Varl gazed out across the dusk settling on the reed-beds and islets of the matt-grey river. Waders and flycatchers darted and warbled over the water and rushes, and the riverside air was crazy with billowing gnats. The great bulk of the Hiraldi road-bridge to the north was just a silhouette.

The rain had eased off. There was a smell of thunder in the air. Varl, with two platoons of Tanith, was sharing defence of the Fort with three platoons of Roane Deepers under Captain Willard, and three hundred Vervun Primary gunners and wall artillerymen answering to Major Rodyin, a junior member of one of the lesser noble houses.

Varl got on with Willard. The Roane was about twenty-five, tanned and shaggy blond, with penetrating, brown eyes and an earthy sense of humour. Like Varl, Willard had a metallic implant – in his case, the fingers and palm of his right hand.

They joked together about their experiences of body automation.

Rodyin was rather more difficult. Although they all faced death here, Rodyin had a more personal stake because this was his home. He was pale, earnest and prematurely balding, though he was only in his early twenties. He seemed utterly mystified by the jokes and quips that rattled freely between his two fellow officers, and he would stare at them myopically though the half-moon glasses that were permanently perched on the bridge of his nose. Varl understood that House Rodyin was one of the liberal families in the hive, more humanitarian and forward-thinking than the old noble houses or the guilders. House Rodyin's fortunes were built on food sources and their harvester-machines grazed the great pastoral uplands north of the Hass, gathering grain for the vast granaries in the dock district.

Varl liked Rodyin, but he didn't seem much of a soldier.

The Tanith sergeant crossed the tower top, slapping gnats off his skin, and toured the emplacements as the daylight faded.

He heard laughter and saw Willard and some of his tan-uniformed troops joking by a rocket station. Rodyin stood a little apart, scoping the river and the road with a high-power set of magnoculars.

Willard greeted Varl. 'But for these bloody flies, Ghost, I'd say we've pulled the best duty here! None of that bloody fighting stuff up here at Hass East, eh?'

Varl had already seen fighting in Vervunhive and was actually glad of the calm and quiet up here on the far eastern side of the city. But still, waiting was sometimes the mind-killer. 'Wouldn't object to a few Zoicans to pop though,' he grinned.

'Hell, no! A few of those bloody yellows to keep my eye in, eh?'

More laughter. Varl saw how Rodyin shifted uncomfortably, unwilling to be drawn in. The major took his duties and his war seriously – too seriously in Varl's opinion – probably because he'd never been in one before.

'See anything?' Varl asked, joining Rodyin at the parapet.

'A little river traffic. Barges, ferries. Most of them are crossing from the north bank with munition hauls. House Command has embargoed all but vital supply runs.'

Varl took his own single-lens scope from his pack and scanned the area. To the north of their position, near the bridge, sat the bulky promethium tanks of the dockside fuel depot, the main facility serving Vervunhive. On stilt legs, pipelines tracked away to the north and east, as far into the distance as Varl could see. They'd once pumped the fuel in from Vannick Hive, before it was lost. Now the only liquid fuel supplies available to Vervunhive were coming from NorthCol.

'Looks quiet enough,' Varl said.

Behind them, Willard finished a particularly coarse joke and the laughter of his men echoed down the battlements into the deepening gloom.

GUILDER WORLIN returned to his guild house at nightfall. He was grinning broadly and his face was shiny with the glow of too much joiliq. An extraordinary guild meeting conducted in an armoured bunker under the Commercia had left his personal resources three times the size they had been that dawn. The considerable promethium reserves he had to bargain with had been snapped up greedily in a bidding war between five major guild cadres, and he'd also managed to draw up a resourcing agreement with representatives of Vervun Primary. His pipeline was still drawing fuel into the massive steel bowsers in the Worlin commercial estates on the river. Vannick Hive might be dead, but its legacy lingered on and Worlin was amassing a trade fortune with every drop of it. By the time the war was over, Worlin was assured of a place in the high circle of the Commercia guilds. House Worlin would affect a promotion to the senior echelon of hive trade institutions. Its stock price alone had quadrupled since the First Storm.

He sat in his private office, at a teak-topped desk with built-in pict-plates, and sipped an overfilled glass of joiliq as he reviewed the messages his communicator had collected during the day.

One stopped him in his tracks. It was a notification of enquiry from some nobody called Curth at Inner Hab Collective Medical Hall 67/mv. It wanted to know his whereabouts on the first day of attack. Had he been anywhere near Carriage Station C7/d? There were irregularities that demanded investigation and they were taking statements from anybody who had been in the area at that time. Monitor viewers along the access ramp had recorded him and two of his houseguard crossing that way during the bombardment of the Commercia. The message was signed 'Curth, A.' and copied to an off-worlder medic named Dorden, one of the Imperial Guard.

Worlin realised his hand was shaking and he was slopping joiliq out of the glass. He set it down and sucked the drops off the ball of his thumb.

He checked his weapon was still in the drawer of the desk. This annoyance would need to be dealt with quickly.

THE CHATTER WAS now so persistent that there was no other sign or meaning to the world. Salvador Sondar spasmed gently in his fluid world, gnawing at his lips. The voice of his worthy Ferrozoican cousin Clatch had been whittled away until it simply repeated two words, over and again. A name. A daemonic name.

Sondar was emaciated and weak with hunger. His feeder tubes had long since run dry and he had not the presence of mind to cycle the automated systems to refresh them. Even his meat puppets were forgotten and slowly rotting as they dangled lifelessly from their strings.

A rich smell of decay filled the High Master's chambers.

He was oblivious.

He knew what the chatter wanted. The notion appealed to him, because the chatter made it so appealing.

He couldn't form a coherent thought. He simply listened. Perhaps he would do it… just to shut the chatter up. Any time now.

LARKIN HAD BEEN perfectly still for over an hour. His eye never left the scope-sight. The Spoil-head manufactory around him was quiet and dark, but he was aware of the Vervun

sniper Lotin crouched behind rubble further down the sec-
ond-storey room.

Ten minutes before, Larkin had sensed movement down
on the Spoil. He'd watched for it again and now he saw it: a
brief flash of moonlight on armour.

He retrained his aim. Breathed.

The Zoicans were advancing up the Spoil. They were well-
drilled and as stealthy as any practised insurgency team. It
was clear they had either switched their distinctive ochre
armour for dull, night-fighting kit or had covered the livid
yellow with soot.

He signalled his intelligence to Mkoll over the vox link,
using only half a dozen code words.

Mkoll ordered the Tanith snipers to address and fire when
they had a target. A second later, Ormon delivered the same
command to his own men.

Larkin saw movement again, clearly in the foggy, green
glow of his scope.

He breathed, squared and fired.

The stinging red pulse whipped down the ore slope and a
black-clad figure was thrown up and backwards.

Larkin immediately dipped under the edge of the rubble
and took a new position. He was certain his muzzle flash
had been discreet, but there was no sense in advertising. He
made his new vantage and aimed again, his extended barrel
hidden inside a broken drain-gutter.

Lotin, ten metres away, fired. His lasgun made a loud crack
and even from where he was, Larkin saw the muzzle flash
and cursed.

He heard Lotin complain over the vox-link. He'd missed.

Move, move and re-aim! Larkin willed silently.

Lotin fired again. His whoop of success was quickly cut
short by a perfectly aimed las-round from the Spoil below.
The Zoicans had been watching for a repeat flash.

Lotin toppled back and slumped into the rubble scree on
the floor, his face gone.

So, thought Larkin, *they have capable and careful snipers too.*
This war just got interesting.

* * *

THE NIGHT WAS on them now and the moons, two large and cream and one tiny and livid red, climbed slowly into a purple sky. Rain clouds, black and woolly, chased along the eastern skyline. Distant thunder rolled out in the grasslands.

The air was sultry and unseasonable, and at Hass East Fort, Varl was sweating freely into his black fatigues. The discomfort was made worse by the static build-up generated by the vast Shield behind them, fizzing and crackling in the dark, a glowing hemisphere of energy.

The plating of his lasgun and his bionic arm tingled with electricity. Varl yearned for the threatening storm to break over them and clear the stifling air.

There was a brutal flash from the north-east and then an ear-splitting bang, followed by an impact that threw Varl off his feet. Voices were shouting in the night, alarms were ringing and someone was screaming in agony.

The sky lit up again. Explosions were rippling along the entire stretch of Curtain Wall between Ontabi Gate and the Hass.

Varl got up, blinking. There was no sign of shelling. That had been... mines.

He ran down the parapet, yelling into his vox-link as more explosions shook the wall. Detonating mines meant one thing only: the enemy was right on top of them, close enough to set charges.

Men were milling all around, confused. Equally useless barks of vox-traffic answered Varl. Varl grabbed the wall for support as another explosion went off close by, flame slicking upwards in a tight ball inside the Wall.

Inside the Wall?

'They've penetrated! They've penetrated!' he bellowed, not understanding it but desperate to get the message out. Almost at once, he came under fire. Las-shots flicked the air around him, coming up from the nearest Wall access stair.

Varl returned fire, rallying the Vervun Primary troops nearest to him. Crackling autoguns began to support him. He saw Zoican storm-troops spreading out onto the battlements from the stair access, their ochre armour dulled by dark, tarry stains.

Varl shot down one or two before realising many more were storming the battlement behind him too. How in the name of feth had they got inside?

A huge blast shook him to his knees. An entire section of Hass East collapsed with a roar and brick dust billowed into the sky, underlit by flame. Further detonations sliced through the top of the wall.

Varl saw gun emplacements ripped apart and exploded and he watched as entire sections of wall-defences blew outwards as mines set off ammunition silos and autoloader hoppers.

Like the wrath of a ruthless god, the war had come to Hass East at last.

TWELVE
DARKNESS FALLS

*'What is the strongest weapon of mankind? The god-machines
of the Adeptus Mechanicus? No! The Astartes Legions? No!
The tank? The lasgun? The fist? No to all! Courage
and courage alone stands above them all!'*

— Macharius, Lord Solar, from his writings

DISTANT THUNDER woke Ibram Gaunt from a dreamless
sleep.

His bedroom, part of a small suite of rooms disposed to
him, adjacent to House Command, was dark except for the
dull amber glow of rune sigils on the small codifier by the
desk.

He turned on the lamp and slid off the bed where he had
lain down only a couple of hours before, fully clothed. Sleep
had overtaken him in an instant.

By the light of the lamp, he crossed to the desk, where
stacks of ribbon-bound papers and data-slates were piled up.
He took a sip of last night's wine from a glass on a side table.

The thunder came again. Somewhere, deadened by the
thick walls, an alarm was ringing.

He activated the call stud of the intercom set into the marble facing of the wall, blankly regarding the great framed portrait over the bare grate opposite. Its thick, time-darkened oils portrayed a pompous-looking man in the Vervun Primary uniform of an older age, bedraggled with braid, one foot raised to rest on a pile of human skulls, a scroll in one hand and a power-sword in the other.

When the intercom replied, Gaunt was idly wondering who the subject of the portrait was supposed to be and who the skulls had belonged to.

'Sir?'

'What's going on?'

'Reports of a raid at Ontabi Gate. We're waiting for confirmation.'

'Appraise me swiftly. I have men at Hass East.'

'Of course, sir. There is… a visitor for you.'

Gaunt checked the clock. It was nearly two in the morning. 'Who?'

'He bears the Imperial seal and says you requested him.'

Gaunt sighed and said, 'Allow him in.'

The suite's outer door slid open and Gaunt went into the sitting room to meet his visitor, activating the wall lamps.

A gnarled, elderly man in long, purple robes shuffled in, peering at Gaunt through thick-lensed spectacles. His hair, where it protruded from under his high-crested, red, felt cap, was grey and unruly, and he leaned on an ebony cane. Behind him came a tall, pale young man in grey cleric's coat, laden down with old tomes and sheaves of paper.

'Commissar… Gaunt?' the old man wheezed, studying the officer before him.

'Colonel-commissar, actually. You are?'

'Advocate Cornelius Pater of the Administratum Judiciary. Your request for legal assistance was received this night and Intendant Banefail directed me to attend you with all urgency.'

'I thank the intendant for his alacrity and you for your time.'

The advocate nodded and wheezed his way over to a leather couch, leaving his assistant in the doorway, swaying under the weight of the manuscripts and volumes he carried.

'Set them down on the table,' Gaunt told him. 'You are?'

The man seemed wary of speaking.

'My clerk, Bwelt,' Pater answered for him. 'He will not speak. He is training for junior advocacy and must perforce learn the protocols of question and address. Besides, he knows nothing.'

'How do we undertake this?' Gaunt asked the advocate.

Pater cleared his throat. 'You will review the matter for my benefit – excluding no detail – you will show me any pertinent transcripts and you will furnish me with a glass of fortified wine.'

Gaunt glanced round at Bwelt. 'There's a bottle on the side table in the bedroom. Fetch him a glass.'

Pater refused to speak further until the crystal glass was in his withered hand and the first sip in his mouth. The cane lay across his lap.

Gaunt began. 'An Imperial Guard General – Grizmund of the Narmenian Armour – and four of his staff officers are charged with insubordination. They're being held in the VPHC stockade, pending prosecution by a VPHC court. The charges are spurious. I want them freed and back to duty immediately. I think the matter founders on a formality – the VPHC cannot prosecute Imperial Guard personnel. If there is a crime to answer, it is an Imperial Commissariat matter. I am the highest representative of that authority on Verghast.'

Pater adjusted his spectacles and studied the data-slate Gaunt handed him.

'Hmm… clear-cut enough, I suppose. You're citing Imperial Commissariat Edict 4368b. The VPHC won't like it. Tarrian, in particular, will hate you for it.'

'There's no love lost between us.'

'Bwelt? What is it? You gurn like a fool or a man with chronic gas.'

'It's 4378b, Advocate. The edict is 4378b.' Bwelt's voice was almost a whisper.

'Just so,' Pater said, brushing off the correction and returning his gaze to the slate. 'It may come to court. Tarrian has a miserable record of dragging cases through all the due processes, even if he is bound to lose. To him, there's some satisfaction in prolonging the agony.'

'I want it thrown out before then. We can't be without Grizmund any longer. In the next few days, Vervunhive's future may depend upon skilled armour.'

'Tricky. But the edict is well-precedented. A brief hearing, perhaps at dawn tomorrow, and we should be able to pull the rug out from under the VPHC.' Pater looked up at Gaunt. 'I'll derive satisfaction from that. The VPHC have deemed themselves above Imperial Law for many years. It's been nigh on impossible to practise clean law in the hive. With your prestige involved, we can win.'

'Good. At least we know the VPHC can't act before then. However they argue it, they know an Imperial Commissar must be present for a tribunal to be conducted.'

'Indeed. Even if they press for a court of their own, we can stall them as long as you refuse to participate. Then – Bwelt? Again, you screw up your face! What now?'

Bwelt paused and seemed to choose every word with great care. 'The… tribunal is in session now, advocate. You told me to collate all information relating to this case before we came here and that fact was diarised in the judiciary case-roll.'

'What?'

'Th-they are proceeding… because they have an Imperial commissar present. Commissar Kowle has agreed to represent the Imperial interests and–'

Gaunt's vicious curse shut Bwelt up and made the old man start. Pulling on his jacket, cap and weapon belt, Gaunt reeled off a colourful and descriptive tirade outlining what he would do to Tarrian, Kowle and the entire VPHC in four-letter words.

'Come with me! Now!' he told the advocate and his trembling clerk, then flew out of the room.

AT THE EASTERN edge of the hive, the sky was on fire. From the outer dark of the river bend, enemy shelling had begun to hammer at the damage done to the adamantine Curtain Wall and the ramparts of Hass East Fort by the mines.

Varl stumbled through the firestorm, trying to regroup his men and get them down into the deep-wall bunkers. Zoican assaulters were everywhere. The defenders couldn't fight this.

Varl tried to vox House Command or Tanith control, but the energy flare of the bombardment had scrambled the communication bands.

He got maybe twenty men around him, mostly Ghosts but some Roane and Vervun Primary, and ran them down the tower steps into the bowels of the fort. The stone walls were sweating as the heat of the burning levels above leeched into them. Plaster facings shrivelled and wilted, and the air was oven-hot and hurt the soldiers' lungs. At one point, a shell-fall punched through the corridor twenty metres behind them and passed on through the opposite wall, slicing stone so it dribbled like heated butter. The superheated air that slammed down the hall from the impact flattened them. They met groups of Zoicans and Varl's men cut them apart.

Two levels down, they ran into a stream of nearly sixty Vervun Primary and Roane Deepers with Major Rodyin amongst them. Several had bad burns.

'Where's Willard?' screamed Varl over the klaxons and the explosive hurricane roar.

'Haven't seen him!' barked Rodyin. One lens of his spectacles was crazed and he had a cut on his cheek.

'We have to get the men down! Down lower!' Varl yelled and the two officers began routing the surviving troops down a back staircase as firestorms billowed down the hallways towards them.

'They mined the Curtain Wall! From inside!' Rodyin bellowed as he and Varl pushed man after man past them onto the stairs.

'I know, feth it! How the hell did they get in?'

Rodyin didn't answer.

ON A SECTION of wall below the mauled fort, Corporal Meryn was leading a straggle of panicking troops to cover. Two squads of Ghosts – Brostin, Logris, Nehn and Mkteeg amongst them – pushed forward past him, but there were twenty or more Vervun Primary soldiers stumbling in their wake. Meryn bawled at them, waving his arms, trying to be heard above the shriek of the shelling and the detonations all around. Flames from the fort were reaching a hundred metres into the sky and billows of soot and burning fabric squalled around them. The heat was overwhelming. Somewhere close, a loader full of ammo had caught fire and heated rounds were firing off wildly, spanking off the stonework and cutting zigzag tracer paths in the air.

A shot hit the Vervun Primary trooper nearest to Meryn and exploded his spiked helmet.

There was a flash and some vast cutting beam drawn up outside the Wall swept over them. Meryn saw it and threw himself flat as the inexorable beam raked the parapet at chest height, vaporising the hurrying line of Vervun troopers in a murderous sequence. They simply vanished in turn, obliterated, leaving nothing but clouds of steam and the occasional smouldering boot behind.

The beam swept right over the prone Tanith Corporal, searing the back of his breeches, jacket and head-hair right off. He winced at the low throb of superficial burns, but he was startled to be alive.

He got to his feet, his black fatigues shredded and falling off his body, and stumbled to the nearest stairhead.

HUNDREDS OF MEN – Tanith, Roane and Vervun Primary – fled the Wall fortifications and Ontabi Gate and ran for cover in the streets and habs adjacent to the docks. Enemy shelling and beam-fire were punching clean through the Wall and the fort structure now and blasting into the edges of the worker habs. The Shield, ignited above them, mocked the scene. What good was an energy screen when the enemy was blasting through ceramite and adamantium?

Stretches of the habs were engulfed in flame and thousands of hab-dwellers filled the streets in panic, mingling with the fleeing soldiery, choking the access routes and transits in a panicked stampede. Hass East Fort convulsed and collapsed volcanically, the great hatches of Ontabi Gate melting like ice. A breach had been cut in the Curtain Wall of Vervunhive more terrible and more extensive than any damage done so far, even than at the brutalised Veyveyr Railhead.

AT CROE GATE, the next main fortification down the Curtain Wall from Hass East, some ten kilometres south of Ontabi, the wall troops and observers watched in incredulous horror as beams of destruction and heavy shelling punished the riverside defences. A plume of fire underlit the storm clouds and blazed up into the sky like a rising sun.

General Nash was at Croe Gate still and he dismally voxed the situation to House Command. He urgently requested significant reinforcements to his position. In the wake of a major breach like this, ground forces couldn't be far behind.

As if on cue, one of his spotters reported movement on the Vannick Highway, twenty kilometres north-east. Nash used his magnoculars on heat-see and gazed out at the shimmering, green phantoms of tanks and armoured vehicles, thousands of them, roaming towards Ontabi in a spearhead formation.

'I have contacts! Repeat, I have contacts! At least a thousand mechanised armour units advancing down the Vannick Highway and the surrounding hinterlands! They'll be on top of Hass East in under an hour! Reinforce my position now! I need armour! Lots of bloody armour! House Command! Do you respond? Do you bloody respond?'

AN ALMOST EERIE silence fell across the main auditorium of House Command. Only the desperate chatter of vox-traffic could be heard, reeling out reports of fearful destruction from a thousand different locations.

His face pinched and pale, Marshal Croe looked down at the chart table on the upper level. Hass East was gone. A mass armour force was approaching from the eastern levels. Artillery was beginning to pound Croe Gate and the eastern wall circuit. Zoican troops were assaulting the Spoil and the defences at Veyveyr. Heavy tanks and infantry columns were hitting Sondar Gate and the wall stretches towards Hass Gate and Hass West Fort. Hass West Fort itself was receiving ferocious ranged shelling.

An attack on all fronts. The defences of Vervunhive were already at full stretch and Croe knew this was only the beginning.

'What – what do we do?' stammered Anko, his face as white as his dress uniform. 'Marshal? Marshal Croe? What do we do, Croe? Speak, you bastard!'

Croe struck Anko across his fat mouth and sent him whimpering to the ironwork floor. Croe looked across at Sturm. 'Your thoughts, general?' There was venom and ice in equal parts in Croe's voice.

'I...' Sturm began. He faltered.

'Don't even begin to suggest an evacuation, Sturm, or I'll kill you where you stand. Evacuation is not an option. You were sent here to defend Vervunhive, and that's what you'll do.' He handed Sturm his ducal signet. 'Go to the stockade. Take troops with you. Release Grizmund and set him to command the armour before its strength is wasted. If that bastard Tarrian or any VPHC resists, deal with them. I expect you back at Veyveyr Gate to assume command there as soon as Grizmund is free. We have spent too much time arguing amongst ourselves. Vervunhive lives or dies tonight.'

Sturm nodded stiffly and took the ring. 'Where will you be, marshal?'

'I will take personal command of Sondar Gate. The hive will not die while I yet live.'

THE SHUTTER HATCH of the stockade remained resolutely shut. Gaunt hammered on it with the butt of his bolt pistol, but there was no response. Gaunt, Pater and Bwelt stood pinioned by the floodlights, locked out in the damp cold of Level Sub-40. Captain Daur was with them, bleary and pale with sleep. Gaunt had dragged the liaison officer from his quarters on his way down to the stockade.

Gaunt turned to the advocate, who was wheezing for breath and leaning on his cane after the exertions of the frantic journey down into the bottom of the Spine. 'Don't you have an override, an authorisation?'

Pater held up his badge of office. 'Administratum pass level magenta... but the VPHC are a law to themselves. They have their own lock codes. Besides, colonel-commissar, do you see a keyhole?'

Gaunt pulled off his leather coat and threw it to Bwelt. 'Hold that,' he said bluntly and swung out his chainsword. The weapon whined as he cycled it up to full power.

He stabbed it at the armoured shutter. It rode aside, shrieking, leaving scratch marks and sending broken saw-teeth away in a flurry of sparks. He dug again and sliced into the metal, cutting a jagged slot a few centimetres across before the sword meshed and over-revved. With the sheer force of his upper arms and his shoulders, Gaunt heaved down, snarling a curse out at the top of his lungs, tearing down another few centimetres.

'Sir?' Daur said sharply behind him.

Gaunt spun around, raising the chainsword, in time to see the armoured lift cage descend and clank to rest. The grill-doors squealed open. General Sturm, flanked by Colonel Gilbear and ten Blueblood stormtroops, emerged from the lift car.

'Sturm, don't make this worse by–'

'Oh, shut up, you stupid fool, and put that weapon away,' snapped Sturm. He and his men approached and surrounded the quartet at the shutter. Gilbear was oozing a dreadfully superior smile at Gaunt.

'Get him out of my face, Sturm, or I'll practise what I'm doing to the door on him.'

Gilbear raised his hellgun, but Sturm slapped it aside. 'You know, Gaunt,' Sturm said, 'I almost respect you. I could do with a few men of your passion in my regiment. But still and all, you are a benighted fool and beneath the contempt of civilised men. You've spent too much time with those Tanith savages and – *what are you doing, you old fool?*'

This last remark was directed at Pater, who was carefully and quietly dictating material for Bwelt to set down on his slate.

'Transcribing your words, general, in case the colonel-commissar wishes to press a slander action against you later on.' The old advocate's voice was utterly empty of expression or nuance: a true lawyer. Gaunt laughed out loud.

Sturm looked away from the old man. He held up Croe's ducal signet. 'If you want to get inside, you need one of these.' He pressed it against the centre of the shutter. There was a dull thunk, a noise of servos churning and the shutter, with its chainsword tear, rose.

The group entered and Sturm opened the inner shutter. They passed on into the sodium-lit inner hall of the stockade.

'Marshal Croe has ordered me to release Grizmund. The world is going all to hell above our heads, Gaunt. Zoica assaults on all fronts. It is time to forget all petty bickering.'

Three VPHC troopers ran forward to confront them. One started to ask what they were doing in the stockade. Gilbear and his pointman cut them down with loose, brutal shots.

Gaunt pushed forward past the bodies and kicked open a set of wooden double doors to the left of the inner concourse.

There was a large circular chamber beyond, lit by bracketed wall-lamps with glass chimneys. Grizmund and his officers, hands tied behind their backs and hoods over their heads, stood on a raised dais under spotlights in the centre of the room. Kowle, Tarrian and nine senior VPHC officers sat on a tiered rank of wooden stalls before them, and a dozen VPHC troops with riot-guns lined the walls.

'What the gak is this?' Tarrian roared, getting to his feet.

Sturm held up the ducal signet. 'By order of the marshal himself, this court is overthrown. The prisoners will be freed.'

Kowle rose too. 'The meeting is in session and obeys the edicts of both planetary and Imperial law. We–'

'Shut your damn face, Kowle!' snapped Gaunt. 'The hive is dying above us and you waste your time persecuting good, honest men for the sake of some political point-scoring. You have no idea what real war is, do you, you bastard? You didn't on Balhaut and you don't here!'

Kowle's face went purple with rage, but the furious Tarrian pushed him aside. 'Interference with VPHC proceedings is a capital offence, Gaunt! Your maverick actions won't get you anywhere except to the sharp end of a firing squad detail!'

'Actually, that's not correct,' said Bwelt firmly. 'Imperial Edict 95674, sub-clause 45, states that an Imperial judicial officer, such as a full commissar, may interrupt and foreclose any planetary legal affair without restraint or penalty.'

'You tell him, boy!' cackled Pater.

Gaunt stared at Tarrian. 'Don't push them, Tarrian.'

'Who?'

'Gilbear and the other Bluebloods. Sturm can't control them and I sure as feth can't either. From me, you'll get tough honesty. From them, you'll get a hell-round between the eyes.' Even as he spat the words, Gaunt felt them all crossing an almost imperceptible line. The line between a precarious confrontation and total mayhem.

'Gak you, you wretched off-world scum!' bawled Tarrian as he pulled his autopistol from its holster. Gilbear dropped him with a shot to the chest. Tarrian's body exploded out through the back of the wooden seating.

The VPHC guards surged forward, racking riot-guns and firing. Gaunt saw a Blueblood fly backwards, hit in the shoulder. Sturm was cursing and blasting with his regimental service pistol. The Bluebloods opened up and sprayed the room.

Grizmund and his officers, blind under their hoods, dropped to the floor in terror. Gaunt wrestled the gasping advocate and his stunned clerk to the ground out of harm's way. Daur's laspistol cracked repeatedly.

Point-blank, in the tight confines of the court chamber, Volpone met VPHC head on, hellgun against riot-gun, filling the air with smoke, blood-mist and death.

SALVADOR SONDAR slumped. A dribble of blood-bubbles fluttered from his ear towards the roof of the tank. He gave in. The chatter filled him, eating into his flesh, his blood, his marrow, his mind.

He did what it told him to do.

He deactivated the Shield.

THIRTEEN
THE HARROWING

'Never.'
— Warmaster Slaydo, on being asked under what
circumstances he would signal surrender

THERE WAS A loud, subsonic bang of pressure as the great
Shield collapsed.

Windows blew out all across the hive. The ambient temperature dropped by six whole degrees as the insulation of
the energy dome vanished and the cold of the Verghast night
swept in. The vortex of collapsing air whisked up the vast
smoke banks collected around the Curtain Wall and blew
them into the hive itself like acrid fog. Disconnected energies crackled up out of the great pylon and the anchor
stations and burned themselves out ferociously in the blackness.

A shuddering and terrifying noise drove in across Vervunhive. It was the unified howl of triumph from the millions of
Zoicans outside.

Marshal Croe, majestic in his robes and armour, had just
reached Sondar Gate with his staff retinue, and he stopped

212

in his tracks, gazing up incredulously into the cold dark. His first thought was mechanical failure or even sabotage, but the Shield generators were the most securely guarded installations in the hive, and he had expressly ordered work-teams to inspect them every hour.

This was unthinkable. Inside the ceramite of his freshly donned war armour, Croe felt his heart grow as cold as the night around him. The ungifted powersword of Heironymo Sondar, most valued of all the hive's war-icons, felt heavy and useless in his hand. He caught himself and glanced around. The bannerpoles of his colour-sergeants drooped and fluttered dismally about him.

'Lord marshal?' whispered his adjutant, Major Otte.

'We...' Croe began, his mind racing, frantic but empty. He was torn. He wanted to return to the Main Spine at once and cut to the root of this disaster, get the Shield back on. It was Sondar, he felt it in his blood. That bastard Salvador had finally gone over the edge.

But the immediate fight was here at the hive wall, in the face of the massing foe. His men had seen his arrival and if he turned around now, just as he had arrived, it would destroy their morale.

The silence that had followed the ghastly massed howl of the Zoicans outside, a silence that in truth could only have lasted a few seconds, was lost abruptly as the ear-splitting bombardment resumed. For leagues, the sky behind the towering shadow of the Curtain Wall that rose above him was lit yellow by the flare of colossal assault. Croe saw a section of turret to the west of the gate explode and collapse down into the Square of Marshals in a shower of sparks and rubble.

He took the tower steps two at a time at the head of his retinue, blazing the sacred sword into life, raging out orders to both the men around him and those unseen on the wall-top via his microbead link.

One of those orders, direct and succinct, coded in House Croe battle language, was for the ears of Izak, Croe's personal bodyguard. The big house warrior, clad in maroon body-armour, faltered at the foot of the tower steps and then turned back, curtly acknowledging his lord's command. He ran back across the square to the armoured staff-track that had brought Croe to Sondar Gate, and he steered it away at full throttle towards the Main Spine.

ALARMS AND KLAXONS began to whoop and wail once again. In the refuges and the camps of the Commercia and the other open spaces of the hive, the multitude seethed in panic. They'd seen the Shield fail. They'd fought their way to the security of the hive and now that too was gone.

Stampeding in places, two and a half million refugees began to surge north towards the river, the deluge of their bodies choking the streets. Their vast numbers were quickly swelled by inner hab citizens, worker families and low guilders, who had all, in a brief few seconds, seen their protection from Zoica disappear. In a matter of minutes, the hive was haemorrhaging people, rivers of panicking, screaming civilians, heading in hordes to a river they couldn't hope to cross.

LORD HEYMLIK CHASS looked up from his scriptorium and gazed out of the ogee window. The stylus dropped from his trembling fingers and made a blot of violet ink on the pages of his journal. He got up, his ornamental chair tumbling over onto its back, and he stumbled across to the window, pressing his hands against the lead glass.

'Oh, Salvador,' he said, tears in his eyes, 'what have you done?'

His daughter burst into the room, still dressed in her nightgown, her terrified maids trying to wrap a velvet robe around her. Outside in the hall, House Chass lifeguards were shouting and running to and fro. Lord Chass turned and saw the look of jolted fear and bewilderment in his daughter's eyes.

He took her in his arms.

'The alarms woke me, father. What–'

'Hush. You will be all right, Merity.' He stroked her hair, holding her head tight to his chest.

'Handmaids?'

The women barely curtsied. They were terrified and half-dressed themselves.

'Take my daughter to Shelter aa/6. Do it now.'

'The chamberlain is preparing the house shelter, lord,' said Maid Wholt.

'Forget the house shelter! Escort her now to aa/6 in the sub-levels!'

'A municipal bunker, lord?' gasped Maid Francer.

'Are you both deaf and stupid? The sublevels! Now!'

The maids scurried around, pulling at Merity. She clung on to her father. She was crying so much she couldn't speak.

'Go, daughter of Chass. Go now. I will follow shortly. I beg you, go!'

The maids managed to drag the sobbing girl out of the chamber and away towards the Spine elevators.

'Rudrec!' At Lord Chass's shout, the chief lifeguard appeared in the doorway. He was still buttoning on his ornate body-armour. His weapon was armed and unshrouded. He bowed.

Lord Chass handed him a small, silk satchel. 'Go with my daughter. See she is brought safe to the municipal shelter. No other will do – no other is deep enough. Take this for her: a few private family items. Make sure she gets them.'

Rudrec tucked the satchel inside the body of his flak-mail hauberk. 'It is my duty to escort you too, lord, I–'

'You are a good man, Rudrec. You have served this house well. Serve it again by doing as I order.'

Rudrec paused, his eyes meeting his lord's directly for the first and last time in his life.

'Go!'

Alone now, the hall outside thundering with footsteps and voices, Chass put on his ceremonial robes, his bicorn hat, his shot-silk gloves. He was shaking, but most of that was rage. He put his ducal seal in his coat pocket, pushed the heavy code-signet ring onto his gloved finger, and slid a compact, single-shot bolt pistol with inlaid grips into his gown's inner sleeve. A handful of shells followed it.

Chass strode out into the corridor, stopping three of his lifeguards short. They saluted uncertainly.

'Come with me,' he told them.

LESS THAN FIVE minutes after the Shield vanished, the first Zoican shells began to wound the inner hive. It was as if their artillery, their Earthshakers, their siege mortars, their missile positions had all been ranged ready, waiting.

Wave after wave of shrieking missiles screamed in over the Curtain Wall and hit the central district. Concussive ripples of explosions blew out along block after block, closing arterial routes with rubble, setting fires that blazed through dozens of high-rise habitat structures. Thousands of habbers, either sheltering in their homes or fleeing through the streets, were obliterated or left crippled and helpless.

Siege mortar shells wailed in across Sondar Gate and punctured the stone concourse of the Square of Marshals. Flagstone sections, whizzing like blades, were flung out, decapitating or mashing wall troopers from behind. The distinguished lines of statues edging the square were toppled by the blasts or disintegrated outright.

Mass shelling pounded the manufactories alongside Croe Gate. Swathes of machine shops and warehousing caught fire, and the flames established a firm hold, licking west into the worker habs. Similar shelling, supported by ground-to-ground rockets, began to systematically hammer the habs and manufactories behind Hass West, and the impacts of their fall crept north into the elite sector. Guild holdings and house ordinary estates were flattened and torn apart.

The shelling and the dreadful cutting beams searing Hass East scored a hole a hundred metres wide where the Curtain Wall and the Ontabi Gate had once stood, and as the beams redirected towards the inner habs and the upper stretches of the Curtain, the Zoican armoured column and massed infantry along the Vannick Highway pressed in through the breach. The Zoican land forces made their first entry into Vervunhive proper thirteen minutes after the Shield came down, though the insurgent forces encountered by Sergeant Varl were, by then, well inside the hive.

Long-range shells – some two thousand kilos apiece, launched from railcars drawn up on hasty, makeshift trackways out in the southern grasslands – whistled and whooped as they dropped on the Commercia and the mercantile suburbs. Barter-houses blew out, their rich canopies igniting in sheets of flame as hot as the heart of a star. Shockwaves crumpled others and the massive shells dug vast craters in the rockcrete footing of the hive. Hundreds of thousands of refugees were still pressing to leave the commercial spaces. Most died in the firestorms or were instantly obliterated by the shelling. Some of the craters were five hundred metres across.

Shelling and missile attacks began to hit the vast Main Spine itself. In hundreds of places, the adamantine skin of the city-peak ruptured and holed. Fires burned unchecked through nine or more levels. House Nompherenti, on Level 68, took a direct hit from a massive incendiary rocket and the entire noble lineage was immolated. They died frenzied, tortured deaths amid the furnace of tapestries, furniture and drapes in their exalted court. Lord Nompherenti himself, ablaze from head to foot, ran screaming for a hundred paces and toppled from the raised balcony of his banquet hall. His burning body, streaming a trail of fire like a comet, plunged fifteen hundred metres down onto the roofs of the central district.

General Xance, with a tattered vanguard of seven hundred NorthCol troops, was pushing through the firestorm chaos west of Croe Gate when pinpoint shells began to rip along his straggle of trucks and Chimera troop carriers. Vehicle after vehicle exploded, showering the street with metal debris, ignited ammunition and plumes of gushing fuel. NorthCol troopers fled the convoy to either side, dying in further shell-strikes everywhere they turned. Xance's truck was overturned by a shell that struck the road alongside it. Blacked out for a few seconds, the general found himself lying twisted in a mangle of ruptured wreckage and the bloody remains of his command team. There was a fine, dark drizzle in the air which he realised was a vapour of blood droplets.

He tried to move, but pain gutted him. A transverse-gear rod had disembowelled him. He was half-buried in splintered body parts.

He moved aside a fragment of leg that lay across his chest, coughing blood. Then a limbless torso that still had the NorthCol insignia on its braids. Then a severed arm.

He gazed at it. It was his own.

Shells dropped all around, lighting the space with flashes so bright they burned out his optic nerves. They made no sound, not to him anyway. His eardrums had been punctured by the initial shell strike. Blind and deaf, he could only sense the carnage around by the quaking of the ground and the shockwaves that buffeted at him.

Xance was almost the last of his seven hundred-strong unit to die. He had bled to death, howling in rage, before yet another shell vaporised him.

IN HOUSE COMMAND, Vice Marshal Anko had fallen silent, his voice robbed to hoarse whispers by the screaming orders he had been issuing. He slumped across the great chart table as the command staff hurried around, stunned and helpless.

The chart table made no sense any more. Runes and sigils flicked on and off, unable to keep up with the progress of the assault, wavering as contradictory data pummelled back and forth through the straining codifiers. After a while, it repeated nothing but default setting repeats of house crests.

Anko got up and backed away from the disingenuous table and its silence. He smoothed the front of his white dress uniform, adjusted the waist buckle under the girth of his belly and pulled out his autopistol.

He shot the table eight times for disobedience, then changed clips and shot two of the aides who ran screaming from him. He tried to yell, but his voice was nothing but a feeble rasp.

He ran to the ironwork rail and began to fire indiscriminately down into the lower deck, killing or wounding five more tactical officers and exploding a cogitator unit. VPHC Officer Langana and two servitors tried to wrestle him to the ground. Anko shot Langana through the left eye and emptied the rest of his third clip into the mouth of one of the servitors, blowing the upper part of its head away.

Anko threw off the other servitor and got to his feet. He turned to face the great observation window, fumbling for another clip as the staff fled in panic all around.

He saw the missile plainly. It seemed to him he could even see the checkerboard markings around its nose-cone, though he knew that was impossible, given the speed at which it must have been travelling.

Even the fluting of the exhaust ducts, the rivets in the seams.

The missile entered House Command through the great window, slamming a blizzard of lead-glass inwards with its supersonic bow-wave before striking the rear wall and detonating.

The storm of glass shards stripped Vice Marshal Anko's considerable flesh from his bones a millisecond before the blast destroyed House Command.

A BRACE OF Earthshaker shells struck the great Basilica of the Ecclesiarchy east of the Commercia.

The two-thousand-year-old edifice – which had stood firm through the Settlement Wars, the Colonial Uprising, the Piidestro/Gavunda power struggle and countless bouts of civil unrest and rioting – shattered like glass. The roof was thrown outwards by the multiple blasts and millions of slate tiles showered the area for kilometres around, whizzing down like blades.

Stone walls, two metres thick, were levelled in the deluge of fire, flying buttresses sundering and bursting apart. Precious relics almost as old as the Imperium itself were consumed along with the priesthood. The streets outside were awash with rivers of molten lead from the roof and the windows. Many devotees of the Imperial cult, citizens and clerical brethren alike, who had survived the initial impact hurled themselves into the building's pyre, their faith utterly destroyed.

AT CROE GATE, General Nash tried to reform his beleaguered units and direct them north to the Ontabi breach, even though fierce Zoican attacks battered the gate position.

House Command was offline and there was no coordination of repulse. Nash reckoned correctly he had 1,500 Roane Deepers and 3,500 Vervun Primary troops. He had been waiting for support from the NorthCol and Xance, but he had a sick feeling it wasn't coming. The hammering of the shells was overwhelming.

Nash had been in the infantry since he joined the Guard and he had seen the very worst dog-soldier work it had to offer. In those first few hours of the Great Assault, his command and leadership was unrivalled in Vervunhive. He set a condensing resistance around Croe Gate that shut the invaders out, and he countermarched two thirds of his forces north to Ontabi and the main breach, which was nothing short of overrun.

Nash's Roane Deepers, never the most celebrated regiment of the Imperial Guard, proved their worth that night at the eastern extremities of Vervunhive's Curtain Wall. They met the Zoican infantry pouring into the hive with determined marksmanship and hand-to-hand brutality.

The Deepers, despite their reputation for laziness and an easygoing attitude, stopped the inrush at Ontabi dead for two and a half hours. A thousand Roane – supported by and inspiring the Vervun Primary residue – took down almost 4,500 Zoican troops and nearly a hundred armour elements.

Nash died in a work-hab ruin just before dawn, shot nineteen times as the Zoicans finally broke his last-ditch defence and swarmed into the hive. Falling back, the Roane and Vervun Primary survivors continued to defend, street by street, block by block, as the Zoican force rolled in on them.

AT SONDAR GATE, Zoican stormtroops raised ladders and siege towers to overrun the wall. Marshal Croe had lost count of the ochre-armoured soldiers he had slain by the time a massive death machine shaped much like a vast praying mantis thundered forward out of the night and hooked its huge arms around the towers of the Sondar Gate, ripping them apart. The great mantis-limbs locked and bridging plates extended between them, forming a huge ramp that allowed the Zoican troops to finally overrun the battlements.

Croe fell as the vast limbs destroyed the entire frontage of the gate battlement.

He was still alive in the rubble outside the collapsed gateway when advancing Zoican troops passed in, bayoneting any living bodies they kicked.

Marshal Croe died – broken, covered in dust and unrecognisable – with a Zoican bayonet through his heart.

FOURTEEN
THE IMPERIAL WAY
OF DEATH

'True to the Throne and hard to kill!'
— The battle-pledge of the Volpone Bluebloods

'ENOUGH!' GAUNT SNARLED. The gunfire which had been shaking the martial court died away fitfully. The air reeked of laser discharge, cartridge powder and blood. VPHC corpses littered the floor and the shattered wooden seating ranks. One or two Bluebloods lay amongst them.

The half-dozen or so surviving VPHC officers, some wounded, had been forced into a corner, and Gilbear and his men, high on adrenaline, were about to execute them.

'Hold fire!' Gaunt snapped, moving in front of Gilbear, who glowered with anger-bright eyes and refused to put up his smoking hellgun. 'Hold fire, I said! We came down to break up an illegal tribunal. Let's not make another wrong by taking the law into our own hands!'

'You can dispense it! You're a commissar!' Gilbear growled and his men agreed loudly.

'When there's time – not here. You men, find shackles. Cuff these bastards and lock them in the cells.'

221

'Do as he says, Gilbear,' Sturm said, approaching and holstering his pistol. The Blueblood troopers began to herd the prisoners roughly out of the room.

Gaunt looked around the chamber. Pater sat against the far wall, with Bwelt fanning his pallid face with a scribe-slate. Daur was releasing the Narmenian defendants.

The room was a ruin. Sturm's elite troops had slaughtered more than two thirds of the VPHCers present in a brutal action that had lasted two minutes and had cost them three Bluebloods. Tarrian was dead, his rib-cage blasted open like a burned-out ship's hull.

Gaunt crossed to Kowle. The commissar was sat on one of the lower seating tiers, head bowed, clutching a hell-burn across his right bicep.

'It's the end for you, Kowle. You knew damn well what an abuse of the law this was. I'll personally oversee the avulsion of your career. A public disgrace... for the People's Hero.'

Kowle slowly looked up into Gaunt's dark eyes. He said nothing, as there was nothing left to say.

Gaunt turned away from the disturbing beige eyes. He remembered Balhaut in the early weeks of that campaign. Serving as part of Slaydo's command cadre, he had first encountered Kowle and his wretchedly vicious ways. Gaunt had thought he embodied the very worst aspects of the Commissariat. After one particularly unnecessary punishment detail, when Kowle had had a man flogged to death for wearing the wrong cap-badge, Gaunt had used his influence with the warmaster to have Kowle transferred to duties on the south-west continent, away from the main front. That had been the start of Kowle's career decline, Gaunt realised now, a decline that had led him to the Vervunhive posting. Gaunt couldn't let it go. He turned back.

'You had a chance here, Pius. A chance to make good. You've the strength a commissar needs, you just have... no control. Too busy enjoying the power and prestige of being the chief Imperial commissar to the armies of Verghast.'

'Don't,' whispered Kowle. 'Don't lecture me. Don't use my name like you're my friend. You're frightened of me because I have a strength you lack. It was the same on Balhaut, when you were Slaydo's lap-dog. You thought I would eclipse you, so you used your position to have me sidelined.'

Gaunt opened his mouth in astonishment. Words failed him for a moment. 'Is that what you think? That I reported you to advance my own career?'

'It's what I know.' Kowle got to his feet slowly, wiping flecks of blood from his cheek. 'Actually, I'm almost glad its over for me. I can go to my damnation relishing the knowledge that you've lost here. Vervunhive won't survive now, not with the likes of you and Sturm in charge. You haven't got the balls.'

'Like you, you mean?' Gaunt laughed.

'I would have led this hive to victory. It's a matter of courage, of iron will, of making decisions that may be unpalatable but which serve the greater triumph.'

'I'm just glad that history will never get a chance to prove you wrong, Kowle. Surrender your weapon and rank pins.'

Kowle stood unmoving for a while, then tossed his pistol and insignia onto the floor. Gaunt looked down at them for a moment and then walked away.

'Appraise me of the situation upstairs,' Gaunt said to Sturm. 'When you arrived, you said the hive was under assault.'

'A storm on all fronts. It looked grim, Gaunt.' Sturm refused to make eye contact with the Tanith commissar. 'Marshal Croe was ordering a full deployment to repulse.'

'Sir?'

Gaunt and Sturm looked round. Captain Daur stood nearby, his face alarmingly pale. He held out a data-slate. 'I used the stockade's codifier link to access House Command. I thought you'd want an update and…'

His voice trailed off.

Gaunt took the slate and read it, thumbing the cursor rune to scroll the illuminated data. He could barely believe what he was seeing. The information was already a half-hour old. The Shield was down. Massive assaults and shelling had punished the hive. Zoican forces were already inside the Curtain Wall.

Gaunt looked across at Grizmund and his fellow Narmenians, flexing their freed limbs and sharing a flask of water. He'd come down here on a matter of individual justice and when his back was turned, hell had overtaken Vervunhive.

He almost doubted there'd be anything left to return to now at the surface.

UNDER THE CO-ORDINATED command of Major Rawne and Colonel Corday, the Tanith and Volpone units holding Veyveyr Gate staunchly resisted the massive Zoican push for six hours, hammered by extraordinary levels of shelling. There was no ebb in the heedless advance of Zoican foot troops and the waste ground immediately outside the gate was littered for hundreds of metres around with the enemy dead. Along the ore-work emplacements at the top of the Spoil, Mkoll's marksmen and Ormon's Spoilers held the slag slopes with relentless expertise.

Mkoll voxed Rawne when his ammunition supplies began to dwindle. Both had sent requests to House Command for immediate resupply, but the link was dead, and neither liked the look of the great firestorms seething out of the hive heartland behind them.

Larkin, holding a chimney stack with MkVenner and Domor, had personally taken thirty-nine kills. It was his all-time best in any theatre, but he had neither time nor compunction enough to celebrate. The more he killed, the more the memory of the Zoican's bared face burned in his racing mind.

At the brunt-end of the Veyveyr position, Bragg ran out of rockets for his launcher and discarded it. It was overheating anyway. His autogun jammed after a few shots, so he moved down the trench, keeping his hefty frame lower than the parapet as las-fire hammered in, and he took over a tripod-mounted stubber whose crew had been shot.

As he began to squeeze the brass trigger-pull of the thumping heavy weapon, he saw Feygor spin back and drop nearby. A las-round had hit him in the neck.

Lesp, the field medic attending the trench, scrambled over to Feygor, leaving a gut-shot Volpone who was beyond his help.

'Is he okay?' Bragg yelled.

Lesp fought with the struggling Feygor, clamping wet dressings around the scorched and melted flesh of his neck and trying to clear an airway.

'His trachea is fused! Feth! Help me hold him!'

Bragg fired a last burst or two and then dropped from the stub-nest and ran to Feygor and the slender medic. It took all of his gargantuan strength to hold Feygor down as Lesp worked. The las-hit had cauterised the wound, so there was precious little blood, but the heat had melted the larynx and the windpipe into a gristly knot and Feygor was suffocating.

His eyes were white with pain and fear, and his mouth clacked as he screamed silent curses.

'Feth!' Lesp threw the small, plastic-handled scalpel away in disgust and pulled out his long, silver Tanith knife. He stuck it into Feygor's throat under the blackened mass of the scorched wound and opened a slot in the windpipe big enough to feed a chest-tube down.

Feygor began breathing again, rattling and gurgling through the tube.

Lesp yelled something up at Bragg that a nearby shell-fall drowned out.

'What?'

'We have to get him clear!'

Bragg hoisted Feygor up in his arms without question and began to run with him, back down the lines.

THE TANITH UNITS that had held Veyveyr two nights before pushed south from their temporary mustering yard as soon as the Shield failed. Corbec led them and Sergeant Baffels's platoon was amongst them.

Lacking orders from House Command, Corbec had agreed to move west while Colonel Bulwar's NorthCol forces moved east, hoping to reinforce the Veyveyr and Croe positions.

In tight manufactory enclaves behind the once-proud Veyveyr rail terminal, Corbec's deployment encountered crossfire from the west. Corbec realised in horror that while Veyveyr might be sound, the enemy were pouring in through Sondar Gate unstaunched. He set up a scarifying resistance in a factory structure called Guild Githran Agricultural and he tried to vox his situation to Rawne or Corday.

Corday eventually responded. It took a while for Corbec to convince him that enemy forces, already in the inner hive, were in danger of encircling the solid Veyveyr defence.

THEY CHOSE A window each, coughing in the dust that the bombardment was shaking up from the old floor boards.

Milo saw las-rounds punching through the fibre-board sidings of the broken building, and he heard the grunt-gasp of flamers. The enemy was right outside.

From the windows, under Baffels's direction, they fired at will. It was difficult to see what they were hitting. Filain and Tokar both yowled out victory whoops as they guessed they brought Zoicans down.

Rhys, one window down from Milo, stopped firing and sagged as if very tired.

Milo pulled round and called out to him, stopping short when he saw the bloodless las-hole in Rhys's forehead.

A falling shell blew out a silo nearby and the building shook.

Colonel Corbec's voice came over the microbead link, calm and stern.

'This is the one, boys. Do it right, or die here.'

Milo loaded a fresh cell and joined his platoon in blasting from the chewed window holes.

MORE THAN THREE hundred Tanith were still resting, off-guard, in their makeshift chem-plant billet when the Shield came down and the onslaught began. Sergeant Bray, the ranking officer, had them all dress and arm at once, and he voxed House Command for instructions.

House Command was dead. Bray found he couldn't reach Corbec, Rawne or Gaunt – or any military authorities. What vox-links were still live were awash with mindless panic or the insidious chatter broadcasts of the enemy.

Bray made a command decision, the biggest he'd ever made in his career. He pulled the Tanith under his charge back from the billets and had them dig in amongst the rubble wastelands behind, wastelands created in the first bombardment at the start of the war.

It was an informed, judicious command. Gaunt had taught tactics thoroughly and Bray had listened. A move forward, towards Sondar Gate and the Square of Marshals three kilometres south, would have been foolhardy given the lack of solid intelligence. Staying put would have left them in a wide, warehouse sector difficult to secure or defend.

The rubble wastes played directly to the Ghosts' strengths. Here they could dig in, cover themselves and form a solid front.

As if to confirm Bray's decision, mortar fire levelled the chem-plant billets twenty minutes after the Tanith had withdrawn. Advance storm-units of Zoican infantry crossed into the wasteland half an hour later and were cut down by the well-defended Ghosts. In the following hours, Bray's men engaged and held off over two thousand ochre-clad troops and began to form a line of resistance that stymied the Zoican push in from Sondar Gate.

Then Zoican tanks began to arrive, trundling up through the blasted arterial roads adjoining the Square of Marshals. They were light, fast machines built for infantry support, ochre-drab and covered with netting, with turrets set back on the main hull, mounting pairs of small-calibre cannons. Bray had thoughtfully removed all the rocket grenades and launchers from the billet stockpile, and his men began to hunt tanks in the jagged piles of the wasteland, leaving their lasrifles in foxholes so they could carry, aim and load the rocket tubes. In three hours of intense fighting, they destroyed twenty machines. The slipways off the arterials were ablaze with crackling tank hulls by the time heavier armour units – massive main battle-tanks and super-heavy self-propelled guns – began to roll and clank up into the chem-district.

Caffran braced against the kick of the rocket launcher and banged off a projectile grenade that he swore went directly down the fat barrel of an approaching siege tank, blowing the turret clean off. Dust and debris winnowed back over his position, and he scrambled around to reach another foxhole, Trooper Trygg running with him with the belt of rockets.

Caffran could hear Bray yelling commands nearby.

He slipped into a drain culvert and sloshed along through the ankle-deep muck. Trygg was saying something behind him, but Caffran wasn't really listening.

It was beginning to rain. With the Shield down, the inner habs were exposed to the downpour. The wasteland became a quagmire of oily mud in under a quarter of an hour. Caffran reached the ruins of a habitat and searched for a good firing point. A hundred metres away, Tanith launchers barked and spat rockets at the rumbling Zoican advance. Every few moments, there would be a plangent thump and another tank round would scream overhead.

Caffran was wet through. The rainfall was cutting visibility to thirty metres. He clambered up on the scorched wreck of an old armchair and hoisted himself up into an upper window space, from which he could get a good view of the rubble waste outside.

'Toss me a few live ones!' he called down to Trygg.

Trygg made a sound like a scalded cat and fell, severed at the waist. Ochre-armoured stormtroops flooded into the ruin below Caffran, firing wildly. A shot hit Trugg's belt of grenades and the blast threw Caffran clear of the building shell and onto the rubble outside.

Caffran clawed his way upright as Zoicans rushed him from three sides. Pulling out his Tanith dagger, he plunged it through the eyeslit of the nearest. He clubbed the next down with his rocket tube.

Another shot at him and missed.

Caffran rolled away, firing his loaded rocket launcher. The rocket hit the Zoican in the gut, lifted him twenty metres into the air and blew him apart.

There was a crack of las-fire and a Zoican that Caffran hadn't seen dropped dead behind him.

He glanced about.

Holding the laspistol Caffran had given her as a gift, Tona Criid crept out of cover. She turned once, killing another Zoican with a double shot.

Caffran grabbed her by the hand and they ran into the cover of a nearby hab as dozens more Zoican troopers advanced, firing as they came.

In the shadows of the hab ruin, Caffran looked at her, one soot-smeared face mirrored by the other.

'Caffran,' he said.

'Criid,' she replied.

The Zoicans were right outside, firing into the ruins.

'Good to know you,' he said.

THE CAGE ELEVATORS carried them up as far as Level Sub-6 before the power in the Low Spine failed and the cars ground to a screeching halt. Soot and dust trickled and fluttered down the echoing shaft from above.

They exited the lifts on their bellies, crawling out through grille-doors that had half missed the next floor, and they found themselves in a poorly lit access corridor between water treatment plants.

Gaunt and Bwelt had to pull Pater bodily out of the lift car and onto the floor. The old man was panting and refused to go on.

Gilbear and his troops had fanned down the hallway, guns ready. Daur had guard of Kowle and Sturm was trying to light a shredded stub-end of cigar. Grizmund and his officers were taut and attentive, armed with shotguns they had taken from the VPHC dead.

'Where are we?' Gaunt asked Bwelt.

'Level Sub-6. An underhive section, actually.'

Gaunt nodded. 'We need a staircase access.'

Down the damp hallway, one of Gilbear's men cried out he'd found a stepwell.

'Stay with him and move him on when he's able,' Gaunt told Bwelt, indicating the ailing Pater.

He crossed to Grizmund. 'As soon as we reach the surface, I need you to rejoin your units.'

Grizmund nodded. 'I'll do my best. Once I've got to them, what channel should we use?'

'Ten ninety gamma,' Gaunt replied. It was the old Hyrkan wavelength. 'I'm heading up-Spine to try to get the Shield back on. Use that channel to co-ordinate. Code phrase is "Uncle Dercius".'

'Uncle Dercius?'

'Just remember it, okay?'

Grizmund nodded again. 'Sure. And I won't forget your efforts today, colonel-commissar.'

'Get out there and prove my belief in you,' Gaunt snarled. 'I need the Narmenian armour at full strength if I'm going to hold this place.'

General Grizmund and his men pushed on past and hurried up the stairs.

'Sounds like you've taken command, Gaunt,' Sturm said snidely.

Gaunt turned to him. 'In the absence of other command voices…'

Sturm's face lost its smile and its colour.

'I'm still ranking Guard commander here, Ibram Gaunt. Or had you forgotten?'

'It's been so long since you issued an order, Noches Sturm, I probably have.'

The two men faced each other in the low, musty basement corridor. Gaunt wasn't backing down now.

'We have no choice, my dear colonel-commissar: a full tactical retreat. Vervunhive is lost. These things happen. You get used to it.'

'Maybe you do. Maybe you've had more experience in running away than me.'

'You low-life swine!' Gilbear rasped, stomping forward.

Gaunt punched him in the face, dropping him to the floor.

'Get up and get used to me, Gilbear. We've got a fething heavy task ahead of us, and I need the best the Volpone can muster.'

The Volpone troops were massing around them and even Pater had got up onto his feet for a better view.

'The Shield must be turned back on. It's a priority. We've got to get up into the top of the hive and effect that. Don't fight me here. There'll be more than enough fighting to go around later.'

Gaunt reached down with his hand to pull Gilbear up. The big Blueblood hesitated and then accepted the grip.

Gaunt pulled Gilbear right up to his face, nose to nose.

'So let's go see what kind of soldier you are, colonel,' the Blueblood said.

* * *

THEY CLIMBED THE dim stairs as far as Level Low-2 and then found a set of cargo lifts still supplied with power. The massive Spine shuddered around them, pummelled from the outside by the enemy.

Crowded into a lift car, the Volpone checked weapons under Gilbear's supervision. Sturm stood aside, silent. Gaunt crossed to Daur and his prisoner.

'Ban?'

'Sir?'

'I need schematics of the upper Spine. Anything you can get.'

Ban Daur nodded and began to resource data via his slate.

'Salvador Sondar has total control of the Shield mechanism,' said Kowle suddenly. 'He exists on Level Top-700. His palace is protected by obsidian-grade security.'

Gaunt looked at Kowle bemused.

'It sounded for a moment there like you were trying to help, Pius.'

Kowle spat on the floor. 'I don't really want to die, Ibram. I know this hive. I know its workings. I'd be the callous bastard you think I am if I didn't offer my knowledge.'

'Go on,' said Gaunt cautiously.

'Salvador Sondar has been borderline mad since I first met him. He's a recluse, preferring to spend his time in an awareness tank in his chambers. Yet he has absolute control of the hive defences. They're hard-wired into his brain. If you intend to turn the Shield back on, you'll have to deal with the High Master himself.'

The lift cage lurched as a shockwave passed through the Spine. Gaunt looked out of the cage door as they ascended and he saw a flickering procession of empty halls, then some thick with screaming habbers beating on the cage bars. They rose past fire-black levels and ones where twisted skeletons, baked dry by the heat of incendiaries, clawed at the lift doors.

One level was ablaze and they flinched as they passed up by its flames.

Daur handed Gaunt the slate with a plan of the upper Spine loaded onto it.

Another four hundred levels, Gaunt thought, watching the lights on the lift's indicator panel, and the High Master and I will have ourselves a reckoning.

LORD CHASS AND his three bodyguards had reached Level Top-700 and forced their way in through the powerless blast doors.

Shots came their way the moment they emerged, killing one of the bodyguards outright with a head wound.

Chass pulled out his gun and fired it as his remaining bodyguards unshrouded their hand-cannons and blasted tracer strings down the plush, marble-walled atrium.

A las-round hit Lord Chass in the left knee and dropped him face down onto the carpet. The pain was extraordinary, but he didn't cry out. His bodyguards ran to him and were both cut down by sprays of las-fire.

His lifeblood was pumping away through his leg wound. Lord Chass knew he was going to die very soon.

He crawled forward, a few centimetres at a time, soaking the priceless carpet with his blood. He couldn't see who or what was firing at him. The atrium was made of green cipolin stone and decorated with House Sondar banners. Light globes hung on chains from the high roof. At the atrium's far end, a wide arch led through into the audience hall, the Sondar chapel and the private residence.

He flopped over behind a sandstone jardinière and loaded a fresh shell into his compact handgun. He thought about reaching for one of the fallen bodyguards' laspistols, but they were exposed in the open, and Sondar's unseen protectors were raking the carpeted floor with steady fire.

Then the firing stopped. Three meat puppets swung into view in the archway: a cloaked female, a naked youth covered in gold body-paint, and something rank and emaciated that was only vaguely human any more. All lolled wretchedly, eyes vacant, lasrifles wired into their hands. They came unsteadily down the atrium, wobbling on the feed-tubes and wires that played out from a recessed trackway in the ceiling. Though their eyes didn't move, they seemed to sense him. Chass knew they were guided by heat and motion systems wired into the palace walls. They fired again, blowing chunks off the jardiniere and hitting Chass in the foot and shin of his already wounded leg. He fired his single-shot piece and the heavy round took the youth's head off. It continued to advance and shoot.

A sudden burst of autogun fire licked down the atrium and tore the puppets to pieces, leaving nothing but a few shreds of flesh trailing from the wires.

Four men came down the hall from the main entrance. Chass knew their maroon body-glove armour made them guards from Croe's personal retinue. Their leader was Isak. He knelt by Lord Chass as his companions moved on to secure the archway. Isak bowed his respect to the nobleman, then reached into his harness pouches for field dressings.

'The marshal sent you?'

'I am instructed to take any action necessary to restore the Shield, lord. That includes the suppression of High Master Sondar and his forces.'

At last Croe is acting with the same purpose as me, thought Chass. He felt no pain from Isak's work on his wounds. He was cold and everything seemed distant. 'Help me up,' he told the bodyguard. 'You'll need the geno-print of a noble to activate the Shield systems.'

Isak nodded and hoisted Lord Chass up by the armpits, as if he was as light as a feather. From beyond the arch came the sounds of renewed gunfire.

In the colonnade beyond the atrium – a long cloister of wooden beams and inlaid upper balconies with a roof of stained glass – Isak's men had encountered more servitor puppets. Some were appearing in the balcony galleries, others moving down the open length of the cloister. The House Croe guardsmen were pinned near the archway.

Lord Chass, leaning heavily on Isak for support, noticed a smell, a spicy taint that stung his nostrils, sweeter and more subtle than the sharp pungency of the discharged weapons. 'What is that smell?' he whispered, half to himself.

'Chaos,' Ibram Gaunt said.

Chass and Isak looked round from the archway where they were sheltering and saw Gaunt leading the team of Blueblood elite down the atrium with silent precision. Daur,

Kowle and Sturm were at the back of the line, Gilbear along-side the commissar. All weapons were drawn.

'It seems we share a mission,' Gaunt said dryly. He gestured to Gilbear and the Volpone moved three of his seven troopers round to cover the far side of the arch. In a moment, they were adding the considerable force of their hellguns to the dispute.

'Sic semper tyrannis,' Chass whispered and smiled at Gaunt. 'I knew you would serve Vervunhive with true valour…'

His voice was faint. Gaunt looked at the wounds that mauled the nobleman's leg. Isak had applied a tourniquet high up on the thigh, but his robes were soaked with blood.

Gaunt caught Isak's look. They both knew how close to death Chass was.

Chass knew it too. 'I'd like to see us victorious before my passing, colonel-commissar.'

Gaunt nodded. He shouted to the Volpone. 'Let's not waste any more time! Take the chamber now!'

Gilbear looked across and tapped the grenade launcher mounted under his hellgun's barrel with a predatory grin. 'Permission?'

'Given!' said Gaunt. 'Tell your men in there to duck and cover!' he told Isak and the bodyguard snarled through his microbead.

Gilbear and one of his point men bellowed the Volpone battle-pledge at the tops of their lungs as they launched grenade after grenade in through the arch. The launcher mechanisms thumped and clacked as they pumped them.

The blast, a series of explosions piled on top of one another, ripped back down the colonnade and blew out the galleries and the glass roof. Debris and ash washed back through the arch.

Before the smoke even began to clear, the Volpone stormed the room, yelling and firing. Whatever else he thought about them, Gaunt had to give the Bluebloods their due. They were finely trained, ruthlessly effective heavy troops. He'd seen their worth on Monthax. Now they were proving it again.

With his bolt pistol and chainsword drawn, Gaunt ploughed into the colonnade after them, followed by Isak and the Croe guards, with Daur and Sturm left to assist Chass. Kowle simply wandered along behind.

The place was a ruin. Dismembered or support-severed servitors littered the wooden wreckage. One puppet, which had been standing on a now-collapsed balcony, swung above their heads like a corpse in a gibbet.

The Bluebloods fanned out, moving down side halls, exchanging fire with lifeless defenders.

'Which way?' Gaunt asked Chass, but the wounded man was only semi-conscious.

'The audience hall is down to the left,' Isak said.

'What did you mean, the smell was Chaos?' asked Chass suddenly swimming awake.

'The filth that corrupted Ferrozoica is here. It's got inside House Sondar, permeating everything. Probably why the bastard turned the Shield off. Kowle said Sondar was wired directly into the hive's systems. I'd lay bets that's how it got to him, infecting him like a disease.'

'You mean the hive systems are corrupted too?'

'No – but Sondar has listened to lies that have come directly into his mind. The fact they say he was mad to begin with can't help.' He checked ahead and saw the large double-doors to the chamber. 'With me!' Gaunt yelled, his chainsword buzzing murderously. The Volpone fireteam formed up behind him and had to run to keep up.

Gaunt burst through the doors and clashed directly with more servitor puppets in the entrance lobby. His chainsword cut through support wires and flesh. He hacked clear of their murderous attentions as Gilbear and his men came in behind, finishing the rest.

The audience chamber was large and softly lit. The air was warm and now so much thicker with the taint-smell. Muslin wall drapes twitched in the ventilator breeze. On the far side of the room sat a large, iron tank – its shell rich with verdigris from its brass fittings – fashioned with a single, baleful porthole in the front.

'I see you. What are you?' asked an electronic voice that came from all around.

Gaunt walked towards the awareness tank. 'I am the agency of Imperial authority on this world.'

'I am the authority here,' said the voice. 'I am the High Master of Vervunhive. You are nothing. I see you and you are nothing. Begone.'

'Salvador Sondar – if you still answer to that name – your power is ended. In the name of the God-Emperor of Mankind and for the continued welfare of this subject planet, I order you to surrender yourself to the Imperial Guard.'

'Surrender?'

'Do it. You will not enjoy the alternative.'

'You have nothing that threatens me. Nothing to tempt me. Heritor Asphodel has promised me this world in total-ity. The chatter has told me this.'

'Asphodel is the spawn of the warp, and his promises are meaningless. I give you one last chance to comply.'

'And I give you this.'

The servitor came into the room through a doorway con-cealed by muslin drapes. Sondar's macabre fascination with his meat-toys was infamous in the noble houses, and many efforts had been made to curtail his surgical whims and clone-farming over the years.

This thing was far more than that, more even than the deluded creation of a mad flesh-engineer. The insanity of the warp was in it: eighteen hundred kilos of scarred meat and gristle, bigger than a Hyrkan antlerdon, a jigsaw of human parts fused into the carcass of a wild auroch from the grass-lands. Limbs twisted and writhed around it, some human with grasping hands, some animal, some wet, glistening pseudopods like the muscular feet of giant molluscs. The massive head was an eyeless mouth full of needle teeth, that smacked slackly and gurgled. The donor auroch's vast horns swept outwards from the low skull crest. A multitude of cables, feeds and wires suspended it, but unlike the other meat puppets, this thing moved of its own volition, pawing and stamping the soft carpet, writhing and pulsing.

The smell was overwhelming.

Gilbear and the Volpone backed off a few paces in aston-ishment. Sturm cried out in horror and one of the House Croe bodyguards turned and ran.

The meat-beast came for them, moving with a speed and fluidity that seemed impossible for something so vast. It howled as it came, a piercing, sibilant shriek of rage. Gaunt leapt aside and was knocked over by a flailing pseudopod. The slime burned through his leather coat where it touched.

Gilbear fired twice, blowing open holes in the lower belly of the thing. These issued spurts of stagnant pus onto the carpet. Then the Blueblood colonel was flying through the air, tossed aside by a twist of the huge horns.

Backing frantically, the other Volpone fired wildly. Blubbery, wet punctures appeared in the creature's flank, some oozing filmy fluid, others erupting with sprays of tissue and watery blood. A cloned human arm was blown right off and lay twitching on the ground.

A screaming Volpone was hoisted into the air and shaken violently to death, impaled through the chest on one of the horns. Another was crushed under the meat-beast's bulk, leaving a trampled mess of blood, bone and broken armour pressed into the carpet. Grasping limbs and curling pseudopods caught hold of a third and began to pull him apart, slowly and inexorably. His agonised wailing drowned out the meat-beast's keening roar.

Gaunt scrambled up, dazed, and shot the clasped Volpone through the head to end his drawn-out death. He fired again and again, until the sickle clip of his bolt gun was empty, the powerful close-range shots blowing chunks of raw meat and translucent fat out of the creature. Blood and ichor spurted from the wounds.

The monster wheeled round at Gaunt, wailing. Head down, it charged him and the horns, one still decorated with the limp corpse of the Volpone soldier, smashed into the chamber wall, gouging the ceramite facing. Gaunt dived aside, swinging his chainsword round with both hands. The purring blade sliced through the top of the skull and chopped one of the horns off. Then Gaunt was rolling away again, trying to stay out of reach of the biting maw that chased after him, drooling spittle. With its attention on Gaunt, the meat-beast had turned away from the remaining Volpone and they resumed firing, ripping into the thing's hindquarters but apparently doing nothing to slow it down.

Gaunt knew that daemonic force pulsed inside the beast, a life-energy that animated it beyond any considerations of physical function. If there was a brain or any vital organs at all, they would be useless as targets. The thing wasn't alive in any real sense. It couldn't be killed the way a human could be killed.

Daur was firing too now, as were the remaining House Croe guards, and Kowle had scooped up the weapon of a dead Volpone, adding his own shots to the fight. Chass was slumped limply in a corner, unconscious. There was no sign of Sturm.

Gaunt hacked into the thing again, ripping through ribs. His chainsword was matted and clogged with the beast's fluid and tissue, and steam was rising from the blade where it was being eaten away by the toxic deposits.

Gaunt cursed. Delane Oktar, his old mentor, now long dead, had given him that sword on Darendara, right at the start of his career, when he had still been green and eager. He had carried it ever since, all through his time with the Hyrkans until his service under Slaydo at Balhaut, and beyond to Tanith and every victory of his beloved Ghosts. Its destruction hurt him more than he could say. It took the past from him, took his memories and victories away.

He jammed the dying blade into the beast's shoulder, kicking out a wash of toxic blood and bone chips. Wedged fast, the sword disintegrated and the power unit in the grip exploded. Gaunt was thrown backwards.

The thing lunged down after him, biting at his kicking boots as he scrambled backwards on his backside. Isak and two of the Volpone surged forward, firing to cover him and draw the thing away. As it wheeled on them, Gaunt found himself dragged clear. It was Gilbear. Blood flecked the front of his armaplas chestplate and there was rage in his eyes. He hauled Gaunt back towards the green bulk of the iron tank.

Another Volpone was caught by the beast's clamping jaws and shredded by savage bites of its teeth. The walls and drapes of the audience hall were sprayed heavily with blood now.

The creature turned on Isak, snapping off his head and shoulders with one crushing bite. His body fell beneath its clawing, stamping legs.

'A gun!' Gaunt yelled to Gilbear.

'Lost mine!' replied the Blueblood colonel, referring to the hellgun that had been tossed aside with him. He had out his powerful sidearm, a long-barrelled autogun plated with chrome. He put shell after shell into the creature's neck.

Gaunt scrambled forward, retrieving his boltgun, and slammed a fresh clip into the receiver. He would kill this thing before he died. By the ghosts of Tanith, he would.

The meat-beast slew one of the remaining Croe guards and flew at Daur and Kowle, trailing meat and blood from its mouth. Both men stood their ground, exhibiting levels of bravery as high as any Gaunt had ever witnessed. They pumped relentless shots into the approaching nightmare. Nothing slowed it.

Hastily they both dived aside. Daur rolled into Chass's crumpled body and frantically tried to reload.

Kowle landed on a Volpone corpse. The creature headed for him.

'Get clear!' Gaunt bellowed. Kowle was apparently fumbling with the dead Blueblood's equipment belts. Gaunt and Gilbear fired again in a futile attempt to drop the thing.

At the final moment, Kowle turned and rose. He faced the rushing beast with his arms held out. He was clutching a canvas web of grenades. The meat-beast bit his arms off at the elbows and Kowle tumbled backwards, blood jetting from the stumps. He didn't make a sound.

The creature convulsed, retched and exploded from within. Its massive torso blew out in a rush of flame and body matter. A spinning section of rib, thrown out by the blast, stuck quivering into the wall near Gaunt like a spear. Flames gouted out of the huge mouth.

The beast collapsed onto the floor, pulling feed lines and wires out of the ceiling. The pool of stinking fluid spreading beneath it began to burn the carpet away.

With Gilbear behind him, Gaunt crossed to the carcass. 'We need a flamer. We need to burn this abomination as soon as possible.'

'Yes, colonel-commissar,' Gilbear answered, turning to the surviving Volpone.

Kowle, on his back in a widening circle of blood, was still alive. Gaunt knelt beside him, soaking his knees.

'Said... you... didn't have the balls,' Kowle said, his voice so weak it was barely audible.

Gaunt had no words for him.

'Envy you...'

'What?' Gaunt asked, bending closer.

'Balhaut... you were there at the victory, with the warmaster. I envy you. I would have given... everything to share in that...'

'Pius, you–'

'Shut up, Gaunt... not interested in... anything you have to say to me. You took my honour away, you... ruined me. I hope the Emperor... will forgive you for robbing Terra of a... great leader like me...'

Gaunt shook his head. He reached into his pocket and pulled out Kowle's rank studs and cap badge. Carefully and deferentially, he pinned them back in place. Kowle seemed to notice what Gaunt was doing, though his eyes were wide and dilated, and the blood was now merely trickling from his ghastly stumps.

'Goodbye, commissar. You gave your best.'

Gaunt saluted, a sharp, smart gesture he hadn't made in a long time.

Kowle smiled, barely, then died.

GAUNT GOT UP from the corpse of the People's Hero and crossed to the awareness tank. 'Get Lord Chass up. Get the Shield back on,' he said to Daur sourly.

Daur nodded and began to raise the feeble Verghast noble.

Gilbear joined Gaunt at the tank. They looked down at the thickly glazed porthole.

'Come up with a way for me to pay you back as soon as you can,' Gaunt said, not looking round at the Volpone.

'What?'

'You pulled me clear of the beast. I don't want to be in the debt of a high-caste bastard like you any longer than I have to be.'

Gilbear grinned. 'I think I may have underestimated you, Gaunt. I had no idea you were such an arrogant swine.'

Gaunt glanced round. It would take another Ibram Gaunt and a whole different universe for there to be any trust or comradeship between him and Gilbear. But for now, in the thick of this nightmare, Gaunt couldn't help respecting the soldier, for that was what he was: a devoted soldier of the God-Emperor, just like Gaunt. They didn't have to like each other to make it work. A measure of understanding and honour between them was enough.

Gaunt bent down to look through the port glass, and Gilbear did likewise at his side.

Through the fog of murky, phlogistic fluid, they could just make out a frail, naked body, withered and corrupted, drifting inside the tank, its skull linked to wires and cables that curled upwards to the roof.

'We can call it quits if you let me finish this,' said Gilbear.

'He's all yours,' said Gaunt.

Gilbear smirked, arming the hellgun he had just retrieved. 'What about your due process? What about taking the law into your own hands?' he asked sarcastically.

'I can dispense it. I'm a commissar. That's what you said, wasn't it?'

Gilbear nodded and fired two shots through the portal window. Filthy green water rushed out in torrents, flooding the floor. Steam rose from it.

Gilbear leaned down once the force of the outrush slackened, and he watched the twitching, spasming form of the High Master trembling in his draining tank. He fired a grenade in through the broken port and turned away.

A dull crump and the sheet of steam that billowed out of the window hole marked the end of Salvadore Sondar, High Master of Vervunhive.

Daur had carried Chass over to the brass console in the wall and he helped the enfeebled lord punch in the override settings. Chass mumbled the codes to Daur just in time. The noble was dead by the time Gaunt reached them.

The runic sigils on the console plate asked for a noble geno-print. Gaunt simply lifted one of Chass's limp hands and pressed it to the reader-slate.

'Sic semper tyrannis, Lord Chass,' Gaunt whispered.

'Did he see victory, sir?' asked Daur.

'He saw enough. We'll find out if this is a victory or not.'

Automated systems cycled and whirred. Deep in the bow-els of Vervunhive, field batteries throbbed. The pylon crackled and the anchor stations that remained intact raised their masts.

With a resounding, fulminating crack and a reek of ozone, the Shield was reignited.

Ibram Gaunt left the audience hall of House Sondar and walked up onto an enclosed roof terrace that overlooked the entire hive. Fires burned below, thousands of them, and streaks of constant shelling lit the air. The Shield overhead glowed and crackled.

Now the Last Ditch had begun.

FIFTEEN
DAY THIRTY-FIVE

'Target and deny! By our deaths shall they know us!'
— General Coron Grizmund, at the start
of the Narmenian counterattack

OVERNIGHT, BETWEEN the thirty-fourth and thirty-fifth days of the war, Vervunhive had come to the brink of destruction. Now, like a clenching muscle, the Imperial forces tightened and backed through the inner habs and elite sectors, resisting the encircling foe. For all their massive numbers, the Zoicans could only attack by land with the Shield reactivated. The dense streets, city blocks, habitats and thoroughfares favoured the defenders, who could dig in and hold the Zoican push.

Corday and Rawne dragged their forces back from Veyveyr into the worker habs a bare half hour before they could be encircled by enemy forces reaching upwards from Sondar Gate. NorthCol and Vervun Primary battalions pushed west to support the retreating Roane, still resisting street by street as they fell back from the Croe and Ontabi Gates. Colonel Bulwar had nominal command of that front.

Five thousand Vervun Primary troopers under Captain Cargin still held the Hass West Fort fast, though looping columns of Zoican infantry were beginning to bracket them through the chemical plant district.

Throughout the inner habs south of the Main Spine, Imperial units tried to stem the advance. Sergeant Bray directed the Tanith in the wastes north of the chem district. Volpone, NorthCol and Vervun Primary sections strung out to his east, where Corbec's remaining Tanith and a force of Roane Deepers under Major Relf had consolidated a wide area of manufactories.

The fighting there was thick, as thick as any in the hive. Guild Githran Agricultural had been held since the small hours of the morning. Corbec's platoons had precious little ammo left and no food. They had been fighting all-out for six hours straight. Enemy flamer-tanks holding the north-south arterial highway tightly were preventing the Tanith from obtaining munitions from the better-provided Roane, just half a kilometre away to the east. The Tanith were forced to scavenge for ammo, running out of cover in twos and threes to loot the fallen Zoicans. At least with the Shield reactivated, they were spared the worst of the shelling, though the enemy armour and field pieces now set up inside the Shield dome were unrelenting.

Baffels whistled a command, and Milo, Neskon and Cocoer dashed from the cover of a derelict abattoir and scurried towards a burning textile mill. Dremmond covered their run with spurts from his flamer. The three Tanith had bayonets fixed. They were all out of ammo, except Cocoer, who had only a handful of shots left.

Six Zoicans lay dead behind the rear wall of the mill. The trio descended on them and stripped them of las-cells. Each corpse had six or seven as well as musette bags filled with stick grenades.

Milo looked up. The air throbbed with las-fire and though the Shield had shut out the rain, the ground was slick and muddy. He pulled Neskon down into cover. Enemy fire chased down the mill wall, cracking holes in the plaster facing and puffing out brick dust.

A fireteam of Zoican stormtroopers was advancing through the ruins to the west of the mill. Cocoer now had a fresh clip in his Guard-issue weapon and he fired twice, missing his targets but causing the Zoicans to duck and cover.

'We're pinned!' Milo hissed into his microbead.

'Stay down,' the voice of Sergeant Baffels crackled back.

They did. Neskon poked his head up long enough to be shot at.

'Come on, Baffels!' Milo added urgently. They could hear the crunching footfalls of the Zoicans barely ten paces from their cover.

'Just another moment,' Baffels reassured his friend.

Loud las-shots cracked over the ruins, single shots, high-powered.

'You're clear! Go!' Baffels squawked.

Milo led the way, Neskon and Cocoer on his heels. He got a glimpse of the Zoicans behind him, sprawled dead from clean head-shots.

Milo smiled.

The trio slid into cover in the agricultural manufactory, safe behind a solid ceramite wall. Baffels and other Tanith crowded round them as they shared out the clip-cells and the stick-bombs.

Milo looked across the roofless factory-space and saw Larkin dug in high up near a vent hatch. The Tanith snipers, along with the Spoilers, had drawn back from the Spoil. Milo had known that the precision killing of the Zoicans had been the work of marksmen.

He flashed a grin up at Larkin. The weasely sniper winked back.

Milo handed a cell to Baffels. 'Your turn next time,' he joked.

'Of course,' said Baffels. Hours before he had ceased to recognise the humour in anything.

'COLM?'

Corbec looked up out of the loophole he was holding, his shaggy head coated in soot and grime. He shot a beaming grin when he saw Mkoll.

'About time you got here.'

'Came as fast as we could. The bastards have the Spoil now. We left it to them.'

Corbec got up and slapped Mkoll on the arm. 'You all make it through?'

'Yeah, Domor, Larkin, MkVenner – all the boys. I've spread them out through our lines.'

'Good work. We need good marksman coverage all along. Feth, but this is ugly work.'

They looked round, hearing angry voices down the burned-out hall. Vervun Primary troops with long-barrelled lasguns were moving in to join the defence.

'The Spoilers, so called,' Mkoll explained to his colonel. 'Dedicated to protecting the Spoil. Took a while to convince them that falling back was the smart choice. They'd have held the slag-slopes forever. It's a pride thing.'

'We understand pride, don't we?' grimaced Corbec.

Mkoll nodded. He pointed out the leader of the Spoilers, a bulky man with bloodshot eyes who was doing most of the shouting and cursing. 'That's "Gak" Ormon. Spoiler commander.'

Corbec sauntered over to the big Verghastite.

'Corbec, Tanith First-and-Only.'

'Major Ormon. I want to lodge a complaint, colonel. Your man Mkoll ordered our withdrawal from the Spoil, and–'

Corbec cut him short. 'We're fighting for our fething lives and you want to complain? Shut up. Get used to it. Mkoll made a good call. Another half an hour and you would have been surrounded and dead. You want a "spoil" to defend? Take a look!' He gestured out of a shattered window at the wasteland around. 'Start thinking like a soldier, and stop cussing and whining. There's more than unit pride at stake here.'

Ormon opened and closed his mouth a few times like a fish.

'I'm glad we understand each other,' Corbec said.

IN THE NORTH-EASTERN corner of the hive, Sergeant Varl and Major Rodyin had command of one hundred and seventy or so men holding the burning docks. Half were Tanith; the rest, Vervun Primary and Roane. Zoican stormtroops were blasting in along the Hass East Causeway under the Hiraldi road-bridge, and the Imperial forces were being driven back through the hive's promethium depots. Several bulk capacity tanks were already ablaze and liquescent fire spurted from derricks and spout-vents.

Firing tight bursts, Varl crossed a depot freightway and dropped into cover beside Major Rodyin, who had paused to fiddle with the cracked lens of his spectacles.

'No sign of support. I've been trying the vox. We're on our own,' the Vervun officer remarked.

Varl nodded. 'We can do that. Just a few of us should be able to keep them busy in these industrial sectors.'

'Unless they move armour our way.'

Varl sighed. The hiver was pessimism personified.

'Did you see the way the Zoicans' armour was smeared with tar and oil?'

'I did,' said Varl, clipping off a few more shots. 'What of it?'

'I think that's how they got in, how they broke us open. They came through the pipeline from Vannick Hive.' Rodyin pointed out across the depot to the series of vast fuel-pipe routes that came in over the river on metal stilt legs from the northern hinterlands. 'The pipes come in right under the Curtain Wall.'

'Why the feth weren't they shut down?' snapped Varl.

Rodyin shrugged. 'They were meant to be. That's what I was told, anyway. The directive was circulated weeks ago, right after Vannick was obliterated. The guilds controlling the fuelways were ordered to blow the pipes on the far shore and fill the rest with rockcrete.'

'Someone didn't do their job properly,' Varl mused. Somehow the information aggravated him. It was way too fething late to find out how they had been breached.

The fight at hand took his mind off it. Persistent rocket grenades were tumbling onto them from a loading dock at the edge of the depot. Varl ordered a pack of Roane down to establish covering fire and then sent Brostin in with the flamer.

He edged the rest of his men along down the devastated depot roadway, sometimes using the litter of metal plating and broken girders as cover, sometimes having to negotiate ways over or around it. A fuel tank sixty metres away blew out with huge, bright fury.

Logris, Meryn and Nehn, working forward with a handful of Vervun Primary troopers, almost ran into a Zoican fireteam in a drain-away under one of the main derrick rigs. The Tanith laid in fearlessly with bayonets, but the Vervun-hivers tried to find room to shoot and several were cut down.

Hearing the commotion over his microbead, Varl charged in with several other Tanith, spiking the first ochre-suited soldier he met with his silver bayonet. Another sliced at him with a boarding hatchet and Varl punched his head off with one blow from his metal arm.

Major Rodyin came in behind, shooting his autopistol frantically. He seemed pale and short of breath. Varl knew that Rodyin had never been in combat like this before. In truth, the man had never been in combat at all before that day.

Three desperate, bloody minutes of close fighting cleared the drain-away of Zoicans. Logris and Nehn set up solid fire positions down the gully, overlooking the dock causeway.

Rodyin took off his glasses and tried to adjust the ear-pieces with shaking hands. He looked like he was about to weep.

'You alright, major?' Varl asked. He knew full well Rodyin wasn't, but he suspected it had less to do with combat shock and more to do with the sight of his home city falling around him. Varl could certainly sympathise with that.

Rodyin nodded, replacing his spectacles. 'The more I kill, the better I feel.'

Nearby, Corporal Meryn laughed. 'The major sounds like Gaunt himself!'

The notion seemed to please Rodyin.

'What now? Left or right?' Meryn asked. He was wearing bulky fuel-worker's overalls in place of the Tanith kit which had been scorched off him. His seared scalp was caked with dried blood and matted tufts of scorched hair.

'Feth knows,' Varl answered.

'Right. We try to push down the river towards the bridge,' Rodyin said with great certainty.

Varl said nothing. He'd rather have stayed put or even fallen back a little to consolidate. The last thing they wanted was to overreach themselves, yet Rodyin was determined. Varl was uneasy following the major, even though the Verghastite had rank. But Willard was dead – Varl had seen his burning body fall from the Wall – and there was no one of authority to back him up.

So they moved east, daring the open firestorms of the docks, winning back Vervunhive a metre at a time.

GENERAL GRIZMUND walked down the steps of the Main Spine exit, adjusting his cap and powersword. Wind-carried ash washed back across the stone terrace of the Commercia where the Narmenian tanks were drawn up: one hundred and twenty-seven main battle tanks of the Leman Russ pattern, with twenty-seven Demolishers and forty-two light support tanks. Their engines revved, filling the air with blue exhaust smoke and thunder.

Brigadier Nachin saluted his general.

'Good to have you back, sir,' he said.

Grizmund nodded. He and the other officers liberated by Gaunt from the hands of the VPHC were more than ready to see action.

Grizmund pulled his command officers into a huddle and flipped out the hololithic display of a data-slate. A three-dimensional light-map of the Commercia and adjacent districts billowed into the sooty air. Grizmund began to explain to his commanders what he wanted them to do, how they would be deployed, what objectives they were to achieve.

His voice was relayed by vox/pict drones to all the Narmenian crews. His briefing turned into a speech, a rousing declamation of power and victory. At the end of it, the tank crews, more than a thousand men, cheered and yelled.

Grizmund walked down the line of growling tanks and clambered deftly up onto his flag-armour, The Grace of the Throne, a long-chassis Russ variant with a hundred and ten-centimetre main weapon. Like all the Narmenian vehicles, it was painted mustard-drab and bore the Imperial eagle crest and the spiked fist sigil of Narmenia.

It felt like coming home. Grizmund dropped down through the main turret's hatch, strapped himself into the command chair, and plugged the dangling lead of his headset into the vox-caster.

Grizmund tested the vox-link and made sure he had total coverage.

He pulled the recessed lever that clanged the top-hatch down, and he saw his driver, gunner and loader grinning up at him from the lower spaces of the tank hull.

'Let's give them hell,' Grizmund said to his crew and, via the vox, to all his men.

The Narmenian tank units roared down through the Commercia and back into the war.

HOUSE COMMAND WAS a molten ruin full of scorched debris and a few fused corpses. The blast that had taken it out had also blown out the floor and disintegrated the Main Spine structure for three levels below. Gaunt viewed it from the shattered doorway for a minute or two.

Searching the adjacent areas, Gaunt appropriated a Ministorum baptistry on Level Mid-36 as a new command centre. Under Daur's supervision, workteams cleared the pews and consecration tables and brought in codifiers and vox-systems liberated from dozens of houses ordinary on that level. Gaunt himself hefted a sheet of flakboard onto the top of the richly decorated font to make a desk. He began to pile up his data-slates and printouts.

Ecclesiarch Immaculus and his brethren watched the Imperial soldiers overrun their baptistry. It was one of the few remaining shrines in the hive still intact. They had been singing laments for the basilica when Gaunt arrived.

Immaculus joined Gaunt at his makeshift desk.

'I suppose you're going to tell me this is sacrilege,' Gaunt said.

The old man in long, purple robes shook his head wearily. 'You fight for the Imperial cause, my son. In such manner, you worship the Emperor more truly than a hundred of my prayers. If our baptistry suits your needs, you are welcome to it.'

Gaunt inclined his head reverently and thanked the Ecclesiarch.

'Baptise this war in blood, colonel-commissar,' Immaculus said.

The cleric had been nothing but gracious and Gaunt was anxious to show his appreciation. 'I will feel happier if you and your brothers would hold vigil here for us, watching over this place as a surety against destruction.'

Immaculus nodded, leading his brethren up to the cele-bratory, from where their plainsong chants soon echoed.

Gaunt viewed the data-slates, seeing the depth of the destruction. He made note marks on a paper chart of the hive.

Daur brought him the latest reports. Xance was dead; Nash too. Sturm had vanished. As Gaunt surveyed the lists of the dead, Major Otte of the Vervun forces, the lord marshal's adjutant, arrived in the baptistry. He was wounded and shellshocked, one of the few men to make it clear of the fall of Sondar Gate.

He saluted Gaunt. 'Marshal Croe is slain,' he said simply.

Gaunt sighed.

'As ranking officer of Vervun Primary, I hand command to you, as ranking Imperial commander.'

Gaunt stood up and solemnly received the salute with one of his own. What he had suspected ever since he led the assault on Sondar's lair was now confirmed: he was the senior surviving Imperial officer in Vervunhive and so overall mili-tary authority was now his. All senior ranks, both local and off-world, were dead or missing. Only Grizmund held a rank higher than Gaunt and armour was always subservient to an infantry command.

Otte presented Gaunt with Croe's sword of office: the powerblade of Heironymo Sondar.

'I can't accept–'

'You must. Whoever leads Vervunhive to war must carry the sword of Heironymo. It is a custom and tradition we have no wish to break.'

Gaunt accepted, allowing Otte to formally buckle the car-rying sash around him.

Intendant Banefail of the Administratum, surrounded by a procession of servitors and clerks, entered the baptistry as Otte was performing the ceremony. He nodded to Gaunt gravely and accepted his authority without question.

'My ministry is at your disposal, commander. I have mobilised labour teams to assist in fire control and damage clearance. We... are overwhelmed by the situation. Most of the population is trying to flee across the river, all militarised units request ammunition supply, the main–'

Gaunt raised his hand. 'I am confident the Administratum will provide whatever they can, whatever is in their means. I trust the astropaths have been maintaining contact with the warmaster?'

'Of course.'

'I will not ask Macaroth for aid, but I want him to understand the situation here. If he deems it worthy of his notice, he will assist us.'

Horns sounded, a pathetic gesture of pomp, and Legislator Anophy shuffled into the baptistry with his retinue: a long train of child-slaves, servitors and guards, some carrying banner poles. The banners and the robes were singed and grubby in places, and the slaves looked wet-eyed and terrified. Representatives of the guilds and high houses flocked in behind the Legislator's procession, shouting and disputing.

Gaunt turned to Banefail. 'You can help me immediately by keeping these worthies out of my face. Listen to their petitions and notarise them. I will review later – if there is an opportunity.'

'It will be done,' Banefail said. 'May the Emperor of Mankind provide for you in this hour.'

As the Administratum staff swept away behind Banefail to head off the angry mob of dignitaries, Gaunt resumed his review of the battle data. The first of the vox-links had just been set up and Daur brought him a speaker set.

Gaunt selected a channel. 'Vervunhive Command to Grizmund. Signal "Uncle Dercius".'

'"Uncle Dercius" given and heard,' crackled the receiver.

'I need you to deny the approaches to Croe Gate and Ontabi Gate. From what I can see here, the main vehicular invasion is pouring in that way.'

'Agreed. But there are tank squadrons coming up through Sondar Gate too.'

'Noted. I'll deal with that. May the God-Emperor guide you, general.'

'And watch over you, colonel-commissar.'

Adjusting his channel setting, Gaunt raised the commander of NorthCol armour groups milling in confusion south of the Commercia. He directed them down towards Sondar Gate. Then he began to systematically contact all the tattered sections of infantry and Guard.

He got through to Corbec at Guild Githran Agricultural.

'Feth, commissar! I thought you were dead!'

'I thought the same of you, Colm. How is it?'

'Bad as anything I've seen. We're holding, just barely, but they're pouring it on. I could really do with a pinch of armour.'

'It's coming your way as we speak. Colm, we need to do more than hold, we have to push them back. The Shield will only work for us if we can hunt them out from under it.'

'You don't ask for much, do you?'

'Never.'

'You'll owe me a planet of my own for this, you realise?'

'I owe you that already, Corbec. Think bigger.'

A servitor brought Gaunt more data feeds from the newly engaged codifiers set up in the baptistry. Gaunt looked through them, his gaze stopped by a report relayed in from Varl.

'Daur?'

'Sir!'

'I want a list of guilds controlling fuel supply and accredited proof from every damn one of them that they closed their pipelines down.'

'Yes, commander.'

Gaunt spent the next ten minutes voxing tactical instructions to dozens of individual troop units throughout the hive. He was unable to reach Varl or any unit north of the Main Spine. As he worked, servitors and staff officers tracked the substance and matter of his battle-plan on a hololithic chart of the city, overlaying it with any data they received from the ground.

For a short while, Gaunt toyed with the settings of the vox-unit, hunting through the bands to locate the low frequencies the Zoicans were using. He still hoped they might intercept and unscramble the Zoican transmissions and eavesdrop on their tactical command net. But it was futile. The Zoican channels were seething with transmissions, but all in that incomprehensible chatter, the chatter that defied translation even by linguistic cogitators, a constant, meaningless stream of corrupt machine noise that gave up no secrets. Either that, or the chanting repeats of the Heritor's name on the propaganda wavelengths. Gaunt had fought Chaos long enough to know not to call in human scholars or astropaths to try to decode the chatter. He couldn't allow that filth to taint any mind in Vervunhive.

A commotion at the door roused Gaunt from his work. A detail of Vervun Primary soldiers was escorting General Sturm into the baptistry.

'We found him trying to join a party of refugees boarding a ferry at the viaduct jetty, sir,' the squad's leader told Gaunt.

Gaunt looked Sturm up and down. 'Desertion?' he said softly.

Sturm straightened his cap, bristling. 'I am senior commander here, Gaunt! Not you! Vervunhive is lost! I have given the signal to retreat and evacuate! I could have you all shot for disobedience!'

'You… gave the signal to evacuate? Then why are all Imperial forces and planetary units still fighting? Even your own Volpone? You must have given the signal very quietly.'

'Don't talk that way to me, you jumped-up shit!' Sturm croaked. The room fell silent around them and all eyes turned to observe the confrontation. 'I am the senior general of the Royal Volpone! I am ranking officer here in Vervunhive! You will obey me! You will respect me!'

'What's to respect?' Gaunt walked around Sturm, looking out at the watching faces with interest. No one showed any sign of leaping to the general's defence. 'You fled the assault on House Sondar. You fled the Main Spine and headed for the river. You gave up on Vervunhive.'

'I am ranking officer!'

With a brutal tear, Gaunt ripped Sturm's rank pins of his jacket.

'Not any more. You're a disgrace. A coward – and a murderer. You know damn well it was your orders that killed five hundred of my Tanith on Voltemand. Killed them because

they managed to win what your Bluebloods could not.'
Gaunt stared into Sturm's blinking eyes.

'How you ever made general, I don't know.'

Sturm seemed to sag.

'A weapon…' he said weakly.

'What?'

Sturm looked up with blazing eyes. 'Give me a cursing weapon, colonel-commissar! I'll not be lectured at by a low-born shit like you! Or punished! Give me a weapon and allow me the good grace of making my own peace!'

Gaunt shrugged. He pulled his bolt pistol from its holster and held it out butt-first to the general.

'Final request granted. Officers of the watch, so note General Sturm has volunteered to exact his own punishment.' He looked back at Sturm. 'I've never even slightly liked you, Noches. Give me a reason to speak of you well. Make it clean and simple.'

Sturm took the proffered gun.

'Officers of the watch, also note,' hissed Sturm, 'that Ibram Gaunt refuses to signal evacuation. He's condemned you all to death by fire. I'm glad to be out of it.'

He cocked the weapon and raised it to his mouth.

Gaunt turned his back.

There was a long pause.

'Gaunt!' Captain Daur screamed.

Gaunt swung around, the powersword of Heironymo Sondar already out and lit in his hand. It sliced through Sturm's wrist before the Volpone general could fire the bolt gun – the bolt gun that had been aimed at Gaunt's skull.

Sturm fell sidelong on the baptistry flagstones, shrieking out as blood pumped from his wrist stump. Nerves spasmed in his severed hand and the bolt pistol fired once, blowing a hole through the ornate prayer screen behind Gaunt.

Gaunt glared down at the general's writhing form for a moment. Then he stooped and retrieved his bolt pistol from the detached hand.

'Get him out of my sight,' he told the waiting troopers with a dismissive gesture at Sturm. 'I don't want to look at that treacherous bastard any longer than I have to.'

* * *

BY EARLY AFTERNOON on that fateful thirty-fifth day, whatever co-ordinated resistance could be made was being made. Gaunt's command post in the Main Spine had contacted and tactically deployed almost two-thirds of the available fighting strength in the hive, a feat of determined efficiency that left both the Administratum and the surviving officers of the Vervun Primary Strategic Planning Cadre dumbfounded. What made it altogether more extraordinary was that Gaunt had driven the work almost single-handedly. After the incident with Sturm, he worked with an intense devotion that was almost terrifying. Latterly, as the cohesion of his plan became clear, he was able to delegate work to the eager tactical staffers, but the core of the resistance plan was his alone.

Ban Daur stepped out of the baptistry a little after midday to clear his head and find water. He stood for a while under a blackened arch at the end of the hallway, watching through glassless windows as flickering areas of warfare boiled through the dense streets below.

Captain Petro, one of the tacticians, emerged from the baptistry too and came to stand with Daur, an old friend from their academy days.

'He's frightening...' Petro said.

'Gaunt?'

Petro nodded. 'His mind, his focus... it's like a codifier. All drive, all purpose.'

Daur sipped his glass. 'Like Slaydo,' he said. Petro raised a quizzical eyebrow.

'Remember how we studied the warmaster's career? The keynote was always Slaydo's singularity of purpose – that he could look at a theatre and plan it in his head, hold the whole situation in his mind. That was military brilliance. I think we're seeing its like again.'

'He served with Slaydo, didn't he?'

'Yes. His record speaks for itself.'

'But as an infantry officer.' Petro frowned. 'Gaunt's reputation's never been for overall battlefield command, not on this scale.'

'I don't think he's ever had the chance to show it before – a commissar, a troop commander, always following the lead of higher ranks. He's never had an opportunity like this before. Besides… I think it may be because he's got everything to prove.'

'What the gak do you mean, Ban?'

'The high commanders are dead… or, like Sturm, disgraced. Fate and his own actions have put Gaunt in command, and I think he's determined to prove he should have been there all along.'

AT A CROSSROADS designated fg/567, in the heart of the eastern central habs, Bulwar's infantry divisions were close to breaking. They had no anti-armour ordnance left and the Zoican tank thrust was burning a spearhead through from Croe Gate, laying waste to hectares of habitat structures.

Bulwar and his NorthCol battlegroup moved south around the crossroads, tackling Zoican troops in the rockcrete tangles that had once been labour-homes. Tank rounds screamed down over them, blowing out sections of wall and roadway, collapsing precarious spires of rubble and masonry.

In the shell of a funicular carriage station, between the ornate marble pillars and the old brass benches, they fought at close quarters with a phalanx of Zoicans. More were pouring in through the ticket booths at the far end or climbing up into the station through the shattered wreck of a carriage train that had made its last stop at the platform. Civilian dead lay all around.

Bulwar led the attack, breaking body armour with his power claw and shooting with his autogun. Men fell around him, too many to count. A las-round struck his shoulder and he was thrown backwards off his feet.

When he got up, things had changed. A fighting force had erupted into the station from the passenger exits and it was tearing into the Zoicans from the side. They weren't NorthCol or Vervun Primary or even Guard. They were workers, hive labourers, armed with captured guns, axerakes, or any other weapon they could find. Bulwar realised they were one of the many 'scratch companies' informally raised by willing habbers to support the defence. He'd heard of many emerging from the ruins to assist the Imperial forces, but not one of this size and organisation. Their vengeful fury was astonishing.

The frenzied fighting lasted about eight minutes. Between them, Bulwar's platoon and the workers killed every Zoican in the station precinct.

There was cheering and whooping, and NorthCol troopers hugged Vervunhivers like lost brothers.

A short, thick-set worker with one eye, bedraggled in muck and blood, limped over to Bulwar and saluted.

'Who are you?' asked Bulwar.

'Soric, commander of the Smeltery Irregulars, sir!'

Bulwar couldn't help smiling. The worker boss had a general's pins, fashioned out of bottle caps, sewn into his jacket.

'I thank the Emperor for you, General Soric.'

Soric paused and glanced bashfully at his insignia. 'Sorry, sir; just a joke to rally the men. I'm just a plant supervisor–'

'Who fights like a warmaster. How many are you?'

'About seven hundred, sir – workers, habbers, anyone really. We've been trying to do our bit for the hive ever since the start, and when the Shield went down, it was run or fight.'

'You'd put us to shame.'

Soric frowned. 'If we won't fight for our own bloody hive, sir, I don't know who should.'

Standing orders required all unit commanders to inform Spine Command of the size and composition of any scratch companies encountered so that they could be designated a marker code and factored into the defence structure. Bulwar called up his vox-officer and called in the details of Soric's Irregulars. He looked to Soric. 'We need to co-ordinate, general. I thank the Emperor for the likes of you, but we'll only win this thing if the military forces and the civilian levies work as one. Get your men to spread the word. Scratch companies must try to make contact with Imperial forces and be accounted for. They'll have to take orders too.'

Soric nodded and called his 'officers' up to brief them.

'You can't be a general though, I'm afraid,' said Bulwar. Soric was already pulling his makeshift rank pins off.

'Take a brevet rank, Soric. State-of-emergency field promotion. You're a sergeant now and you'll answer to me.

Designate one man in every twenty a corporal, and fix a chain of command. You choose them; you know them.'

Soric nodded again, lost for words with pride.

Explosions thundered across the station, throwing some of the men to the ground. One of Soric's freedom fighters was yelling out. 'Enemy tanks! Enemy tanks!'

Bulwar and Soric scrambled over to the station's east entrance to see. The huge shapes of Zoican storm-tanks, long-barrelled and heavily armoured, were scything in towards the station and the surrounding habs. Others, including fast-moving light assault tanks and squat, super-heavy flamer platforms, were pushing round onto the transit streets leading to the Commercia and the Shield Pylon.

'We have explosives, sir,' said Soric, saluting again for good measure. 'Mining charges we lifted from the stores behind the smelteries.'

'Static charges with no launchers... against tanks?'

'It's how we've been doing it so far, sir: a man takes a wrap of charges and runs with it, anchors it to the tank hull–'

'Suicide!'

Soric frowned. 'Duty, sir. What other way is there?'

'How many tanks have you taken out with that method?'

'Twenty-four, I think.'

'How many men has it cost you?'

Soric shrugged. 'Twenty-four, of course.'

Bulwar wiped his mouth on the back of his glove. Incredible. The devotion, the determination. The sacrifice. The workers of Vervunhive, who had built this place with their sweat, were now buying it back with their blood. It was an object lesson in loyalty and devotion that even the finest Imperial Guard regiment could admire.

The tanks were closing now, hammering the station, blowing sections of the overhead trackway down. Sheets of fire leapt through the terminus hall.

'Throne of Earth!' Soric gasped, pointing.

Mustard-drab battle tanks, moving at full power across the rubble scarps, some of them bursting through sections of wall, were thundering forward from the west. They were firing freely, with huge accuracy, maintaining a cycle rate of fire that the Zoican armour, turning to the flank to greet them, couldn't even begin to match.

Neither Bulwar nor Soric had ever seen a mass armour charge before, certainly not one undertaken by a crack Imperial tank brigade like the Narmenians. They opened their mouths in awe, and nothing but wild cheers came out.

GRIZMUND CALLED IT 'Operation Dercius.' He'd sent his sentinel recon units and foot-troop spotter units forward towards Croe Gate as he composed his tank brigade in the Commercia. The spotters couldn't fix the position of the moving Zoican armour, but they could assess its force and direction. Grizmund had compiled the data and sent his main columns first south into the habs and then turned them east at full speed, to catch the enemy's flank. Grizmund truly understood the power of armoured vehicles, not just the physical power, but the psychological strength. If a tank was a threatening thing then a tank moving fast, and firing accurately and repeatedly, was a nightmare. The tank strike was his forte and he only admitted into the Narmenian cadre drivers who could handle thirty-plus tonnes of armour at speed, and gunners and layers who could fire fast, repeatedly and make kills each time.

In the command chair of *The Grace of the Throne*, Grizmund watched the picts on his auspex slate wink and flash as they marked hits on the glowing target runes. The interior of the turret was a red-lit sweat-box, alive with the chatter of the vox and the efficient call and return of the gun team. Fresh brass-stamped shells clanked down into the greased loading rack from the magazine over the aft wheels, and the layer primed them and shunted them forward to the gunner, who was hunting through the glowing green viewer of his scope. Every few seconds, the layer eased the muzzle recoil brake and the main gun fired with a retort that shook the tank and welled smoke into the turret, smoke quickly sucked out through the louvres of the outlets.

Grizmund's driver, Wolsh, was one of the finest and he kept them moving even when firing. He had a master's eye

for terrain and seemed to know exactly what to ram and
what to steer around, what to drive over and what to avoid.
The Narmenians joked that Wolsh could smell a mine a kilometre off.

Operation Dercius threw forty fast-moving Narmenian
heavy tanks down through fg/567 and cut through the neck
of the Zoican column spread. Grizmund's forces had killed
or crippled seventy-two enemy vehicles by the time they
doubled back, swinging around without breaking speed to
re-engage the shattered Zoican armour from the other side.
By then, the Zoican armour was milling and fracturing in
confusion.

Now came the part that required true skill, a manoeuvre
Grizmund had dubbed 'The Scissors'. As his tanks came
around to re-engage, another fifty under Brigadier Nachin
charged the enemy from the other side, from the direction of
Grizmund's original strike. A textbook disaster in the hands
of less able commanders, but at the turn, Grizmund's forces
had begun to send identifying vox beacons to distinguish
them from the enemy, and Nachin's forces did the same. The
rule was anything caught between their charges that didn't
broadcast the correct beacon was a target. Grizmund had
used this tactic nine times before and never lost a tank to his
own fire.

That fine record was maintained at Vervunhive. Like the
jaws of some vast beast, the opposing Narmenian armour
charges tore in towards each other, crushing and destroying
everything between them. Grizmund and Nachin's speeding
tanks passed through each other's ranks, some vehicles missing others at full speed by only a hull's span.

And they had just begun. In the course of the thirty-fifth
afternoon, the Narmenian divisions executed three more
precision scissor manouvres, looping back and forth onto
each other, slowly chewing the head, neck and shoulders off
the vast Zoican incursion.

By four o'clock, the Zoicans had lost nearly two hundred
tanks and armoured battle-hulks. The Narmenians had lost
only two.

By nightfall, the Narmenians had driven the Zoican
armour back into the inner habs, less than ten kilometres

from Croe Gate, and cut a slice down the spearhead from Ontabi. With the routes behind them clear of enemy armour, efforts to resupply the Imperial ground troops were now no longer suicidal. Labour forces of the Administratum, the cargo guilds and Vervun Primary spread out in convoys and brought fresh ammunition to the dug-in infantry forces. Many, like Bulwar's, now resupplied with rockets, launchers and grenades, followed the Narmenian thrust out towards the great eastern gates, killing every Zoican tank the Guard armour had missed.

RISING FROM HIS seat at the font-desk in the baptistry, Gaunt took the data-slate Petro held out to him and smiled a weary smile as he read the reports of Grizmund's sally. He felt... justified: justified in his faith in the general, justified in fighting for him in the stockade, and justified in his tactical plans to hold the hive.

Towards Sondar Gate and Veyveyr, the position was less heartening. The NorthCol armour lacked the genius of leadership or the combat-experienced skill that shone in the Narmenians. Major Clodel, commanding the North-Col units, had done little more than grind his tanks into a slugfest with the Zoican armour penetrating the hive from the south. He had stopped them, though, halting them at the edge of the southern manufactories, and for that he would get Gaunt's commendation. But now a blistering, static tank-war raged through the southern skirts, and there was no possibility of driving the invaders back and out or of sealing the gates. North of Veyveyr, the NorthCol were losing as many tanks as they were destroying. Gaunt wished for another of Grizmund's ilk to lead them, but he couldn't spare any of the Narmenians from the eastern repulse. He would be content with what he had.

And what he had was a shattered hive spared from the brink of defeat at the eleventh hour. He wasn't winning, but he wasn't losing either. To the east, he was driving the foe out. To the south and west, he was holding them hard. There was still a chance that they could win out and deny Heritor Asphodel and his Zoican zealots.

The baptistry hummed with activity and Gaunt wandered away into the side chapel as tacticians filled in for him at the hololithic chart. Daur was orchestrating the command work-force. A good man, Gaunt thought, rising courageously to his moment in Imperial history.

Can the same be said about me, he wondered?

The side chapel – a sacristy, peculiarly calm and softly lit given the apocalypse currently unleashed outside the Spine walls – seemed to welcome him. He was dead on his feet with fatigue. He'd spent all day at a desk, with a data-slate in one hand and a vox-horn in the other, and yet he'd fought the greatest and most exhausting battle of his career so far. This was command, true high command, wretched with absolutes and finites. He pulled his newly bestowed power-sword from its sheath and leaned it on the edge of the gilt altar rail so he could sit down. Above him, a great, golden statue of the Emperor glowered. The air was full of the con-tinuing song of the Ecclesiarch.

He made no obeisance to the Emperor. He was too tired. He sat on a bench pew in the tiny chapel, removed his cap and buried his face in his hands.

Gaunt thought of Oktar, Dercius, Slaydo and his father, the men who had moulded his life and brought him to this, equipping him, each in their own way, with the skills he now used. He missed them all, missed their confidences and strength. Oktar had trained him, and Gaunt had been at the great commissar-general's side when he had passed, wracked with ork poison on Gylatus Decimus, over twenty years before. Slaydo, the peerless warmaster – Gaunt had been at his deathbed too, on Balhaut after the finest victory of all. Gaunt's father had died far away when he was still a child. And Dercius – bad, old Uncle Dercius; Gaunt had killed him.

But each, in their own way, had made him. Oktar had taught him command and discipline; Dercius: ruthlessness and confidence; Slaydo: the merits of command and the self-lessness of Imperial service. And his father? What he had gleaned from his father was more difficult to identify. What a father leaves to his child is always the most indefinable quality.

'Lord commander?'

Gaunt looked up from his reverie. Merity Chass, dressed in a simple, black gown of mourning, stood behind him in the arch of the sacristy. She held something in her hands.

Gaunt got up. 'Lady Chass?'

'I need to speak with you,' she began, 'about my father.'

SIXTEEN
THE LEGACY

'That our beloved hive should be conquered, or should fall into the controlling hands of unwise or unfit masters, I greatly fear and sadly anticipate. For this reason, I entrust this ultimate sanction to you. Use it wisely.'

— Heironymo Sondar, to Lord Chass

'IT HAS BEEN in the trust of my family since the Trade War,' she explained, her voice broken and exhausted.

Gaunt took the amulet from her hands and felt it purr and whisper between his fingers.

'Sondar made this?'

'It was his provision for the future. It is – in its own way – treachery.'

'Explain it again. I cannot see how this is treachery.'

Merity Chass looked up into Gaunt's tired eyes fretfully.

'Vervunhive is a democratic legislative. The High Lord is voted in by his noble peers. It is written in the sacred acts of constitution that absolute power should never be allowed to rest with any one individual who could not be unseated by the Legislature should it become necessary.'

'Yet the hive has suffered under one individual: Salvadore.'

'Precisely the kind of evil Heironymo dreaded, commander. My father told me that after the Trade War, great Heironymo wished to vouchsafe the future security of Vervunhive. Above all else, he feared a loss of control. That an invader – or a ruler not fit for the role – would seize control of Vervunhive so entirely that nothing could unseat him. What usurper or tyrant observes the mechanisms of constitution and law?'

Gaunt began to understand the far-reaching political dilemma attached to the device in his gloved hand. 'So this was his failsafe: the ultimate sanction, so very undemocratic, to be used when democracy was overturned?'

'And so you understand why it had to be a secret. Heironymo knew that by constructing such a device he would lay himself open to accusations of tyranny and dictatorship.'

She gestured towards the amulet. 'He made that and entrusted it to House Chass, whom he considered the most humanitarian and neutral noble house. It was never made to fall into the hands of any ruler. It was the safeguard against totalitarian rule.'

'And if House Chass became the High House?'

'We were to entrust it to another, as surety against our misuse of power.'

'And you give it to me?'

'You are the future of Vervunhive now, Gaunt. Why do you think my father made such efforts to evaluate you? He needed to be certain such insurance would not be handed to one who might abuse it. He knew you were no tyrant in the making, and I see that too. You are a soldier, true and brave, with nothing but the survival of our hive in your dreams.'

'Your father died well, Merity Chass.'

'I am glad to hear it. Honour him and the duty borne by his house, Ibram Gaunt. Do not prove him wrong.'

Gaunt studied the amulet. It was a system-slayer and, from what the girl said, quite the most powerful and formidable example of its kind he had ever heard of. In the time of Heironymo, House Sondar had specialised in codifier systems and sentient cogitators, and they had enjoyed long-term trade partnerships and research pacts with the tech-mages of the Adeptus Mechanicus. This was the masterpiece: in the event of anyone achieving total technological mastery of Vervunhive, the activation of this amulet would annihilate the command and control systems, erase all data and function programs, corrupt all codifiers and lobotomise all cogitators. It would cripple Vervunhive and allow the device's wielders to free the hive from would-be conquerors now rendered helpless.

In its peculiar way, it was more potent than atomics or a chapter of the Adeptus Astartes. It was an ultimate weapon, forged for arenas of battle far beyond the remit of a dog-soldier like Gaunt. It was war on a refined, decisive level, light years away from the mud and las-fire theatres that Gaunt regularly experienced.

Still, he understood it. But he didn't like it. Such ancient high technology was a fearful thing, like psyker witchcraft.

He set it down on the pew next to him. It gurgled and hummed, system patterns reconfiguring like sunlight on moving water across its smooth casing.

'We don't need it.'

Merity Chass stiffened and stared up at the stained-glass rosette of the sacristy.

'I was afraid you'd say that.'

She turned to face him. Her face was pale, and her eyes were angry and dark. Multi-coloured light from the window behind her created a halo around her slim form. 'My father agonised about using it. When I reached the shelters and found he had hidden it in my belongings, I agonised too. Even as I came here to find you, I realised we had left it too late. You have already unseated cursed Salvador. Our dire situation is no longer a matter of control.'

'We have control,' Gaunt agreed. 'The problem is now simply one of physical warfare. Though Vervunhive stands at the brink of doom, it is not the doom Heironymo feared or planned for with this.'

She sat down next to him, smouldering with rage. 'If only I had brought it sooner – or urged my father to do the same. We could have used it to overthrow Salvador–'

'Praise the Throne we did not!'

She glanced around at him sharply.

Gaunt shrugged. 'We'd have crippled ourselves, crippled the hive systems, left ourselves with nothing to use to regain control. A system-slayer is an absolute weapon, lady.'

'So, my soul-searching, my father's painstaking deliberations... were all pointless anyway?' She laughed a thin, scratchy laugh. 'How fitting! House Chass, so gakking intellectual and refined, agonising over nothings while the hive bleeds and burns!'

He pulled off his gloves and tossed them aside. 'Heironymo's legacy was never to be taken lightly. That we can't use it now does not reflect badly on the care and devotion with which House Chass held that trust.'

She reached out her hand and clasped his callused fingers. 'What happens now, Gaunt?

Slowly, he looked round at her. 'We fight a simple war, men and machines, lasguns and shells. We fight and try to drive them out. If we win, we live. If we lose, we die.'

'It sounds so bleak.'

'It's all I know, the crude equation of battle. It's not so bad. It's simple at least. There's no deliberation involved.'

'How long?'

'How long what?'

Her eyes, more alive than anything Gaunt had ever seen, gazed into his. 'How long before we know?'

Ibram Gaunt exhaled deeply, shaking his head. 'Just hours now. Perhaps a day, perhaps two. Then it will be over, one way or another.'

She pulled him to her, her arms stretched tightly around his broad back. He could smell her hair and her perfume, faint and almost worn away but still tangible despite the odours of cold and damp and dirt she had been exposed to in the shelters.

Gaunt had long forgotten the simple consolation of another's body warmth. He held her gently, swimming with fatigue, as the low voices of the Ecclesiarch choir ebbed through the sacristy. Her mouth found his.

He pulled back. 'I don't think–' he began.

'A common soldier messing with a high-born lady?' She smiled. 'Even if that mattered once, it doesn't now. This war has made us all equals.'

They kissed again, neither resisting. For a while, their passion was all that mattered to either of them. Two human souls, intimate and wordless, shutting the apocalypse out.

MIDNIGHT WAS long past. Bray's Tanith units, after a day and night of tank-busting in the slag-reaches of the chem plant district, fell back through the battered central hab zone towards the Shield Pylon. All the Zoican southern efforts seemed to be directed at the pylon and Bray knew that its strategic importance was unmatched by anything in the hive. Bray had about two hundred and eighty Tanith left, augmented by four hundred more Vervun Primary, Volpone, Roane and NorthCol stragglers, plus around six hundred hivers. The hivers were mostly non-coms, who looked to the troops for protection, and Bray and his colleague officers found themselves managing more of a refugee exodus than a troop retreat.

But some of the hivers had consolidated into scratch units, adding about one hundred and seventy fighting bodies to Bray's forces.

More than half of the scratch companies were made up of women, and Bray was amazed. He'd never seen women fight. Back on Tanith war was a masculine profession. But he couldn't deny their determination. And he understood it. This was their fething home, after all.

Bray's immediate command chain was formed by Vervun Primary and NorthCol, but though some of them outranked him, they looked to him for leadership. Bray suspected this was because Gaunt was now field commander. Everyone deferred to the Tanith now the endgame had begun.

Shells from Zoican armour whooped over his head and Bray sprinted into a trench-stretch between a blown-out meat-curing plant and a guild estate mansion. In the trench, Sergeant Zweck of the NorthCol and Major Bunce of the Vervun Primary were directing the men around the curing plant to engage the enemy's forward push.

Las-fire zagged down at them. Most of the Imperial shooters fired from shallow foxholes at the ranks of Zoican assault troops advancing, bayonets fixed, across the rubble. Mortar shells rebounded off the rockcrete slag and exploded as airbursts, causing significantly more damage

Behind the toppling lines of Zoican infantry, tanks rumbled in, many carrying troops clinging to the hull netting like apes.

Bray fired his weapon over the trench lip. Beside him, Zweck was decapitated by air-burst splinters. Blood saturated the side of Bray's dark fatigues.

He reached for another clip.

'WHAT ARE THEIR names?' Caffran yelled over the pounding thunder of the tanks. He had Yoncy under one arm and was leading Dalin by the hand. Tona hurried after him.

Scratch companies to their west were holding the Zoican front back, and they were struggling to keep up with a straggle of civilian refugees fleeing into the northern sectors. Caffran yelled again.

Tona Criid was busy and didn't answer Caffran.

She was firing her laspistol at the Zoican assault troops crossing into the street behind her. But she was in trouble. There was no one to cover her.

'Hold tight to your brother and get down!' Caffran cried at Dalin, pressing the swaddled baby into the boy's arms. 'I'm going back for your mother!'

'She's not my mother. She's Auntie Tona,' said Dalin.

Caffran glanced back confused and then ran on as lasbursts flickered around him.

He fired his lasgun wildly and dropped into the shell-hole where Tona cowered.

'Fresh clip!' she called.

He tossed her one. Reloaded, both rose and sent a stinging waft of kill-fire down the street at the Zoicans. Ochre bodies crumpled.

'Good shots. You're scary, Tona.'

'I do what I do. Fresh clip!'

He tossed her another.

'So they aren't yours? I thought you looked too young.'

Tona swung round to him, her face hard. 'They're all I have! Gak you! You won't take them from me, and neither will these bastards!'

She swung up and fired her gun, killing one, two, three...

* * *

SAVAGE FIGHTING CONTINUED unabated on all fronts right through into the early hours of the thirty-sixth day. By then, two thirds of the hive's immense civilian population were packed into the north-eastern sectors and docks, making desperate efforts to flee to the north bank. The flow was far beyond the abilities of the river ferries to manage. Working through the night, with only brief pauses to refuel, boats like the *Magnificat* shuttled back and forth across the Hass. Over two million refugees were now in the outhabs of the north shore or clogging the Northern Collective Highway. The night was cold and wet, and many – wounded, shocked, or unfed – suffered with exposure and fever.

In the hive it was worse. Millions choked the approaches to the wharves or lined the river in ranks as thick as the crowds on the terraces of the stadium watching a big game. Brutal battles broke out as citizens fought to win places on the approaching boats. Thousands died, almost two hundred of them aboard a ferry that they overloaded and capsized in a panic rush to get aboard. Hundreds more were trampled or simply crushed in the press or were pushed into the river by the mounting weight of bodies behind them. Those that didn't drown immediately died slowly, floundering in the cold of the water, unable to find enough room on the docks to clamber back ashore. An entire pier stretch collapsed under the weight of the refugees, spilling hundreds into the Hass. Rioting and panic fighting spread like wildfire back through the crowds. Like a wounded, enraged animal, Vervunhive began to claw and tear at itself.

Every small boat or craft that could be found was stolen and put to the water, usually overfilled and often guided by men or women with no idea of watercraft. Hundreds of others elected to try to swim or paddle across, clinging to packing bales or other items of floating material. The Hass was almost three kilometres wide, icy cold and plagued with strong currents. No one who tried to swim made it more than halfway before perishing, except for a very few who were pulled out of the water by passing ferry crews.

Streams of evacuees made it up from the docks onto the great viaduct and crossed on foot. The density of foot traffic on the railbridge was so great that many were pushed off and

fell screaming into the river far below. Just after midnight,
Zoican rockets ranged down the dock basin from the invad-
ing forces at the Hiraldi Bridge end to the east. Some fell on
the docks or hit the water. Four blew out the central spans of
the viaduct, toppling three of the great brick pier supports
and killing hundreds. The viaduct as an evacuation route
was finished, and those pressed on to the southern spans
who had survived the rocket strike were trapped, unable to
retreat back into the hive and reach the docks because the
pressure of bodies behind them was so great. One by one,
they were pushed off the shattered end of the viaduct.

A little after the destruction of the railbridge, Folik, steer-
ing his ferry on a return run across the Hass, saw lights and
movement on the north shore to the east. Zoican motorised
brigades were sweeping in along the far shore from the
pipelines and the Hiraldi road, pincering round to deny the
escape route. The Zoicans clearly intended no one should
survive the destruction of the hive. By dawn, the Zoican
army groups were assaulting the tides of refugees on the
north bank. The hordes who had been lucky enough to get
across the river were now systematically massacred on the far
side. Perhaps as many as half a million were slaughtered outright. Hundreds of thousands fled, their numbers dissipating
into the inhospitable hinterlands or the ruined outhabs.

Now there was no way across. The ferries returned to the
south docks, many under fire from Zoican forces on the
north side, and tied up. They were as trapped as the hosts on
the banks now. A fearful hush of realisation fell across the
multitude when they saw flight was no longer an option. The
Zoicans began to fire across the river into the tightly packed
refugees. Despite the wholesale killing, it was a matter of
hours before the civilian masses began to draw back into the
hive. It took that long for the message to filter back through
the press of humanity to adjust their tidal flow.

Folik sat with Mincer on the foredeck of the rocking *Magnificat*, sharing a bottle of joiliq. They had decided not to
flee. There seemed little point, especially now they were both
roaring drunk. Sporadic enemy fire from across the Hass
stippled the waters around them and smacked off the hull.
Parts of the docks were ablaze now. Folik expected a rocket

or mortar to blow them out of the water at any moment. He fetched another bottle from the wheelhouse and a las-round punched straight through the cabin window and out the other side over his shoulder as he stooped to reach into the steerage locker. It made him laugh. He stumbled back to Mincer. They decided to see if they could finish the bottle before they were killed.

HASS WEST FORT was encircled by the enemy and under siege. By dawn, it was close to destruction. Shells and rockets rattled into it from outside the Curtain Wall, and enemy troops and light armour pounded it from the manufactories and habs within. Captain Cargin, badly wounded, held his men together, barely six hundred of the five thousand with which he had started the night. There were virtually no gunners or artillerymen left alive, but that hardly mattered because all the munitions for the Wall and fort gun emplacements and missile racks were spent. The Vervun Primary troopers and their lasguns were all that remained. The fort itself was rattled with damage and lower levels were blocked or ablaze.

Cargin adjusted his spiked helmet and limped down the gate battlement, urging his men with a voice hoarse from hours of shouting. The rockcrete deckways were littered with dead. One of his men, Corporal Anglon, called to him. Through the smoke and flame, he had sighted something approaching through the outer habs.

Cargin took a look. Through his scope, he saw a colossal shape crawling through the suburb ruins fifteen kilometres south of the fort. Another death machine, he thought instinctively.

But this was different – larger, slower. A huge pyramid structure, five hundred metres high at the apex, its mechanical sides painted Zoican ochre and decorated with vast, obscene symbols of Chaos. It moved, as far as he could see, on dozens of fat, wide-gauge caterpillar units that crushed everything in its path. A gouged trail half a kilometre wide scored through the habs in its wake. Its flanks bristled with weapon turrets and emplacements, and huge, brass speaker-horns on its summit, with Chaos banners fluttering from poles between them, boomed out the Heritor chant and crackled the inhuman chatter.

'What is it?' Anglon hissed.

Cargin shrugged. He was cold and weak from blood-loss and pain. Every word, movement, or thought was an effort of superhuman concentration. He unstrapped the handset of the vox-unit he had been carrying over his shoulder since his comm-officer had been killed some hours before.

'Cargin/Hass West to Baptistry Command. Marker code 454/gau.'

'Received and recognised, Hass West.'

'We've got something out here, approaching the walls. Massive mechanised structure, mobile, armed. I'm only guessing, but unless there's more than one of these things, I'd lay real money it's the enemy's command centre. I've never seen a mobile unit so big.'

'Understood, Hass West. Can you supply visuals?'

'Pict-links are down, Command. You'll just have to take my word for it.'

'What is your situation, Hass West? We are trying to direct troop forces to support you.'

Cargin sighed. He was about to tell Baptistry Command he had less than a thousand men left, most of them wounded, at the end of their ammo supplies, with no artillery support, and an ocean of enemy on all sides. He was about to estimate they could hold on another hour at the most.

The estimate would have been inaccurate by fifty-nine and a half minutes. Anglon grabbed Cargin's arm, shouting out as fierce lights blinked and fizzled in dark recesses down the centre of the pyramid side facing them. The vast Zoican vehicle shuddered and then retched huge, searing beams of plasma energy at Hass West Fort: cutting beams, like the ones that had dissected Ontabi Gate, but larger still and far more powerful, energy weapons of a scale usually seen in the fleet engagements of naval flagships. The roar was deafening, sending out a shockwave that was felt kilometres away.

Hass West Fort and the gate it protected were obliterated. Cargin, Anglon and all the remaining defenders were disintegrated in one blinding instant. As the cutting beams faded, rocket and gunnery platforms all across the pyramid opened fire and piled destruction on the ruins. The air stank with ozone and static and fycelene. For half a kilometre in each direction, the Curtain Wall collapsed.

The pyramid machine began to trundle forward again, inching towards the dying hive, blaring the Heritor's name over and again.

GAUNT WOKE WITH a start, his mind spinning. Sleep had taken away his immediate fatigue, but every atom of his body ached and throbbed. It took him a moment to remember where he was. How long had he been asleep?

He clambered to his feet. The sacristy was chilly and silent, the Ecclesiarch choir long since finished.

Merity Chass stood nearby, gazing at the friezes of the Imperial cult. She wore his long overcoat and nothing else. She looked round at him and smiled. 'You'd better get dressed. They probably need you.'

Gaunt recovered his shirt and boots and pulled them on. He could still taste her on his lips. He stared at her for a moment more. She was... beautiful. If he didn't have a reason to fight for Vervunhive before, he did now. He would not allow this girl to perish.

He sat down on the pew and laughed to himself dryly.

'What?' she asked.

Gaunt shook his head. Such thoughts! He had committed the cardinal sin of any good officer. He'd placed his emotions in the firing line. Even now, he could hear Oktar's dirty chuckle in his mind, scolding him for becoming attached to anyone or anything. Over the years they had spent campaigning together, Gaunt had seen Oktar leave many tearful women behind as he moved on to the next warzone.

'Don't get involved, Ibram, not with anything. If you don't care, you won't care, and that makes the hardest parts of this army life that much easier. Do what you must, take what you need and move on. Never look back, never regret and never remember.'

Gaunt buttoned his shirt. He realised, perhaps for the first time, that he had broken with Oktar's advice a long time since. When he had met the Tanith and had brought them as Ghosts from the deathfires of their world, he had started to care. He decided he didn't see it as a weakness. In that one thing, old Oktar had been wrong. Caring for the Ghosts, for the cause, for the fight, or for anyone, made him what he was. Without those reasons, without an emotional investment, he would have walked away or put a gun-muzzle in his mouth years before.

Gaunt got to his feet and found his cap, his gloves and his weapon belt. He was trying to remember the furious notions that had woken him. Ideas, whirling...

Daur burst into the sacristy. 'Commissar! Sir, we–' Daur saw the naked woman cloaked in the overcoat and stopped in his tracks. He turned away, flushing.

'A moment, captain.'

Gaunt crossed to Merity.

'I must go. When this is over–'

'We'll either be dead, or we'll be a noble lady and a soldier once again.'

'Then I thank the Emperor for this precious interlude of equality. Until the hour of my death, however far away that is, I will remember you.'

'I should hope so. And I hope that hour is a long time coming.'

He kissed her mouth, stroked his fingers down her cheek, and then followed Daur out of the sacristy, pulling on his jacket and weapon-harness. At the door, he put on his cap and adjusted the metal rose Lord Chass had given him for honour. It was drooping in his lapel and he straightened it.

'Sorry, sir,' Daur said as Gaunt followed him down the hall.

'Forget it, Ban. You should have woken me earlier.'

'I wanted to give you all the rest you could get, sir.'

'What's the situation now?'

'A holding pattern as before. Intense fighting on all fronts. The enemy has taken the north shore. And Hass West fell a few minutes ago.'

'Damn!' Gaunt growled. They strode into the bustle of the Baptistry Command Centre. Additional cogitators and vox-sets had been added over night. Over three hundred men and women from Vervun Primary, the Administratum and the guilds now crewed them, working in concert with dozens of servitors. Major Otte was occupying 'the Font,' as the command station was now known. Intendant Banefail and members of his elite staff assisted the major.

Many saluted as Gaunt entered the chamber. He acknowledged the greetings while taking in the details of the main hololithic display.

'Just before it fell, Hass West reported seeing a massive mobile structure moving in towards them. We're fairly sure it is their main command vehicle.'

Gaunt spotted the marker on the display. The thing was certainly huge, and now close to the western extremity of the Wall. 'The marker code... "spike"?'

Banefail joined them. The distinguished lord was almost dead on his feet with fatigue. 'My fault, commissar. I referred to it as a bloody great spike, and the word stuck.'

'It'll do. What do we know about it?'

'It's a massive weapon, but slow moving,' Major Otte said, crossing the floor to Gaunt. 'I guess we can assume it's well armoured too.'

'What makes you think it's the command element?'

'It's the only one we've sighted,' Daur said, 'and its size clearly indicates its importance.'

'More than that,' Banefail said, gesturing at a vox-set manned by a female Administratum cleric, two servitors and a withered astropath. 'It's the source of the chatter.'

Gaunt glanced at the woman operating the set. She dialled up the speaker and the air filled briefly with the coded, incessant growl of the enemy.

'The enemy vox-traffic unites them all,' lisped the pallid astropath thickly. Gaunt tried not to look at him and the festoon of data-plugs stapled into his translucent scalp. The astropath lifted a bionically augmented, wasted limb and pointed to data runes flashing across the instrumentation. 'We knew it was coming from outside the hive and we suspected the source was Zoica. But it's mobile now and audio scans confirm it is being emitted by that structure.'

Gaunt nodded to himself. 'Asphodel.'

Banefail glanced around at the name. 'He's there? So close?'

'It matches his recorded behaviour. The Heritor likes to be near to his triumphs, and he likes to maintain intense control. He commands by charisma, intendant. Where his legions march, we will not find him far behind.'

'Golden Throne...' Otte murmured, looking at the display with frightened eyes.

Gaunt forced himself to look at the astropath. The stink of the warp hung about the cadaverous wretch. 'Your opinion? This chatter: could it be the control signal of the Zoican forces? An addictive broadcast that maintains the Heritor's hold over his zealots?'

'It is certainly patterned and hypnotic. I find myself reluctant to listen to it for any length of time. It is a Chaos pulse. Though we can't – daren't – interpret its meaning, the flow of the enemy troops and armour seems to match its rhythmic fluctuations.'

Gaunt turned away, deep in thought. The idea that had woken him reformed in his mind.

'I have a notion,' he told Daur, Otte and Banefail. 'Send word to Major Rawne's units and to Sergeant Mkoll and his scout platoon.' He ordered other preparations to be made, and then told Daur to fetch him a fresh box of bolter shells.

'Where are you going? We need you here, sir!' stammered Otte.

'You have my full confidence, major,' Gaunt said. He gestured to the hololithic display. 'The defence strategies are set in motion. You and this staff are more than able to direct them. I'm a foot soldier. A warrior, not a warmaster. It's time I did my job, the job I'm best at. And with the grace of the Emperor shining on me, I may take this field yet.'

Gaunt took Heironymo's amulet from his pocket and felt it whisper and chuckle in his hand. The flickering light patterns on its carapace roiled like the twisting flashes of the Immaterium.

'In my absence, Otte and Daur have field command. If I fail to return, intendant, you should signal Warmaster Macaroth and plead for salvation. But I believe it won't come to that.'

The amulet gurgled and quivered.

This could work, thought Gaunt. *God-Emperor save us, this could fething work!*

SEVENTEEN
OPERATION HIERONYMO

'I believe this Gaunt fellow is singularly overrated.'
— General Noches Sturm to Major Gilbear,
during the assault on Voltemand

A SCRATCH COMPANY met them at 281/kl to guide them in. The company was forty strong and had been conducting guerrilla work in the southern outer habs before the Shield fell. Their leader, a powerful, saturnine ex-miner called Gol Kolea, saluted Gaunt as he approached. Gaunt looked every centimetre a leader, though the braid of his cap had been rubbed with ash to dull its glint. He wore the powersword at his waist and his boltgun in a holster across his chest, under a short, black, leather jacket. On top of that, draped expertly as Colm Corbec had instructed him during the first days of the Ghost regiment's existence, was his Tanith stealth cape.

The roar of battle thundered down the ruined streets beside them, but this sector was clear and quiet. Cold, morning light filtered in through the crackling Shield. Gaunt signalled his units up to join Kolea's scratch company: thirty men, all Tanith, pale-skinned, dark-haired warriors in black fatigues and stealth capes, their skin decorated with various, blue tattoo symbols. They were the cream of Rawne's unit and the pride of Mkoll's stealth scouts. Amongst them, Bragg, Larkin, Domor, MkVenner, Dremmond, Genx, Neskon, Cocoer, the medic Gherran – most of the very best.

Gaunt was beginning to outline 'Operation Heironymo' to his waiting squad when Rawne heard movement down a side street. The Ghosts and scratches fanned out and made ready, arming weapons freshly supplied for the mission.

A fireteam of ten Volpone advanced down the side street, led by Colonel Gilbear. They were all Volpone elite troops from the 10th: massive, carapace-armoured and holding hellguns ready.

Gaunt walked out into the rubble-strewn open to meet Gilbear. They saluted each other.

'Not going in without the Bluebloods, I hope, colonel-commissar?' Gilbear said archly.

'I wouldn't dream of it, colonel,' Gaunt replied. 'I'm glad you got my message and gladder still you found your way here. Join us. We're about to move out.'

Gaunt crossed to Rawne and Kolea as the Volpone meshed into the column spread.

'I don't fething believe you invited them,' Rawne cursed.

'Keep your thoughts to yourself, major. The Bluebloods may be bastards, but I feel I have reached an understanding with them. Besides, we'll need their muscle when it comes to it.'

Rawne spat in the puddles and made no reply.

'I understand you're command now,' Kolea said bluntly to Gaunt. 'May I ask what the gak you're doing here? Gnide and Croe never got their hands dirty.'

'Their command ethic was different, Kolea. I hope you'll appreciate my method of doing things.'

'Can you sign?'

'What?'

'Most of my company are deaf. Can you sign your commands?'

'I can, sir,' Mkoll piped up.

Gaunt gestured to the scout sergeant. 'Mkoll can relay my instructions to your fighters. Good enough?'

Gol Kolea scratched his cheek. 'Perhaps.'

Gaunt could tell Kolea had been through hell in the last thirty-odd days. Courage and determination seemed to ooze out of him like sweat. He was not a man Gaunt wanted to be on the wrong side of.

THEY FOLLOWED dingy, battle-worn streets out through the southern extremities of the hive, and they left the shattered Curtain Wall behind them. Mkoll's scouts led the way, directed by Kolea's troops. The bulky Volpone struggled to keep up with the swift, silent advance. Clear of the Shield, they were all exposed to the bitter rain.

'You know these quarters well, Kolea. I guess they were your home,' Gaunt remarked softly to the miner.

'Correct. Just half a kilometre from here, I could take you to the crater where my hab once stood.'

'You lost family?'

'A wife, two children. I don't know they're dead, but – gak! What are the chances?'

Gaunt shrugged.

'How many did you lose coming here?' Kolea asked.

'Troops?'

Kolea shook his head. 'Family.'

'I didn't have any to lose. I don't know which of us is luckier.'

Kolea smiled, but without any light or laughter in his face. 'Neither one, commissar. And that's the tragedy.'

'I DON'T KNOW about the girls,' Larkin muttered as they moved through the scorched-out, rain-pelted ruins. Bragg, his missile launcher and autocannon slung over his shoulders, raised his eyebrows and made no reply. There were eight females in Kolea's scratch company, none older than twenty-five. Each held a captured Zoican lasgun or a Vervun Primary autorifle and carried an equipment pack over their ragged work fatigues. Most of them, like the men, wore salvaged military boots wadded with socks and wrapped tight with puttees made of cargo tape to keep them fast. The women moved as silently and as surely as their male comrades. A month of intense guerrilla war in the outhabs had trained them well. Those that had not learned had not made it.

'Women can fight,' Rilke murmured, holding his sniper rifle with the stock high in his armpit and the long barrel pointing downwards. 'My sister, Loril, used to hold her own against the rowdies when it got to chucking-out time in my father's tavern back home. Feth, but she could throw a punch!'

'That's not what I meant,' growled Larkin, rain dripping off his thin nose. 'It doesn't seem right, sending women in like this, all gussied up in combat gear and waving lasguns. I mean, they're just girls. This is gonna get nasty. No place for women.'

'Keep it down!' Dremmond hissed, lugging his flamer with its weighty, refilled tanks. 'They'll hear you, Larks!'

'You heard what that big, bastard miner said. They're all shell-deaf! I can speak my mind without insulting no one! They can't hear me!'

'But we can read lips, Tanith,' Banda said, moving past the chief sniper with a smirk. Some of the other scratches nearby laughed.

'I– I didn't mean nothing by it,' Larkin began, moving his mouth over-emphatically to make sure she could hear. Banda looked back at him, a mocking expression on her dirty face.

'And anyway, I'm not deaf. Neither's Muril. And neither are the Zoicans. So why don't you clamp it and do us all a favour?'

They moved on, the eighty-strong assault group splashing down a damp, debris-strewn side road.

'That told you,' Dremmond whispered to Larkin.

'Shut up,' Larkin replied.

MKVENNER SCOUTED ahead as part of Mkoll's recon deployment. In his immediate field of vision was Scout Bonin and the scratch company guides: a girl called Nessa and a Vervun Primary sergeant named Haller, who was second in command of Kolea's makeshift group. Haller was one of nine Vervun Primary survivors to have found their way into the scratch company, though with his dirty, patched uniform and the woollen cap he wore in place of his spiked helmet, he didn't look much like a Primary infantryman any more. He seemed content to be commanded by a miner rather than a military officer. MkVenner knew the members of the scratch company had weathered the very worst of the war, and he couldn't begin to understand their loyalties or the circumstances that had brought them together.

Nessa guided them through a series of torched manufactories, covering the ground quickly, keeping low and making curt, direct gestures they could read easily. They crossed an arterial highway where the rockcrete was crumpled by a series of shell-holes, and they skirted the wrecks of two Zoican battletanks and an infantry carrier that had been flipped over onto its back.

Across the highway, they fanned through textile mills where the constant rain trickled in through the holed roofs and rows of iron-framed looms stood silent and shattered. The loose ends from hundreds of bales of twine rippled in the breeze. MkVenner stopped in a doorway and scanned around. He watched with idle fascination as droplets of rainwater crept down taut feed-threads over one loom, glinting like diamonds and thickening before dripping off the hanging brass bobbin onto the weaving frames beneath.

MkVenner realised he'd lost sight of the woman. Haller appeared behind him.

'You have to watch her,' Haller mouthed, signing at the same time. He knew full well MkVenner could hear, but the practise was now instinctive.

Bonin joined them and they edged down the length of the mill, until they found Nessa in an open loading dock at the far end, crouched behind an overturned bale-lifter. Outside, in the bright, thin light of the cargo yard, a quintet of Zoican flamer tanks grumbled by, heading north. The foot soldiers could smell the coarse stench of the promethium lapping in the tanks' heavy bowsers.

Once the tanks had passed, Nessa made a punching motion in the air and the troops hurried on, across the open yard and into the razorwire-edged enclosure of a guild's freight haulage plant. The rusting bulks of overhead cranes and hoists creaked in the wind above them. Rainwater had formed wide, shallow lakes across the rockcrete apron. They moved past rows of plasteel cargo crates and produce hoppers flaking paint. Near the haulage site office, a small Imperial chapel built for the workers had been desecrated by the advancing Zoicans. They'd shot out the windows and soiled the walls with excrement. A dozen site workers had been crucified along the front porch on gibbets made from rail sleepers. The bodies were little more than ghastly, stringy carcasses now. They'd been nailed up three weeks before, and the steady rain and the carrion birds had done their best to erode the flesh.

Haller's boot clipped an empty bottle and the noise of it tinkling away across the ground startled the birds, who rose in cawing, raucous mobs, revealing the gristly horrors beneath. Some of the birds were fat, glossy-black scavengers, the others dirty-white seabirds from the estuary with clacking pincer-bills. Black and white, the birds made a brief checker pattern in the air before flocking west to the haulage barn roof and settling. The open ground was peppered and sticky with their droppings.

There was a break in the fence behind the chapel. MkVenner held position long enough to check, via microbead, that the main force was within range behind them. Gaunt and the column were just entering the haulage site.

The land south of the freight-holding was a mass of chalky rubble and sprouting weeds. There were dark driver holes in the ground at intervals and the area was littered with thousands of gleaming, brass shell cases. In an earlier stage of the war, massive Zoican field pieces had been braced here, trained at the Wall. MkVenner was about to move on, but Nessa stopped him.

He made the gesture for question, and she signed and mouthed back at him.

'In our experience, the Zoicans trap-wire their sites when they move on.'

MkVenner nodded. He signalled back and Gaunt sent Domor forward. Haller helped Domor lock his sweeper set together, and then the Ghost began to creep away from them, playing the head of the broom back and forth over the dirt. Domor liked to do this work by sound and MkVenner smiled to see him closing the shutters of his bionic ocular implants by hand. The time when Domor could simply close his eyelids was long passed, way back on Menazoid Epsilon.

Domor had a path cleared in under five minutes, playing out a fibre-cord to mark its zigzag path. By the time he had finished, the assault force had caught up with them and were waiting with MkVenner, Haller, Nessa and Bonin at the fence.

'He found nothing?' asked Haller, pointing over at Domor on the far side of the area.

'No, he found plenty, but we're not here to mine-lift. Follow the cord,' replied MkVenner.

Single file, the eighty soldiers crossed the ex-artillery emplacement and moved down along a reinforced walkway that crossed one of the hive's main drainage gullies. Swollen by the heavy rains, the gully was in full flood. It was partially dammed in places by slews of debris rubbish and bundles of corpses.

Up the other side, they climbed the chute slope by a metal stairway and hurried in small packs across another highway. The ruined remains of bodies littering the road stretched as far as the eye could see. Most tried not to look. Larkin stared in horrified fascination as he crossed the road. Nothing more than bundles of rags, the bodies were those of workers and habbers slaughtered as they had tried to flee inwards towards Vervunhive. They had fallen weeks before, and no one had touched or moved them, except the mashing tracks of Zoican war machines heading north towards their target.

Gaunt called a halt-period in the broken habitats on the far side of the highway. His motley brigade set up defence watches all around as he climbed to the third storey of a hab block with Kolea and Gilbear.

'I smell smoke,' Gilbear said suddenly. He moved ahead, down the dirty, dank hallway, his weapon raised, and kicked open the rotting door of a worker flat.

Gaunt and Kolea, weapons ready, moved in behind him. All three stopped short.

The flat was thick with trash and overrun with vermin. The smoke issued from a small fire set in a tar bucket over which swung a metal pot on a wire frame that had once been a clothes hanger. The five inhabitants of the room, a mother with three children and a much older woman, cowered in the far corner. They were emaciated and filthy, just terrified skin and bone clad in dirty tatters. The old woman whined like a caged animal and two of the children cried silently. The mother, her eyes bright and fierce in her soot-black face, held out a shank of metal, sharpened to a point.

'Back off! Now!' Gaunt told Kolea and Gilbear, though Kolea needed no urging.

'It's all right… I'm sorry,' Gaunt told the mother, his hands raised, open. The shank remained pointing at him.

'Leave them,' Kolea said. He pulled a wad of ration cakes from his pack and went over, dropping them on the floor in front of the group when the mother refused to take them.

They went back out into the hallway and Kolea pulled the door back into place.

'Throne of Earth…' Gaunt hissed, shaking his head.

'Quite,' joined Gilbear. 'What a waste of rations.'

Gaunt looked round at him, began to speak, and then just shook his head. Explaining the real nature of his horror to Gilbear might take a lifetime.

And that time, however it could be measured, was all Gaunt had left to do something far more important than drum compassion into an aristocratic warrior like the Blue-blood colonel.

Kolea had heard Gilbear's remark and he glowered at the man with utter disdain. Kolea doubted even the colonel-commissar understood what it was like to claw and scrape for survival in the shelled ruins of your home, day after day. Gol Kolea had seen enough of that misery since the Zoicans came, enough to last a hundred lifetimes. There were thousands of hab families out here still, slowly dying from starvation, disease and cold.

The trio of officers climbed out onto a fire escape at the eastern end of the hab block, and Gaunt and Gilbear pulled out their scopes.

Five kilometres south, across the ruins, through the smoke and rain, rose the bulk of the Spike. It was moving at a slow crawl, up towards the main hive. Gaunt swung his scope

around and looked back at the vast, glinting dome of the
Shield and the massive Spine and hab structures within.

Gaunt offered his scope to Kolea, but the man wasn't
interested. Gilbear gestured, suddenly and sharply, to them
both and pointed down at the highway below, the one they
had just crossed. A host of Zoican troopers, escorted by a
vanguard of carriers and light tanks, was advancing towards
them. Chaos banners flopped lankly in the rain and the light
shone off the wet, ochre-coloured armour.

Gilbear raised his hellgun, about to turn, but Gaunt
stopped him. 'We're not here to fight them. Our fight is else-
where.'

The commissar keyed his microbead. 'Mass enemy formation approaching along the highway outside. Stay low and
stay silent.'

Rawne voxed back an acknowledgement.

It took half an hour for the Zoican column to go by. Gaunt
estimated there were a little over two thousand foot troops
and sixty armoured vehicles – reserves, advancing to bolster
the assault. He wished to the Emperor himself he had
reserves of such numbers to call upon. Feth, he wished he
had such strengths in his active units!

Once the column was safely past and clear, the Operation
Heironymo assault cadre left the habitats and moved on
through rain-swilled ruins, towards the Spike.

THE CLOSER THEY got, the bigger it grew, dwarfing all the
building structures around. Larkin bit back deep unease – it
was big, so fething big! How in the name of feth were eighty
souls going to take on a thing that size?

They were cowering in rubble. Larkin raised his head and
saw Banda grinning back at him.

'Scared yet, Tanith?' she hissed.

Larkin shook his head and looked away.

Mkoll, MkVenner and Gaunt moved forward with Kolea,
Rawne and Haller in a line behind them. Now they could
hear the throbbing grind of the Spike's enormous track sections, the deep growl of its engines. Gaunt noticed dust and
ash trickling down the rubble around him in sharp, rhythmic blurts. He realised the vast machine, still a kilometre

distant, was vibrating the earth itself with its weight and motivation.

The rain grew suddenly heavier. An incessant patter filled the air around them, accompanied by a regular, tinking chime. It came from a broken bottle wedged in a spill of bricks, sounding every time a raindrop hit its broken neck.

Gaunt wiped water droplets from the end of his scope and studied the Spike.

'How do we do this?' he asked Mkoll.

Mkoll frowned. 'From above. Let's get ahead and find a suitable habitat overlook – unless it changes course.'

Gaunt took the group across the wide, pulverised trail behind the advancing Spike, a half-kilometre strip of soil and ash compressed by the vehicle's weight into glinting carbon. The Spike didn't steer around buildings. It flattened them, making its own path.

The Imperial strikeforce overtook the great war machine on the right flank and pressed ahead, hugging the ruins and the rubble. Mkoll indicated a pair of worker hab blocks ahead of them that promised to intersect the Spike's course. Gaunt detailed his troopers into two units and sent one ahead under Gilbear, leading the other himself.

Gaunt's troop was climbing up the stairwell of the nearer hab, five hundred paces ahead of the crawling target, when the Spike fired again. Its awesome spinal weapon, the cutting beams, howled vast energies above and past them at some target in the main hive. The sound was louder than their ears could manage. The hab shuddered thoroughly, and a harsh light-flash penetrated every crevice and opening in the stairwell for a moment. A second later there was a pop of pressure, a wall of dissipating heat and the stink of plasma.

Gaunt and his troop exchanged glances. It had been like standing too near a star for a millisecond. Their eyes ached and the energised stench burned their sinuses. Gaunt wiped a thread of blood from his lip.

There was no time to waste, however. Gaunt and Mkoll led the party up to the fifth floor, to the flats at the far end. The Spike was almost on them. Half a dozen ragged habbers fled past them, running like beaten dogs from their hideaways.

Gaunt got a signal from Gilbear in the other block. The second unit was in position. He looked out of the end window, glassless and burned, and saw how close the massive machine now was.

Its lower slopes swiped the edge of the hab block and tore it away, rubble cascading down under the tracks. Gaunt moved his soldiers back as the passing armour wall tore the end off the room they waited in. Then they moved.

In pairs and trios they leapt clear of the ripped-open building and dropped seven metres onto the sloping sides of the Spike. Most slid down the ochre-painted hull before managing to cling fast to moulding projections, rivets or weld-seams. Gaunt landed hard, slid for a moment, then braced against a row of cold-punched bolt-heads. He heard a cry from above and looked up to see Larkin slithering down the armoured slope, his hands clawing uselessly at the tarnished metal. Gaunt snagged the sniper by his stealth cape and arrested his slide, nearly throttling him with the taut fabric. Larkin found purchase and crawled up beside Gaunt.

'Saving my arse again, Ibram?' Larkin stammered in relief.

Gaunt grinned. At a time like this, he hardly minded Mad Larkin's informality.

'You're welcome. It's my job.'

Ten metres down the Spike's side, Haller also lost his grip. He slid, barking out a helpless curse and slammed into Dremmond, who was barely holding on himself. The two of them tore away and started to slide much more swiftly down the flank, thrashing for handholds.

Bragg drew his Tanith blade, punched it into the Spike's plating to provide a firm anchor point, and caught them as they tumbled past. He captured Dremmond by the harness of his flamer, and Dremmond held tight to Haller. By then, they had barrelled into Muril – one of the scratch company loom girls – too, and Haller held on to her. Secured by one meaty fist around the hilt of his knife, Bragg supported three dangling humans.

'Feth!' he grunted, his arm shaking under the weight. 'Get a grip! Get a grip! I can't hold on much longer!'

Muril swung around and grabbed the edge of an armour plate, digging her fingertips into the seam. As soon as she was secure, Haller let go and slid down beside her. Bragg heaved the kicking Dremmond up next to him by the man's flamer's straps.

'Good fething catch,' Dremmond gasped, gripping tightly, trying to slow his anxious breathing.

'I don't always miss,' replied Bragg. He didn't dare voice his relief. For a moment, he had been close to dropping them – or being pulled away with them.

Gaunt's unit, forty bodies, clung to the sloping side of the gigantic Zoican war machine and slowly began to climb up it. The Spike's pyramid form was punctuated by shelflike terraces, like some step-temples of antiquity Gaunt had once seen on Fychis Dolorous. The soldiers crawled up over the lip and made themselves fast on the nearest horizontal shelf.

The progressing Spike, oblivious to the human lice now adhering to its hide, moved on and slammed over and through the hab block where Gilbear's team was waiting. Gaunt watched in horror as the metal slopes demolished a large chunk of the hab's lower storeys.

Then he saw Gilbear and his team leaping down from a far higher level. They'd clearly moved up a floor or two when the impact of the Spike's course had become evident.

The troopers, led by Gilbear, dropped far further than Gaunt's unit had done. They impacted on the hull above the shelf Gaunt and the others occupied, and most slid down onto that safe landing. Some clung on where they found purchase on the slopes above. Two – a Volpone and the Tanith scout Bonin – bounced away like rocks down a mountainside and dropped past Gaunt, disappearing a hundred metres below under the lip of the hull. Gaunt looked away. If the sheer fall hadn't killed them outright, they were dead under the massive caterpillar carriage.

Gaunt signalled around and made contact with the remaining troopers. They were all rendezvousing on the shelf-lip. The Curtain Wall of Vervunhive was now only minutes away and their time was disappearing fast. Weapons ready, reaching out hands to steady themselves against the motion of the Spike, the strike team followed Gaunt down the shelf.

* * *

THE DIFFICULT PART remained: how to find a way inside this armoured monster.

The hull was solid. Domor pulled out the head of his sweeper kit and pressed it against the throbbing metal.

'Dense – no cavities,' he growled disappointedly.

Gaunt sighed. They could blast or cut the hull open if there was a chance of accessing a hollow space within, but Domor was positive. It stood to reason a machine like this would be thick-skinned.

Two of Gilbear's Volpone returned along the shelf from scouting the far end. Gilbear heard their reports and edged along to Gaunt.

'The main weapon ports along the forward face. They're open, ready for firing. It's that or nothing.'

'And if they fire while we're entering?'

'Then we're dead. You want to stay out here for the rest of the war?'

Gaunt barked out a laugh at Gilbear's attitude.

'No. I guess we won't know anything about it if they fire.'

'It'll be quick, certainly,' Gilbear agreed.

Gaunt notified the squad leaders and led the single-file team along the shelf.

They were about to make the turn onto the forward face when the beam weapons fired again. The light flash was even more brutal out in the open and the sucking roar monstrous. The whole Spike shook.

'How long since the last salvo?' Gaunt asked Larkin as soon as his ears stopped ringing.

'Eight minutes, just about, boss.'

'I'm working with the idea it takes a while for the batteries to recharge. We've got eight minutes to get inside.'

'It sounds so easy when you put it like that,' snarled Rawne.

'Shouldn't we be moving rather than debating?' Kolea asked, shaming them all.

Gaunt nodded. 'Yes. Now. Go!'

Always, always lead from the front. Never expect a man under your command to undertake an action you're not prepared to make yourself. It was one of Delane Oktar's primary rules, drummed into Gaunt during his years with the Hyrkans. He was not about to forget his mentor's advice now.

Gaunt led the way around the corner of the hull and hurried towards the huge, main-weapon recesses below him. Visor hatches the size of the Sondar Gates were pulled up from the ports like eyelids. The air was sweet and tangy with burnt plasma and fluorocarbons.

Gaunt reached the edge of the emplacement recess and grabbed hold of one of the shutter stanchions, a heavy-weight hydraulic limb at full extension. His leather glove slid off the oiled, shining metal. He pulled the glove off and took hold with his bare hand, arming his bolt gun in the other.

Gaunt leapt and let himself fall, swinging down and around like an ape by one hand. Using his body weight's pendulum momentum, he threw himself in through the weapon hatch, letting go of the hydraulic limb at the same moment.

He fell, rather than jumped, inside the hull, landing and stumbling on a grilled cageway that ran alongside the massive snouts of the beam cannons. Rolling, he saw two black-clad Zoican gunners leap up from their firing consoles, and he shot them down.

Three Zoican soldiers in full battledress charged up onto the cageway, blasting at him. Gaunt lost his footing and fell, the las-shots screaming over his head. The shots blew apart the torso of the Volpone leaping in behind him and threw his corpse back and outwards so it fell away down the slope of the hull. Recovering, Gaunt resumed firing, aiming precise head-shots at the Zoicans, exploding their full-face helmets with high-explosive rounds.

Then Gilbear, Mkoll and three other Tanith had made it inside behind him. Mkoll opened up with his lasrifle, supporting Gaunt's fire-pattern, and Gilbear turned back to pull others of the strike force in through the huge awning.

Gaunt and Mkoll advanced with Crothe and Rilke, partly to secure the weapon deck and partly to make room. The commissar and his three Tanith troopers scoured the gun-control position, blasting dozens of Zoican personnel.

Within moments, the Zoican troopers set up a flaying return of fire. Crothe was blasted off his feet and Mkoll took a hit in his hip. He slammed back into the wall and fell, but somehow maintained his fire rate.

Now Gilbear and three of his elite Blueblood were coming in behind, laying down a field of fire with their hellguns. Behind them on the cageway, Haller and Kolea were dragging the other squad members in through the hatch.

Gilbear's fire team advanced and secured the gunnery deck behind the colossal beam emitters, slaying everything that moved. The air in the chamber was dense and rich with gunsmoke. The grilled deck was strewn with Zoican dead.

Somewhere an alarm began to wail.

Inside four minutes, Gaunt's strike team had entered the Spike via the gunports, all seventy-eight of them. Three had died in the initial engagement. Gaunt checked on Mkoll. His wound was superficial and he was already back on his feet.

The strike force spread out to cover all the exitways on the gloomy gundeck.

He led the way to a main blast door that gave access to the Spike's inner cavities. It was locked fast.

'I can blow it,' said Kolea at his side.

Gaunt drew the powersword of Heironymo Sondar, activated it, and sliced the incandescent blade through the hatch. A further three sweeps and a kick left the hatchway open, the cut section of metal clanging as it fell on the deck outside.

'Move!' cried Gaunt. 'Move!'

THE SPIKE'S MAIN weapon deck was linked to the primary command sections by a long, sloping accessway wide enough for a Leman Russ to drive along it. It was painted matt red, the colour of meat, and thick bulkhead frames stood at every twenty metres. The floor was a metal grille and in the underfloor cavity, pipes, tubing and feeder cables could be seen. Off to either side, just on the other side of the blast door, stood service elevators with metal cage frames, set in circular loading docks. The elevators were heavy-duty freight lifts designed to haul shells from the munition stockpiles deep in the belly of the Spike up to the artillery blisters on the upper slopes. The metal walls of the accessway were covered with intricate emblems, the curious, nauseating runes of Chaos. Gaunt realised they had been fashioned from bone that had been inlaid into the metal and then polished flat with the wall so they glowed and shone like pearl.

Human bone, he guessed. The Heritor would demand such details.

A team of Zoican heavy troopers in segmented ochre body armour greeted them in the accessway as they entered, firing up the sloping tunnel from cover at the far end. One of the scratches, a man whose name Gaunt would never know, was sliced apart by the initial shots. His blood sprayed the bone icons on the wall, and the symbols began to squirm and shift.

Larkin saw this and fell back in horror, his guts churning. The eldritch symbols were alive, excited by blood. He knew he was about to vomit with fear.

'Taking a breather?' Banda asked sourly as she pushed past him, firing down at the enemy position. The Imperials were hugging the walls and using the bulkheads for cover, edging down the accessway as far as the enemy fire would allow.

'A breather?' Larkin gulped. He was incredulous. No smirking girl from the hab looms would show him up.

Forgetting his fear, he knelt in cover, shook out his neck, raised his sniper-variant lasrifle and put a hot-shot between the eyes of a Zoican heavy twenty paces away.

'Nice work,' Banda growled from her position and blew Larkin a cocky kiss.

Larkin grinned and made another kill-shot. Either he was beginning to like this woman, or he'd kill her himself.

Another of the scratches fell, ripped open by the mauling heavy weapons the enemy had trained on them. They were caught too tightly between the hall and the entry point Gaunt had cut open. His men fanned round into the side loading docks, but they were packed in.

Rawne hurled a tube charge down the tunnel, but the Zoicans had enough cover to shelter from it.

'Dremmond!' Gaunt yelled.

The flamer-trooper was still trying to pull his bulky tanks through the narrow opening Gaunt's powersword had sliced. Las-rounds peppered the metal around him. A Ghost nearby, Lonner, collapsed with the back of his neck blown out.

Dremmond was clear. Gaunt and Kolea physically dragged the big Ghost to the front of the line and Dremmond braced his scorched flame-gun, ensuring the feed-pipe wasn't twisted and the igniter was sparking.

He squeezed the trigger grip and billows of white-hot flame sheeted down the tunnel, incinerating the Zoican heavies. The scourging flame bubbled the paint off the walls and the twitching bone-runes began to shriek.

He washed the hall with another gout to be sure, and then Rawne, Haller and Bragg led off to secure the hall. Bragg reached the position the enemy had been holding and he stepped over the black, fused corpses. There was another accessway to his left and he sprayed bursts of autogun fire through the door mouth.

Haller moved to the right and went over hard as a half-burned Zoican soldier threw himself at the scratch officer. The blackened thing, its ceramite armour part-melted into its flesh by Dremmond's flames, tore at him in a frenzy. Haller screamed out, frantic. Rawne grabbed the Zoican and threw it off Haller. It bounced off a wall and, before it could rise, Rawne had shot it four times with his lasgun.

'I owe you, Ghost,' said Haller, getting up.

'No, you don't, habber. I don't like it when any one owes me anything. Forget it.'

Haller paused, as if slapped in the face. He hadn't much liked the look of the Tanith major when they had all first assembled. Banda had whispered Rawne had 'toxic eyes.' It seemed true. Even the haughty Volpone seemed to be making more of an effort to be comradely than this Tanith bastard.

'Suit yourself,' Haller said.

'He always does,' mocked Bragg. The big Ghost knew it was neither the time nor the place to bring Haller up to speed on Rawne's history, the fact that Rawne hated Gaunt with an inhuman passion precisely because 'he owed him.'

'Shut it and get soldiering!' Rawne snorted to Bragg. Already there were noises from the side tunnels and fresh Zoican forces were firing on them.

The main strike force had moved up by then. Gilbear swung a party of Bluebloods to the right and cremated a side-tunnel with grenades from their under-barrel launchers. MkVenner hurried right with four Tanith and a number of scratches, moving to secure their advance from enemy prosecution. A las-round hit him in the arm and spun him to the deck. Domor, right behind him, knelt over the injured scout and sprayed las-fire down at the hidden shooter, calling for a medic. Beside him, Vinya, one of the loom-girls, rebounded off the wall as a brace of las-shots caught her in the belly. Several troopers pushed past Domor to hold the side-tunnel, flaying las-fire down into the dark.

Gherran joined Domor, running low, holding a las pistol in one hand, the other hand curled around the narthecium kit to stop it jolting.

'It's MkVenner—' Domor began. The medic dropped to his knees beside the scout. The las-shot had exploded MkVenner's left elbow and disintegrated his biceps. He was curled up, crying with pain, but he forced his voice to work.

'Her first – her!' he said, nodding over at Vinya.

'Let me look at it, MkVenner,' Gherran said.

'No! You know fething triage: serious cases first! She's gut-shot! See to her!'

'Give him this,' Gherran told Domor, handing him a gauze-packed inoculator full of high-dose painkillers. He scrambled over to the sprawled scratch soldier. She was twisted like a broken puppet, her chin forced into her chest where she lay with the back of her head against the wall. Blood oozed out of her in a wide pool. The wound itself had self-cauterised in charred, knotty lumps, but the damage had shredded her insides, and she was bleeding out rapidly.

'Oh, feth!' Gherran spat. 'Someone give me a hand here!'

Kolea was beside him. 'Tell me how.'

'Pressure: here and here. Hold it tight. No, tight like you mean it!'

They were both sodden with her blood. She stirred, moaning.

'Vinya… s'okay… Stay awake…' Kolea murmured to her, his hands clamping hard on her ruined organs.

He looked around at Gherran as he worked frantically.

'She's not going to make it, is she?'

'Major trauma,' Gherran explained as he worked. 'I can sta-
bilise her, but no, it's just a matter of time.'

Kolea nodded. He let go and leaned down to whisper in
her ear, 'You fought well, Vinya Terrigo of Hab 45/jad.
Vervunhive will never forget your courage. The hive loves
you for your devotion.'

Then he reached down with huge, gentle hands and
snapped her neck.

'Oh, God-Emperor!' Gherran cried, recoiling in horror.

'There's a man you can save,' Kolea said, pointing at
MkVenner with a bloody hand. 'I love my people, and I will
fight for them with every last measure of my strength, but
this would have uselessly wasted the time of a good medic
when there are better causes. Her pain is over. She has found
peace.'

Gherran wiped his mouth.

'I–' he began.

'If you were going to tell me you couldn't begin to understand what we habbers have gone through to get here, save
it. I don't want your pity.'

'Actually, friend, I was going to tell you I do understand.
And admire your courage, to boot. Our lives are all on the
line fighting for your home. Me, I don't have a home any-
more. So, feth you and that oh-so-noble crap.' Gherran
gathered his kit-pack and moved over to MkVenner.

Kolea picked up his lasgun and strode past, rejoining the
fight.

COCOER, NESKON AND Flinn had made it to the corner of the
right hand side access, and they drove the gathering Zoicans
backwards. Gaunt, with Genx and Maroy, crawled up behind
them.

'Access?' asked Gaunt.

'Not a fething hope, sir!' sang out Cocoer. The air was flickering with las crossfire.

'Bloody bastard hell!' Neskon cried as his gun jammed. He
shook it. Gaunt grabbed him and yanked him down into
cover just as laser blasts pummelled the wall above his head.

'Never forget the drill, Neskon. Gun jams: duck and cover.
Don't stand there playing with it.'

'No, colonel-commissar.'

'I like you better alive.'

'Me... me too, sir.'

Rilke, reckoned to be the best sniper in the Ghosts after Larkin, and the scratch woman Nessa moved up to flank them. Rilke wasted two shots trying to hit a Zoican in cover down the tunnel. Nessa, with her standard-issue lasgun, picked him off and the Zoican behind him.

'Where'd you learn to shoot like that?' Rilke protested, but she didn't hear him. She couldn't hear him.

Gaunt looked across at her, waiting until she saw his face. 'Good,' he said.

She grinned.

A CEILING PANEL ten metres back slammed open and Zoican stormtroops began to drop down out of it like grains of sand through the neck of an hourglass. They sprayed shots in both directions. Four Ghosts, two scratches and a Blueblood went down. Bragg wheeled and decimated the spilling Zoicans, his withering autocannon supported by Haller, Rawne, Genx and a dozen others.

The Zoican dead lay in a heap under the ceiling drop. Bragg raised his muzzle and began to fire up into the roof, his heavy rounds punching smooth-edged holes through the sheet metal. Blood began to drip down through some of them.

'We're bottled in!' Mkoll yelled at Gaunt.

Gaunt knew as much. Gilbear had blocked the left-hand access, but the right was still thick with Zoicans. And now they were coming down through the ceiling, for feth's sake! At this rate, his strike cadre would exhaust themselves simply maintaining a perimeter. If they were going to do anything of note, they had to focus.

'Mkoll?' Gaunt called.

Mkoll knew what was being asked of him. Gaunt had always valued the chief scout's unnerving ability to find the right way. It wasn't a gift, really. Somehow, sometime back in the shifting, drifting forest ways of Tanith, he had come to understand the logic of structure, the underlying sense of any environment.

Mkoll's gut said straight ahead and down.

'Through the blast shields, sir,' Mkoll announced.

That was good enough for Gaunt. He crawled back, under heavy fire, to the shields. 'Rawne! Tube charges here!'

'What are you doing?' bellowed Gilbear, moving up. 'That way will lead us off into the right hand side of the structure!'

Gaunt looked at Gilbear, las-shots whizzing around them. 'After all we've seen, Gilbear, do you trust me?'

'Very probably, but–'

'If you were constructing this Spike, would you put the main command deck in the dead centre where anyone would expect it to be?'

Gilbear thought for a moment and shook his head.

'Then humour me. I've learned to go with Mkoll's instincts. If I'm wrong, I'll stand you a case of wine. You can choose the vintage.'

'If you're wrong, we'll be dead!'

'Why do you think I made the bet?'

Gilbear laughed out loud.

'Cover and clear!' yelled Rawne, hastening from the bundle of tube charges he had glued to the shield hatch.

The channelled blast tore the doors inwards like paper. Whatever else you could say about him, Rawne knew explosives. There was barely a shockwave on the Imperial side of the hatch.

'For Tanith!' yelled Gaunt, hurling himself through the opening.

'For Volpone!' bawled Gilbear, right beside him.

'For Vervunhive!' mouthed Nessa to herself, close on their heels.

Guild Githran Agricultural had fallen. Corbec drove his Tanith back towards the base of the Main Spine with all hell following. Milo and Baffels guided their survivor company out of the ruins, chased by Zoican tank groups. Bray's mixed units wilted in retreat as divisions of Zoican stormtroopers drove up into the inner habs.

The Shield Pylon shuddered as it took shell after shell.

At Croe Gate, Grizmund's valiant counteraction finally reached a stop. Flat crabs and spider death machines lumbered in at them, in strengths even the crusade's finest tank regiment could not withstand.

On the dock causeway, Varl and Rodyin began to pull their infantry back, facing an ochre host ten thousand strong.

Along the edge of the Commercia, where one of the war's bloodiest battles had been waged, Bulwar ordered his North-Col and scratch companies to retreat. Overhead, the Shield flickered and waned. It would not last much longer. In the middle of a horrendous brawl in a side trench, Soric hammered his axe-rake into the foe. He was one of the last to heed Bulwar's retreat order.

Corday's Volpone unit was pincered by Zoican detachments. The Bluebloods were slaughtered by crossfire in the rubble wastes that had once been the inner-sector habs. Corday died with his men.

In a lost pocket in the wastelands, Caffran held Tona Criid tight, Yoncy and Dalin curled between them. The sky was on fire and shells fell all around. It was just a matter of time, Caffran knew. But until then, he would hold her and the children as tight as he could.

In the baptistry, Ban Daur set aside his headset and sat back in his seat. The workers and staff servitors were still milling around, trying to maintain some semblance of control.

It was over. Daur got up and crossed to Otte at the Font. Windows blew in down the hall and the Main Spine shuddered as shells struck it.

'We gave it our best,' Daur said.

'For Vervunhive,' Otte agreed, weeping quietly with fatigue.

Intendant Banefail joined them. 'High Legislator Anophy has just been carried out. A heart attack.'

'Then he's been spared,' Daur said callously.

Otte looked at him reprovingly, but Banefail seemed to agree. 'This is the end, my brave friends. The Emperor love you for your efforts, but this is the end of all things. Vervunhive is lost. Make your peace.'

Daur looked round at Immaculus. The minister stood nearby with his robed clergy.

'Begin the mass, sir,' Daur told him. 'The requiem. I want the last sound I hear to be a psalm of loss voiced by the Emperor's own.'

Immaculus nodded. He led his brethren into the celebra-
tory and the soft dirge, a haunting melody, began to lift
above the baptistry and the high stations of Vervunhive.

IN THE ABANDONED hall of her house, high in the Spine, Merity Chass heard the low plainsong welling through the walls.
She had put on a long, formal gown and her father's ducal
chain and signet ring, which Daur had brought to her.

She had spent an hour putting the House Chass ledgers in
order and encrypting all the family documents onto storage
crystals. At the sound of the mass, she frowned.

'Not yet... not yet...' she murmured. 'He won't fail us...'

EIGHTEEN
THE LAIR OF ASPHODEL

'A friend of death, a brother of luck and a son of a bitch.'
— Major Rawne, of his commander

ITS SOUNDS AMPLIFIED by the thick, metal walls around, carnage exploded into the Spike's command level. Savage fighting boiled through the dark, mesh-floored chambers. The strikeforce were engaging crew now as well as troops. The crew members wore loose flak-tunics and work-fatigues, and their heads were generally exposed. Gaunt's troopers could see for themselves the horror that had disturbed Larkin so at Veyveyr Gate. It wasn't the implants fused and sutured into their eyes, ears and scalps, linking their senses and brain patterns to the insidious chatter. It was the fact that they were men and women of all ages: hab workers, parents, guilders, older children, the elderly. The entirety of Zoica's population had mobilised for war, just as Gaunt had assessed. The bald proof was overwhelmingly tragic. With blank expressions, somehow even more lifeless than Sondar's servitor puppets, the people of Ferrozoica threw themselves at the attackers.

Gaunt hacked through a pair of Zoican troopers with his powersword, fighting to cut a route down onto the main bridge area. Through the seething press, the smoke and the flashes of las-fire, he could make out a wide, open platform of polished chrome, surrounded by black towers of control instrumentation. In the centre of the platform, the glowing, pinkish ball of a coherent light field, ten metres in diameter, coalesced up from an emitter ring in the floor. He fought his way to it, channelling his deepest reserves of aggression and determination.

Suddenly, he was on the platform itself, virtually alone, lit by the pink radiance. His last frenzied efforts to break through had been almost too successful. He'd effectively separated himself from the rest of his party, still locked into the mayhem in the adjacent bridge areas.

Gaunt was breathing hard and shaking. He'd lost his cap somewhere, his jacket was torn and he was splattered with blood. An almost painful adrenaline high fizzled through him like electricity glowing through fuse-wire. He had never been pushed to such an extremity of raw fury before in his life. His mind was locked out in a paroxysm of battle-rage. Everything had become distant and incomprehensible. For a moment, he couldn't remember what he was supposed to be doing.

Something flickered behind him and he wheeled, his blade flashing as it made contact. A tall, black figure lurched backwards. It was thin but powerful and much taller than him, dressed in form-fitting, glossy-black armour and a hooded cape of chainmail. The visage under the hood-lip was feral and non-human, like the snarling skull of a great wolf-hound with the skin scraped off. It clutched a sabre-bladed powersword in its metal-gloved hands.

Gaunt had seen its like before, on Balhaut. He'd glimpsed its kind distantly on the fields of war, during the final stage of the battle, and then seen several corpses closer to after the victory. It was one of the Darkwatch, the elite retinue of Chaos champions who had been gifted to the warlord, Asphodel, as his personal bodyguard. The thing flickered again, employing its monstrous, innate control of the warp to shift its location around him. Gaunt yelled and blocked the incoming blade of the repositioned horror. The cold blue energies of Heironymo's powersword clashed against the sparking, blood-red fires of the Darkwatcher's weapon.

It flicker-shifted again, just a few paces to the left, and sliced its sword around at him. Gaunt evaded, stumbling in his haste, rolling and then springing up in time to block the downward swing of the Chaos-tainted blade.

But this was not the same weapon. This was longer, straighter, incandescent with smoking green fire. A second Darkwatcher, shifting in to assist the first.

Without looking, Gaunt threw himself sideways, knowing the original fury was now behind him. Red energy sliced a gouge in the gleaming chrome deck.

He backed as they came at him together, both flickering in and out of reality. One was suddenly to his left, but Gaunt threw all his force behind a blocking strike that bounced the blade away. The other sliced in at him and caught Gaunt's right shoulder.

There was no pain. A cold, nauseating numbness ached into his wounded limb.

Gaunt hurled himself forward in a tuck roll, avoiding two more slashes. He knew he had never been this outmatched before, not even face to face with howling World Eater Chaos Marines in the underworld of Fortis Binary or surrounded by the Iron Men in the crypts of Menazoid Epsilon. He should be dead already.

But something kept him alive. Partly his elevated battle-edge, partly his determination, but also, he was sure, Heironymo's sword. It seemed to smell the shifting creatures and forewarn him – by a tingle – of their impossible movements.

Their shifting was localised, as if they were moving in and out of corporeal reality. Every time they became solid to strike, the sword twitched in his grip, moving him to block.

He ducked a scything arc of green energy and stabbed upwards, shearing one Darkwatcher's head off in a flurry of blue sparks. Lambent, frosty smoke jetted out of its tall form as it collapsed in upon itself, flickering and fading. A inhuman scream rang around the bridge.

The other lunged at him, flickering into being right in his face, and though the powersword pulled at him, he wasn't quick enough to avoid the deep gouge the red blade sliced in his left thigh.

Gaunt fell.

A spray of autocannon split the air above him. Bragg had made it to the edge of the platform and was blasting at the Darkwatcher on full auto. The thing shuddered under the impacts, flickering in and out of real-space, its chain cloak whipping as it turned to face the new attack. Kolea and Mkoll were there too, heaving up onto the edge of the chrome level, opening fire at the beast. A second later, Neskon, Haller, Flinn, Banda and a Volpone called Tonsk had also reached the edge of the platform. Sustained fire from all of them drove the raging Chaos-thing backwards – and targeted the other two that had manifested in the last few moments. Bragg's unrelenting fire-cone gradually disintegrated the red-bladed Darkwatcher, which advanced on him, despite the colossal wash of bullets, before finally exploding a few flicker-steps from him.

One of the others, wielding a pike-axe which smoked with orange lightning, chopped Tonsk in two and severed Neskon's left leg at the knee with one stroke. Haller snatched up the Blueblood's fallen hellgun, pumped the under-barrel launcher and blew the thing's head off with a rocket-grenade.

The others, supported by more of the strike force just making it to the platform, caught the remaining Darkwatcher in a crossfire. The thing shrieked and flickered, twisting in the las-hail.

Behind them, the remaining elements of Gaunt's brigade fought a desperate rearguard at the Zoicans pouring into the command area from all around.

Gaunt clawed at one of the instrumentation towers at the edge of the platform and pulled himself to his feet. Hololithic screens projecting from the domed roof above showed fuzzy, amber-tinted views of the onslaught outside. The Spike, with its supporting armoured legions, had exploded in through the Curtain Wall just east of Sondar Gate, and the war machine's vast batteries, presumably recrewed after Gaunt's entry assault, targeted and demolished the Shield Pylon in a blaze of fire.

Sections of the huge structure crashed down across the Commercia, like a titanic tree being felled, wreathed in great washes of flame instead of foliage. Rather than being deactivated as before, the Shield collapsed, its massive energies unsecured and arcing out. The energy flare, designed to protect the city of Vervunhive, ripped the top ten levels off the Main Spine, and all the anchor stations around the city perimeter exploded.

The powersword loose in his hand, Gaunt searched the instrumentation around him for some system he could recognise. It had been built by the tech-wrights of Ferrozoica, so its essential patterns were Imperial, but the markings and format were wretched and alien.

Gaunt staggered across to the next tower and resumed his search. He found what appeared to be a vox-terminal and a pict-link displayer. But nothing else he could understand.

Behind him, the last Darkwatcher exploded, taking Trooper Flinn with it.

The third tower. Halfway down, what could only be a data-slate reader with a universal hub: standard Imperial fitting.

Gaunt felt himself sag, his leg wound pulling at him. Blood from his shoulder wound soaked his sleeve and dripped off his hand.

'Gaunt!' yelled Kolea, at his side, supporting him. Mkoll was there too, and Genx, Gherran and Domor.

'Let me see to your wounds!' Gherran was yelling.

'No t-time!'

'Let him help you, Gaunt!' Kolea growled, trying to keep the struggling commissar upright. 'Let me–'

'No!' Gaunt shook the big miner off. If this was the final act, it would be his.

He pulled the ticking, chuckling amulet from his pocket and fitted its link ports to the reader's hub.

It engaged, purred and turned twice like a kodoc beetle burying its abdomen in the sand.

The lighting and instrument power in the command section shorted on and off two, three, four times. A mechanical wailing of tortured, over-raced turbines welled up from the vast machine pits below them. The chatter cut short.

Then the lights went out altogether.

* * *

SUDDEN, TOTAL DARKNESS; sudden quiet. In the stillness, the groans of the dying and wounded; the bright, brief crackle and fizz of torn cables. A flash of las-fire.

Gaunt's eyes grew accustomed to the gloom. The heart of the Spike was dead. Smoke wafted, full of the rich, animal smells of war. Men stirred, blinking.

The force field in the centre of the platform had vanished.

A huge form, dark like a shadow, crouched where the field had been. It rose, unfurled, grew larger. In the half-light, Gaunt saw the richly embroidered silk of a vast cape spilling away from the figure as it stood. He saw an immense, metal-gloved hand reach out and beckon to him. He saw the shivering flame-light throw into relief a long, smooth armour-cowl split by narrow eye-slits. The cowl fanned up and out into massive, hooked steeples of polished horn.

Heritor Asphodel, Chaos warlord, daemon-thing, fuelled by his dark gods in the Warp, standing fully six metres tall, lunged at the human worms who strove to defeat him. He made no sound. Darkness, which he seemed to wear and pull around him like a great cloak, sucked through the air as it moved with him.

Kolea buried his axe-rake in the Heritor's flank. A second later, he was flying sideways across the platform, most of his ribs shattered.

Firing and making two hits, Mkoll was knocked sideways, his shoulder broken.

Domor's lasgun exploded in his hands, blowing him up, back and off the platform.

Gherran was lacerated by an ebbing fold of darkness, sharp as a billion blades. His blood made a mist that drenched Gaunt.

Genx was pulverised by the concussive force of the daemon's fist as he tried to reload his weapon and fire.

Gaunt met Asphodel head on. He slammed the blazing blue spike of the powersword into and through the monstrosity's chest.

At the same moment, the massive bolt pistol clenched in the Heritor's left hand shot Gaunt through the heart.

NINETEEN
MOURNING GLORY

'With this act we have richly denied the Darkness and made trophies of its creatures. A dark lord is dead. So, this holy crusade, blessed by the Emperor, is advanced with glory.'

— Warmaster Macaroth, at Verghast

THEY CAME LIKE ghosts at dusk. Phantom forms, impossibly large, underlit by the dying sun as they settled down through the smoke-filthy upper atmosphere of Verghast. Warships, bulk troop transports, the might of the Sabbat Worlds Crusade, the pride of the Segmentum Pacificus Navy.

It was the fiftieth day. Learning via the Astropathicus that Vervunhive faced not an inconsequential rival hive but a hunted Chaos commander, Macaroth had made best speed for Verghast, arriving after twenty-seven days of urgent transit through the warp.

The hazy sky was full of metal and looked like it should fall. The awesome power of the Imperium was there for every Verghastite to see: ten thousand ships, some the size of cities, some bloated like ornate oceanic turtles, some slender and serrated like airborne cathedrals.

Macaroth unleashed his might on the planet below: six million Guardsmen, half a million tanks, squads drawn from three chapters of the Adeptus Astartes, two Titan Legions. Troop dropships, bulk machine-lifters and shuttles dropped in a swarm on the Hass valley. For a while, the sky did fall.

Mass destruction followed, lasting for five days, thought it was brutally one-sided. Heironymo's amulet had done its work and cut the insidious chatter for all time. By the time the warmaster's immense forces arrived, the Zoicans were already in total rout. Aimless and lost, they broke off the final assault. Many committed suicide or wandered blindly into the defenders' fields of fire to be massacred. Millions of others woke as if from a dream and stumbled, without purpose or motive, back into the grasslands.

Under Grizmund's command, the battered Imperial forces that had held Vervunhive for over a month reformed to drive the pitiful, bewildered invaders out. Narmenian and NorthCol tank brigades chased down and annihilated Zoican motorised units threading back across the grasslands towards their own hive. Guard infantry, co-ordinated by Colonel Corbec, Colonel Bulwar and Major Otte, utilising every troop-carrying machine they could raise, hunted out and slaughtered the fleeing troop elements in vast numbers. There was no question of mercy. Ferrozoica's taint had to be expunged.

By the time Macaroth's armada made orbit, the Zoicans had been driven back six hundred kilometres into the plains, leaving vehicles and equipment scattered and abandoned in their wake.

In the crippled hive itself, scratch companies slowly weeded out the last, feral pockets of Zoican resistance.

The warmaster followed up with unstinting vigour. He politely but determinedly requested the assistance of the Iron Snakes Space Marines to overtake and neutralise the fleeing enemy. His armoured brigades poured down the main highways and decimated everything that lived. Skeletal Titans, shrieking like wraiths, stalked the grassland horizons, incinerating the retreating foe.

On the fifty-fourth day, crusade warships torched Ferrozoica Hive from low orbit. The blinding flame-flare filled the southern horizon.

But by then, the fight was out of the Zoicans and had been since the thirty-seventh day. Without the hypnotic chatter to unify their cause and drive them on, they had crumbled. Imperial Fist Space Marines ceremonially destroyed the Spike and incinerated the Heritor's corpse.

THE FINAL BATTLE was one of humanitarian support. Intendant Banefail, along with the hive elders and noble houses, laboured to accommodate the millions of wounded and homeless. By day sixty, the true scale of the human cost was undeniable. Vervunhive was a necropolis: a city of the dead. Meeting with the surviving nobility, Macaroth signed the Dissolution Warrant that formally acknowledged Vervunhive's extinction. The hive was dead. All population elements were to be absorbed by the Northern Collectives or shipped to Ghasthive and the Isthmus Steeples. Two new hives were to be founded, one ruled by a clique of noble houses under House Anko, the other a collective governed by Houses Chass and Rodyin. Names would come later. It would be generations until these municipal structures would begin to establish themselves, and it would be decades before the bulk of the dispossessed population could be given new, permanent homes.

Lord Anko, siting his new hive's foundations higher up the Hass waters from dead Vervunhive, planned to exploit the prometheum reserves once controlled by Vannick. Lady Chass, the first woman to govern a collective on Vervunhive, set her foundation in the grasslands far to the south and turned to mining and servitor engineering. Their future rivalry and confrontation would be long and complex, but is not pertinent to this history.

At the time, an air of disillusion fell hard on the survivors of Vervunhive. Many felt they had given everything in defence of the city only to see the city abandoned anyway. When this mood was made known to the warmaster, he spoke publicly about his decision and made law an Act of Consolation.

THE WARMASTER'S STAFF faced a thousand duties as they tidied up the mess of the Vervunhive War. One of those was the

prosecution of all those who had acted in a manner disloyal
to the Emperor during that period of great hardship.

The reports of the Tanith Sergeant Varl, as logged by his
commander, Gaunt, were sorted and processed by the
Administratum during the latter stages of the purge. On day
fifty-nine, prosecuting war-crime charges, Vervun Primary
troops stormed the halls of Guild Worlin. Amchanduste
Worlin was not to be found.

'THEY SAY HE wants to see you,' Corbec said, leaning back
against the sill of a vast stained-glass window in Medical
Hall 67/mv.

'He can wait.'

'I'm sure he can,' Corbec grinned. 'He's only a warmaster.'

'Feth. They're really abandoning the hive – after everything
we did?'

'I think maybe because of everything we did. There's not
much left standing.'

Ibram Gaunt heaved himself upright on his cot. The pain
of his shoulder and thigh wounds had long since faded, but
the burning ache in his chest still plagued him. He coughed
blood, for the third time since Corbec had arrived.

'You should probably lie still, sir,' Corbec ventured.

'Probably,' returned Gaunt. It was the sixty-second day. He
had been unconscious for most of the previous month and
had undergone repeated surgery to repair the wound Heritor
Asphodel had dealt him. Gaunt still didn't know – and never
would – if it had been dumb luck or fate that had saved him.
The Heritor's bolt had hit him directly on the steel rose Lord
Chass had made him wear. Though the collapsing petals had
been driven into his chest, it was certain he would not have
survived otherwise.

'You heard about the Act of Consolation?'

'I heard. What of it?'

'Well, sir, you wouldn't believe the number of new Ghosts
we've recruited.'

UNDER THE TERMS of the Act of Consolation, any disillu-
sioned Vervunhiver anxious to leave Verghast to find a new
life was offered the possibility of training for a place in the

Imperial Guard. Upwards of forty thousand elected to do so. Some made their choice of unit a condition of their acceptance.

Motor convoys carried them north with the regular army to board bulk carriers that had put in at Kannak Port. Sergeant Agun Soric oversaw the embarkation of his brave Irregulars. All of them were yet to be issued with their Tanith fatigues and camo-capes. Soric moved past the ship's payload doors and greeted Sergeant Kolea, who had also joined up, along with most of his scratch company. Kolea was walking on crutches, his torso encased in mediplas bindings.

'We'll never see it again,' said Soric.

'What?'

'Verghast. Take a last look.'

'Nothing here for me now anyway,' Kolea said. Under his breath, he uttered a last goodbye to his lost wife and beloved children.

Half a kilometre away, Bragg supervised the loading of other Ghosts. Many, like Domor and Mkoll, were walking wounded. Along with the soldiers came the inevitable wave of camp followers, lugging their possessions: clerks, cooks, armourers, mechanics, women.

Bragg caught sight of Caffran leading a girl and two children up the ramp. One was just a babe in arms. He noticed that the girl, along with her piercings and surly look, wore the temporary badge of a Guard recruit. Another female trooper. Bad enough Kolea's fighting women had been given a place. Larkin would have a seizure.

Jumping down from his transit truck, Ban Daur took a last, wistful look at the land around him. He felt like a lost soul given one last chance to haunt the place that had raised him.

That was appropriate. He wasn't Captain Ban Daur of Vervun Primary any more. He was a Ghost.

'I KEPT THESE for a long while,' Ana Curth said. She held out the dog tags that had been in the pocket of her apron since Veyveyr Gate. 'I knew there would be no good time for you to see them, but maybe now...'

Dorden took the tags. He read them, sighing.

'Mikal Dorden. Infantryman. Yes, I... they told me...'

'I'm sorry, Dorden. Really I am.'

Dorden looked up from where he sat, his eyes wet with tears. 'So am I. You know I was the only Ghost to have a relative in the Tanith regiment? My son. A fragile, last link to the world we lost. And now… that's gone too.'

She held him to her as he shuddered and wept.

A door banged open and a guilder peered in at them. He was dressed in rich robes and had a driven intensity about his face.

'Whatever you're looking for, it isn't in here,' Curth told him, holding Dorden tightly.

'Surgeon Curth?'

'Yes? What?'

The guilder entered the swab-room. He smiled. 'I was looking for, erm, Surgeon Curth and Medic Dorden.' He unfolded a scrap of vellum. 'I had a request to talk to me… about that terrible incident at the carriage station weeks ago. God-Emperor, it was awful!'

Curth let go of Dorden and turned round to the guilder.

'I'm Curth,' she said, stepping forward. 'Thank you for coming. I need to know: what did you see?'

'I want Dorden here too, before I speak,' Worlin said.

'That's me,' Dorden said, rising and wiping his eyes.

'Both of you? Dorden and Curth?' Worlin grinned.

'Yes? What did you want to tell us? What did you see?

Worlin pulled out his needle pistol and grinned. 'This.'

Dorden threw himself at Curth as Worlin opened fire. The first shot punched through Dorden's right hand, the second through his left thigh. The third hit Curth in the shoulder and threw her across the room.

Worlin advanced on Dorden, aiming the sleekly murderous pistol, eyes burning.

'Let's keep this between ourselves, doctor,' he hissed.

A bolt round blew Worlin's head off in matted chunks. Gaunt, gun raised, limped into the swab-room, supported by the bewildered Corbec.

'I heard shooting,' Gaunt said as he passed out.

ABOUT THE AUTHOR

Dan Abnett lives and works in Maidstone, Kent, in England. Well known for his comics work, he has written everything from Mr Men to the X-Men in the last decade, and currently scripts *Legion of Superheroes* for DC Comics and *Sinister Dexter* and *Durham Red* for 2000 AD.
His work for the Black Library includes the popular strips *Lone Wolves* and *Darkblade*, the best-selling Gaunt's Ghosts novels, and the acclaimed Inquisitor Eisenhorn trilogy.

More Warhammer 40,000 from the Black Library

THE GAUNT'S GHOSTS SERIES
by Dan Abnett

IN THE NIGHTMARE *future of Warhammer 40,000, mankind is beset by relentless foes. Commissar Ibram Gaunt and his regiment the Tanith First-and-Only must fight as much against the inhuman enemies of mankind as survive the bitter internal rivalries of the Imperial Guard.*

FIRST AND ONLY
GAUNT AND HIS men find themselves at the forefront of a fight to win back control of a vital Imperial forge world from the forces of Chaos, but find far more than they expected in the heart of the Chaos-infested manufactories.

GHOSTMAKER
NICKNAMED THE GHOSTS, Commissar Gaunt's regiment of stealth troops move from world from world, playing a vital part in the crusade to liberate the Sabbat Worlds from Chaos.

NECROPOLIS
ON THE SHATTERED world of Verghast, Gaunt and his Ghosts find themselves embroiled within a deadly civil war as a mighty hive-city is besieged by an unrelenting foe. When treachery from within brings the city's defences crashing down, rivalry and corruption threaten to bring the Ghosts to the brink of defeat.

HONOUR GUARD

COMMISSAR GAUNT AND the Ghosts are back in action on Hagia, a vital shrine-world of the deepest tactical and spiritual importance. As a mighty Chaos fleet approaches the planet, Gaunt and his men are sent on a desperate mission to safeguard some of the Imperium's most holy relics: the remains of the ancient saint who first led humanity to these stars.

THE GUNS OF TANITH

COLONEL-COMMISSAR GAUNT and the Tanith First-and-Only must recapture Phantine, a world rich in promethium but so ruined by pollution that the only way to attack is via a dangerous – and untried – aerial assault. Pitted against deadly opposition and a lethal environment, how can Gaunt and his men possibly survive?

STRAIGHT SILVER

ON THE BATTLEFIELDS of Aexe Cardinal, the struggling forces of the Imperial Guard are locked in a deadly stalemate with the dark armies of Chaos. Commissar Ibram Gaunt and his regiment, the Tanith First-and-Only, are thrown headlong into this living hell of trench warfare, where death from lethal artillery is always just a moment away.

™

INFERNO! is the indispensable guide to the worlds of Warhammer and Warhammer 40,000 and the corner-stone of the Black Library. Every issue is crammed full of action packed stories, comic strips and artwork from a growing network of awesome writers and artists including:

- William King
- Brian Craig
- Gav Thorpe
- Dan Abnett
- Graham McNeill
- Gordon Rennie

and many more

Presented every two months, Inferno! magazine brings the Warhammer worlds to life in ways you never thought possible.

For subscription details ring:
US: 1-800-394-GAME   UK: (0115) 91 40000

For more information see our website:
www.blacklibrary.co.uk/inferno